SERIOUS FUN
with

WHITE HOUSE SECRETS

and
STATE DEPARTMENT ANTICS

SERIOUS FUN
with
WHITE HOUSE SECRETS
and
STATE DEPARTMENT ANTICS

LIBBY HUGHES

iUniverse, Inc.
New York   Bloomington

Serious Fun with WHITE HOUSE SECRETS
and STATE DEPARTMENT ANTICS

Copyright © 2009 LIBBY HUGHES

iUniverse books may be ordered through booksellers or by contacting:

iUniverse
1663 Liberty Drive
Bloomington, IN 47403
www.iuniverse.com
1-800-Authors (1-800-288-4677)

ISBN: 978-1-4401-8117-7 (pbk)
ISBN: 978-1-4401-8119-1 (cloth)
ISBN: 978-1-4401-8118-4 (ebk)

Printed in the United States of America

iUniverse rev. date: 10/23/2009

DINNER

Suprême of Pompano à la Meunière
Fleurons

Broiled Tenderloin of Beef
Béarnaise Sauce
Soufflé Potatoes
Broccoli in Lemon Butter

Saint-Paulin Cheese
Endive and Watercress Salad

Pear Williams Bombe
Petits Fours

Ventana
Chardonnay 1981

Ridge
Amador
Zinfandel 1980

Almadén
Eye of the Partridge
Cuvée 1979

THE WHITE HOUSE
Tuesday, October 12, 1982

H.E.The President of the Republic of Indonesia
and Mrs.Soeharto

WHITE HOUSE SECRETS
By Libby Hughes

CONTENTS

Prologue i. Leaving Paris   xi
Prologue ii. The Secret Discovery   xv

PROLOGUE I

LEAVING PARIS

Paris, France, May of 2025.

Author Parker Lloyd holds a press conference at l'Orangerie Museum.

"I'd like to make a brief statement and then open it up for your questions," I said. "After thirty years in Paris as an author of books on Voltaire, Proust, de Tocqueville, Gide, Sartre, Camus, Napoleon, Monet, and De Gaulle, I feel it is time for me to return home to the United States."

"Why would you ever want to leave Paris?" asked the reporter from Le Monde.

"That's what all my friends ask when they hear my wife and I are leaving."

"Are you crazy?" the reporter asked incredulously as his colleagues joined in his laughter.

"I assure you that we will always have a place in our hearts for France, but it is time to go home."

"Don't tell us you're going back to Alabama? Alabama? Is there one ounce of culture in that state?" inquired the man from the AFP wire service in a very haughty manner.

I felt my throat tightening and anger creeping up my neck, reaching to the tips of my ears. They were attacking my home state. I was now sorry I had agreed to the press conference.

"If it weren't for Alabama, I would never have come to Paris—never have stayed here so long—never have spent my career writing about France."

"What do you mean?" asked the American from the AP wire service.

I launched into an emotional self-justification. "First of all, my mother was of French origin and we were a bi-lingual household in the heart of Birmingham, Alabama." The French reporters nodded with approval. "My wife came from Louisiana and grew up speaking French, too." They were unresponsive.

"But France is the only real place to live," the Le Monde reporter argued. "The best food, the best art, the best history, the best men—the whole of Europe is all around you. What more could you possibly want?"

They wouldn't listen to my explanation and I seriously doubted if they would ever understand my point of view, so I plowed through their questions, persisting to defend my life, my Alabama, and my country. "Let me tell you that Birmingham, like Paris, was and is full of literary salons, mostly for ladies, discussing the latest books or exploring the meaning of the classics. Young men from my state regularly attend Harvard, Dartmouth, and Yale. Young southern ladies frequent Sweetbriar or the University of Virginia. A few attended Radcliffe or Smith. My father's aunt had spent her school years in Switzerland and spoke six languages. Throughout her married life, during the summers, she took young American ladies all over Europe to introduce them to the Louvre, the Uffizi, and the Prado museums." The French newsman was impressed by my attempt to extol the intellectualism of people from Alabama, but, nevertheless, he and the European correspondents were entrenched in their own nationalism. It was imprinted like a map on their faces.

"You are more French than the French," he insisted. "Your accent is perfect and your understanding of our culture is innate."

I swallowed this backhanded compliment, but still, I felt the need to explain. I so wanted them to understand I could never really leave France. It was part of me, just as the United States is. "Did you know that the third largest collection of Marcel Proust books and memorabilia in the world is in the library at the University of Alabama in Birmingham? That's why I went there--to study French Literature and where I met my wife. I had read Proust's 'Remembrance of Things Past' (A la Recherche du Temps Perdu) in French by the time I was fifteen. It is the longest novel in the world—seven volumes to be exact. I helped to reduce it to three and then, two volumes." At last, they began to listen and maybe to understand. "When I graduated and contacted a French publisher, they took me on as a translator, editor, and author." I doubted if any of them had read any of my books. Reporters weren't known for their expertise in literature or economics—only politics and feature stories.

"Mr. Lloyd, sir, what do you want to do back in your young and brash country?" asked someone from the BBC.

"My heart's desire would be to write a novel. My whole career has been in non-fiction. Now I want to turn to fiction. Of course, it won't be as long as Proust." Polite laughter rippled through the hot room. I suspected none of them had ever read the whole novel.

"What would be the subject matter, sir?" asked the BBC correspondent in a follow up question.

"I don't know, yet."

"You don't know?" he said. This reply captured everyone's attention. Parker Lloyd, the famous author, didn't know what he was going to write? Skepticism filled the room.

"Fiction will be different," I said. "With all my biographies I knew where I was going and what research was required. Fiction is to be discovered—unexpectedly."

"What if you don't ever discover it?" he asked patronizingly.

"Oh, I will. Believe me, I will."

"Why not write here, basking in the glories of Paris. Many American writers come to Paris for inspiration. And you—Parker Lloyd—are famous and truly accepted here. You can go any place in Europe and write fiction," stated another French reporter.

"We have had a good life here. My wife, Lisa, has had the good fortune to freelance for travel magazines for thirty years, and we've gone to every conceivable location in Europe. I don't know my own country. Now it's time to learn and we are yearning to return to our roots."

"But you have a stunning eight room apartment, overlooking the Eiffel Tower at the Place de Victor Hugo. Not many have such a magnificent place with high-ceilings and four bathrooms. Do you really want to give that up?" asked the Le Monde correspondent.

"It is hard to give up our living quarters, but Lisa and I are ready to conquer new frontiers. We don't have children and our work means everything to us."

"Is your plan to return to Alabama?" asked the BBC journalist with a hint of sarcasm.

"No. We will go somewhere new and different," I said.

"And where might that be, may I ask?" he persisted.

"We're not sure. Thank you for your interest."

"Will you ever come back here?" asked the man from the AP wire.

"Of course. We leave half of our hearts here," I admitted. "I thank you for coming today." I turned and left the room, annoyed at their condescending questions. Deep inside I knew I should have expected them to not understand. It is their country, just as the United States is mine. Yet, they somehow made me feel like a traitor. Only the AP man shook my hand and wished me luck.

In a glum mood, I walked back to the office to pick up my box of books and gifts. Earlier that morning, the publisher and assistants gave me a farewell party. There were red, white, and blue balloons--symbolic colors of both our countries—strong coffee, flakey pastries, and a thoughtful gift of the latest John Grisham thriller to inspire my first novel. They presented me with miniature French and American flags put together on a small wooden stand on my writing desk. At that point, everyone dissolved into tears and I left as quickly as possible and couldn't look back.

When I arrived at the apartment, Lisa was packing some of our breakables. She asked about the party and the press conference. I told her about both. She distractedly nodded, but her mind was on all the boxes and the packing deadline quickly approaching. The place no longer looked like our home. It was sterile and in disarray. It was now cold and uninviting. I went to my spacious study and added the last of everything to boxes and briefcases. Emotionally spent, I sat down in my familiar swivel chair and stared out the balcony window to the Eiffel Tower in the distance. I just stared. I felt a pang of regret cross my chest. Paris had been my mistress for three decades. It was hard to let her go.

As dusk filtered through the lace window curtains, Lisa broke my reverie. "Hon, let's go for an early dinner and get ready for the movers tomorrow."

"Okay. Where shall we go?" I asked.

"Down the street to…" she said with a devilish glint in her eye.

'Not the most expensive restaurant in Paris?"

"We deserve it on our last night!" she said with a bright smile.

"Yes, we do," I agreed--now thoroughly convinced she was brilliant.

We walked two blocks and were greeted with open arms. They knew me and my books. We always received great service there. They brought over champagne to celebrate our new life and teased me about leaving Paris for the backwoods of America.

Vive le Parker Lloyd! Vive la France!" they chanted.

"Vive l'Amerique!" I sang.

Everyone laughed. They wouldn't let me pay. We kissed everyone on both cheeks.

There was a soft mist in the warm air as we left the restaurant. Lisa and I locked arms and strolled down the Champs-Elysées for one last look at the shops and at lovers wandering the avenue as we were. We never said a word to each other. We were lost in our own thoughts. It was a Paris night we would always remember. Who would know if it were tears or mist rolling down our cheeks? We didn't care.

Back at the apartment that had been our home for decades, we watched the Eiffel Tower blink its lights before spending our final night in Paris.

The movers would come early in the morning, and we would board the night flight to our next land of adventure—the United States of America.

Prologue II

The Secret Discovery

As the Air France plane soared into the inky sky above Paris, Lisa and I leaned in close to the window for our final glimpse of the Eiffel Tower in silhouette. There in the darkness below, the outline of jeweled lights faded as we climbed higher and higher above the earth.

We gazed into the black night for a long time and then settled back into our seats. We were exhausted from packing, but excited about our new life across the ocean.

"Do you want to see the city brochures again from the Chamber of Commerce?" Lisa asked.

"Why not?" I kissed her on the forehead. She leaned over and poked through her tote bag, pulling out a sheaf of colorful and seductive pamphlets. Each shamelessly extolled the virtues of the charming towns we might call home. Knowing I was content, she then turned away from me and pulled the blanket over her head to black out my reading light. Soon she was asleep.

*   *   *   *

My thoughts turned inward. I recalled her visits to each place we were considering for the next chapter in our lives. I remembered her telephone calls to me in Paris after she had seen and researched each location months earlier. Lisa had contracted to freelance with a magazine to write a story on the three most desirable places to live and retire in the United States. The angle, criteria, and places for the article were completely up to her. Of course, we selected the three gems of most interest to us. She flew to all three to do extensive research. They were Oxford, Mississippi; Annapolis, Maryland; and Cape Cod, Massachusetts. She spent two weeks in each, exploring the surroundings, talking to locals, and wandering the main streets while taking massive amounts of pictures and notes. Her phone calls to me about each place were full of excitement, and her delight was utterly contagious.

"What is Oxford like?" I asked over the long distance line.

"Charming. It's a college town with a typical southern square full of wonderful restaurants and atmosphere. The wrought iron balustrades are almost like those in New Orleans. Oh, and the southern food is good enough to rival French food." I raised an eyebrow because I knew she had gone a bit overboard. "Guess what? John Grisham's yellow Victorian House is in full view from the highway. William Faulkner's plantation, Rowan Oak, is nearby and open to the public. It is humble, but surrounded by large pin oak trees. Perhaps you might want to do a biography about him," she suggested rather flippantly.

After I sighed, I said, "No, Lisa, I'm through with biographies—you know that. I'm burnt out."

"No harm in asking," she said.

"Be sure to call me from the next place." It had been quite awhile since we had been apart this long. "In case you don't know, I miss you."

"I miss you, too, honey."

As I hung up, I had a suspicion we wouldn't be calling Oxford home although I do love college towns and cities with universities. One's brain never goes stale or stagnates where there are young people and young ideas. I guessed the nearest big city to Oxford was either Memphis or Birmingham. Surely there was plenty of Civil War history around Oxford, plus the shadows of two exceptional American writers. But somehow, I wasn't sure whether we would spend our sunset years there. I would wait for Lisa's next call.

She phoned a few days later. "Well, I'm here," she shouted over the long distance of an ocean.

"Where's here?' I teased.

"Annapolis."

"Watch out for those Naval-types," I warned.

"Don't worry, they're all locked up behind those 1845 thick, white stone walls," she laughed. "Besides, all of them are young enough to be my sons!"

"Well, what's the verdict?"

"It's charming, too. There are many narrow streets to explore and a quaint city center where we could shop and dine out. It has miles of waterfront."

"Like the Seine?" I joked.

"Don't be silly. It's not that metropolitan. However, it is only 27 miles from D.C., which is a plus. Pierre Charles L'Enfant designed the capital's layout. He was a French architect and civil engineer. You know, George Washington asked him to do it. Are you interested?"

"Lisa, I have no interest in doing a biography of L'Enfant. I know he nearly died in poverty and never received the recognition he deserved until long after his death, but this writer's heart is not moved."

"Oh and the Treaty of Paris was signed in Annapolis." I was sure she added this to stir my curiosity.

"Nice try. I'm really not a sailor who yearns to be near a marina," I said.

"Okay, okay. I'm on my way to Cape Cod."

"Call me when you get there." She hung up. I knew she was annoyed at my ruling out the first two places, but I somehow sensed, these two charming towns weren't for us.

I waited for her next call. If this place fails, I'll have to reconsider Oxford. Maybe we shouldn't leave Paris. What am I thinking?

When the phone finally rang ten days later, I crossed my fingers.

"This is it."

"What's it?" I asked.

"Cape Cod. You'll love it. Beaches on the Atlantic side and beaches on the Bay side. Six miles between them."

"What else?"

"Gray, weathered cottages, breezy salt air, and wild pink roses cascading over fences."

"Sounds promising."

"Promising? It's absolutely enchanting. I've driven from Sandwich to Provincetown. Without a question, this is a great place to write a novel!"

"Stop pouring on the persuasion. Is Boston the nearest city?" I asked.

"Yes. It's about two hours away. It's not Paris, but it has the old world feeling of it with brownstones on cobblestone streets and rich history woven throughout. Longfellow and the Transcendentalists left their written words in the area. By the way, I'm not suggesting you do any biographies," she said in a playful and mocking voice.

"Good," I said as a smile crossed my face.

"The symphony and theatres and Boston Ballet are all here."

"So what's the population of Cape Cod?" I asked.

"A million and a half in summer and 450,000 year-rounders. It really is perfect for us."

"Sounds reasonable. Have you narrowed it down to a particular town or found a house?"

"Well..."

"Lisa?"

"As a matter of fact, I selected a house in a wonderful small town. It's halfway down the Cape and it is the nearest thing to a French name."

"What's it called?" I asked.

"Orleans. You'll love it."

"Why didn't you wait for me to see it?"

"I was afraid the house would be snatched up." There was a slight quiver in her voice.

"What's the location?"

"It's down a long private road that opens to a panoramic view of long fingers of sand, bracing the Atlantic. There are three acres and a long marsh that stretches out to the shoreline where we will be able to hear the sounds of the ocean from our deck," she said.

"Sounds nice. What about the house?"

"Well, it's quintessential Cape Cod—gray shingles, a deck that wraps around one side to capture the view. It will seem smaller inside than we're used to, but perfect for us—a nice study for you and one for me."

*　　*　　*　　*

As I stirred in my tight airline seat, I realized I had dozed off. For how long, I wasn't sure. Suddenly, the pilot turned on all the lights and the flight attendants became very busy dispersing the breakfast trays. In an hour, we would be landing.

The minutes dragged on forever. From the square window, we saw dawn breaking over the Boston horizon. The landing was a bit bumpy, but no one cared. We were all glad to be on the ground and anxious to be out of the plane and finally back home.

Surprisingly, the line through customs went quickly. It was nice to be officially in the United States. Lisa went across the international arrival terminal to the car rental while I groggily pulled our luggage off the moving belt. Between the two of us, we had five bags to start off our new adventure. I thought about the rest of our worldly belongings that would arrive in Boston on a freighter and then be transferred to a moving van, headed for the Cape.

Although we were still sleepy from the flight, Boston's crisp salt air hit our faces as we found our car in the rental lot. Now we were fully awake.

"It seems pretty cold for late May," Lisa complained.

"They say New England doesn't have a spring. It jumps right into summer in June. No chestnuts in bloom here," I mumbled.

"Do you feel like spending a few days in Boston, honey?"

"No. Let's go to Cape Cod and see the house we own. Besides, we'll get ahead of Memorial Day traffic and the start of the summer season if we go now," I said.

"You'd think you were an authority?" Lisa said.

"I remember how people left Birmingham in droves to get to the Florida panhandle. The highways were mobbed on Thursdays and Fridays. We're lucky this is Wednesday—just the right time to hit the road."

"Here's the map and directions in case I goof."

"Darling, you've done this before. I trust your navigational skills implicitly," I teased.

I slid down and settled in my seat and sighed. The jet lag had tugged on my eyelids. Yes, we were home. It felt new and strange, but I could hear the heartbeat of the land underneath the wheels. This wasn't my beloved France, but it was my country. The highways were wider and the cars bigger. Fast food places were everywhere, but no patisseries, no cafes, no fields of growing crops or plows drawn by horses trotting up and down the rows.

"Parker, wake up!"

"What? Where are we?"

"At the bridge," she said.

"What bridge?"

"The Sagamore Bridge, over the Cape Cod Canal."

"So?"

"So, we're about to drive down the Cape Cod peninsula to Orleans. You don't want to miss it," she laughed.

"No, indeed." I sat up straight to observe everything. "The light is different."

"Different how?"

"Brighter, I guess. A glare—the kind of glare you get when you're on the beach. The light turns the leaves to platinum. The sky seems closer, like you can reach up and touch it and grab a cloud."

"Does that mean you like it?" Lisa asked plaintively.

"I don't know yet, but I like the feel."

"People told me this highway was turned into six lanes in the year 2023 to accommodate all the increasing summer traffic. It used to be just two lanes on both sides and then one lane each side from exit 9," Lisa told me. "The population in summer used to be well under a million, but not now. Apparently, you can't find waterfront property anymore."

At last we came to exit 12, the gateway to Orleans. It was an abrupt turn-off from the highway. Lisa and I became quiet. I looked critically at everything along Route 6A, known as the Cranberry Highway. It was seaside rustic, but definitely not Deauville. She cut down a side street that brought us to Main Street. The shops were quaint and not commercial looking. I spotted a library, post office, and market—the essentials.

"We're turning onto Tonset Road. The house is just off of it," she said.

"That's an interesting name. Is it Indian?"

"I think so. There are American Indians on the Cape. You'll see some Indian and English names on street signs. In fact, in some areas, the Indian culture is still alive."

Near the end of the Tonset Road, Lisa turned down a narrow lane that elbowed to the left and straight into a long driveway, with the little house blocking the ocean's view. We opened our car doors and walked to the front door. As Lisa opened it, the vista straight through the inside glass slider was breathtaking. The Mediterranean blue colors and sun-bleached sand sparkled like a painting. It was a moment immediately frozen in my memory.

"Oh my God," I said. "You were right. It is spectacular." Almost in a trance, we stood out on the deck while Lisa pointed out Snow Shore, Nauset Beach, and the Atlantic beyond. I was so mesmerized by this beautiful spot, I wanted to feast my eyes on it forever, but Lisa was anxious to show me the house and reluctantly tugged on my arm. Once inside, I could see it was small, but all we needed.

"I'm glad you didn't wait for me to see it. Someone would have bought it for sure." After a full tour of the house, we returned to the deck and gazed at the view with our arms around each other.

"Do you know anything about the previous owners?" I asked.

"Jack, I have a feeling this house is full of… secrets," whispered Lisa.

"Secrets? What do you mean?"

"I'm not quite sure, but there is something about this place. I can't put my finger on it, but I sense something unusual. According to the realtor, Ginny and Jack Hunter moved here after Jack left The Boston International, where he was a correspondent for them in Africa and Asia before being called back to Boston to become editor. Apparently, Jack had wanted to own and run a small newspaper. When The Orleans Weekly was for sale, they bought it and worked together with their pre-teen and teenage children at the paper. After a few years, Jack was invited to Washington to work for President Russell Rowland's administration. He couldn't turn down such an honor, so they moved and spent almost four years in D.C. After a year back in Orleans, they divorced, sold the papers, and went their separate ways. That's it in a nutshell."

"Who bought the house once they sold it?" I asked.

"I don't know, but that doesn't matter. Mr. Hunter remarried and moved west. Mrs. Hunter became an author. After 25 years apart, they came back and bought their old house for their grandchildren," Lisa said. "This spot must have meant a great deal to them. I don't know very much more than that, except the grandchildren decided to sell it to us—Thank God."

"Interesting," I mused. "Mind if I wander around again?"

"Go ahead. I'll start visualizing where all our furniture will fit into la petite maison."

I went upstairs and found a perfect location to place my writing desk. I soon realized that minor renovations would be needed. I would put in big windows to take advantage of the view for inspiration. I wondered if I ever would find something to write about or would I just stare at the panorama in front of me?

What Lisa had told me about the Hunters was somewhat intriguing. Their sketchy story aroused my curiosity; Perhaps it was because Jack Hunter was a writer and for that matter, so was Mrs. Hunter.

I surveyed the room again to figure out where my files and bookcases would go. The space was small compared to my large study in Paris. Briefly, I had a moment of nostalgia until my eyes became riveted on a black, metal latch on the side wall under the slope of the roof. Unlatching it, I found it opened to a long narrow storage area under the eaves. I bent down and stuck my head inside to look to the right and to the left. It appeared to be empty. Just as I was about to close the door, I caught sight of something white at the far end. Without a flashlight, I would have to crawl to find out what it was.

While my eyes adjusted to the dark, I made my way on all fours, scuffing up the dust, until I reached a black plastic crate, stuffed with white folders and tattered, old notebooks. I twisted it in front of me and slowly pushed it to the open door, giving it a final shove into the room. Then, I stood up, stretched, and coughed from the dust in my nostrils. After brushing the dirt from my trousers, I moved the crate to the center of the room where I sat down cross-legged on the wooden floor.

Curious about the contents, I fingered through the tightly stuffed papers. There appeared to be a number of plays in report folders. I extracted three and was amused at the titles: SIN IN THE ATTIC; SEX UNDER THE COLLAR; and WHITE HOUSE SECRETS.

"White House Secrets?" I exclaimed out loud. I noticed the name of Ginny Hunter on all of them.

Before I thumbed through the rest. I saw a faded red spiral notebook, squeezed into one side of the crate. It looked like a student's five-subject notebook. As I wiggled it out very carefully, some cards spilled onto the floor. Picking them up, I discovered they were Christmas cards from the White House. Stunned, I saw President Russell Rowland's name and that of his wife,

Noline Clare Rowland. Their names were embossed on each one; there were formal menus also. Most of those were from the State Department.

Suddenly, a million questions went racing through my mind. I opened the cover of the notebook to the yellowed pages within and found a journal in printed handwriting. I assumed this must be Ginny Hunter's account of the couple's time in Washington. The first date of entry was 1981, describing a telephone call for Jack Hunter to ask if he would come to D.C. as a political appointee. Quickly, I riffled through to the last page. The final entry was dated 1984.

Placing the notebook on my lap, I started randomly reading. I was amazed at secrets that she openly uncovered. Some of the events concerning Mrs. Hunter were very funny. I found myself chuckling and fascinated. Instinctively, I knew this was an inside look at the White House and State Department. My author's juices began flowing, and I wanted to know more. Maybe the play, called WHITE HOUSE SECRETS, might tell me more.

In my excitement, I shouted for my wife. "Lisa? Lisa!"

"Parker?"

"Honey, come upstairs."

Reacting to the excited tone of my voice, she ran up the narrow stairs quickly and stared at me on the floor with the crate. "What's that?" she asked.

"Secrets!" I said.

"Secrets?"

"To this house and the people who lived here. You were right. There is some sort of mystery in this house," I said.

"Where did you find this?"

"Under the eaves in the storage area," I said, pointing to the latched door. "Sit down with me," I said, patting the floor. She sat down across from me.

"Okay, what are the secrets?" she asked.

"From the White House!"

"The White House?" she asked.

"In this old notebook."

"Whose is it?" she wanted to know.

"Ginny Hunter's from 44 years ago. She seems to have recorded lots of tidbits during their time in Washington. I can't wait to read it."

"Oh, my God!" Lisa exclaimed.

"Look at these."

"What are they?" she asked.

"Christmas cards from President Rowland and the First Lady to the Hunters. These are calligraphy menus from the State Department and some from the White House," I said, handing them to her.

"I don't believe it! Where did you find it?"

"At the far end of the storage area. I almost didn't see it because it was so far back," I said.

"Do you think it might be something that she didn't want anyone to know about and hid it there?" she asked.

"Maybe, because I almost didn't see it. Be careful. It's old and ready to fall apart," I said.

Lisa propped the journal on her knees and skipped through it, smiling here and there. "I think she had a sense of humor."

"Definitely."

"What are those other folders?" she asked.

"Plays."

"You mean stage plays?"

"That Ginny Hunter wrote," I said.

"She certainly was creative! Do you think we should mail the notebook and plays to the Hunter children?"

"NO!" I said rather possessively.

"No? Why not?"

"Not yet," I replied.

"Why?"

"Because I need them," I said.

"What for?"

"My novel," I stated nonchalantly.

"Your novel? About what?"

"About White House secrets!" I laughed.

"You've found it!" she said, looking into my eyes.

"I have."

"What's the time frame of the entries?" she asked.

"1981 through 1984."

"But that's so long ago. I mean, it's now 2025. Will anyone be interested in something that old?" she asked.

"Russell Rowland was an icon in history," I said. "And Ginny Hunter gives us the inside story, based on this journal—at least for one term."

"Will it be non-fiction?"

"Fiction. So I can invent and enlarge upon events. Before our furniture arrives, I think I need to go to D.C. to do some research and get to know my country and its government. Would you mind?" I asked her.

"This is your mission! Of course not."

"Okay, let's check into our B & B," I said. I put everything back in the crate, except the journal and one play. Then, I used my foot to push it back in the storage area. Lisa clapped her hands and gave me a big hug and kiss.

"You're holding the journal as if it were the Mona Lisa!" she said.

"It is."

We laughed and headed downstairs and out to our car.

"My research into D.C. secrets has just begun," I said.

"What a great discovery," she said as she started the engine.

I took out a pocket notebook to jot down some notes. "What did Ginny and Jack look like? Did the realtor describe them?"

" Let's see," she said, trying to remember. "I think she mentioned they were a handsome couple. He was tall and suave with a dry sense of humor and she was thin like a model, kind of naïve, but fun and extremely honest. I really wasn't paying much attention because the house was my main focus. Is that any help?"

"A big help," I said, scribbling notes.

"How are you going to use Ginny's journal?"

"Probably as a framework. I'll try to be true to some of the quotes and events, but create fictional names for the politicians and invent funny episodes for Ginny," I mused.

"Parker Lloyd, are you going to become Ginny Hunter in this novel?" she asked.

"I guess that's how it works in fiction."

"But you've only written about men up until now!" she declared.

"If I need a feminine point of view, I'll sit at your feet and ask for advice!" We both laughed.

"Maybe I can find out more about the Hunters when you're away," she said.

"Fantastic," I smiled. "Once I've read the journal, her play, and get to know about the State Department, I'll be flying over the keys of my computer as Ginny Hunter and every other character in the novel. I can't wait to start writing White House Secrets!"

"I can't wait to read it," Lisa said with a touch of anticipation.

CHAPTER ONE

▼

THE FBI SNOOPS AROUND

Orleans, Massachusetts, in June of 1981.

Jack and I led an enchanted life. We had lived in Africa and Asia when Jack worked for The Boston International. Who could ask for anything more than to experience those two exotic continents: one with raw, untapped beauty and the other with centuries of unyielding classical architecture and history.

Hong Kong was a magical city. Our apartment overlooked the jade-green waters of the South China Sea at Repulse Bay. Through the mountain saddle to the downtown side, the skyscrapers were so close, they almost whispered to each other. Every inch of land, except the cricket field, was occupied by banks, hotels, and soaring office buildings. Apartment buildings for Europeans were terraced at different levels of the mountainside. At night, it was a fairyland. Western traditions melding with Eastern. The lights sparkled, and Chinese junks were silhouetted at sunset as the Star Ferry plowed through the inscrutable waters of the Hong Kong Harbor, landing on the Kowloon side and its cacophony of Chinese life.

Our lifestyle was one of idyllic dreams. We had an amah for the children, and a full time cook, who could prepare home style western menus or native exotic Chinese dishes. Each of his pastries was a work of art. We were spoiled. When the four day Chinese New Year holiday rolled around, all the westerners could barely cope with cooking and caring for their own children. Most of the journalists' wives were left alone in Hong Kong for 50 percent or more of every year while their husbands covered stories all over Southeast Asia as well as being China watchers. The ex-pat community was very close-knit.

I became a friend of <u>The New York Times</u> bureau chief's wife. Together, we wrote a musical about Mao Tse Tung and his power-hungry wife, Chiang Ching. On the side, I wrote a travel article about Bali for The Times. A British publisher saw it and hired me to write a book about that enchanted island.

At the time, I thought the worst day of my life had happened when we had to leave Hong Kong for Jack to become editor of <u>The Boston International</u>. I couldn't imagine what it would be like in the States after six years in Asia. I had come acclimated to the bustle of Hong Kong with its sights and sounds. I would miss the modern skyscrapers abutting centuries-old temples. And I would miss the multi-national cuisines that shaped and satisfied our taste buds.

Adjusting to American life was a huge hurdle at first. Tending to two growing children, though, made the time pass quickly. After almost ten years in a suburb of Boston, it was time to fulfill Jack's dream—owning a small newspaper on Cape Cod.

We pooled our resources and bought the <u>Orleans Weekly</u>, the town's namesake. It was in a typical gray, weathered, shingled building. The old rickety, one-story structure had rooms like a rabbit warren, but it was on the main thoroughfare at a great location. This humble piece of real estate housed a small press in the basement. When it began to hum, the blood in our veins, like ink on the presses, made the juices flow with excitement. Many a night we had to spend stuffing papers and bundling them with string when staffers walked off the job. Nevertheless, it was a good life—a satisfying one.

The house we found was a little Cape Cod jewel. Just five minutes away from the office, it was hidden down a long narrow drive and opened to a panoramic view of Nauset Beach and its sandbars, facing the Atlantic. There were three acres and a beautiful marsh that changed colors with the seasons. The house was small, and we shared a study, which wasn't ideal, but bearable since we lived seven days a week at the newspaper.

After four great years there, a life-changing telephone call came for Jack from Washington, D.C. The Russell Rowland administration was considering Jack as a political appointee to Secretary of State, Gavin Stanley. Jack was in contention to serve as his spokesman under the formal name of Assistant Secretary of State for Public Affairs. The news was so unexpected, we were stunned. A battery of D. C. telephone calls came to our newspaper office. For privacy, Jack had to go either into the closet or bathroom. The walls were paper thin. Everyone always heard each other's conversations.

"Ginny, THEY want my fingerprints," whispered Jack.

"THEY?"

"The FBI."

"How is that done?" I whispered back.

"They want me to go to the local police station."

"You can't. They will be so suspicious and start spying on you."

"I know. Wait a minute." Jack picked up his mail and quickly shuffled through it. "Guess what?"

"What?"

"They said they had sent a fingerprint card to me in the mail." He ripped open the brown government-looking envelope on his desk. "This is it."

"Now what?"

"Go ask Betsey if she has an ink pad." I went to the front desk and snatched away her ink pad without asking—for the sake of National Security! When I came back, I closed the door to Jack's office. He took the pad and rolled his fingertips on it. Then, I put the special card on his desk and he placed each finger in the noted space until it was full. Naturally, the tops of his fingers were covered in ink. He washed his hands in the bathroom sink and used a paper towel to rub off all traces of the ink stains. As I watched this process, I was struck by its symbolism. Jack was wiping the slate clean by exchanging the ink of a newspaper office for the global arena of the State Department. This seemed to be part of Jack's destiny, and we would treasure each step as it unfolded.

Jack held up the fingerprint card and said, "Looks professional to me."

"Me, too. If it doesn't work out at the State Department, you can always transfer to the FBI!" I teased.

'Thanks for your undying confidence!. We'll drop this in the mail on the way home."

"You can stop whispering!" I said.

The telephone rang again.

"Jack Hunter. Yes. Since 1945? That's a long time ago. I can't remember everything. I will. My books? I might have a couple of spare copies. What for? There's nothing provocative in them—just the truth. Where should I send them? I certainly will. Goodbye."

I asked, "What do they want from 1945?"

"All the places I've lived since then."

"Do they know that we lived in 41 different places during just six years in Africa? I can't remember all of them. What do they want your books on Africa and Indonesia for?" I asked.

"To go over them with a fine toothcomb to see if there is anything subversive in them," Jack said.

"They're thorough, I'll say that about them."

"Let's go home."

That was early spring. We had sent the very professional-looking fingerprint card and all the items and information they had asked for. We didn't hear anything else for a couple of months, but kept working, as if it weren't going to happen. Still, every once in a while, we found ourselves staring at each other and wondering if we would be leaving our home and our business. If it were to be, Max, our youngest, would go with us and finish high school there. Wanda would be entering college, living away from home. Would the Rowland administration be in office for four or eight years and would we be gone for the same? Would all our roots be pulled up once again? Could we adjust back to big city living? It was a lot to think about. And yet, the prospect was so exciting. As we waited for the next step, we kept one ear listening for the telephone to ring, bringing us news from Washington.

One afternoon we went home for a leisurely lunch on the deck. Jack installed an extension cord on our phone and pulled it out beside his chaise lounge. As we were drifting off into a semi-slumber, the telephone rang.

"Mr. Hunter, sorry to disturb you, but there's someone important at the front desk asking for you," said the receptionist.

"Who is it?"

"A Diplomatic Security Officer from the State Department."

"A State Department Security Officer?" Jack asked. I immediately sat up. "Should I come back to the office?"

"He says they don't want to talk with you, but to speak alone with everyone in the office."

"Of course. Okay. Just be sure our people cooperate. Use my office," said Jack calmly looking directly at me. He hung up and we stared unbelieving at each other. "Well, it's no longer a secret."

Little did we know, and didn't find out until hours later, that at the same time the officer arrived at the newspaper, he had help from the local FBI field agents, and they had set up a post at the elbow bend in the road, leading to our driveway. Instead of heading back to the office, we decided to stay put. Jack paced back and forth for hours until he finally went to work at his desk in the house. I couldn't concentrate and just lounged on the deck with a multitude of thoughts rushing through my mind.

The three FBI men in typical dark suits and conservative ties had the back of their black van open, so they could adjust all of their electronic devices, used for recording. They stopped and name-checked everyone who came down the road. There were only four or five houses on our secluded lane, so the activity couldn't have been that great. After an hour of no movement, one of the men decided to begin knocking on the neighbors' doors. A few moments later, our most elderly neighbor, a woman in her seventies, asked who was there. She had no idea that he was ready to take her statement.

"Excuse me, ma'am, we're from the FBI. Could you spare a few moments to talk with us?"

She skeptically opened the door, but wouldn't come out. "May I see your badge?" He politely, but authoritatively, showed it to her and she reluctantly came out on her porch. "How may I help you and what's this about?"

He said, "Your neighbor, Jack Hunter, is being considered for a high-level post in Washington, D.C."

"Washington, D.C.? That's awful," she blurted out.

"I beg your pardon?"

"Washington is such a rat race. I spent forty years there. Why would anyone want to leave paradise and go there?" she queried.

"Do you know Mr. Hunter?"

"Sadly I don't, but please give him my condolences," she said and turned to reenter her house and close the door. As far as she was concerned that's all she was going to say on that matter.

The agent smiled and went to join his colleagues to recount what had just happened. They all laughed. One of them said, "She could be right. It's pretty nice here." They nodded and waited for the next victim. Just as they were about to pack up, a bushy-haired teenager skidded around the corner on his blue bike. He was whistling and nearly ran the men down. They put up their hands to stop him.

"Hello there, young man, do you mind if we ask you a couple of questions?"

"Okay."

"Do you know the Hunters? Jack and Ginny Hunter?"

"Yep."

"Do they have any close relationships with any of your neighbors?"

"Nope."

"How old are you?"

"Fifteen."

"Well, do they have any friends?"

"Nope—no friends."

"No friends? Why not?"

"I dunno. Maybe because they work all the time—seven days a week."

"How do you know?"

"I know."

"Who are you?"

"Their son."

"The Hunters' son?"

"Yep."

"What's your name?"

"Max. Max Hunter."

"I guess you know who we are."

"The police or the FBI. Would you excuse me? I need to do my homework, and get to my job," said Max.

"Where do you work?"

"At a local restaurant, washing dishes," Max answered.

"Good for you. We won't keep you any longer."

"Thanks. By the way, my Dad's a pretty terrific guy—for what it's worth."

With astonishment they watched him ride to his house, take off his knapsack, and go inside. They packed up and went for coffee.

The front door slammed.

"Mom?"

"Max? I'm out on the deck," I said.

"Guess what?"

"What?"

"I just got stopped by the FBI."

"We heard they were around. What did they ask you?"

"If you and Dad had any friends," smiled Max.

"Good Lord, what did you tell them?"

"That you didn't."

"Oh Max!" I exclaimed.

"Well, it's the truth."

"I know, but…"

"Don't worry, I told them it's because you guys work all the time."

"Did you really tell them that?" I asked.

"Yep."

"Thank God."

Just then, Jack walked back on the deck to greet Max. "How's it going, son? Any news?"

"Nothing, except the FBI stopped me."

"Did they ask you a lot of questions?" Jack asked.

"Not really. They were only interested in your friends. I told them you didn't have any."

"Good answer," Jack said.

"Oh, Jack," I said.

"You know how I feel about people. They are clawing at me all day. I deserve some peace and privacy in my own home with my own family."

"It just doesn't make sense. You're a newspaperman, who is making news this week. By the way, you are the most charming and witty person ever. You could attract any friend on earth," I said.

"You're prejudiced. Anyway, I save all my charm for you!" Jack said.

"Ridiculous."

"Don't worry, Dad, I told them you didn't have any friends because you and Mom work so hard," Max volunteered.

"I think the other answer was more fun," Jack said with tongue in cheek.

"Oh, Jack, you're impossible," I said, shaking my head.

"Guess who just called me?" said Jack.

"Who?" I wanted to know.

"Bill Banner at The Boston International."

"What did he want? To beg you to come back?" I asked.

"The FBI agents are swarming all over the offices, finding out about their ex-editor. Bill said he gave them all the dirt."

"What do you mean?" I asked.

"They wanted to know if I took drugs."

"What did Banner say?"

"Hell, no, he hardly takes an aspirin," Jack stated.

I laughed really hard. So did Max before going upstairs to do some homework and get ready to wash dishes downtown.

"Well, I'm going to the office for a while. Want to come?" asked Jack.

"Nothing could stop me," I answered.

As we drove in our Ford Bronco, we joked all the way about the State Department and FBI spreading its men across Cape Cod and Boston and who knows where else. Swinging in front of the office to park, we noticed that everyone was about to leave for the day. One agent, who had conducted the interviews, looked like a young Marlon Brando.

"Mr. Hunter?" asked the agent movie star.

"Yes?"

"I understand my colleagues have been posted on the road near your house."

"My son informed me," Jack replied.

"By the way, he's a cool customer, according to my men. Mr. Hunter, if all the things your employees say about you are true, you may be going to Washington very soon," he smiled.

"They were all coached," Jack quipped.

"If so, you did a great job."

"I didn't do the coaching, it was my lovely wife." Everyone laughed, and the handsome agent firmly shook my hand.

As the agents left, Jack and I headed for his office. Everyone--reporters, ad people, and production staff-- crowded into the small room and asked him a million questions about the job he would be taking. Their eyes were shining with excitement. And of course, they wanted to know who would be running the paper in Jack's absence.

"You all should know that nothing is final. I haven't received a formal offer from D.C. But if it all works out, our capable manager, George Dwyer, will take the helm. We will be in constant contact, and Mrs. Hunter will probably return in summers to run the office. I'll come as often as I can. I know you are all capable of keeping everything running in tip-top condition. Otherwise, I wouldn't consider this new position if I didn't trust each and every one of you. You are the stars in my Orleans universe." They all responded with laughter and applause.

"Can we put an announcement in our paper?" asked the young editor.

"Only if you bury it on page six as a local interest story due to agents running around," insisted Jack.

"Not the front page?"

"Absolutely not!" Jack demanded.

"Why not?"

"It would not be appropriate since nothing is firm yet," said Jack.

They were really happy for Jack and congratulated him while they collected their things to go home for the evening. Chatter and whispering followed them out the front door. After they were gone, George Dwyer leaned against the door frame and looked at Jack with a twinkle in his eye.

"So, you trust me to run the littlest show in town?" asked Dwyer.

"Don't worry, I'll be snapping the whip from the Washington Monument," Jack retorted. "I'll want a weekly report from you on Sunday mornings to keep me apprised. Agreed?"

"Agreed, boss," smiled George as he swaggered to his back office.

Jack turned to me and said, "Let's grab a pizza and salad for dinner and take it home."

"Good idea." We strolled across the street to the Villa Pizza. As we entered, two of our reporters stood up and yelled, *Mr. Smith Goes to Washington.* Hey everybody, this is our boss, Jack Hunter, and he's going to D.C. to work for the President." Everyone in the restaurant stood up, cheered, and clapped.

"Nothing is official," said Jack. Embarrassed by this public announcement, Jack let me order the pizza. We talked with the reporters while we waited. When it came, they wouldn't let us pay. They waved and cheered as we left and wished us good luck.

It wasn't long before the news ripped through the little town of Orleans like wildfire and spread throughout the Cape. The telephone started ringing and ringing and didn't stop.

In less than a week, a formal letter came from Secretary of State Gavin Stanley, congratulating Jack on his selection as Assistant Secretary of State for Public Affairs as his spokesman. He expressed the State Department's good fortune in having someone with such a wide range of experience. Secretary

Stanley concluded by assuring Jack how much he looked forward to working with him.

✳   ✳   ✳   ✳

A few nights later, Jack came into our study, looking at me curiously, and asked, "Ginny, what's that notebook? What are you doing?"

"I'm going to start writing down what's happening to you and us. All these letters and phone calls are fascinating. It's unforgettable now, but twenty or thirty years down the road, we may forget," I said. Jack nodded and turned back to his desk. I assumed his nod of agreement gave the go ahead, so I took out a large red, school-like notebook and my favorite blue pen to begin describing this awesome journey. I started with recording the FBI investigations and many of the local comments from Cape Cod friends and colleagues.

COMMENTS:

1. Jack, you must be crazy to do this.
2. Good God, why would you do it?
3. What an honor! Why Jack? Why was he selected?
4. You people are doomed to that kind of life. You can't stay away from it.
5. Tell the President to keep us out of war.
6. Jack will certainly be in his right place.
7. Leaving Cape Cod? God, that's awful. What a shame.
8. Jack has done so many wonderful things. This is one more star to add to his resume.
9. My God, I hear the FBI even went to Alaska to interview someone about his character. Why didn't they use the telephone and save some money—our money.
10. It's a natural for him.
11. He's a heck of a guy.
12. This is the biggest thing to happen to Cape Cod since JFK.
13. How exciting.
14. What a bombshell.
15. The best appointment Russell Rowland has made.
16. Congratulations. When does the Oval Office devil want you down there?
17. It's the best thing to happen to Mom and Dad. They're city people. They don't know how to relax in a resort place.
18. One reporter at <u>The Boston International</u> was asked this question. "Does Mr. Hunter have any weaknesses?" "Yes, he has one. Before

God and my country, I say it. He has a weakness for Labrador Retrievers."

19. The publisher of the rival newspaper in Orleans said this, "Jack, you're a glutton for punishment. I came up here to get away from all that."

During all the excitement, we had forgotten about Jack's mother, Clarissa, who lives in a condo across town. Jack called her after he hung up from the last call.

"Mother, are you sitting down?" Jack asked.

"Yes."

"We have some news. Can you guess?"

"Ginny's not pregnant again, is she?"

"No, of course not. Wait a minute, let me ask her. Ginny, are you pregnant?" asked Jack. I shook my head vigorously from side-to-side.

"She's not pregnant. We're moving to Washington, D.C.," Jack couldn't hold her in suspense any longer.

"Washington? Why?"

"The President and the Secretary of State want me to serve as the State Department's spokesman."

"Oh my goodness. That's wonderful. Will Ginny go, too?" she asked.

"Ginny and Max."

"What about Wanda?"

"She'll be going to college," Jack said.

"I'm overcome."

"Will you be all right by yourself here in Orleans?" he asked. After all, she had just moved here to be near us and now we were leaving.

"Certainly. Friends will take me around, I'm sure."

"Ginny will be here in the summers, and we'll come back for Christmas and holidays," Jack assured her.

"This is indeed an honor," she said.

"There will be a short announcement in our paper on Thursday and maybe in The Cape Codder."

"Congratulations, dear. I'm very proud of you."

"If all goes as planned, the Sunday Cape Cod Times will have a front page story with pictures. A reporter and photographer came out to the house for the interview. The Cape Codder may have a story as well.

After the stories appeared, Clarissa Hunter had many telephone calls with these comments:

1. You must come and have tea with us.

2. You must be very proud of your son.
3. We didn't realize he was a Pulitzer Prize winner.
4. Come down to my condo and tell me all about your son's appointment.
5. Are you going to be leaving us?
6. When will they go?
7. Where will they live?
8. Your son is going to be working for the worst people in the world!
9. I knew your son and his wife couldn't stay buried on Cape Cod.
10. They will have to entertain a lot.

Of course, I added them to my red notebook for posterity's sake. The invitations flooded in. Everyone wanted to entertain us. We just didn't have the time. But we made time for one group, who were D.C. aficionados and wandered in and out of every administration, wielding their power in one way or another.

We invited them to dinner at our house. We needed to learn from their experiences and knowledge. I wanted to make it a special night. This was our first foray into the D.C. way of life. I prepared shrimp cocktail and made an exotic Chinese stir fry with chicken and cashew nuts. For dessert, I made a cooling watermelon pie that was too delicious for words.

One of our notable male guests said in a slight southern drawl, "You are going to be a famous hostess in Washington, my dear. I just wish I were there to see it. Who knows, maybe I will. I think our hostess deserves a toast."

I positively melted and became totally embarrassed.

That was our last dinner party in our Orleans oasis. We decided to buy secondhand furniture in D.C. and leave our house intact. It had taken a great deal of thought to blend our African and Asian décor into our New England seaside cottage. We didn't want to disrupt our dream house and view. It would be there to welcome us back—whenever that might be.

The next thing was for me to fly to D.C. and look for a place to live--another place to call home. My friend, Georgia, knew a realtor, who was licensed in both Virginia and D.C. She was sure Nancy Barr could help.

CHAPTER TWO

▼

TOURING D.C.

D.C.

Off I went to the cherry blossomed capital of our country. I was disappointed not to see the blooms this year, but I couldn't wait for next April to view them firsthand. I heard the sight was absolutely spectacular.

I took a Plymouth & Brockton bus from Hyannis to Boston's Logan Airport to catch my flight to D.C. The bus ride was so easy and I boarded the plane to settle comfortably into my seat. As we approached the airport in D.C., the pilot swung us around the familiar picture-postcard sights of Washington. For this aerial view, I pressed my face against the window to absorb everything I could. Originally, the District was carved from a ten mile square piece of land, ceded from both Virginia and Maryland. Now, this beautiful place was going to be our next home. I felt butterflies and pride on this perfect, cloudless sunny June day. Fleetingly, I wondered if the politics would match the purity of the shimmering white memorials and the high-minded quotations engraved on their walls. I knew, in time, I would enjoy finding the answer to that question from an insider's point of view!

D.C., here we come.

With a small overnight bag, I landed at National Airport across the Potomac River from the District. Once in the arrival area, I began searching for Nancy Barr, the realtor and personal friend of Georgia's on the Cape. I soon spotted the sign with my name on it. I waved to her and we embraced as if we had been friends forever.

Nancy was from Illinois and had that irresistible warmth most mid-westerners exuded. Her accent, similar to that of a Texan, had a bit of a lilt—a voice you would never forget. One's name had a prolonged ending to it or the end of a sentence hung mysteriously in the air. Her hair wasn't blonde or gray. It was a combination of both—the exact color of sand. Her au currant layered haircut meant that whichever way it swung from the River breezes, it would fall in perfect place. Her pale blue eyes slanted downwards and seemed connected to her upturned smile. She was impeccably dressed in light beige to match her hair. However, I was to discover that Nancy had a personality that was far from beige!

"Ginnyyyyyyyyy!

"Nancy!"

"Welcome to our beautiful townnnnn!"

"Thank you for coming to meet me. Georgia will be so pleased we've connected," I said.

"Let's get in the car and start our missionnnnnn—unless you have more luggage?"

"This is it. I'm ready!"

As we sat in her fancy late model Mercedes convertible with the top down, she said, "This is the agendaaaaa—if you approve. I'll give you a little sight-seeing tour to orient you. Then, I'll give you a verbal rundown with spec sheets on the houses and condos in D.C., Maryland, and Virginia. From there, you can rule out what you don't like and we'll set off to see what you dooooo."

"Sounds good to me."

Nancy Barr swung out of the airport in a confident manner. I was surprised how close we were to the heart of D.C.

"Perhaps you know the District was originally a fort owned by Maryland to defend against Indians. At the Philadelphia Convention in 1787, the parcel of land was designated ten miles square (100 square miles). In 1788 and 1789, Virginia and Maryland ceded land to the District," she said. "Where that fact came from, I'll never know!" We laughed together.

"I knew some, but not all, of it!"

We crossed the Potomac over a concrete European style bridge, which I later learned was the Arlington Memorial Bridge, with magnificent sculpted horses on either pillar in gilded bronze, inviting us to the political side of the river. One horse was the winged Pegasus. There were 36 gilded bronze stars to represent the number of states at that time. I was astonished to see the Lincoln Memorial loom just behind the horses like a huge backdrop. It was overpowering.

"I'll swing you by the monolithic State Department where Jack will be spending most of his time," she said.

"Oh, do you mind if we stop at the Lincoln Memorial first? It is so imposing. I can't resist it!" I exclaimed.

"No problem. It's right in front of us. We'll park, so you can see it on foot," she said.

Enthusiastically, I jumped out of the car and Nancy joined me as we skipped up the steps. "The other day, I went to the little Snow Library in Orleans to learn something about these memorials. Are you interested?" I asked.

"Of course. Give me as much as you know!"

"Let's see, the architect was Henry Bacon and the sculptor Daniel Chester French. It was started in 1914 and finished in 1922. The 36 column Greek Doric Temple is made from Indiana limestone and Yule marble, discovered by mining engineer, George Yule, near Marble, Colorado. The Lincoln statue is made of Georgian marble. On the walls are quotes from the Gettysburg Address and Lincoln's second Inaugural Address. Also, Martin Luther King, Jr.'s 'I have a Dream' speech is on another wall."

"Well, you've told me more in one minute than I have ever known about the monument."

"If I'm wrong, you can blame the reference books in Snow Library!" I said. I hoped that I didn't mix up the facts in trying to learn so much in a short time.

"I'll take your word for it. Do you want to see where the Vietnam Veterans Memorial will be near the Lincoln Memorial?"

"Maybe in a couple of years when it's built," I said.

"Did you find out anything about ittttt?" she asked.

"A little. President Jimmy Carter signed the project into law in 1980, last year, and a Yale University student entered a contest for a design and won."

"Do you remember the nameeee?" she asked.

"Only because I read about it yesterday!" I confessed. "Her name is Maya Ying Lin."

"Will it indeed be a black wall with names of the fallen on it?" asked Nancy.

"Exactly. It will be polished black granite from Bangalore, India."

"It should be a stirring sight--hauntingly so--in black and at eye-level with all those soldiers' names," Nancy said. We both agreed.

"Now, shall we drive two blocks over to the State Department?" She asked.

"Fine."

"You do know that political appointees actually work seven days a week, 24 hours a day!" she laughed. "There it isssss." Before I could answer her joke, she pointed to the State Department.

"I don't know what I expected, but the architecture doesn't have the flair of the other buildings on the mall. It is more like a poor man's Parthenon in rectangular slabs of limestone," I said. "However, Thomas Jefferson was the first Secretary of State and today there are over 30,000 people who work on the eight floors. The Secretary's offices are on the seventh floor. The eighth is for entertaining. There are three Diplomatic Reception rooms: the Jefferson, Franklin, and John Quincy Adams. I learned all that yesterday because I wanted to know what I was getting into."

"That's interesting. Perhaps Jack will bring the flair and drama that it needsssss!" We looked at each other and laughed.

As we were turning around, I said, "Wait, there's something on the side of the road at the side of the State Department."

"Where?"

"There."

"That, my dear, is a homeless man, sleeping on the steam heat grid. He's been there forever and refuses to move," stated Ginny.

"Won't someone run over him?"

"Everyone knows he's there and is extra careful," said Nancy.

"That's terrible; especially in the nation's capital. Pull over."

"Now?"

"Yes. I won't be long. I have to give him something." I dug out a ten dollar bill from my bag.

"But…"

I rushed out to the figure wrapped in tattered ponchos and stooped down. "Sir, I hope I'm not disturbing you."

He opened his bulging brown eyes and tried to focus on my face. "Of course not, madam. Pardon me for not standing up for a lady."

"Quite all right. May I ask your name?" I inquired.

"Lord Byron."

"You are a poet!"

"And an actor."

"Could you quote me a few verses from 'Don Juan'?"

He stood up with his fists on his waist and said, "Would you mind stretching across my grid so that no one else can steal my place while I'm emoting?"

"I'd be happy to," I said, following his request.

He bellowed out in a Shakespearian voice some verses. Passers-by stared in amazement.

"Absolutely beautiful. Thank you."

A policeman looked at me suspiciously, so I quickly stuffed the bill in Lord Byron's hand. "This is to feed you in between your meditations," I whispered like a conspirator.

"Madam, you have made my year. May the magnificent blessings from above fill your being!"

Spying the policeman getting closer to me and the homeless man, Nancy literally stood up in the car. "GINNY! Let's gooooo."

The policeman was looking at me intently. I quickly ran to the car. "Let's get out of here before they take your license plate number," I said out of breath. Nancy's tires screeched as we turned around.

"Ginny, what possessed you to do such a thing?"

"The homeless aren't invisible, Nancy. They are people and deserve respect," I answered.

"What did you say to him?"

'I asked his name. It's Lord Byron."

"Is he a looney?"

"Oh, no. I asked him to quote from 'Don Juan.' "

"Did he?"

"Verbatim. Nancy, I didn't do anything wrong. I spoke to a homeless man and gave him money. That's not a crime," I said.

"But if a reporter got hold of the story, it might have been an interesting start to Jack's job."

"Oh." I began to think about Jack's reaction to this little incident.

"This can be a vicious town."

"Sorry. I didn't mean to embarrass you," I said.

"Shall we go to the Jefferson Memorial? It's one of my favorites," Nancy said.

"Yes!"

As we came closer, Nancy said, "You can imagine how beautiful it is during cherry blossom time. The wind blows the pale pink petals off the branches as they fall gracefully to the ground, creating a moving carpet or they float on top of the Potomac's waters."

"It must be incredible," I said. "It's breathtaking even without the blossoms."

"Tell me some facts about the Jefferson Memorialllll," Nancy said with a slight twinkle.

"Let's see what I can recall on this one. It was started in 1937 on eighteen acres in a Classical Revival style with a shallow dome, like the one on his Monticello home. The architect was John Russell Pope and it was dedicated in 1943. Jefferson's bronze statue was finished in 1947. The Declaration of Independence is on the wall inside the portico. I can't really remember anything else, but it is impressive."

"Innnnsppppirrrring," she said.

"Can we drive over to the Washington Monument and take a look?" I asked.

"We certainly can," she said.

The Monument wasn't far. It was almost in the middle of the mall. We parked and looked up at the soaring obelisk. Lots of people were walking around and standing in line to go inside to climb to the top. Seeing so many children, families, and folks of every age and nationality was a source of pride as an American.

"Do you have any idea how tall it is?" asked Nancy.

"Don't ask me tomorrow, but today I think it is 555 feet and five inches."

"And the architect?" she asked.

"Robert Mills. They worked on it from 1848 to 1881, but because the funds ran out, it wasn't finished. Apparently, when the light is right, one can see the difference in the color of the marble, due to a different quarry stone used when the building commenced," I said. "And that's the extent of my knowledge."

"Nothing else?"

"Well, there is one fact that will never make it to the history books," I conceded.

"What's that?"

"Jack Hunter proposed to Ginny Parks right here at three o'clock in the morning after we had been to see the late show of Sophie Tucker performing in a local nightclub. We were on our way to Alabama to see my parents."

"Oh, my heavensssss. Maybe that's why you are returning to Washington," smiled Nancy. "To reestablish your engagement ties."

"Who knows?"

"We'll swing by the Capitol. Any facts you can share?"

"Not many," I replied. "It was designed by Dr. William Thornton in an American Neoclassical style. Started in 1793, President George Washington laid the cornerstone. However, the Capitol was set on fire by the British in the War of 1812. It was rebuilt and has since evolved into the beautiful structure we see today. "

"Thanks, Ginny, for the tourrrr!" Nancy giggled.

"I hope it wasn't too boring."

"Very informative. Now we'll start house huntinggggg."

"Perfect," I said.

Ten minutes later we were in a totally different part of town without monuments. It is an area that looks and feels something like Boston with its townhouses on tree-lined streets.

"This is Georgetown, a very upscale neighborhood close to everything. Jack and Jackie Kennedy lived right there," said Nancy.

"Charming. What's the price range in this area?"

"$700,000 and uppppp."

"And up and up and up?" I asked.

"Yes."

"Although it's beautiful, let's scratch this area from our list," I said. "Anything in this price range, we can skip."

"What is your range?"

"Between $150,000 and $175,000. Should we stop looking?" I asked half joking and half serious.

Nancy laughed. "Of course not. That helps to narrow our focus to Virginia. Forget D.C. and Maryland. Let's go to McLean and meander. I have a few listings. Are you hungryyyy?"

"A sandwich or salad would be perfect," I mused.

We found a local, non-descript place with a private booth and sat down. Over lunch, I asked Nancy some personal questions. Since we hit it off, I didn't think I would be overstepping my bounds.

"Nancy, are you married?"

"Divorceddddd."

"Children?"

"Two. A daughter at West Point and my son in a small Midwestern college. And you?" she asked.

"Two. One about to go to college and the other needs to finish two years of high school here," I said.

"McLean has a wonderful high school—Langley High School. It's big—2,600 kids. Many are the sons and daughters of diplomats and Congressmen."

"Sounds interesting," I nodded. "How did you get into real estate?" I asked innocently.

Nancy stared at her tall iced tea glass and turned it slowly with her fingertips, leaving marks on the glass's frosty condensation.

"Did I ask something I shouldn't?"

"No." She looked up and slowly answered. "When my children were in their pre-teens, I asked my husband for a divorce, even though I didn't have any of my own financial resources. He was a skillful lawyer and immediately took custody of the children. I was allowed to see them once a month under supervision.

"What did you do?"

"Fortunately, a friend let me live in her basement. It took me six months to get myself together emotionally," she said.

"Any alimony?"

"None."

"Any skills?"

"None. My mother sent me a little something from her Social Security. I was grateful for her help, but knew I shouldn't rely on her kindness."

"And then?"

"Then, I found a job as a receptionist in a real estate office. One day, there wasn't anyone in the office to show a young couple some houses, so…That was it. Now I have my own company and am able to be part of my children's lives."

"What a great story! I'm impressed."

"Let's finish our search and see what turns up."

"Good idea. Let me pay for this," I said.

"Not on your life. I'm successful nowwww," she said and paid the bill.

We drove around McLean, by the school, the shopping area, and the residential section. It was manicured, clean, stylish and full of energy from the powerbrokers and policy makers that live side-by-side. At that moment, she drove into a circular drive of a brick colonial house with a nice shady yard. She opened the lockbox attached to the front door and we walked into a spacious center hall.

"It's empty," I said surprised. "I thought people left furniture to sell a house."

"Every four or eight years when the administration turnover starts, people are anxious to return to their permanent homes. Realtors are in heavennnn. They can sell and resell the same houses over and over," Nancy stated. "We thrive on the changing of the guard."

"This is one of them?"

"Yes." We walked through. It was lovely, but a bit big for the three of us. I asked the price.

"Somewhat higher than you had hoped--$450,000."

"This is beyond us," I sighed.

"There is one condo that might fit your needs," she said.

"In McLean?"

"A cluster of condos at Lewinsville Square near the McLean Inn where the Sunday buffet is scrumptiousssss," Nancy laughed. We were back in the car and racing to the u-shaped parking area where the condos were—all attached like two-story townhouses; some built from brick and others in wood-siding and fairly new. We entered the one for sale.

It was like a tunnel with no windows on the sides. There was a long hall to the small living room and a deck, big enough for outdoor dining, overlooking a small enclosed yard. The tight, indoor dining room was to the right of the front door, and it had a nice modern kitchen next to it. Upstairs was a master bedroom with its own bathroom like a master suite. Above the living room was a small guest room and guest bathroom at the head of the stairs. The basement was unremarkable and grounded in a beige carpet. It had one bedroom, a large bathroom, and a living area big enough for a pullout sofa and desk.

"What do you think?" asked Nancy.

"This is it," I said without thinking, because I knew it was perfect for the three of us. "Whoops, I haven't asked the price?"

"$165,000."

"Really. Humm. It sounds like a deal or maybe we can make an offer of $160,000?" I asked timidly.

"Let's go write out an offer agreement," she said.

We raced back to her car with a feeling of accomplishment and headed to her office. I was happy and she was happy. I had the checkbook and put down the deposit. I even signed a purchase and sale with the next installment, full of hope that the owner might accept the offer. It was late afternoon and we had seen and covered a lot of ground.

"Nancy, do you know a place that sells secondhand furniture?"

"I certainly do. It closes in 45 minutes, so grab your purse, and we'll go," she said.

We went up and down the aisles in lightning speed and I furnished the condo in thirty minutes. Nancy was amazed. I paid half and put everything on hold.

"You are amazingggg!"

"Deadlines help," I said.

"Now what, wonder woman?"

"I'll be spending the night at a friend's and go back to Boston tomorrow on an early flight," I said.

"Is the friend's house in McLean?"

"Yes, do you happen to know Nora French?"

"The Nora French at the World Bank?" she asked.

"That's the one."

"A friend of mine sold her that exotic house. I know exactly where it is," she said.

Nora was waiting and welcomed us to her palace. It was a secret jewel hidden in a maze of trees and dirt roads. I made the introductions and thanked Nancy profusely. She offered to take me to the airport, but Nora had already made plans to drop me on her way to the office. Nancy then bid us goodbye.

"Do you have my telephone number?" I asked.

"Yes. I'll be in touchhhh."

Nora and I changed into something more formal for dinner. It gave me a chance to catch my breath and freshen up. Nora then drove us to a famous Chinese restaurant on K Street, Mr. K's. Through the more than seven courses, Nora talked about her job and the ups and downs of her love life. It was the mantra of many successful women—thwarted in the search for love and a lifelong partner.

As I sympathetically listened to her sad tale of love gone wrong, I looked up and saw a man at a rear table in distress.

"Oh no!" I exclaimed. Before Nora could ask why, I rushed to his table.

"Stand up, sir!" I said in a quick, commanding voice. He stood up and from behind I put my arms around him to perform the Heimlich maneuver. As I squeezed forcefully a second time, an actual chopstick with a piece of sweet and sour pork shot out of his mouth like a torpedo and landed in a lady's beehive hairdo. In what seemed like slow motion, I chased the wooden stick and carefully extracted it from the stiff hairspray, holding her upswept style in place. All the customers cheered. I handed the waiter the chopstick and calmly sat down again with Nora as if nothing had happened. In reality, my heart was racing.

The man I had just helped came to the table. He took my hand and gallantly kissed it. "Mademoiselle, please accept this as a very small measure of my gratitude." He pressed a $100 dollar bill in the palm of my hand.

"Sir, I couldn't possibly accept your kind gift. I didn't do it for money," I said.

"But you saved my life."

"It doesn't matter."

"Then, I insist you be my guest at the Embassy. I am Robert Marchant, France's ambassador to the United States."

"Oh, Mr. Ambassador, that's so kind. I am Ginny Hunter. May I introduce my friend, Nora French?"

"Mon Dieu! Mademoiselle French of the World Bank?" he asked. Nora nodded as he kissed her hand, too.

"When can you both come to the embassy?"

"Well, my husband and I will be moving here in September," I said.

"Excellent. How do I contact you?"

"My husband, Jack Hunter, will be the spokesman for the Secretary of State."

"I will contact you through him in September," he said.

"Thank you very much."

"It is I who should be thanking you," he bowed, smiled, and returned to his table.

"Ginny, I can't believe what just happened," said Nora.

"I know, it feels like a dream."

At the conclusion of our very strange dinner, the waiter never brought the check to our table. So, I went to the cashier to pay, but they refused to take any money. The French ambassador had taken care of it.

Nora, still speechless, drove us around the Washington Mall and memorials at night. It was quite a different experience than the day and somehow more thrilling. The white exteriors against the black of night were more dramatic. I didn't bother to expound on the history because Nora probably knew it already. After all, she was a graduate of Stanford in economics with a global perspective on everything.

As we drove back to her house, I turned to her and said, "I'm getting a disease.

"What disease?" she asked in a fearful voice.

"Potomac Fever!"

"It's contagious," she said with relief. "Try to get over it."

"I can't. I've fallen in love," I sighed.

"Ginny, you must try to get over it!"

"Why?" I asked.

"You might be disappointed. Look at me, I have Cape Cod fever. I wish I were going there with you tomorrow," Nora said.

"Maybe next summer when I'm there looking after the business," I said.

"It's a deal!"

CHAPTER THREE

▼

SWEARING IN

From Orleans to D.C.

"Ginnyyyyyy!" sang the voice on the other end of the phone.

"Nancy Barr! How are you?" I said with a smile and not needing to ask who was on the other line.

"Fabulous. What did Jack say about the condo in McLean?" she asked.

"Well, he knows it's not a mansion, but perfect for us and close to the State Department. He also likes the idea of Langley High School for our son," I said.

"Then, I have some good news for you."

"About the condo?" I said almost rhetorically.

"Exactly."

"Have they accepted our offer?"

"Not only have they accepted it and the Purchase and Sale agreement, but miraculously they have skipped the sixty day waiting period and offered it to you whenever you're ready," she said without taking a breath.

"That's incredible."

"Can you speed up the loan process?" she inquired.

"I'll have Jack work on it today."

"When do you plan to come?" she asked.

"We'll all drive down on July 6 in a convoy of two cars. After Jack's swearing in ceremony, I'll come back to the Cape with the kids. They both have jobs for the summer, so I should be up here until the end of August or just after Labor Day."

"Would you like me to have your furniture moved into the condo on the 3rd or the 5th of July?" She asked.

"Nancy, that's a very generous offer, but don't you have plans for the 4th?"

"I'm not going out of town if that's what you're asking and would love to do this. Why don't you send me a check for the rest of the furniture, and I'll send you keys to your new home!" she said.

"I'll do that right away, but are you sure this isn't an imposition?" I asked. "How can I ever repay you?"

"Don't worry, I'll think of something. It will be terrific to have you in the area. By the way, did you tell Jack about the homeless man?"

"No! I forgot," I admitted.

"Maybe it would be a good idea to keep forgetting," she laughed.

"You could be right."

"I know I am. Washington feeds on these innocuous bits of nonsense until they become gigantic anecdotes. So we'll keep it to ourselves. Bye, sweetie, we'll be in touch."

"Bye."

Nancy hung up and bit her lip. She hoped Ginny wouldn't be fodder for baseless gossip of vultures. She would hold her breath and pray. In fact, she might give Nora a call and get her to take on this rare innocent bird and figure out how to protect her.

Day after day I went from room to room to organize the packing. It took longer than I thought, considering we vowed to take very little to D.C. Our shared study was the most important. I lined up boxes for Jack to sort his papers, books, and files. I decided not to take any books, but only my manuscripts and typewriter. I let Jack select his own formal clothes and a few casuals. I packed my formals, which I never wore on Cape Cod, but hoped to in Washington although I did pack a few informal things like cotton pants and shirts. The rest of my Cape attire, I left hanging in my closet. I stacked suitcases and boxes up in Max's room. Except for his summer-job-clothes and paraphernalia, he would need almost everything for Virginia. Wanda's packing would be for college. She could wait until August to empty her drawers. Thank goodness.

One day it was so hot, I flopped out on the deck with some lemonade and stared at the view. Four-wheel drives--pick-ups, jeeps, campers--were parked on the outer beach with tailgates open for an afternoon of picnics. A few dogs were joyously jumping in the surf. Sailboats of all sizes and small motor boats raced to and fro along Snow Shore. There wasn't a cloud in the sky. For a few moments, I wondered if we were crazy to give all this up and live as transients in D.C. I soon returned from those musings and knew we were in for the time of our lives.

July 4th was suddenly upon us. All of us took time off from preparations to go to Rock Harbor to watch the fireworks off the sands of Skaket Beach along Cape Cod Bay. Some people stayed in their cars. Others spread a blanket on the beach for snacks and drinks. When it was over, the traffic was snarled for 30 or 40 minutes, a virtual traffic-jam on Cape Cod! We didn't bring our Yellow Labrador Retriever, Ginger, to the beach. Her ears were too sensitive to the noise of popping fireworks.

On Saturday morning, we picked up Clarissa to dog sit at the house and then loaded the cars. Jack had all his clothes and necessary papers in his car. I had everybody else's belongings in mine. The kids and I would return Tuesday night. The fridge was full of people food and plenty of dog food that I had made from a special concoction.

Sunday morning we left at 8:00 a.m. sharp. We calculated it would take ten hours from door to door. Jack led the way in his car. Max decided to ride with him while Wanda and I followed. We had a plan to honk twice if we needed to stop for gas or food or if Jack pulled off, we would stay right with him. Wanda played her music tapes most of the way.

Around 6:00 p.m., we drove into Lewinsville Square--right on time. We slowly opened the front door and thanks to Nancy Barr, the furniture was there. She had done a great job of placing our secondhand furnishings in every room. The kids were anxious to see Max's downstairs suite. He was thrilled. It gave him the privacy he wanted as a teenager--away from his parents! Jack was pleasantly surprised. It met all our requirements. The electricity was on and a telephone hooked up. Nancy had thought of everything.

We called her to invite her for dinner. She came by and took us all in her convertible to a restaurant at Tysons Corner—the biggest shopping mall we had ever seen. Nancy, of course, was our guest. Afterwards, she offered to drive us from our front door to the State Department so that Jack could find his way in the morning. The Department was only fifteen minutes away. Then, she thought Max and Wanda might like to see the memorials illuminated at night. They were speechless at the beauty. Jack was, too. Wanda almost regretted that she couldn't live in D.C. It would be fun to have her, but at least she could visit.

After Nancy dropped us back at the condo, we unloaded the cars and exhaustedly piled into bed after a long day. The condo already felt like home. So did Virginia and D.C.

On the edge of sleep, I thought what a great honor Jack's appointment was for him and for all of us. At the swearing in ceremony on Monday, he would be taking the oath of office to support the Constitution. This town and our time here would be exciting.

I couldn't resist saying in a loud whisper to Jack before he drifted off to sleep, "This is going to be an adventure."

"Indeed it will," he replied in a drowsy voice.

In the morning, Jack put on his best dark suit and white shirt with a silver and blue tie. He looked sharp. He looked ready. He looked like a man in charge. I was proud of the man I had fallen in love with. After he left, the kids and I began to unpack suitcases and boxes. Next, Wanda, Max, and I went shopping for groceries and stopped at Langley High school on the way. We found the front office and made sure Max was registered. Someone very kindly showed us around the maze of rooms and steered us to where the junior class's homerooms would be. It gave Max a feel for where he would be in the fall.

On the way back, I ran into the familiar secondhand store to see if I could find a carpet for the living room. There were two affordable Orientals that looked almost presentable and were perfect.

We fixed a late lunch at our new home. With anticipation, I dressed in a simple black suit with a flattering pink blouse and sensible, black patent pumps. Wanda wore a short black skirt and burgundy cotton sweater. Max dressed in a dark blue suit, blue Oxford shirt, and dark blue and white tie. He looked like his father's son. Except for his mop of bushy, wavy hair, he looked quite handsome in a suit, as opposed the beach boy attire, living the Cape Cod lifestyle.

Just before we left, Jack called to say we should have our driver's licenses with us to check into the building. Fortunately, Max had just passed his test before we left and had a temporary one. At 2:30 p.m., the three of us drove to the State Department. As we went into the parking garage underneath, security was there to check our identifications and call the Secretary's office for confirmation of our appointment. The lobby upstairs was impressive with a terrazzo floor and flags from all nations. We told the receptionist and attending officer our purpose for being there. They nodded and made a telephone call. Someone came down from the seventh floor and escorted us to the Secretary of State's large, yet comfortable office. Jack made the introductions and we all shook hands.

"Shall we move to the lobby outside my office for the swearing in ceremony?" asked Secretary Stanley. He was tall and friendly; his dark hair was just starting to recede. It made him look distinguished and seasoned. He led the way and beckoned the staff to serve as witnesses. At the side of the lobby, a blue velvet curtain behind the lectern was set up. An American flag was to the left and a blue and gold state department flag with its seal was to the right from where we were standing. This was called Pipe and Drape by the inner circle and used as a backdrop for all sorts of events. The Secretary then directed me behind the lectern and handed me a Bible. Secretary Stanley stood to the right of the lectern while Jack and the two children were to the left.

"Mr. Hunter, would you raise your right hand and place your left hand on the Bible, being held by Mrs. Hunter?"

"Yes, Mr. Secretary," said Jack.

"Please repeat after me. "I, Roger Jackson Hunter, do solemnly swear that I will support the constitution and laws of the United States…"

Jack repeated the words flawlessly.

"And that I will faithfully and impartially discharge and perform all the duties incumbent upon me as Assistant Secretary of State for Public Affairs…"

Jack managed to remember every word.

"…according to the best of my ability and understanding, so help me God."

Jack finished the oath with confidence.

"Welcome to the State Department," smiled the Secretary and shook Jack's hand as a photographer stepped forward to capture the moment for posterity.

"Thank you, Mr. Secretary." Jack leaned over and kissed me on the cheek. I put the Bible inside the shelf of the lectern.

"Why don't we all adjourn to my office for a few refreshments to celebrate this laudable moment?"

"That's a very kind offer," said Jack. The Secretary, Jack, the two children, and staff/witnesses walked back into the office, shaking Jack's hand. Everyone was in a jovial mood. While the group was chatting, I quickly opened my purse to check my hair and lipstick. As I started to follow everyone, I lurched forward and bounced backward like a weighted, plastic, punching bag clown. I discovered I couldn't move. My shoes seemed to be stuck to the floor for some reason. By now, the Secretary, staffers, Jack and the children were in the Secretary's office. I tried to call Jack in a loud whisper, but it was useless. I tried to move my shoes, but they were stuck. I slid down on my haunches to find out why this was happening. I saw a clear liquid oozing up through the floorboards. "GLUE!" I said out loud. "I'm glued to the floor!" But why? Was this a deliberate trap? Oh Ginny, stop being so paranoid. This isn't the CIA. It's the civilized State Department. I think. I stood up and noticed the clear liquid was in a two or three foot circle around me. I panicked. Should I scream? Don't be silly. Act like a lady and don't embarrass your husband. Just keep silent and no one will miss you, I kept telling myself. Looking at my black patent pumps, I knew there was no point in stepping out of my shoes because my stockings would stick, too. Was this an omen of things to come? Would I be known as the Glue Girl? No, it's just a freak accident. At least, I hope so. God help us if it's not! I tried not to cry. Men hate women who cry. Frozen to the floor, I dared myself not to cry. To stop the tears, I pulled my eyelids straight out until they hurt.

Suddenly, I could hear Secretary Stanley's booming voice, "Jack, where is your wife? Did she leave?"

"Why, no, she was right behind us. Excuse me." Jack retraced his steps out of the office into the hall lobby and came back to the lectern. "Ginny, what are you doing? Why didn't you come to the office?"

"I can't."

"What do you mean you can't? Are you alright? Come on, you're embarrassing us!"

"I can't move. Really, I can't."

"What? What do you mean? Don't be silly," he said. By now he could see my distress and was becoming concerned.

"My shoes are glued to the floor," I said, biting my lip.

"Then, step out of your shoes."

"I can't. The glue is everywhere and my stockings will stick, too. How come you didn't get stuck and I did?"

"If this were going to happen to anyone, it would happen to you!"

"Can't you get someone to help me?" I asked plaintively.

"How did this happen?" he asked distractedly. Stroking his chin, he wondered what to do. On his first day, he didn't know the building or the system for emergencies.

"I honestly didn't know there was fresh glue here, Jack. I'm sorry—really sorry. I know it couldn't be happening at a worse time."

"You can say that again," said Jack.

"It couldn't be happening at a worse time."

"Okay, okay. Stay where you are," he said distractedly.

"Do I have a choice?"

"I'll get someone to help." Jack walked briskly back into the office and whispered to the Secretary's assistant.

"Oh no! I'll get maintenance up here right away," she said and moved off in a flurry.

Sensing something was amiss, the Secretary asked, "Is everything all right?"

"It will be, sir," said his assistant.

"Is Mrs. Hunter all right?" he inquired, looking into the hallway.

"She will be shortly."

"What can we do?" he asked.

"Just wait here and she will join us in a few minutes. Please excuse me," the assistant said assuredly.

I was waiting alone for what seemed hours, but in fact, was only minutes. I could feel my face flush red and tears welled up. I willed myself to keep calm. Just when I couldn't fight back tears any longer, two muscular men stepped off the elevator. I could see Stanley's assistant greet them and explain the situation. Jack hovered around them. The burly men looked at me and then the dais and moved it carefully out of the way, surveying the floor around me.

"Ma'am, stretch your arms out straight from your sides. We're going to lift you out of your shoes and over the glued floorboards. Keep your arms stiff and don't bend them. Ready?"

I heard myself saying, "Yes." But I was still in a foggy state. I pretended to be a gymnast with arms straight, strong, and posture perfect. I lifted my arms and before I knew it, they each had grabbed an arm and lifted me out of my shoes and flew me through the air to the dry floor for a perfect landing. When my stocking feet touched the non-sticky surface, I was in heaven. At last, I was free—free from my glued prison.

"We will try to unglue your shoes and return them as soon as we can to Secretary Stanley's office. We apologize for this terrible mistake before the swearing in."

"That's all right," I said, trying to smile, so no one would be reprimanded.

"Are you all right?" asked the assistant with an unperturbed face.

"Fine. Just fine," I said. "But embarrassed to be like this." I gazed sadly at my torn stockings.

"Walk right behind me as if nothing has happened, and Mr. Hunter, you take her arm. No one will look at her feet and I'll lead you to a chair behind the sofa where she can sit and her feet won't be exposed. No one will be the wiser," said the assistant.

"Thank you very much," I said. "I'm sorry to put you to so much trouble."

"We should be the ones to apologize by putting you in that miserable situation. Usually this doesn't happen at the State Department of all places. This is a mark on us, not you, Mrs. Hunter. Please follow me and I'll take care of everything."

As we entered, people were curious about my mysterious disappearance, but the assistant smoothed it over without any explanations and had me seated in safety. A tart punch and some cookies were brought over to me, and the Secretary proposed a toast to Jack.

"Will you join me in welcoming Jack Hunter and his lovely family to Washington and to Jack himself for accepting this very sensitive and important post as my spokesman," he said, raising his glass. "We look forward to a long and beneficial association."

"Hear, hear!" everyone chimed in.

Suddenly, Max asked the Secretary a direct question. "Mr. Secretary, could I ask you what the difference is between a political appointee and someone like yourself, who is also appointed by the President?"

"A very good question, young man. In regards to a State Department political appointee, like your father, he is investigated thoroughly by our internal Security Division, together with the FBI. It is to attest to his impeccable character and background, so that he qualifies for top level security clearance."

"I know. They were crawling all over Cape Cod and it wasn't much of a secret." Everyone laughed, including the Secretary, Jack, Wanda, and me.

"Well, a proposed Secretary of State goes through a similar investigation, but also rigorous senate hearings. It can be a grueling and lengthy process. The Secretary designee also has to be investigated by the White House Cabinet Affairs. Then, the President, the State Department, and the FBI have to sign off on the clearance. It is a worthy process so that the President is protected by having people of integrity surrounding him."

"Thank you, sir," mumbled Max.

At that very second, the maintenance man appeared at the door. "Sorry to interrupt, sir, but Mrs. Hunter's shoes are ready."

"Her shoes?" asked the Secretary puzzled.

I turned beet red as people looked at the maintenance man and then at me. The assistant rushed to retrieve them and then to hand them to me. As I quickly slipped into them, Jack and I both expressed our thanks.

"May I ask what's going on?" asked Secretary Stanley.

"Sir, perhaps you don't want to know," said Jack.

"Of course I do."

The assistant rushed to Jack's rescue and mine by explaining the whole situation in hushed tones. Seeing the room was silent, her hushed tones carried the story. I turned red again. Everyone was shocked and apologetic; especially the Secretary. Some people were actually laughing as they covered their mouths, but they weren't laughing at me. They were laughing at the situation and that it happened in their impeccable State Department. Once the incident was out in the open, I realized it wasn't all bad—and not all good either! I felt like Winnie the Pooh caught in a pot of glue.

It seemed appropriate for me to say something, "Since I can walk in shoes again, I think the children and I should let you all get back to work, now that this domestic drama is over!" Everyone laughed, including me. We said our goodbyes and Jack walked the three of us to the elevator.

"We'll see you tonight, Jack, unless I get glued to the elevator floor!" I said. He nodded and went back to the office.

No one in our family or the rumor mill, would ever forget Jack's swearing in ceremony. As we drove out of the underground parking lot, I turned left instead of right.

"Mom," exclaimed Max. "You're going the wrong way to go back to McLean."

"I know."

"Where are you going?"

"You'll see." I quickly pulled the car over and near to the familiar steam grate. I jumped out with a $20 bill in my hand. "Lord Byron, do you remember me?"

"How could I forget the Lady of Mercy?"

"I'm sorry I don't have time to listen to your poetry today, but I have something for you. Don't bother to get up. It's just something to feed the soul," I said and smiled, handing him the money.

"Blessings, dear lady, showers of blessings on you."

I turned and ran back to the car.

"Mom, what are you doing?" Wanda and Max asked. "Who is that?"

"Lord Byron."

"Who?" They both asked.

"He's a homeless man who has been here for years. That's his name. He can quote reams of poetry."

"Is he crazy?" asked Max.

"No, he's a genius," I said.

"I don't know if Dad would like it," said Max.

"What would he think?" said Wanda.

"To give money to a homeless man is not a crime. It's something I want to do. We might not be rich, but we have more than that poor soul," I said with conviction.

Jack arrived home late--the first of many long nights to come. So the kids and I had an early supper. We, of course, saved some for him. That night, we went to bed early for our ten hour drive back to Cape Cod.

Before I crawled in, I wrote the day's events in my diary. As I described the glued-to-the-floor incident, I put my hand over my mouth to smother my giggles. What had seemed a total disaster was now quite funny—hilarious, in fact, but oh my Gosh, I wish it had happened to someone else.

I never heard Jack come in and didn't stir when he arose. He left before any of us woke up.

We left by 8:00 a.m. The kids slept in the back seat. The long drive gave me time to absorb what happened in the last couple of days. It was going to be wonderful. I was sure of it.

Goodbye, D.C., at least for the hottest two months of the year.

CHAPTER FOUR

▼

PARTIES AND
WHITE HOUSE RECEPTIONS

Cape Cod in summer is heaven, but it also can be a traffic nightmare unless you know the back roads and shortcuts. The tourist population swells to six or seven times larger than the year-round residents. Artists have been working all winter preparing their wares for the selling period of two to three months. Even the weekly newspapers double in size with ads designed to attract visitor dollars.

There is a reason for all this migration. The scenery is intoxicating-- the same sights and sounds that enticed Jack and me--button-sized, wild pink roses cascading over driftwood fences around weathered gray-shingled cottages and the refreshing salt air. All of that and more lure people back every summer. Everything exudes charm and is designed to shelve business worries away while vacationers stretch out on a beach or swim in the chilly surf. Realtors are desperate to seduce the summer population into buying a dream house or condo for their secret escape. Around this time of year, I think of a poem that captures the essence of Cape Cod, written by a local resident, who wants to remain anonymous, but perhaps you can guess who it is!

CAPE COD

On the flowing skirts of sand,
hedged by pines and marshland,
rests the bent arm of Cape Cod.
A playground of summer sport

is the Cape—where tides and surf,
cottages and pink roses,
dawns and florid sunsets
are one's greatest playmates.

Cape Cod offers nature as balm
to the society-weary,
to business burdens,
to marital thorns,
to the scarred conscience.

Here, one can graze freely
in serene mental pastures
as Cape Cod restores the soul.

Those words rumble around my brain when I am driving. Then, I remember the summer light on Cape Cod, which is another wonder. In July, the evenings are light until almost 9:00 o'clock. As summer winds down in August, fifteen to twenty minutes fall away every week until dusk turns to dark by half past seven. During the final days of August, the earlier nights are an omen for summer's end and fall's hint of September, which fill the evening air. I begin to think--didn't summer just begin with its promise of sunlight and warm days? How can it be September so soon? What happened? It went too fast.

That's exactly how the children and I felt that summer. Wanda was waitressing at Kadee's in East Orleans, making tips for college spending money. Max worked at the local drugstore and a restaurant, saving his money for Virginia. I was covering theatre on Cape Cod for the newspapers and interviewing celebrities as they came every week to perform in the famed Cape Playhouse in Dennis. I was in and out of the newspaper office constantly and keeping tabs on the kids. Max would often go with me to interviews and take photos of the celebs for the newspapers. Pearl Bailey, appearing at the Melody Tent in Hyannis, was horrible to him at a press conference. Other journalists there came to his rescue, so I, as a mother, didn't have to do the obvious.

Jack only made it back for two weekends. Actually, I was surprised he made it back at all. Life in D.C. was hectic. He told me in detail what it's like to be an insider in government, where much of the news is created, as opposed to hunting in the world of journalism, working day in and day out to gather bits and pieces of information to make a complete story. We sat out on the deck after dinner, watching the shadows of night fall across the beach and horizon.

"So, how are you feeling about your job at the State Department?" I asked.

"At first, I felt like a rowboat among aircraft carriers. It was kind of frightening. I kept a low profile, but after a few days, I was forced to make global decisions, and my honeymoon pass was over. It feels good, being back in the swing of international affairs."

"What's your daily life at the office like?" I asked.

"The days are much longer," he said.

"What time do you get to your office?"

"Between 5:30 and 6:00 a.m."

"Why so early?" I asked.

"The world doesn't sleep all at once. The State Department has diplomatic corps offices on every continent around the globe and the news keeps moving. It never stops and I am in charge of the message. Public Affairs secretaries are there at 5:00 a.m. to read the newspapers and highlight them for me. Then, I read them and do some more highlighting. If something earth shattering happens, I track it down to get confirmation before I meet with Secretary Stanley to review events from the world and all the newspapers. We discuss pertinent points plus all the events from intelligence reports that journalists are not privy to. I'll meet with him again before I give my daily press briefing. Much of the information I convey to the Secretary comes from the briefing book that is prepared for me every day by my public affairs staff," he said.

"Do you ever disagree with the Secretary?"

"If I do, it's usually from a journalist's point of view—my newspaper background helps here. You can't control information, but you can give the press as much as you're able without giving away privileged information. After the briefing, we can always discuss things on background. I never lie to the press. If I can't provide information for security reasons, I'll say so and they respect that."

"Do you like the people you work with on a daily basis?" I wanted to know.

"For the most part, I have great respect for them. On the other hand, they are career foreign service officers, who will spend several decades serving their country. They have seen many political appointees come and go. They very often hold them in contempt and await their term to be over."

"Contempt?" I asked.

"And with suspicion."

"Why?"

"Because they think they know the system inside out, they regard a group of novices as incompetent and knowing nothing. They have to baptize him or her again and again. Since they assume they know everything, they resent the appointees who are not as knowledgeable as they. In fact, they practically hold the appointee hostage and maneuver him or her to do their bidding. There are code signals among them," he chuckled.

"Code signals? What do you mean?"

"Well, no one is ever judged as good, average, or poor," Jack said.

"Why not?"

"If someone is classified as 'very good' that actually is the code description for 'mediocre or very poor.' The word 'unmatched' can mean something devastating. Codes mean everything to the insider and causes tremendous humor for those in the know."

My heavens, who told you this?" I asked, bursting out laughing.

"My deputy—once he trusted me."

"How do you get anything done in that atmosphere?"

"Carefully. Show a little steel and a lot of diplomatic muscle. The selection of words is important and so is grace," he replied.

For a while, we were silent. I was digesting what he had just told me. It was shocking and yet, understandable from both sides. I began to think that Washington was much like fencing. One had to wear mental armor and watch every vulnerable spot in order not to be stabbed verbally or always be ready to joust.

"Have you been to any parties and if so, what are they like?" I asked.

"Because I'm so exhausted at the end of the day, I mostly just go home to sleep, but I've been to a couple," he said.

"What happens at them?"

"Well, Giles Roberts of USIA and I went to a small one at his colleague's home. There were maybe fourteen guests. Before dinner, it was very social— just chit chat among wives and spouses. Once we sat down, the men were striving for one-liners to top each other, followed by waves of laughter. A lot of insider humor, which became overused and mangled. After dinner, the men gravitated to one corner and the women to another."

"Did women participate in the policy conversation?" I asked.

"Not much. They were there to take the intensity out of the conversation. Women are necessary, but not for anything important. They are just on the fringes."

"Jack, that's awful," I snapped.

"It's the truth—the sad truth," he said.

"Do you think I really need to come?"

"Of course."

"Why?"

"I need you in every way. To keep me company and lick my wounds," he laughed. "You'll see for yourself when you come after Labor Day."

After the kids finished their summer jobs, feeling rich with their savings, Jack came back for Labor Day weekend, and then we headed to Wanda's college to deposit her with her worldly goods in her freshman dorm. It was traumatic for us—our firstborn was leaving the nest. The goodbyes were emotional for us, but liberating for her.

The dog and the three of us drove to McLean to take up full-time residence. It was sad to be leaving Wanda and the Cape, but we were filled with expectancy for this new adventure. The biggest adjustment would be for the dog—no beach runs or freedom to roam over our Orleans' three acres, but she was family and all of us would adjust.

After a couple of weeks in McLean, we all settled into a routine. Sometimes Jack would take Max to school. Other times Max took the bus. He seemed to fit in, making some interesting friends among the offspring of diplomats and members of Congress. He loved his grown-up suite in the basement of our new home.

Although Jack turned down ninety percent of the invitations because of his workload, he accepted the necessary ones. His friend Giles Roberts invited us on a yacht that cruised down the Potomac. The owner was a supporter of Giles' agency. It was a dressy, but casual affair for cocktails and dinner. The night was beautiful and still warm. A full-bellied moon was hidden behind the Washington Monument, showing a perfect round slice on either side of the obelisk.

I was staring at the beauty of that natural pose and illumination when a woman I didn't know whispered in my ear, "This is a man's town!"

"A man's town?"

"Look at them. They've been as polite to us ladies as long as they could bear to, and now they've gravitated to their clique of male colleagues. See how happily they're talking shop," she said, rolling her eyes.

"Shop?"

"Politics. I guess you haven't been here very long?"

"Only a couple of weeks," I said.

"I thought so. Well, you'll get used to being a non-entity. This is also a city of tuxedoes. Except for the semi-informality of this party, men are attending formal parties, clad in the black and white armor of tuxes, throughout the city. Their behavior is the same. A little social chit chat before the purpose of attending—gathering information," she informed me.

"Like journalists?" I asked.

"No, like politicians or like curious foreign and civil servants. They want to seize on a new nugget and deliver it to their bosses and colleagues, wrapped in intellectual humor."

"I had no idea about all these undercurrents," I exclaimed. Of course, Jack had told me some of the same things.

"Oh yes, keep your ears and eyes open," she whispered. "By the way, what does your husband do?" she asked.

"Spokesman for the Secretary of State."

"Really. How interesting. My husband was observing him."

"What does your husband do?" I asked.

"Oh, it doesn't matter," she smiled and turned away from me. I suddenly realized that she was one of those she had talked about. Her husband probably sent her over to me to extract information. She took me in her confidence and then pounced. Once she had what she wanted, she left. Just then, Jack came over and took my arm. "Want something to eat?" he asked.

"Sounds like a splendid idea."

We picked up our plates and gazed down the buffet table with its wonderful array of food. There was turkey, roast beef, and rock lobsters for starters. Side dishes included broccoli, cauliflower, potatoes, and salad. For dessert, the choices were cheesecake, pecan pie, chocolate mousse, and cheeses. Coffee was the postlude.

Some of the men joined the ladies for eating. Once the meal was over, the men were back to their groups, laughing and sharing thoughts in muted tones. I saw the lady who had spoken to me. She pointed to the men. I nodded at her knowingly. I still couldn't figure out whom she belonged to. Jack had joined a group of Giles' colleagues, so I couldn't ask him. I sidled up to some women and sat down without saying a word.

When we docked, the moon was now a halo around the tip of the Washington Monument. I was so engrossed in looking at it that I didn't watch my step and fell overboard into the Potomac. Everyone gasped.

"Ginny!" shouted Jack.

"Mrs. Hunter!" shouted our host.

"Oh my God," said Giles. "Where is she?"

The water was black and really cold. I seemed to go straight down and just couldn't propel myself upwards. I was frantically out of breath and thought my lungs would burst. I could tell the people were shouting from the boat, but their voices were so far away. Finally, I surfaced, gasping for air. I tried to grab onto the boat, but there was nothing to wrap my hand around.

"Can you swim, madam, to the ladder?" a crew member asked. I nodded as he pointed.

The crew guided me around to the ladder. They were ready with towels. The host was most apologetic, but I told him it was my fault for being distracted by the moon. I knew Jack was dying a thousand deaths. I saw that woman again. She shook her head at me and mouthed 'No' with downcast eyes. I guess I had made an unforgivable mistake. I thanked our host and apologized for the mishap. He was very kind.

Understandably, the ride back to McLean was a bit frigid, both literally and figuratively!

"How could you be so stupid?" Jack asked through gritted teeth.

"It was pretty clumsy. I'm sorry to have been the evening's closing entertainment."

"You should be," he said.

"At least they were strangers," I said.

"Don't worry, it will get around. These things are told and retold through the years."

"Oh dear. Thankfully, there were no photographers."

"Thank God."

Before we went to sleep, I apologized again. My midnight baptism had introduced me to the tip of Washington society and its more sinister side.

An exciting invitation came. It was to attend a small White House reception. I wanted to look perfect. It was suggested I go to Loehmann's, where women could find bargains. I rushed down Route 50 and combed through all the racks and found something sparkly, but not overdone. I bumped into some ladies, who were wives of men from Voice of America. They were offering me unsolicited advice, but in the end I found and bought what I wanted.

As they turned away from me, I heard one whisper to the other, "That's the young woman who fell off the yacht into the Potomac."

"Really?" she turned back to look at me. "I bet she got a dunking from her husband." They both smothered their giggles. I pretended not to pay any attention to them, but my heart sank. Jack was right, it did get around. I didn't know those women, but they had heard the story. I felt awful for Jack.

The following morning when I was fixing breakfast for my two men, Jack made an impassioned plea.

"Ginny, I have a tremendous favor to ask of you."

"What's that?"

"At the White House, would you please be on your best behavior?"

"What do you mean?" I asked. Of course, I knew what he meant.

"I mean, would you try and stay out of trouble?"

"Trouble?" I asked.

"You know—like not falling in the Potomac or getting glued to the floor."

"Jack, I, of course, never intended for those things to happen," I said.

"I realize that, but if you would be extra careful to avoid any unforeseen accidents?"

"Yes, Mom, be very careful," said Max.

"This is none of your business, young man!" I said.

"Please try," said Jack as he picked up his briefcase.

"I'll try." Poor man, I knew he was still smarting from those incidents.

"See you later," he said, leaning down to kiss me.

"Bye, Mom."

"Bye, Max." The two men looked at each other and shrugged.

Anyway, late in the afternoon, Giles sent an office car to pick up his wife, Janine, and me in McLean. We had on our finest. I was able to wear my special jewelry from Hong Kong. The sunburst pendant in gold with bits of blue sapphire on the tips of the gold rays was a perfect complement to my dress. Janine admired it. We met our husbands on Pennsylvania Avenue at the Northwest Gate to the White House. Somehow, there was a mix-up at the check point. Neither Jack's nor my name was on the list of cleared guests. This time it was Jack's turn to make quite a scene. They examined our driver's licenses several times and finally let us through after many telephone calls. Giles was getting impatient while Janine was amused.

At last, we were on the other side of the gate. We walked to the door of the White House. As we entered, there was very tight security. The women went through one security line and the men through another. The ladies' purses were examined. Mine only had a small comb, red lipstick, potent mints, and my driver's license with a very unflattering picture. Janine and I sailed through.

While we waited for our husbands, we were entranced by the China collection, and Remington bronzes, which I had read were on loan from Walter Annenberg to the White House. They were magnificent. I leaned down to get a closer look at a Remington horse and rider. My long hair fell into the metal ropes of the rider. I tried to jerk my hair away, but it got caught and tightened. There was nothing I could do. The hair wouldn't come loose. My promise to Jack at breakfast made me gag with guilt.

"Janine," I whispered. She was at the next marble table, looking at a blue and white Chinese vase. "Janine, help!" I said more loudly.

She rushed over to me. "Ginny, what's wrong?"

"My hair is caught in this Remington statue. I can't move. Can you get somebody to help," I said in desperation. She ran over to the military Social Aide and explained my predicament. The Marine came over and examined the tangled mess.

"Just hold still, madam," the young man in a stiff and tight uniform said.

"Janine, stand to my side, so no one can see," I said. By now, Jack and Giles walked over to us.

"Ginny, what's going on?" asked Jack.

"My hair got caught," I said through a corner of my mouth.

"Oh my God, I should have known," exclaimed Jack and this time without a smile on his face.

"Don't worry, sir, I'll have your wife free in a few seconds," said the Marine.

"Jack, would you and Giles make a little circle around us, so no one can see," I pleaded.

"Too late, Ginny, everyone is looking," Jack said through clenched teeth, trying to control his anger.

"There you are, Madam," smiled the young Marine.

"Oh, thank you. Thank you so much. You saved my life," I said.

"And mine, too," echoed Jack.

"Glad to be of service." He turned and went back to his station at the door.

"Why don't you two go upstairs and we'll join you shortly," said Janine. "I think Ginny should see the Gilbert Stewart portrait of George Washington in the Library. We'll be fine."

"Don't be long," said Giles.

"We won't," she said.

"And be sure to stand up straight, Ginny," said Jack. "No more hair entanglements!"

"Don't worry," I said.

Janine and I hurried to the rose-colored Library. I couldn't believe how perfect the portrait was. I wouldn't have wanted to miss it. Then, we raced up the curved stairway, carpeted in brilliant red. As we entered the Cross Hall, a six piece Marine band was playing classical music. They looked handsome in their uniforms.

Jack and Giles were waiting for us and anxious to be ushered into the Blue Room with its dark blue carpet, pale blue silk chairs, beige silk wallpaper, and Wedgewood colored drapes. On white marble table tops were bowls of white carnations and white gladiolas. A fire was blazing. It was surreal to be standing in the oval space of the White House, and we weren't on a tour. We were invited guests at this party!

As Janine and I edged over to the table where the flowers were, she whispered to me, "Shall we each take a little carnation?"

"After what happened to me downstairs? I'm in enough trouble already. We might get arrested or the First Lady would know what we did. No, Janine, NO!" She nodded, but I knew she'd love to have a small bloom to add to her ensemble.

Instead, we walked slowly past the table of hors d'oeuvres, ranging from perfect pink salmon, glazed Smithfield ham, miniature quiche to ideal fan-tailed shrimp. I indulged in the shrimp.

Just as I was swallowing the last morsel, it went down the wrong way. I couldn't stop coughing. At the same moment, the President and First Lady entered the room of twenty guests. The President came over to me and patted me on the back and said, "Could someone bring this young lady a glass of water?" One of the stewards was at my side immediately with a tall, slender glass of iced water. I sipped it and stopped the coughing.

"Thank you, Mr. President. Oh, you're much handsomer in person than on television and your wife is much prettier!" I said. All the guests laughed.

"Why, thank you. Next time I see you, I want you to start coughing again, so we can repeat this conversation," he winked at me.

"You aren't mad?" I asked.

"Enchanted," he replied.

"Sir, if I could say one more thing. I want to tell you what a wonderful job you did in the interview with Don Raymond last night on network television," I said.

"You know, after I finished the interview, I went upstairs and watched it. At its conclusion, I thought we looked like two people who had a big argument. I was sure I could have answered the questions in a better way." He snapped his fingers and shook his head in an 'oh well' gesture. I guess, even the President wanted a second chance to do better.

At that moment, Giles came over and introduced us. "Mr. President, may I present Mr. and Mrs. Jack Hunter. Mr. Hunter is spokesman for our Secretary of State. The President shook Jack's hand and took mine and patted it.

Giles moved down the line, introducing everyone. Half way down, Russell Rowland reached into his pocket and pulled out a little, clear plastic box with an inch square, green book in it that had "Rowland," stamped in gold.

"What do you think of this?" asked the President as he held it between his fingers to show everyone.

A guest quipped, "Is that from 'This is Your Life?' "

"Good retort," laughed the President. "I hope my entire life isn't this small."

I couldn't help noticing how athletic President Rowland looked. He was tall and his chest seemed muscle-bound like the football player he once was. The quality of his black suit and maroon paisley tie was first rate. Combed impeccably, his hair was black with salt strands throughout, making him ever so distinguished. His years as a governor had given him political grace and skills. The First Lady, Noline Clare Rowland, was petite and thin like the model she once was. Her voice had a certain lilt to it. Her hair was still blonde and straight, pulled back with a midnight blue headband in a sort of Grace Kelly style. Her eyes were a starlit blue. When they looked at each other, the love of forty years was apparent. No one could enter their circle. You knew they had secrets no one could ever invade. What they had was rare—something to be cherished and envied. The First Lady moved gracefully in her sapphire-blue, silk Halston, belted with a Chanel gold chain.

Janine provided introductions to the First Lady. When she came to me, I shook her hand and asked, "Mrs. Rowland, do you know Ginger Rogers? She is a very dear friend of ours."

"In fact, she came to our house on Cape Cod," chimed in Jack.

"Of course we know her, and she was here recently at the White House. We marvel at the accomplishments of hard-working stars such as Ginger and Anne Miller," Mrs. Rowland said.

"They certainly make no concessions to age," I remarked.

"I hope I'll be like them when I reach their age," she joked.

"I don't think you have anything to worry about!" I said. Everyone within earshot laughed, including the First Lady. "If you will forgive me for saying so, but I think the press unfairly criticized you for accepting Swedish glass goblets for the White House."

"Hear, hear!" chanted the group.

"Is there anything more beautiful than Swedish glass?" I asked.

"I don't think so," stated Mrs. Rowland. "But of course, I'm prejudiced! I only meant to add to the beauty of the White House and my husband's administration."

At the end of the line, the President thanked the guests for sponsoring the satellite film <u>Let Poland Be Poland.</u>

"We beamed the film to 52 countries, who celebrated Poland's right to freedom," said the President. "Our government thanks each one of you for your support."

All of us applauded as the President took his wife's hand and exited. Of course, Jack and I had not contributed. We were the guests of Giles Roberts. When the President and First Lady were gone, Giles came over to me and whispered some words into my sunburst pendant.

"Is that an electronic bug?" he asked.

"I was afraid the metal detector would catch it on the way in, but it didn't," I joked.

"That's a joke, everybody. This is a piece of jewelry," he announced.

Some guests made another swing past the food, but the rest of us left. As we departed the Blue Room, the Marine Band had switched from classical music to Scott Joplin. Perhaps they were happy the occasion was over.

And that was our first White House reception. I was thrilled. So was Jack. He had already forgotten the earlier incident of tangled hair in the Remington sculpture. I hadn't, but I was relieved and felt somewhat redeemed.

*   *   *   *

The next invitation to a White House reception was to honor Preston Hazib, an envoy, who spent four months negotiating peace agreements between Israel and the Palestinian Liberation Organization in Lebanon.

At 4:15 p.m., we were outside the Southeast Gate, going through the process of identification and name checking. This time they had our names. Thankfully, we were on the list. Next we were passing through the metal detectors and the handbag search. This was a much bigger crowd than our first visit. There were at least 300 people who swarmed up the curved staircase. It seemed like the same Marine band was playing. This time we were ushered into the State Dining room for champagne, soft drinks, and hors d'oeuvres of bite-sized sausage rolls, tantalizing scallops wrapped in bacon, petite éclairs and other desserts along with a choice of cheeses.

Later, we were directed into the East Room for the ceremony. Somehow I ended up at the end of the line. Jack and I were separated. I was shoved near a fireplace where the media stood on bleachers. I couldn't find Jack or see a thing. It was amazing how well-dressed and well-mannered people could be so aggressive to be first in line. I decided I could be one of them, so I crouched down on all fours to be exact, clutching my purse handle in my teeth and started crawling towards the center front. Remarkably, this tactic worked quite well, considering the circumstances! One lady had stepped out of her shoe and I had to hold my breath. My ribs were slightly knocked by kneecaps. One man stepped on my fingers. I had to clench my teeth around the purse handle to stop from screaming. Finally, he shifted off my hand and I wedged myself to the front row and knelt on my knees to place my head between a lady's long skirt and a man's dress pants. I unclenched my purse and it dropped in my lap. I had a perfect view of the lectern.

As I looked down the frontline of guests, I saw Secretary Stanley staring at me. My jaw dropped open. He smiled and winked at me. I half-smiled back and winked at him. I drew an imaginary zip across my lips. He nodded. Then, the President, First Lady, Ambassador Hazib and his wife came to the lectern. Both women were in white dresses. I strained my neck upwards to get a good glimpse of the foursome. The applause was overwhelming. I noticed the three torpedo-shaped chandeliers of crystal and gold that were reflected in giant mirrors.

The President made some generous remarks about Mr. Hazib's patience and courage when spending months in Beirut sorting out the differences between Israel and the PLO, the bombing, and eventual evacuation of the PLO back to various Arab countries. President Rowland said that Ambassador Hazib more than deserved the Medal of Freedom presented to him yesterday in the Oval Office. He thanked him.

"I wish my parents, who originated from Lebanon, could be here to know I had the privilege of restoring peace to my country of origin," said Hazib with emotion. Everyone clapped and moved towards the Blue Room to form the receiving line.

Finally, Jack and I found each other. "Where were you?" he asked.

"Near the media."

"I lost you," he said.

"I know. I looked everywhere. I guess there were too many people."

"I guess so. But I heard a rumor going around," Jack said.

"What rumor?"

"That some woman had crawled through the crowd to get a better view of the speakers. That wasn't you, was it?" he asked.

"I wish it had been."

"Ginny!" he said in an exacerbated manner.

"I was in a lousy spot. Jack, do you think the President will remember me?" I innocently asked.

"Not a chance in a million. He meets thousands and thousands of people every week and month!"

"You're probably right," I nodded.

"When you get to the social aide, give him your name, so he can introduce you to the President."

"Okay." When it came to my turn, I did what Jack said.

"Hello, Mr. President." I shook his hand.

"You look awfully familiar," he said.

"Really?"

"Yes," he said looking intently at me.

"Well, I must have one of those faces, but I wanted to ask you how your vacation was?" I said quite seriously.

He stopped the whole line to answer me. "Wonderful."

"I'm glad. You deserved it." Jack was nudging me in the ribs to stop asking questions and move on. Well, how could I tell the President of the United States not to tell me anything more because we were holding up the line? It would be impolite and ungracious.

"As a matter of fact," said President Rowland. "There should be a decompression period."

"I agree. They should give you more time to readjust," I said.

Mrs. Rowland was now staring at me and probably wondering what we were talking about and why it was taking so long. In fact, I was sure everyone wondered what was holding things up. They might even wonder who I was to spend so much time with the President. I gave my name to Mrs. Rowland's aide, shook hands with her, and mumbled something innocuous.

As Jack and I turned to go, we bumped into Secretary Stanley and his wife, Olivia. I liked her so much because she was down to earth.

"Did you enjoy the ceremony?" asked Secretary Stanley with a twinkle in his eye. I prayed he wouldn't spill my secret and I was sure he wouldn't.

"We did indeed," said Jack.

"Afterwards, I asked Mr. Hazib why he wasn't wearing his Medal of Freedom?" said the Secretary.

"What did he say?" I asked.

"He said it was pinned to his pajamas and he forgot to take it off!" We all had a tremendous laugh. "He also told me that when he was in Lebanon having breakfast with the representative from Israel, they were talking about border lines. Hazib started to draw the lines on a napkin. The Israeli was not pleased and asked the waiter for some paper. Out came a brown paper bag. Hazib drew a set of border lines and the paper bag became the agreement." We laughed again, amazed by such a simple solution.

Jack said to the Secretary, "Sir, there is a rumor I heard a few minutes ago that a woman crawled on the floor of the East Room to get a better view of the ceremony."

I felt a sick feeling in my stomach and looked down at the floor. I dared not look at the Secretary.

"Really?" said Stanley. "I didn't hear that rumor, Jack."

"I guess it was just a rumor," said Jack somewhat relieved.

★　　★　　★　　★

Our next visit to the White House was for a State Dinner, honoring President Suharto of Indonesia. This had a special meaning for Jack and me. Jack had covered the coup d'etat of Sukarno, Suharto's predecessor, for The Boston International—for which his press coverage won the Pulitzer Prize-- and then, a publisher asked him to write a book about the coup.

That was an exciting prospect. Once the contract was signed, we gathered up our baby son and toddler daughter to spend several months in Jakarta for Jack to do the research. We loved Indonesia and its people.

Anyway, this was a black tie affair. I wore a black velvet skirt, feminine pink ruffled blouse, and matching black velvet vest. My hair was swept up in a French twist. I guess my outfit was the subject of amusement because I saw a famous designer whispering behind her hand to a colleague. They obviously were making comments and laughing. Suffering only a slight twinge of dismay, I decided to ignore them and savor these precious moments in the White House.

When we entered the reception room, the Social Aides greeted us and introduced us to the press as the photographers snapped our pictures. Previously, Jack would have been part of the press. Now it was he who was the subject of scrutiny, which was a new and uncomfortable role for him. We both knew we would not appear in the newspapers because we were too low on the totem pole of dignitaries, but it was a new experience for us to be on the other end of the lens.

Once again, we climbed the red-carpeted, marble staircase. Another Aide greeted us at the top of the stairs. He took my arm and escorted me to the East Room with Jack following. There, we were announced. Jack and I were given instructions and separate table numbers. Then, we joined the receiving line to greet President and Mrs. Rowland and President and Mrs. Suharto. I observed President Suharto had on a dark western suit with a black fez-type hat, blending the two cultures handsomely. Mrs. Suharto wore a beautiful purple silk with a gold design in keeping with her country's traditional dress. Mrs. Rowland was elegant in a white dress and sparkling amethyst earrings.

"Good evening, Mrs. Rowland, you and Mrs. Suharto are a perfect blend of colors," I said, while shaking her hand.

"Why, thank you," she said.

"I wonder if you happen to know a dear friend of mine from Malmo, Sweden—Countess Hedvig Hamilton," I asked her.

"Hedvig? Yes, indeed. She is a darling," said the First Lady.

"And her daughter, Madeleine?"

"Of course. She used to work for *Vogue* magazine over here and then became a literary agent in Stockholm. How do you know them?" Mrs. Rowland asked.

"Through a mutual friend, we became good friends and visited them in Malmo," I said.

"How very interesting. Thank you for mentioning them to me," she said. She smiled and I moved on.

There were many celebrities in attendance that night, including Mabel Mercer, Alexis Smith, and Arnold Palmer. Corinne and Jim Andrews stood near us in line. We had known them in Indonesia when Corinne was writing a book about Sukarno just before the coup. They both were humorous and we enjoyed chatting with them. Corinne and I discovered, much to our delight, we were sitting at the same table. At least, I would know one person!

While we were standing in the receiving line, something funny happened to me. I saw Secretary and Mrs. Stanley across the room as they were advancing towards me. Mrs. Stanley wore a broad smile and opened her arms. I smiled back and stretched out my hand. She brushed right past it and embraced a woman behind me and then hugged a young lady, who turned out to be her daughter. They were the Beckers—longtime friends of the Stanleys. It was a Charlie Chaplin moment! I was embarrassed. I don't know if Mr. Stanley witnessed this funny moment, but he was kind enough to introduce us to the Beckers. Jack didn't say a word. Either he didn't see my faux pas or was becoming immune to them.

Once the receiving line was finished, we all moved into the State dining room where twelve tables were elegantly arranged. Jack was at table nine and Corinne and I were at twelve. Did that mean the unimportant people were at the last table? We had a mix of businessmen, wives of the President's staff and cabinet, protocol officer, and Corinne and me. It didn't matter. We were in a place of history and this was indeed an honor of more importance.

The decorations were beautiful, consisting of pink tablecloths, napkins, and tall centerpieces of peach-colored roses and baby carnations; completing the design was red & gold china paired with Swedish goblets and ornate silverware—appropriate for such a stately occasion.

Corinne was the center of attention. She had had plastic surgery since last we saw her in Jakarta and she looked gorgeous. Her dress was a red and white batik print from either Indonesia or from India. She wore an exotic red turban and had on solid white make-up, which was the rage among models and designers at the time. Her false eyelashes curved up to her eyebrows. Her eyes were the color of midnight ink. Everyone was mesmerized by her; she was absolutely charming to all, especially to the two men either side of her.

The menu was simple, but delicious. The first course was fish, followed by the main course of roast beef, mushrooms, broccoli, and puffed potatoes; Belgian endive salad came next. For dessert, there was a rich white cake and a poached pear set in a chocolate cup.

Once the meal was over, Corinne leaned over to me and said, "Let's go to the ladies room."

"No. Corinne, we can't," I said.

"Why not?"

"Because it would be impolite."

"No it wouldn't. When you have to go, you have to go," she declared.

I gave a side glance to the protocol officer who shook her head. "Corinne," I said, "the President is about to make a toast to the President of Indonesia. We can't leave." She turned away from me in dismay. At that very moment, the President stood up and offered a toast to Indonesia and its President and First Lady. Everyone clinked their glasses.

After the reciprocal toasts, Jim Andrews immediately began hobnobbing with the President, and it appeared as if they were exchanging jokes. Corinne saw Secretary Stanley staring at her. She rose and walked to his table.

"I'm told you wrote a book about Sukarno," he said before she could say hello.

"Yes. What a naughty boy he was to flirt with the communists," she smiled seductively. Stanley's eyes never left her face. He smiled, too.

"Very naughty!"

"You know, Mr. Secretary, I knew Jack Hunter in Indonesia."

"So, I understand. We are very fond of him and are extremely glad he is on our team," he said.

"I'm writing a column about this occasion for a New York publication," she said. "Would you give me a quote?"

"The United States is grateful to have such a fine leader in President Suharto. We expect our relationship to Indonesia will continue to grow," he said. "How's that, Mrs. Andrews?"

"Perfect. Thank you, Mr. Secretary."

Corinne came back to our table, turning male heads along the way. She beckoned me and we went downstairs to the Vermeil Room, leading to the ladies powder room, which was elaborately decorated. As she retouched her make-up, she described her encounter with the Secretary.

Upstairs, we rejoined our husbands and moved into the East Room for a short concert by opera singer, Frederica Von Stade, who was dressed in a breathtaking scarlet evening gown. The performance was excellent, but I could tell that Jack was anxious to go home. When Miss Von Stade finished, the President announced a new American Ambassador to Indonesia.

At the conclusion of his remarks, we headed to the foyer and exit. The Marine band was playing for those who wanted to dance in the Cross Hall. Secretary Stanley had a passion for ballroom dancing and was spinning the Becker daughter around the marble floor. Reluctantly, Jack, who was a really good dancer, took a few dance moves with me until he reached the top of the staircase. We quickly descended and walked out the door.

CHAPTER FIVE

▼

WOMEN, GRIDIRON, AND TENNIS

Observing and learning about women on the D.C. scene was an eye-opening experience and helped prepare me for when Jack and I moved to the city. One day, when Jack was at work, I sat at my desk and thoughtfully began to examine the different aspects of women's circles around town, one-by-one.

About eight years ago when we were at an editor's conference in D.C., I sat next to a senator and I was quizzing him about life in Washington, especially for wives.

"What's Washington like for a senator's wife?" I asked him.

He looked directly at me before speaking and said, "Awful."

I wasn't expecting this answer and repeated, "Awful?"

"They have no life of their own. Yes, they go to parties with their spouses, but they are extraneous. They are nobodies. They have no power, no influence. Most do not have careers outside the home. That's why many of them drink," he said.

I tucked that piece of information away and decided not to respond. Instead I asked him, "What about cabinet wives?"

"They have a little more clout because there are fewer of them and they have proximity to the President, so people pay attention to them and to what they say. For wives of most Congressmen, they are persona-non-grata. I think it would be better to have the families stay at their homes in the state where they come from."

"That's shocking," I said a bit outraged and disappointed.

"But true. Be glad who you are, that you have a career as a newspaper writer," he said.

As I'm thinking back on that episode, I'm looking at women from a different perspective now that I'm a wife of a political appointee. Where do I fall in the pecking order? I am not a Congressman's wife and not a Secretary's wife, but an Assistant Secretary's wife. Of course, Jack had told me something similar recently about the wives and families of the Washington powerbrokers. But here I am in the role he was talking about—a persona-non-grata.

Surprisingly, another group of women heavily influence the direction of issues, their timing, and outcome. They are the secretaries of those in high positions, who have tremendous influence and power. And most are not afraid to wield it. Many of them have been around the political circles for decades and know the ropes and all the diplomatic nuances from administration to administration. In general, many employees work very hard during long hours, out of a sense of duty and dedication.

One very trend-setting, savvy Washington woman, who is an exception to this whole female issue, is Karen Grenthem. Her father bought The D.C. Gazette and worked tirelessly as publisher. When he stepped aside, her husband took the publishing reins. Tragically, he committed suicide and she assumed the top position because of her family ties. She knew very little about the administrative end of newspapers and began her own intensive study of learning the business end. Financial wizard, Wesley Barnes, helped her. As the new publisher, she commanded instant respect because the paper was the most prominent and influential in Washington.

Socialites of Washington, who come from old money, play a prominent role in the town's hierarchies, too. Even without that pedigree, one can still be invited to one of their parties and consider it a coup. Sometimes these individuals can act as facilitators of power. They provide the atmosphere and privacy for deals to be discreetly made. To be invited to a Perle Mesta party or Pamela Harriman's home was definitely moving in the circles of power.

Then, there are women on the fringes, who can't get inside the circles of power no matter how hard they try. They make every effort to associate themselves with people in the know, usually through the wives. They offer to take them to the City Tavern Club in Georgetown or the Cosmos Club on DuPont Circle with the intention to flatter and impress. The University Clubs and prestigious Sulgrave Club are included in this list. They pick up crumbs of information from someone who actually is involved and can pass it along as if it comes from their direct contact, not from their luncheon partner. These once-removed associations pump up their egos. The hope of these want-to-be women is to capture an invitation that will catapult them to the real center, so they can rub shoulders with the names appearing on the front page, not just the Style section.

- Also helping to make the town tick are the single, professional women. Their stories are similar in many large cities. They keep growing in number and making their way up and down the corridors of power. Many come to D.C. to build their careers, find a husband, and have it all. Some find it and some don't. Their jobs are fascinating and they can support themselves, but home and family seem to elude them.
- Washington is such an interesting place. So many nuances and groups. After my observations about women, I wondered where I fit in? As time passes maybe I'll figure it out and maybe I won't. I kept returning to what that senator had told me about women turning to drink since they are without any purpose or stature in D.C. One thing for sure, that would not be me!

In reflecting over the plight of women in Washington, I wanted to record a true, but sad story of a woman I met at a party, who was typical of someone that senator had described. Without naming names, Jack and I witnessed something that could have come right out of a Scott Fitzgerald novel or a one-act play:

The Setting: The infamous Watergate complex, situated across from the Kennedy Center and along the banks of the Potomac.

A Stunning Apartment: The living room had glass on two sides with the view, featuring the Kennedy Center close up and across the river—the twinkling lights from high-rise apartments in Arlington, Virginia.

The Star of the Show: Our hostess. She easily could have been Zelda Fitzgerald. She was a true southern belle and made people feel immediately at ease by introducing each new guest to the others. Irresistibly, she flirts with men—grabbing their arm and rolling up to them and then away from them—all very seductive. Amazingly, though, she does not ignore the women. She was known for creating a comfortable, yet fun, social environment.

Supporting Role: A supportive husband. He was a gentle soul and a southern gentleman to the core.

The Cast of Characters: Interesting. Guests ranged from Washington elected and appointed officials, a sculptress of Lucite; a Prussian woman with a PhD in French and German literature; a young author writing a book about the State Department.

Once the party was well underway and had taken on a momentum of its own, the hostess suddenly disappeared at the instant the conversation was getting animated. Unless you were paying attention, you wouldn't quite notice, but you would sense something unusual in the room. Her husband dutifully stepped up and assumed the role of both host and hostess. He graciously guided us to the buffet table of spicy shrimp New Orleans style, crabmeat soufflé, salmon, and turkey.

And as the festivities began to wind down, he diplomatically left his guests to retrieve his wife. In those farewell moments, she was still the belle she had been in greeting us.

We were the last couple to leave. Before I stepped over the threshold, I remembered my evening shawl that I had left in the bedroom. I told Jack I would be out in a minute. He and the husband stood chatting in the open door. I rushed quickly in the bedroom and found my wrap. As I turned to leave, there was our hostess, sitting on the floor of her closet with a wig perched precariously on her head.

"Mrs.-------!" I said.

"Are they gone?" she mumbled.

"All but me," I whispered. "I forgot my shawl."

With slurred speech, she said, "And I forgot my wig. I had a bad hair day and couldn't find it, but here it is in my hat box right where I left it. My best friend also resides there all snuggled beneath and tucked in."

"Your best friend?" I asked.

"This!" She brought out a large, half-filled bottle of Vodka. "Shake his hand. He's Russian, you know, and a big, bad boy." She held up the bottle for me to wrap my hand around. I had no choice, but to stoop down to be level with her eyes and to extend my hand. She laughed hysterically as the wig slipped to a cockeyed position. After she unscrewed the Vodka, she threw her head back to drink, and the wig tumbled off to land on a pair of black evening pumps as the liquid dribbled down her face.

"Should we put him back in the box?" I softly asked.

"No, no, dear. He and I are now out of the closet—because of you," she said as she started giggling. "You made us come out of the closet; yes ma'am--out of the closet. I should write a song called 'Out of the Closet.' You made us come out. Isn't that funny?" Now she was doubled over in hysterical fits of laughter.

"Can I help you up?" I asked.

At that moment, a southern voice bellowed forth, "Darling! What are you doing? Mrs. Hunter is our guest. Get up." Our host had come into the bedroom and witnessed his wife guzzling the contents of the bottle. He leaned down to pick her up and the Vodka spilled over him.

"Excuse me, I must be going. My husband is waiting. Thank you again for a lovely party," I said, trying to retreat backwards as quickly as possible, out of this embarrassing scene that I had stumbled into so innocently.

"I'm sorry you had to see my wife in this condition, Mrs. Hunter. Please accept my apologies," he said in a voice cracked with emotion. It tore my heart in two.

"No apologies are necessary," I said. "Washington takes its toll on many." I rushed to the front door with tears in my eyes. I took Jack's arm and we went to our car.

Later, I found out that her reputation was well-known; especially hiding bottles of liquor in the master bath toilet tank. Her checkered high school education, compared to her husband's stellar college accomplishments, gave her a great sense of inferiority and fear, so she regularly retreated out of sight, once the niceties of introductions were completed. One can only assume this was her way to hide her doubts and low self-esteem. Her husband was patient and understanding, and they remained a devoted couple.

I felt saddened because I don't think D.C. started the drinking. I had heard that it was a long-standing problem.

*　　*　　*　　*

Among many traditions in Washington is the Gridiron Club dinner held annually in the spring; it is considered a four-star event for journalists and politicians. The Club was founded in 1885 by reporters, columnists, and bureau chiefs from the D.C. area for the purpose of producing skits and songs that skewer the president and congress. Then, ripping remarks, in the guise of great good humor, are delivered by those in white tie and tails. The president retorts with a humorous speech as do ranking members of both political parties. Usually, the president takes it in good stride. By 1958, the Club established a foundation to raise funds for journalism scholarships.

Jack was invited by <u>The Boston International</u> bureau chief to attend the Gridiron dinner. The event was extremely high profile and only a select few actually attended. In fact, wives were not allowed to attend those Saturday evening productions. Instead, they could, and often would come to the Sunday afternoon repeat performance at the Capitol Hilton. The same faces and new ones were often seen at these matinees. Although it was disappointing not to see the reactions of the president and other politicians to those roasted comments, the skits were still uproariously funny. It was quintessential Washington fun.

Anyway, we went to a roped off area down front to watch the less formal repeat matinee. We sat next to two unassuming elderly couples. A gentleman came over to congratulate Jack on his new position. At the same time, he introduced us to the two couples. You never know who is going to know whom. Washington is a small town at heart. As it happened, they were Justice and Mrs. Barrett and Justice and Mrs. Branson from the Supreme Court. We shook hands all around. Since I was seated next to Justice Barrett, he wanted to know Jack's whole biography in a few short minutes. I delivered and he was impressed.

"Where do you live?" I asked.

"Alexandria. The worst investment I ever made," he confessed to me.

"May I ask why?"

"Because I've been renting for twelve years. I should have bought the place, but the landlord won't sell. We're staying because my wife really likes the floor plan and I like the proximity to work."

"What kind of hours do you work as a Justice?" I asked.

"From seven to seven. Then, after dinner I work until midnight."

"Every night?"

"Exactly. Seven nights a week," he replied.

"And how many cases do the Justices handle in one day?"

"Up to one hundred."

"No wonder you work so late!" We both laughed.

"We sit on the bench for two weeks, listening to arguments, and then take two weeks off to consider opinions in a quiet atmosphere," he said.

"How is your new lady Justice coping?" I asked.

"She's surviving very well. She doesn't give any favors and she doesn't take any. Because of the novelty of her appointment, she is swamped with social invitations. Only now is she discovering how to weed them out and decline. She has a good mind, but the adjustment is not easy. It took me five years to really feel comfortable," he said.

"You mean as a Justice?"

"Yes," he said.

"When you go on vacation, do you ever get away from it mentally?" I asked.

"No, but it's never boring."

At that moment, the show was about to begin. The newsmen sang new humorous, revised lyrics to old songs. There was one about the new woman justice on the Supreme Court. As we were applauding, Justice Barrett and I smiled a knowing smile at each other. The First Lady made a surprise appearance and sang a very self-deprecating song, which everyone enjoyed. A couple of journalists played stand-up comics and took pot shots at various cabinet members to everyone's delight. Journalist Carlson Reeve played Tip

O'Neill with a white wig. Hysterical! When the show was over, we parted on a friendly note with the two Justices and their wives.

✱   ✱   ✱   ✱

TENNIS!

Tennis is a sports obsession with women in D.C. They talk about it; they dream about it; and they do it—they play. Men dream about the games of squash, golf, or gaining more power. Squash is quick and strenuous. Slamming the ball against a wall relieves huge amounts of tension. Golf is a four hour indulgence to forget worries, do a little business on the course, and try to drain that little white ball into a tiny, flagged hole on the green. The power game is not for the faint at heart and played every minute of every day by those who crave it.

Up until this point, my D.C. days were mostly spent at the typewriter, pounding out my plays and revising them multiple times. I guess I'm a perfectionist in my own way!

Imagine my surprise when the telephone rang one morning as I had settled at my desk.

"Ginnyyyyyy!"

"Nancy Barr, how are you?"

"Fine, but I need some help," she said.

"What kind of help?"

"We need a fourth for tennis in an hour."

"Uh oh, I know what's coming," I said.

"Can you?"

"You know I'm a first class dud. I haven't played in twenty years, and I don't have a fancy white skirt and top—just an old pair of red shorts and a tee-shirt," I said, hoping she would call someone else, but I did owe her for having placed the furniture.

"We'll take you with all your flaws! The game must go on!" she sighed with delight and relief.

"You may be sorry," I told her.

"See you up at the Club at 10:00 a.m. We'll have lunch there afterwards."

"Okay. We're on." As the words tumbled out of my mouth, I was amazed at what I had agreed to. Was I truly ready for this? I don't think so.

"See you there and thanks a million," she said.

I quickly showered to clear my thoughts for this friendly competition and changed into my non-conformist, not correct tennis togs, grabbed my racquet, and drove to the tennis club. Inside it was surprisingly huge. There were six courts. I saw Nancy hitting balls to Janine. I wondered who the third player was. Nancy waved. She and Janine came over.

"Ginny, hi," said Janine.

"I didn't know you were a tennis player," I said.

"She's terrific and thanks, Ginny, for answering our call!" said Nancy.

"I'm really rusty."

"Forget about it. We're here to have fun," said Janine. "Does Jack know you're here?"

"Nope. He'll be shocked," I said.

"Here's Kitty West," said Nancy. "Kitty, come meet Ginny Hunter. She's filling in for Vera Lynne."

"Hi, Ginny, nice to meet you. I just saw Vera with a friend. Her arm is all bandaged. I guess she wants to watch," said Kitty.

"Oh, dear," I swallowed. "Nancy, could you and I hit some balls to get me warmed up?"

"Sure. The court next to us is free, so we'll practice. Kitty and Janine can do the same," said Nancy.

"Okay, girls, get the limbs moving," said Kitty.

Well, Nancy and I performed a so-called volley, but my balls went high and wide, sending Nancy all over the court. They were wild and not within the lines. I felt sorry for her, but she knew what she was getting! When I served, they loftily went over Nancy's head or directly into the net. It was a disaster. After fifteen minutes, the foursome assembled. The battle was about to begin. The deal was that we would rotate sides and partners every two games. This way no one would be stuck with me too long!

Nancy and I were partners for the opening two games. I was at the net and she served. They had to remind me that reaching over the net to hit the ball was not how it was done. They were really good sports. The three of them couldn't stop laughing at my not so stellar shots. I tried as best I could to keep my racquet under control, but to no avail. At one point, not wanting to miss another ball, I leapt into the air to hit the ball and fell awkwardly right into the net. At that very moment, I realized I wasn't Billie Jean King, as someone's distant camera flash went off.

When I untangled and righted myself, I announced to no one in particular, "I think I have a hole in my racquet," They thought this was hilarious, but I wasn't going to quit.

There was another opportunity for me to jump four feet into the air and catch the ball in the center of my racquet and drop it neatly on the other side so no one could return it. I did it although I still fell into the net again. That distant camera flashed again. Everyone applauded. I thought maybe they clapped out of pity, but I felt better, helping my partner score.

Now it was my turn to serve. There were double faults and wild balls high above the court. They tried to stifle their laughter. I was mad at myself, knowing I really could do better, and right then, I decided to become a tiger on the court. I tossed the ball in the air, swung my racquet over it, and crushed it with all my might as it came down and hit the inside corner of Kitty West's court. She was stunned as it whizzed past. The jaws of my fellow players had dropped. I had redeemed myself. They looked at me as an equal. I was victorious in a DC women's sport of choice. At last, I had arrived.

Once our time was up we went to the picnic area. Nancy had brought her homemade chicken salad and green beans for us, and Janine had brought a strawberry shortcake dessert. Kitty had a jug of iced tea. Vera Lynne and her friend joined in. We all exchanged bits of our life stories over lunch. They seemed like a nice group. While Vera's arm was healing, I would be her substitute.

Vera was intrigued by my playwriting and wondered if we could chat at my house afterwards. She's a feature writer for a local weekly newspaper. I told her about our newspapers on Cape Cod and my work as a drama critic. She suggested she would like to do a feature story on me. I hummed and hawed about whether I should let her without consulting Jack. She said it would be a harmless piece. Reluctantly, I agreed. They followed me home. Little did I know that one of my luncheon partners, her friend, was a photographer.

Before we entered the condo, her friend clicked a shot of the outside.

"Great location," said Vera.

"Nothing special. Just a home away from home," I said.

"What's your dog's name?"

"Ginger," I said.

"She looks like a Ginger," said Vera.

"She's a great dog, but she misses running around our three acres and the beach," I said.

"Why would you leave Cape Cod to come here?" the photographer asked.

"Service to our country. When it's time, we'll go home."

"Could we see your study?" Vera asked.

"Sure. It's up in the guest room." I showed them my desk and typewriter as Vera thumbed through the manuscripts. "Shall we sit down?" Her friend was taking a variety of pictures. I suddenly felt uneasy, but dismissed it. After all, she was Nancy's friend and we had just played tennis and enjoyed a nice lunch. We sat on the sofa.

"What are you working on now?"

"SIN IN THE ATTIC," I said.

"Sin in the Attic?" asked Vera with surprise. "What's it about?"

"It's about an 80-year-old mother who comes to live with her middle-aged daughter and her family—husband and teenage daughter. They fix up the attic for her with a separate entrance, so she can come and go as she likes and keep some semblance of freedom."

"What's the sin?"

"Well, she meets a drunken man in the park and brings him to the attic to sober him up. Of course, the daughter doesn't know that and she spies on them with binoculars through the floorboards, assuming her mother and the stranger were moving closer to the bed. Obviously, the daughter treats her own mother like a child. The grandmother and sixteen-year-old join forces and run away," I said. "That's a quick summary. By the way, it's a comedy."

"Where did you ever get the idea?" asked Vera.

"One time I was in an apartment hotel and witnessed a 50-year-old daughter berating her elderly mother in the center of her living room. I was so shocked that I thought it would make a good play by using comedy instead of tragedy to expose this kind of abuse," I replied.

"Amazing."

"What's THE TORTURED TRIANGLE about?" asked the photographer.

"A father and son are in love with the same woman. The two men have been estranged for years after the death of the father's wife. He is a landscape painter and lives on Cape Cod with a woman half his age. The son returns unexpectedly. A situation develops where the father finds the son and his lover together. In a jealous rage, he kicks them off his land, having made the decision on false appearances. After the lover explains, the relationship between father and son is finally mended."

"That's a twist. Well, I think we should go. Maybe one shot of you at your typewriter," said Vera.

"Okay," I said. Still I had a negative feeling about this whole visit.

They thanked me and left. For the next two days I could hardly move. Muscles that had not spoken to me in twenty years were yelling. I felt some satisfaction in knowing I had held my own with that server's ace.

About a month later, Jack came home from work with a clipping of an article about me. He was steaming. I obviously was caught off guard, since I had no idea what he was talking about. There were two photos side-by-side—one of me falling into the tennis net and then another of me at my desk. There were descriptions of me flubbing on the tennis court and more copy, ridiculing the two plays Vera had asked about. The biggest blow was the headline: **Wife of Government Spokesman Snared in D.C. Net.**

I felt hurt and betrayed by Nancy's so-called friend, who had set me up. I hoped Nancy hadn't been involved because it was she who invited me to play that day. I had to believe that she had nothing to do with it. Neither the game of tennis nor the DC games seemed so much fun to me anymore, mainly because they hurt Jack more than they hurt me.

There was hell to pay for that one. Gentle journalism on Cape Cod is nothing compared to the razors of Washington.

A couple of months later, when Jack had recovered from the mangled publicity about me, we were invited to join three other couples for a round-robin of tennis on a Saturday afternoon. I was apprehensive because of my last experience, but I didn't want to disappoint Jack.

Jack is a pretty good player—far better than I. We played 30 minutes with one partner and then moved to the next. Jack and I were a disaster together because I was so nervous. I couldn't stop thinking of that photo of me, falling into the net—literally and figuratively. When I played with Giles and then Nelson West, my game improved. Those two were the best players.

As we were about to finish, I sailed into the air to smash a ball into an alley. As I landed, there was a crack and crunch as I rolled over on my foot.

"This is the only way I could help my partner—by injuring my foot, so he can find someone new and exciting," I quipped. "Now my husband has to wait on me hand and foot!" Giles and Nelson chuckled. Even Jack found it kind of funny.

That was it. I hobbled off the court and climbed into the first row of bleachers until the match was over. Despite the foot, it was so much fun!

Tennis with the ladies continued on and off during our stay, but I never once played with Vera again.

CHAPTER SIX

▼

THE PRESIDENT'S BOX AT KENNEDY CENTER

On the D.C. side of the Potomac's banks is The Kennedy Center for the Performing Arts, a magnificent building in white marble. From an aerial view, it looks like a giant, horizontal ice cream sandwich—a very pronounced top and bottom with some type of filling in the middle.. Upon closer inspection, it has real design and the style of a modern Parthenon. Its purpose is to bring culture to a town myopic about politics.

Sometimes I would sneak off on my own to see performances in the smaller venues. There was Jean Stapleton in "The Late Christopher Bean;" Emlyn Williams in a one-man show about Charles Dickens; Zoe Caldwell in "Medea;" and Katharine Hepburn in the "Last Waltz." Because I was the drama critic for our home newspapers, I occasionally would review a Kennedy Center show for our readers. I thought Miss Hepburn would be of interest, so I tried to interview her without success.

In preparation for writing articles for our Cape Cod newspapers, I had researched the Center's history and learned that although the Kennedy Center opened officially in 1971, the original idea came from First Lady Eleanor Roosevelt in 1933. She envisioned it between Capitol Hill and the Supreme Court and wanted it named after her husband. The Depression and Second World War prevented the idea from moving forward.

President Eisenhower tried to promote the idea in 1959, but it wasn't until John F. Kennedy became president that the idea actually began to materialize.

President Kennedy asked Roger L. Stevens to help him. Jacqueline Kennedy and Mamie Eisenhower became Honorary Co-chairmen. It took $70 million to build, with federal funding supporting it in perpetuity. It was officially named The Kennedy Center for the Performing Arts in 1964.

To deafen the noise of the planes from nearby National Airport, the Center was built as a box within a box. Architect Edward Durrell Stone designed the 100 foot high, 630 foot long, and 300 foot wide structure. There is red carpeting laid against white marble for a truly dramatic effect. The massive sixteen Swedish Orrefors crystal chandeliers are beyond beautiful and description. The Hall of States and the Hall of Nations are 250 feet long and 63 feet high.

The three main theatres each have a Presidential box in the center of the first balcony, reserved for the president and his invited guests. The Opera House seats over 2,000 people and the Concert Hall with almost the same number of seating. The chandeliers are from Norway. Then, there is the cozy Eisenhower Theater, seating a little more than 1,000 ticket holders. Five smaller theaters are scattered throughout and at the top is a cafeteria.

Jack and I were invited twice to attend performances, seated in the Presidential box. They were both thrilling events.

The first invitation came from the First Lady's Chief of Staff. The president and his wife were going to be away, and Mrs. Rowland offered the tickets to him. They selected five couples to be their guests at the National Symphony in the Concert Hall. It was a rainy day and of course, I needed something to wear. I braved the rain and bought a cocktail length skirt for the occasion.

I drove to the State Department to pick up Jack. The only place to park was in front of a fire hydrant. A long, black limousine had taken up two parking spaces. I saw a familiar face as Giles stepped out of the limousine.

"Giles," I shouted from the car window, "can you tell Jack I'm here?"

"In a minute," he said. "Come meet a very special couple."

I hopped out of the car as a very handsome young man started smiling at me. I recognized him immediately. Giles introduced us while he helped his wife out of the limo.

"Patrick Benson, I'd like you to meet Ginny Hunter. Her husband is the State Department spokesman for Gavin Stanley and this is Eve Benson," said Giles.

"I'm thrilled to meet you both, and Mr. Benson, you are my favorite singer," I said like a real fan.

"Why, thank you, Mrs. Hunter."

"In fact," I said, "I just saw your parents yesterday morning on the 700 Club, telling how they found the Lord through the Bible."

"I'm so glad you saw it, because we missed it," said Patrick. "Can you tell us what you thought?"

"For one thing your father is so humorous," I said.

"Our household was and is a very happy one, and my Dad makes us laugh a lot."

"How wonderful," I said.

"Our children grew up with Giles' kids. We've known them for twenty years," said Patrick."

At that moment Jack appeared, Giles introduced the Bensons and we got back in our car and drove to the Kennedy Center. We parked in the garage underneath the building before taking the escalator to the lobby and then the elevator to the roof-top restaurant.

Over a light supper, Jack told me about the speech he gave at the State Department to celebrate a year of the new leadership program at the United States Information Service, USIS.

Jack explained how he introduced his speech. "There are two kinds of people: talkers and writers. I'm a writer, so I'm going to read what I've written. Scotty Reston was a respected writer. Reston has been quoted as saying, 'How do I know what I think until I read what I've written.' "

And Jack added, "Giles couldn't resist saying from the audience," 'There are plenty of talkers who don't say anything.' " "Everyone laughed," said Jack.

By then, it was time for us to go down to the Concert Hall. We arrived ahead of our host, and the usher appeared very skeptical, demanding to see our tickets. Upon very close inspection, the tickets must have passed the test as we were permitted past the red velvet ropes that stretched across the prestigious box's entrance. Upon entering, I was surprised by a well-appointed sitting room, with another door on the opposite wall that opened to the Presidential box.

While we waited for our host and the others, I tried to memorize everything in the sitting room in case I would never be there again. If only I had my camera to show the kids my pictures. To record the details in my memory, I said to myself, "It is about ten or twelve feet square. There is a gold table in the center with four Victorian chairs around it in rose and beige stripes. The carpet is a bright red, and the walls are carpeted, too, in woven-looped beige to absorb the sound." I paused for a moment to pinch myself!

I continued to talk silently to myself, "To one side is a marble-topped table with an ornate clock over it. On the opposite side is a slim table with a mirror over it. There were Murano glass jars with M&Ms and jellybeans." Just then, others from our party started to join us.

Our hosts showed us a secret--a gold-colored telephone for the president's use if he were needed during a performance. It was well concealed, but exceedingly accessible. Jack and I looked at each other in amazement. They had obviously been here before.

I was still absorbed in mentally recording the décor, so I wouldn't forget. "The Presidential Seal is on the left wall before entering the balcony. On the right wall are a series of small paintings of flowers, four geese, and a small Japanese painting. Off to one side of the ante room is also a closet for coats, as well as a refrigerator for soft drinks at intermission. Of course, there was a powder room, too. Very sensible," I said silently to myself.

Once we all assembled, friendly introductions were made. There was a local attorney, a couple from Columbia University, and personal friends of our host. As we were seated for the performance in the Presidential box, everyone in the theatre turned to see if we were famous. When they discovered our faces were unrecognizable, the curious public lost interest. We happily settled into the best seats in the house.

The elegant box has a central aisle, flanked on each side by two rows of six, for a total of twelve seats in the box. We were separated from our spouses during the first half and reunited during the second half.

Conductor/composer Leonard Bernstein was conducting three selections, played by the National Symphony orchestra. The first was his original composition, full of dissonance and occasional melodic strains from a rolling tympani and a staccato castanet. Slight in stature, Bernstein waved his arms like a proud eagle and made a joyous leprechaun leap off the platform to hug and kiss the soloists—flute and viola, first violinist, and others at the first act's conclusion.

At intermission, we re-grouped in the ante room, sipping soft drinks and commenting on Bernstein's theatrical performance. Most of us remember him for the melodic music from "West Side Story." The second act had a much more traditional style. I liked the final selection of the evening—Sir Jonathan Elgar's "Variation on an Original Theme." It was sweet, melodic, and triumphant.

When it was over, the evening seemed a bit surreal. We collected our coats from the closet and slipped them on as we shook hands with the guests and thanked our host profusely.

We were the last ones to leave. I whispered to Jack, "I have to stop in the powder room. I won't be long."

"Ginny, can't you wait? We'll be home in fifteen minutes."

"Sorry, Jack, this can't wait." I slipped into the powder room, which was so elegant. I had to look at everything. A gold framed mirror was above a marble sink with flecks of gold and gold-colored fixtures. Hand towels had gold embroidery. The Kleenex box was covered in an 18th century tapestry design. Individual soaps were in the shape of the Kennedy Center. The wallpaper was of cream and gold with cherubs and musical instruments between gold stripes. A rush of perfume filled the entire space after flushing the commode. I washed my hands with the Kennedy Center soap and dried them on one of the luxurious hand towels.

Just as I was looking in the mirror, there was a knock on the door. I froze. Was there another lady waiting to come in? Was it an usher? For some reason, I felt like a child caught with her hand in the cookie jar. I was afraid to answer.

"Ginny?"

It was Jack. "Yes?" Thank goodness it wasn't a stranger.

"What's taking so long?" he asked.

"I'll be out as soon as I can," I said.

"Well, hurry up. The Center is almost empty and the lights are being turned out. I'll wait for you in the lobby."

"Okay."

Taking one last look in the mirror to tidy my hair, I proceeded to open the door, but it wouldn't open. It wouldn't even budge. The levered handle was stuck. Oh no! I knew I was in serious trouble. This couldn't be happening after such a wonderful evening. I put my lips to the crack in the door and whispered, "Jack?" No reply. "JACK!" I shouted. No one answered. I wished I had that secret gold telephone with me right now. I could write a scenario of how I might be rescued, but in reality, I knew there would be no dramatic rescue. I would have to figure out something.

Jack had gone down to the lobby. Now what do I do? I could sleep on the carpet with my raincoat over me. What if Jack gets fed up and goes home? No one will find me until tomorrow night—if then. This was the last night for Bernstein's concert and I didn't know when the next performance would be. I pushed and pulled the handle. I tried the door dozens of times, but it wouldn't open. I examined the hinges, but they couldn't be unscrewed. I flopped down on the carpet, wondering how this predicament would be resolved. I thought I heard the knob begin to open. I stood up. Maybe it was Jack. As I called his name, I heard a click and all the lights went out.

"Help!" I shouted. "Somebody, anybody? HELP!"

Silence. I fumbled for my handbag to see if I had that key chain flashlight. I did. It was a small beam, but enough to see. There were no candies in here. I wondered if Jack would ever come back.

Meanwhile, Jack was downstairs pacing and constantly looking at his watch. The center was closing down and his frustration was beyond tolerance. He finally got in the elevator to go up to the tier box's ante room. Halfway there, the elevator stopped and all the lights went out. He, too, was stuck. He fumbled in the dark for the panel and pulled every switch he could find. Suddenly, a siren went off and a loudspeaker was activated.

"If you are in distress, please respond to this message."

"I am definitely in distress. The elevator has stopped and I cannot get out. I was trying to get to the ante room of the President's Box at the Concert Hall where my wife is. I know something has happened to her. Please bring me down to the lobby," demanded Jack.

"As soon as the power is turned on, we will assist you, sir. Until then, try to be patient."

They switched off communication before Jack could reply.

Every minute seemed like an hour. Jack leaned against the back of the elevator wall and eventually slid down to sit on the floor. He had no idea how long he would be there. He was seething. Finally, after what seemed forever, the lights came on. He pounded on the doors and noticed the elevator was going to the basement.

The doors opened and a security officer greeted him, "I'm sorry, sir, about this unexpected failure of power. Please accept our apologies."

"My wife is lost," Jack said.

"Lost?"

"She went into the powder room of the President's box. We were guests there this evening. She was supposed to meet me in the lobby, but she never came," Jack said.

"Let's get back in the elevator and go up there."

"Is the elevator safe?" Jack asked.

"Quite safe and I have a ring of keys that can fix anything," said the confident officer.

They both walked into the elevator and pushed the button to go up to the President's Box. The security man walked ahead and tried to open the ante room door. "It's locked," he said.

"My God, she's been locked in there for almost two hours!" Jack shouted.

The man pulled out a ring of keys and carefully unlocked the door and turned on the lights.

"Ginny? Ginny, where are you?" Jack knocked on the powder room door. "Are you in here? GINNY, answer me?"

I had fallen asleep on the floor and thought I heard Jack's voice in a dream, calling me. "Jack?" I said weakly.

"Ginny, open up."

"I can't. It's locked. That's why I couldn't come downstairs." I said in a sleepy voice.

"Well, there's a man from security here with me. Try it again," Jack said.

I stood up and tried the door, but nothing happened.

"Madam, do you see the little gold stick alongside the knob?"

"Yes."

"Push it down all the way."

"Okay," I said. I pushed it down.

"Did it come up?"

"No."

"Try again," he said.

I pushed hard and it popped up. "It's up!" I said excitedly.

"Excellent. Now, pull the handle down and pull it toward you."

"Not away from me?"

"No. Pull down, pull it toward you, and then push it away from you."

I tried again, but nothing happened.

"Don't let go of the handle as you push it forward. Try again," he said.

I did what he instructed me to do and the door opened. I rushed into Jack's arms.

"Oh, Jack, I thought you'd gone home without me and I'd be here for days," I cried.

"It's okay, you're free," Jack said with relief.

"Thank you, sir, for saving me," I said to the security officer.

"That door can be very tricky. We've had problems before. Now, let's get you to your car, so you can go home and forget this nightmare," said the security man.

"Thank you. Maybe you should consider changing the door handle," I said.

"I think you're right," he said.

We took the elevator to the parking garage and drove home in silence. It was a long night and too emotional; especially when Jack told me that he was stuck in the elevator trying to get upstairs to me.

At the office the next day, Jack was asked how the evening at the symphony was. He hesitated and then said, "Wonderful." This was going to be our own Washington secret.

$$* \quad * \quad * \quad *$$

We were asked one more time to the President's Box at the Kennedy Center. The invitation came from the Secretary of State to us and two other couples: Stanley's Deputy, Leonard Easton and his wife Myriam; Phil Wolfe and his wife, Myra. This time it was to see the musical <u>Annie</u> at the Eisenhower

Theater. And we had the pleasure of having a box supper together beforehand at the State Department. I wanted to wear something chic to the theatre. This was a hit musical on Broadway and we would be sitting in the President's box. I pulled out my black cocktail length, shantung silk black skirt and a beautiful dove gray silk blouse. I quickly dressed.

I was looking forward to the evening and the company. Easton was a maverick. He was direct and totally honest in his opinions. His wife was exactly the same. They were a refreshing couple. Wolfe was a young Foreign Service Officer—very sweet and very bright. His wife was quiet, but delightful.

When I arrived at the State Department, the lobby was swarming with reporters and photographers, waiting for any news on the Arab/Israeli situation. One of Jack's five assistants came down to escort me to his office. The corridors were very confusing. So much so, a former Secretary of State had the corridors color-coded, so that he could find his way. Jack's assistant was from Japan and as we waited in his office, we discussed how the Japanese served meals in beautifully decorated lacquer boxes, filled with rice cakes, tempura, and sushi appetizers.

Because Jack was still in a meeting, someone kindly escorted me to Secretary Stanley's office. The wives were already there, sitting in a happy grouping on a yellow sofa and rose silk chairs. Mrs. Stanley was wearing a striped chartreuse dress, which was so becoming. The Secretary was the first to join our group from his office. He greeted all of us and then gave his wife a hug and kiss on the forehead. Mr. Easton was the next to come in from an interview with one of the networks. Then, Mr. Wolfe arrived.

While we waited for Jack, we examined the Foreign Policy Kit on the coffee table. The Stanley children had given it to their father once he became Secretary of State. In the brown cardboard box were a whistle, a flashlight, a compass, dice, Band Aids, and aspirin. Although given as a joke, the contents might be useful at some point.

After Jack came, the box suppers were distributed. Inside were roast beef sandwiches on rye bread, potato chips, a pickle, and a small brownie. The conversation ranged from Massachusetts to the Middle East. During dessert, the discussion turned to female reporters.

The Secretary asked me, "Do you miss your newspaper offices on Cape Cod?"

"It's very discouraging because they are running very well without us," I said with a smile.

He laughed. "I understand weekly newspapers are in a boom right now unlike other aspects of journalism. Tell us, Jack, how do you like standing up at the briefing session every day?"

"Well, sir, I try to visualize the ocean view off our deck on Cape Cod and that keeps me sane," Jack replied. Another surge of laughter.

The Secretary asked me if I knew how to break a banana in three sections, which I didn't. Just as he was about to show me, Mrs. Stanley said that time was marching on and we had to head to the theatre.

Everyone crowded inside a private elevator with the two Department of State security agents. We stopped in the basement of the Department. Instead of going with Jack, Mrs. Stanley beckoned me to come with them in their limousine. The Secretary, Mrs. Stanley, and I sat in the backseat. The driver and one Security man sat in front.

As we pulled out of the garage, we went past the homeless man and I waved to him. He waved back.

"Do you know that man?" asked Stanley.

"Oh yes. His name is Lord Byron," I said.

"Really?" said Mrs. Stanley.

"He is so nice and he can quote all of Byron's poetry."

"How do you know that?" asked the Secretary. The Security agent was now looking at me intently.

"Well, when I first arrived here, a friend showed me all around Washington. As we approached the State Department, I saw him sleeping on the grid and I asked my friend to stop for a few minutes. I walked over to ask his name. When he told me Lord Byron, I requested that he quote a few verses of 'Don Juan.' He stood up with his hands upon his waist and exactly quoted the opening verses in a grand, Shakespearian style. I thanked him, gave him money, and ran back to the car."

The Stanleys looked at each other in amazement. The agent rolled his eyes. "Was there some reason you were compelled to do this?" asked the Secretary.

"Of course. I've been researching homelessness on Cape Cod and Boston in a series of articles for our newspapers," I said.

"What did you discover in your research?" the Secretary inquired.

"You know, the biggest thing homeless people want is respect. Passers-by treat them as if they are invisible. They give them haughty glances and dismiss them as nobodies. They would prefer to have a smile and a few kind words from people rather than money," I said.

"Interesting," commented the Secretary.

Within minutes, we arrived at the Kennedy Center and were ushered into the sitting room of the President's box. This one was not as ornate as the one at the Concert Hall. Everything was in red—the carpet, the walls, the silk, striped covered benches and red chairs. The Presidential Seal was also on the wall. I dared not even think about using the powder room.

We sat eight across, split by the center aisle. The two Security agents sat behind us on the second tier. As the curtain for the first act came down, Mrs. Easton let out a loud whistle and applauded. I was so startled that I added my loud boy whistle to hers. We smiled at each other. Although Jack has always been embarrassed by my whistle because it was not very ladylike, I decided that if the Deputy Secretary of State's wife could whistle with abandon, so could I. At intermission, we had drinks and talked about the acoustics of the theatre as well as structures in Egypt.

The second act was as much fun as the first. The little red-headed Annie was adorable and she had a powerhouse singing voice. At curtain call, Mrs. Easton joined the standing ovation with her whistle. Once again I did the same, but somehow I lost my balance and the top half of my body fell over the balcony's railing. Just then, the audience gasped as did the actors and actresses. Everyone was looking to the balcony.

"Ginny!" shouted Jack. He grabbed my leg that was closest to him. "Mrs. Easton, grab her other leg!" She did. There I was, hanging half upside down with my beautiful black skirt falling over my head, exposing my red panties with white hearts. The Secretary and Mrs. Stanley were frozen in horror.

The quick-thinking Mrs. Easton grabbed my skirt and pulled it up.

In split seconds, the two security officers came to the rescue. Each grabbed my waist and turned me right side up. The audience and stars clapped like crazy. Everyone in the President's Box was stunned and couldn't move. Jack took charge and hustled me to the ante room, so I could sit down in private. The guests asked if I were all right. I nodded my head, which was still beet red from being upside down, mortified, and embarrassed beyond belief.

"Please forgive me, Mr. Secretary and Mrs. Stanley, for embarrassing you and your guests. I must have lost my balance in my enthusiasm for the show," I said. "Please accept my apologies."

"We're grateful you didn't completely topple over into the crowd and injure yourself. That was our main concern," said Mrs. Stanley. "Come and ride back with us in the limousine."

"Thank you, Mrs. Stanley, but I think it's best that we go straight home," said Jack.

"Perhaps you're right," said the Secretary.

We bid everyone goodnight. I felt so awful for Jack. He was humiliated, and I don't blame him. I suppose the story would run like wildfire throughout the State Department. I hoped the press wouldn't get hold of it. Jack might have questions at his press briefing. I felt guilty, really guilty--extremely guilty.

CHAPTER SEVEN

▼

THREE UN FIASCOS

On the 37th anniversary of the United Nations, Washington celebrated at the Kennedy Center with a concert by the Baltimore Symphony Orchestra, conducted by Joseph Silverstern. Yes, the Kennedy Center once again. All the festivities started at 6:00 p.m. Even though the rule of no black-tie before seven was rigid, men still wore their tuxes and ladies were elegant in floor length gowns for this special occasion. There were four main speakers of note, including Secretary Stanley. Although the tickets were $250 per person, we were fortunate to come as guests of the Secretary.

Once the event was over at 8:30 p.m., there was a mad dash to cars and limos to rush to the Washington Hilton for dinner and dancing. I know Jack would have preferred a quiet night at home, but I was hyper excited. In my desperate search for a long dress suitable for the evening, Wanda loaned me her prom dress from high school. It was a pretty wine color, slinky, and simple—surprisingly just right for the UN party. My hair had just been cut to a chin length with a slight flip at the ends. This was the current style about town. I was looking more and more like a Washington woman!

Jack took the long way around, so by the time we reached the hotel, it was a mob scene. White and black limos and town cars were discharging political celebrities and their spouses at the grand entrance. Jack couldn't get near it, so he let me out while he searched for a place to park. I stood to one side of the entrance, wearing a velvet jacket over my dress and waited for Jack to appear. Suddenly, I saw a woman staring at me. She looked familiar. Finally, she came up to me. It was Mrs. Easton--the whistler from the President's box. I really wanted to hide when I recognized her.

"I was just thinking to myself, I wish I looked like that and then I realized who you were!" laughed Mrs. Easton.

"Look like me?" I asked.

"Yes."

"But you look beautiful," I replied stunned. "Why would you want to look like me?" I asked.

"If you don't know, you're nuts. Here's my date. Enjoy the evening," she said and waved goodbye.

Once Jack arrived, we went inside and stood in line for the seating list. Our table was number 78. As we entered the Grand Ballroom, it was dimly lit in a blue atmospheric light. An orchestra was playing and round tables surrounded the dance floor. Our table was positioned right next to it. Just before joining our table, we ran into Don George from Communications and exchanged views on the tough questions at the press briefings and the long hours.

Our table was made up of lawyers, but in fact, I think they were mostly spooks, throwing their clandestine lives to the winds. The wives were no slouches either. They were lawyers, too. One woman was head of volunteers at the White House. When we mentioned Cape Cod, one couple confessed to having a house in Centerville on the Cape where they commuted in summer with their six kids.

There were gifts for each guest: a tote bag and a silver picture frame. It was a fabulous dinner with appetizers before the main menu, starting off with fancy spaghetti in a tortilla shell; a tender filet mignon; artichoke hearts with tomatoes; shredded zucchini; salad; and cheesecake.

After dinner, one of the bald CIA types began dancing with each lady at our table. The man next to me was also bald and wore black-rimmed spectacles. He appeared very friendly.

"What does your husband do?" he asked.

"He's spokesman for Secretary Stanley at the State Department," I said.

"No wonder he looks familiar. I've actually watched him on network news. He's very good," he said.

"Yes, he is a gifted speaker," I said. Secretly I beamed and intended to pass along the praise to Jack.

"Where are you from?" he asked.

"Cape Cod."

"How could you bring yourselves to leave?"

"A sense of duty—to serve the President."

"Of course," he nodded. "And what exactly do you do, my dear?" He asked this in a rather condescending tone.

"I'm a playwright," I said nonchalantly.

"A playwright? I've never met one before. What kind of plays do you write?" he asked.

"Every kind. Comedies, dramas—mysteries."

"Mysteries I love," he smiled. "What are you working on now?"

"A play called WHITE HOUSE SECRETS," I said.

"White House Secrets?" he asked. He seemed disturbed—shocked.

"Yes."

"What's it about?" He turned to face me directly.

"Well, it's about the Russians trying to kidnap the Secretary of State. They capture a theatre and take the audience hostage because the Secretary is there attending a performance."

"What do the Russians want?"

"He has the blueprints for a new invention, which they want," I said.

"What's the invention?" he inquired wide-eyed.

"Aren't you interested in the juicy love story between a Russian soldier and a young lady or the capture of the Secretary's wife to force him to give them the secret plans?" I asked.

"I'm more interested in the invention. It sounds to me as if the plot is nothing without it," he stated.

"That's true," I said. "It's a CamVac."

"A what?"

"A Camera Vacuum," I said.

"What does it do?"

"Well, it's like a tube from a satellite that beams into the inner sanctums of the Kremlin or Peking or Istanbul. It sucks up information and conversations like a vacuum cleaner and takes photographs as well."

He pushed his chair back and stared at me. His eyes were round—full of shock, surprise, and fright. "How did you know?" he asked.

"How did I know what?"

"It exists," he whispered.

"It doesn't. I just made it up. It's fiction," I said.

"Don't ever tell anyone you know me. Forget you've ever heard my name," he stuttered. But I had noticed his name on his place card. He stood up to leave and slipped the name card in his pocket. Before he disappeared for the rest of the evening, he whispered something to one of his colleagues.

At the very moment of his departure, the exuberant dancer came to my chair. "Mrs. Hunter, I would be honored to have you join me on the dance floor." My first instinct was to decline, but it would be grossly impolite to refuse. I looked helplessly at Jack, but he was absorbed in conversation with a very attractive lady.

I arose and followed him to the center of the dance floor. He held up his left arm, crooking it at the elbow. I put my left hand on his right shoulder and slid my right hand into his strong left hand. He clamped down on mine as if they were glued together. Like a wild Russian dancer, he spun me around like a rag doll. Then, he would switch to an animated jitterbug, crashing into other couples with abandon. Many showed anger on their faces. During one spin that seemed to go on and on, my high heel locked into another lady's heel and the shoe was wrenched right off my foot. I limped over to where the woman threw it in disgust and I stepped back into it. Before I could stand up straight, my partner grabbed me and crushed me to his chest. Everyone on the floor moved to the sides. We began the dizzying spins again. My dress kept dropping off one shoulder. My belt moved off center. My hair now covered my face and strands were caught in my mouth. All the loops and strings inside the dress were now hanging out from the cap sleeves. Finally, the music stopped to put me out of my misery. People clapped and sniggered. I peeped through my hair to find our table. I saw the Vice President, the Secretary, and cabinet members staring at me. I wanted to die and crawl into a hole. I went straight to Jack.

"You better go to the ladies room and pull yourself together," he said.

"Can you ask someone to pass my handbag over?"

They did and I practically ran to the ladies room. What I saw in the mirror was a horrible apparition of what had once been presentable elegance. I straightened the dress and belt, tucked in the strings, and combed my hair. I never wanted to leave this room. Then, I remembered being locked in the Presidential Box powder room and took back my wish. Anyway, I held my head high and returned to the table. People were giving me amusing side glances as I walked past them.

My dancing partner ignored me as if nothing had happened. He was out on the dance floor with another victim, but he seemed more civilized. Maybe his wife chastised him.

By midnight, everyone left.

There was a traffic jam in Georgetown from Halloweeners, marching through the streets.

"Ginny, how could you make such a fool of yourself?"

"Jack, it wasn't my fault."

"Well, it was embarrassing to say the least," said Jack.

"That jerk who asked me to dance made a fool of me."

"Why didn't you refuse to dance with him?"

"Because he was our host. I couldn't be impolite," I said.

"Everyone will be talking about this tomorrow. I guess that's the story of my life."

"I can't help it," I said almost in tears.

"Thank God the <u>The D.C. Gazette</u> didn't take a picture," Jack sighed.

It was a UN night that I would never forget.

✶   ✶   ✶   ✶

After that encounter with the CIA man, who said my fictional invention, called CamVac in my play, was real, I began to feel increasingly uneasy in my condo. I was sure I was being watched. The condo across from us was vacant. I kept feeling someone was there with powerful binoculars and maybe some kind of listening device. Occasionally I would peep out one of the front windows. These days the only time I went out was for shopping, tennis, or the occasional coffee or luncheon. Also, it was a quiet time on the international front and perhaps the CIA didn't have enough to do, except spy on me even though they didn't have US jurisdiction. Well, what did it matter, they were, after all, the Central Intelligence Agency, the most secret of secretive organizations.

One day I was going to be away for four hours. They must have known, which means our telephone was tapped. Anyway, I forgot something and came back unexpectedly. As I unlocked the front door, the back door closed. Just as I reached the back door, I saw the outside gate close, too. Now I was really spooked. Besides that, the dog was chewing on a heap of dog biscuits. I ran upstairs and there was my manuscript on WHITE HOUSE SECRETS spread out on the floor. I imagined that one of those tiny cameras, probably made to look like a cigarette lighter, was used to take pictures. It had to be the CIA, and I assumed my fictional CamVac truly must be real. I didn't know if I should tell Jack or not. I decided not to tell him, so I could protect him. If any reporter asked him about CamVac, he could truthfully say he had no knowledge of it. Unbeknownst to me, I was proven right. In a few days, I had a feeling that whoever was in the vacant condo had left. Maybe they got what they wanted from the manuscript and figured it was harmless, but it was a creepy feeling.

✶   ✶   ✶   ✶

Every September, the Secretary of State takes a whole floor at the UN Plaza Hotel in New York City, across from the United Nations, which overlooks the East River. For two weeks, the Secretary and his entourage hold meetings with prime ministers or foreign ministers to discuss policy differences or negotiations about mutual interests prior to the President's visit to the UN General Assembly later in the month. It is a productive time for all and also a time of socializing in the evenings.

President Rowland spoke before the General Assembly. The Russian leader also spoke and gave a somewhat anti-American speech. Relations were not good. There was a reception at the Waldorf Astoria that was interesting to watch. The Israelis were in one corner; the Russians in another corner; and the Americans moving diplomatically between the two. The world's relations could be detected by watching those in one small ballroom. There was much whispering and conferring.

I happened to be chatting with a man I recognized, but couldn't quite remember his name. Afterwards, it occurred to me that it was Prince Sihanouk of Cambodia. I had gone to Cambodia in 1969 with a friend as a tourist because Sihanouk wouldn't let any correspondent from The Boston International enter the country. He had some editorial dispute with them, but on this social occasion, he was charming.

One evening, the Secretary and Mrs. Stanley gave a splendid post reception, private dinner party in a sumptuous suite for a group of eight. Most were from the State Department. The only outsider was the former Chairman of Citicorp, Winthrop Walton, a personal friend of the Secretary's. I was sitting between Mr. Walton and Mr. Stanley. Somehow, the conversation with Walton turned to Martha Covington and Bob Albert of the Barber Corporation.

"They were in the same company and were having an affair," said Walton.

"Not true," I said emphatically.

"Of course they did. It was common knowledge," Walton replied.

"Actually, I interviewed her recently for our newspapers over the summer on Cape Cod, and she told me the whole story," I said. "They were both married to other people at the time. She was a Harvard Business School graduate and had been hired by Albert because of her brilliant intellect and honesty. She helped him pull Barber out of the financial hole. Because they were seen together all the time as colleagues, people made a false judgment about their relationship."

"Don't you think that's a bit naïve?" he asked.

"No."

"Why not?"

"Well, these rumors brought the company to a standstill. She was forced to resign," I told him.

"And he resigned, too," he said.

"I know."

"And they got married," he smiled.

"Not right away. They were both getting divorces from other people."

"And then they got married to each other!" he said.

"It was only after they divorced did they get together romantically," I insisted.

"You really believe that?"

"I believe it because she was raised a strict Catholic girl, and she just wouldn't do such a thing," I declared.

As the discussion dominated the table, Secretary Stanley interrupted our exchange. By now, everyone was listening. "All right," said the Secretary, "we're going to take a vote here and now to see how many believe Martha Covington and Bob Albert had an affair while they both were working at Barber Corp."

Each guest voted that they did commit adultery. When Stanley came to Jack, he threw back his arms and voted in favor of the affair. It was seven to one. I was the only one who voted against it. Just then, Mrs. Stanley said we had to get ready to go to the theatre.

Jack's deputy cornered him and said, "Your wife is dangerous."

"What do you mean?" asked Jack.

"To have someone that honest in this town--Washington-- is downright dangerous," he said.

"What if she's right?" asked Jack.

"She's not. Cunningham must have conned her. Even you believed that she was having an affair."

"I know."

"Was she like this when you first married her?" asked the deputy.

"Let's say, our honeymoon might have been an omen of things to come," said Jack.

"What do you mean?"

"I mean, when we were on our honeymoon going down the east coast of Africa in a small British cruise ship, she did the impossible," said Jack.

"What did she do?"

"We were at a port in Portuguese East Africa. I couldn't leave the ship because I was writing a story, on deadline, so she got off and went to a museum and a hippo pool. She knew she had two hours before the boat would cast off," Jack told him.

"She didn't miss the boat?" asked incredulously.

"Indeed she did," nodded Jack.

"Oh my God. What happened?"

"I thought she was back on board, but when I looked down and saw her pitiful figure on the pier as the boat was pulling away from the dock, I rushed up to the Captain and asked him to stop—that my bride didn't have a passport or money."

"Too bad," said the Captain.

"She was so trusting, so innocent—I knew she was sure something would work out. That's who she is," Jack told his colleague, trying to explain the behavior of his wife.

"But what happened?"

"As the ship moved parallel to the dock, sliding gently out to sea, the crew grabbed her hands from the boat and tried to pull her through a porthole. Even though she only weighed 98 pounds, she couldn't fit."

"So?"

"So, they threw her a rope ladder from the cargo hold. She caught it, stood on the bottom rung, and slammed into the side of the ship. She climbed up the rope ladder into the cargo hold, and we were reunited," said Jack.

"I guess you were furious."

"I was livid, but relieved."

"What did you say to her?" he asked.

"I told her to write the captain a letter of apology, which she did. He wrote a very nice note back and said Anglo-American relations would survive the incident."

"Why was she late?" he asked.

"Her watch was slow."

"Jack, why don't you send her home—back to Cape Cod for her own good? The vultures in this town could tear her apart."

At that precise moment, Mrs. Stanley said, "Come on folks, we don't want to be late for the show."

We all went downstairs and rode to the theatre in two limos with the State Department security cars in front and in back of our convoy with sirens blaring. We were a little bit late for the musical, 42nd Street, but they held the curtain for us. As we settled into our seats, I sat next to Winthrop Walton. I was surprised he would want to sit next to the babe of innocence--me. At intermission, he said I could be right about Martha Covington and why didn't I send him a copy of my article. He handed me his card. I figured that his wife had talked to him in the car for being so hard on me. I did send the article and his lawyer wife wrote a five page letter back, supporting my view. Naturally, I showed it to Jack.

After the show, we were all invited onstage to greet the actors/dancers and then we were returned to the hotel. What an evening!

The next morning I slept in. Jack's meetings with the Secretary were scheduled for all day. I would join them for another reception at 6:00.

Knowing this, I had arranged meetings with agents and play publishers to interest them in my plays.

It was a great September morning, full of autumn sunshine and a slight crispness in the air. I made my rounds in the Times Square area and Sixth Avenue. There were some rejections and some interest. I also arranged to have lunch with Katharine Hepburn's niece, Katharine Houghton. I had reviewed her at the Cape Playhouse one summer and a friendship evolved.

By 5:15, I made it back to the hotel in time for a shower and to put on a cocktail dress for the reception. Jack picked me up in the room. As we walked down the corridor, Secretary Stanley emerged from his suite. He and I walked shoulder to shoulder towards the elevator. I asked him about his day. Just as we were stepping into the elevator together, Jack tapped my shoulder.

"Ginny, let the Secretary go in first!" he said.

"That's all right," said the Secretary.

What happened next seemed to take place in slow motion. I turned to look at Jack when my eye traveled down the corridor.

"Oh no!" I screamed. I saw a gunman with a revolver pointed at the Secretary. Instinctively, I put my arm around the Secretary's neck, pulled him down in the elevator while in a kissing motion. The gun discharged and the bullet hit the wall of the elevator where the Secretary's head had been seconds before. The security agent muscled the man to the ground and handcuffed him.

Once the man was subdued, Jack and the others helped us to our feet. Everyone was stricken by shock. I was trembling all over and could barely speak.

When I recovered my voice, I turned to the Secretary and said, "Mr. Secretary, I'm so sorry, but I didn't know what else to do to stop him. Please tell Mrs. Stanley that there was nothing personal. I just had to save you." I almost burst into tears. Everyone could see my distress, but the Secretary came to my rescue.

"Look at this hole," he said. He put his finger in it. "No need to apologize, Ginny. You're my hero. I'm the one to thank you!"

"Oh," I said, completely embarrassed.

"Jack, you should be proud of your lady," Stanley said.

"I am. Indeed I am. Are you all right, sir?" Jack asked.

"As a former Marine, I am. Shall we go to the reception?" The Secretary said.

"Yes, if you're sure."

The incident didn't seem real—as if it were a dream and never happened.

As it turned out, I wasn't dreaming. The man was from the IRM—
International Revolutionary Movement or the REVOS. How he got through
security onto the floor remained a mystery. They speculated that he was
dressed as a waiter or hid under someone's unused bed. They marveled that
he could have avoided the Marine guards, who search every room. A reporter
somehow did get hold of the story and snapped a single picture of me at the
reception. I tried to avoid being interviewed that night.

It wasn't until the reception was over that I had a reaction and began
to shake all over. I retreated to our room and went to bed. Throughout the
night, I had recurring nightmares about the whole thing. Maybe it would go
into a play.

The next morning the headlines filled the whole front page: **THE KISS;
THE KISS THAT LAUNCHED 1,000 FEARS; THE KISS THAT
SAVED STATE DEPARTMENT; ASSASSIN FOILED BY KISS; SAVED
BY A KISS; AMERICA'S JOAN OF ARC.**

CHAPTER EIGHT

▼

BREZHNEV'S FUNERAL

One day, long after the assassination attempt, Secretary Stanley spoke to one of his secretaries, "Miss Peterson, would you ask Jack Hunter to come up to my office for a few minutes?"

"Yes, sir, I think he's just finished his daily briefing," she replied.

"Leonard?"

"I'm still here, sir," said Leonard Easton.

"How are the plans progressing for the trip to the Soviet Union?" Stanley asked.

"Progressing well."

"Good. I want you to stay while I ask Jack Hunter a couple of questions relating to the trip."

"Mr. Hunter is here, Mr. Secretary," said Miss Peterson.

"Send him in," he said. The Secretary got up from his leather chair and came around his desk to greet Jack. "Jack, how was the briefing?"

"Lots of questions about the Brezhnev funeral, sir. How was your visit to the Soviet Embassy?" Jack inquired.

"Mobbed. Every ambassador to the U.S.A. was there, along with the Vice-President and me. The Russian ambassador expressed appreciation for our presence as we signed the guest book. He asked if we would be going to Moscow for the funeral, and we told him we would. He seemed pleased even though our relations are strained," said the Secretary.

"Did they serve caviar?" Jack asked out of curiosity.

"Nothing but the best. We tasted it and left. Other ambassadors stayed around the buffet table, obviously enjoying themselves, drinking Vodka mid-morning," laughed the Secretary. "Tell me, Jack, has your wife recovered after that dramatic incident at the United Nations?" he asked.

"She's doing much better," said Jack.

"I've been thinking about her and the heroic role she played and wondered if she'd like to come to Russia with us—a sort of thank you from my wife and me," he proposed.

"Well, sir, I can't answer for her, but I think she would be thrilled."

"Her presence would be company for my wife while we have meetings with Brezhnev's replacement, the Russian foreign minister, and military generals," the Secretary said.

"May I talk with her tonight and get back to you tomorrow?"

"Of course. Leonard, do you think there would be a problem?"

"Not that I can think of, sir," said Easton. "However, Jack should keep her away from the press, regarding her Joan of Arc kiss!" Jack and Stanley couldn't help but laugh. Easton had a sharp wit.

I was in the process of preparing a home-cooked dinner for Max and Jack that evening, when Jack popped a surprise question.

"Ginny, how would you like to go to the Soviet Union with me?" Jack asked.

"Russia? Why?" I asked with a surprised look on my face.

"For the Brezhnev funeral."

"Are you teasing?" I asked.

"No. The Secretary asked me today. Mrs. Stanley would love to have you there while we are locked in meetings," he said.

"Why does he want me to come?"

"I just told you," said Jack.

"Does he want to pay me back for the famous savior kiss?" I asked.

"Partly. However, there is one promise that he wants from you."

"What's that?" I asked.

"You are not to talk with the press or allow yourself to be interviewed," Jack said in all seriousness.

"Okay." That was fine with me because I had no desire to be interviewed. I like being the interviewer, not the interviewee.

"You promise?'

"I promise. What will Russia be like in mid-November?" I asked.

"Cold, very cold. Go buy some long underwear tomorrow."

"I will. This is exciting," I said.

After buying necessities and digging out my winter clothes, hats, and gloves, I packed my suitcase as if I were going to Siberia. Well, I practically was! On a late Saturday afternoon, Jack and I parked the car in the State Department garage and transferred to the Secretary's limousine, ready to go to Andrews Air Force Base.

I greeted the Stanleys enthusiastically. They both seemed pleased I was joining them on the trip. Once we were aboard the airplane, I was amazed at the accommodations. It was like no plane I had seen, rather more like a huge resort hotel, combined with a plush office. There was a bedroom and office/living room for the Stanleys; a small bedroom for Jack and me; a tiny conference room to hold private discussions; a private dining area; a press area for 25 journalists in the rear that looked like a first class cabin on a commercial flight.

Choosing the reporters was always difficult. There was a pool rotation that selected the wire service, television, newspaper, magazine, and radio correspondents. They were asked first. It was considered the fairest system. Despite this, some felt slighted, but Jack always included as many as were allowed. Some of them were his friends, and if he didn't select them, sometimes there were still hard feelings. Jack didn't want me to be visible because as a matter of custom, wives of non-principals don't usually go on official trips. To prevent rumors and unnecessary speculation, I was happy to keep a low profile. My escapades thus far might be a hindrance.

"Jack, as soon as you and Ginny are settled, let's meet in our office area," said the Secretary.

"We'll be there shortly," said Jack.

Jack and I unpacked a few things from our suitcases and freshened up before joining the Secretary and his wife in their private quarters. As we entered, the Secretary greeted us warmly.

"Ginny, how do you like your accommodations?"

"They are better than the Waldorf!" I joked.

"The government has a few planes like this for the President and Vice President. When the planes are not in use by them, cabinet members are permitted to request them for official overseas flights," he said. "Sit down— make yourselves comfortable. I thought it would be appropriate to discuss our upcoming schedule and plans. When we arrive in Moscow tomorrow morning, you two ladies will be taken to the train station to go to St. Petersburg, a lovely city, to see the Hermitage Museum and general sights. It's an eight hour train ride. Jack and I will begin our meetings with lower level courtesy calls in Moscow, and eventually, meet with Yuri Andropov, Brezhnev's successor. We will go to Spasso House, the American Ambassador's residence, where he will receive us and where Olivia and I will stay. Jack will stay with and regularly be accompanied by the Press Attache. There will be press conferences with the Soviets and then with only Americans. Jack can handle his own press meetings with the American reporters. When you return from St. Petersburg, the American Ambassador's wife will show you around Moscow. We will all attend the Bolshoi Ballet that evening and then attend the funeral in the morning. The Vice President's own secure bullet-proof, Cadillac limousine is on the car plane. He will take us all back to the private side of Vnukovo airport to our respective airplanes and we will fly home. Any questions?"

"I brought a tourist guidebook. Would Mrs. Stanley like to hear about some of the highlights?" I asked.

"I certainly would," she said.

"Why don't you ladies retreat to the conference room, and we'll meet in the dining room at 7:30 for dinner. How does that sound?"

"Fine," I said. Mrs. Stanley and I found the two leather chairs facing each other with a little table in between. I brought out my compact guidebook. "Shall we learn a few things in an attempt to erase the ignorance factor?"

"Good idea," she smiled.

"To start with, St. Petersburg is on the Neva River at the head of the Gulf of Finland and the Baltic Sea. It was founded by Peter the Great in 1703. In 1914, the city was renamed Petrograd and called Leningrad in 1924. Then, in 1991, it reverted back to St. Petersburg," I said.

"I'm glad. St. Petersburg is much more suitable," she said.

"Exactly."

"I do know it has been called the 'Venice of the North' because of its network of canals," she said.

"You know more than the guidebook!" I said. We both laughed.

"And of course, I have heard forever about the Hermitage Museum, which was the Czar's Winter Palace. I can't wait to see it," she added.

"I agree. The book says there are three million works of art and antiquities!" I said.

"We'll never get to Moscow if we look at them all," she responded.

"We could get lost and they'd never find us," I declared.

"That won't happen because the curator will be our guide," she said.

I continued to read. "There are six buildings of the Hermitage on the Palace embankment and none of them can be higher than the Winter Palace. Look, you can see it in this picture."

"It looks like a long architectural train!" she said.

"You're absolutely right. It says, the major collections include Michelangelo, da Vinci, Rubens, Rembrandt, Impressionists, and Faberge eggs."

"We have to see those!" Mrs. Stanley said.

"Oh, I forgot to say that Catherine the Great added more paintings and a Voltaire collection in 1765. She was a major patron of the arts and created a private theater for performances. Do you think that's enough for us to remember?" I asked.

'Enough for my brain," she said. "Let's eat."

We entered the dining area where the men were waiting for us. The stewards served us dinner. Afterwards, we retired for the night before our arrival in Moscow. They would be waking us early for breakfast.

The knock came at 4:30 a.m. We showered and dressed in our warm clothes before meeting our hosts at the table. It was a monster American breakfast to keep us going forever!

When we arrived in Moscow, and the Stanleys met their Russian counterparts, I was taken to a Soviet car and waited for Mrs. Stanley. We were whisked off to the train station. A special train car had been added for us that included a dining room and a compartment for each of us. Even our security man had a private room nearby, in case the train was hi-jacked. By the end of the day, we were in St. Petersburg. We couldn't see very much at night as the white nights are only in summer. The canals looked dark and murky and there were only a few street lamps. The hotel was huge. A concert by Russian dancers and a jazz band played for our benefit after dinner. Once it was over, we retreated to our rooms.

After breakfast the following morning, we were taken to the Hermitage. The entry of marble and gold with an ornate staircase was breathtaking. The curator, Mr. Greggori, met us. We went to his office and he asked what we would like to see.

"Rembrandt, the Impressionists and Post-Impressionists, and the Faberge collection are highest on our list. Then we can consult again," said Mrs. Stanley.

"Excellent idea, madam," he replied.

We did see our favorites, swooning uncontrollably. As Greggori and his three assistants guided Mrs. Stanley to the next collection, I collapsed on a sofa to drink in the Impressionists.

Just as they were entering the Faberge section, an aide of Mr. Greggori's handed him a note.

"Madam Stanley, I have some sad news," said Greggori.

"What do you mean?" asked Mrs. Stanley.

"There is a message from your husband. He wants you and Mrs. Hunter to return to Moscow tonight. A private airplane will be put at your disposal," he said. "We will take you back to the hotel to collect your things and go directly to the airport."

"Where is Mrs. Hunter?" asked Mrs. Stanley, looking around for me.

"She was here a few minutes ago." Greggori directed his aides to go back through the halls they had already visited, and they ran all the way.

"Mrs. Hunter," they called. As they entered the Impressionists room, they stopped to listen. Suddenly, they heard a snore. Astonished and amused, they tiptoed over to the sofa and peeped over. There I was sound asleep, snoring like a pig. "Mrs. Hunter," they whispered. I sat up straight and looked all around and saw the three faces at the top of the sofa.

"I must have fallen asleep. Where is Mrs. Stanley?" I asked.

"With Mr. Greggori. Her husband has asked you ladies to return to Moscow immediately," one of the aides said. "We must catch up with them."

"Lead the way," I said. We all sprinted to the place where Mrs. Stanley and Greggori were waiting.

"Oh, Ginny," said Mrs. Stanley, "are you all right?"

"Sorry, I fell asleep in the Impressionist section. It must be jet lag. I apologize."

"Have you heard the news about our return to Moscow?" she asked.

"Yes."

"Before we leave, I have a favor to ask Mr. Greggori?"

"Yes, madam?"

"Could we rush through the Faberge collection quickly in order not to miss this precious art of Russia?" asked Mrs. Stanley.

"Follow me."

We practically ran through the rooms as he gave us a few words about each case. We said our goodbyes and expressed our unending gratitude. Once back at the hotel, we packed and met in the lobby for another car to speed us to the airport.

During the two hour flight, I told Mrs. Stanley about Moscow even though we would not see it.

"I hope you're not too disappointed not to sightsee in Moscow," I said.

"Very," she said.

"If you want, I can tell you a few things we'll miss."

"Go ahead," she replied.

"Well, Moscow is set on the Moscow River and it's the largest city in Europe with ten million people," I read.

"That fact I won't miss."

"We'll miss the Bolshoi Ballet," I said.

"I definitely will miss that," she sighed.

"And St. Basil's Cathedral, but we'll see the outside from Red Square."

"It's so pretty with all those onion domes," she said.

"Nine domes and nine chapels. Ivan the Terrible had it built from 1555 to 1561 for St. Basil of the Russian Orthodox Church."

"I will look at it nostalgically," she said.

Soon, we were back in Moscow. An American car met us and took Mrs. Stanley and me to Spasso House. Jack came out and got in the car, so we could go to the Press Attache's residence.

"Why did we have to cut our trip short?" I asked him.

"The funeral has been changed to tomorrow morning," he said.

"Oh."

Our hosts had dinner waiting for us and other American officials. After a short conversation, Jack and I excused ourselves to retire.

"Did you and the Secretary speak to the State Department from The Bubble at Spasso House?" I asked.

"Just the Secretary. I am intrigued by the notion that the RSO and the military have to check for bugs regularly because Russian workers are always trying secretly to install electronic equipment to catch conversations," he said.

"Too bad they don't know about CamVac!" I laughed.

"What?"

"Oh nothing," I said. I never told Jack about my conversation with the CIA agent at the UN dance.

"Look what I bought you," he said with a huge smile. He brought out a bag that said GUM on it—the one shopping mall in Moscow, selling both western and Russian gifts.

I peeked in the bag. "A warm Russian hat—just what I wanted. Can I wear it to the funeral?"

"You'll need it. The temperature will be below freezing tomorrow," he said.

"Jack, that was so thoughtful of you. I really wanted a hat just like this. Thank you," I said, hugging him.

"I'm glad you like it."

I put on the hat and pranced around the room, looking in the mirror. No one would take me for an American. I slept with it on my pillow and had dreams of being pursued by Omar Sharif in the movie 'Dr. Zhivago.' "

The next morning I respectfully dressed all in black: a black wool suit, black sweater, black fur-lined boots, and a black wool scarf to wrap around my face if the weather felt bitter. Jack wore a black suit, a long black coat, and a black fedora hat. He advised me not to wear the Russian fur hat until just before we stepped out of the limo. We packed our bags and took them downstairs for the driver because we would be going immediately to the airport once the funeral was over, but not in the Vice President's limo as originally planned. Our hosts provided a hearty American breakfast for which I was grateful.

The limo picked us up first and then to Spasso House for the Secretary and Mrs. Stanley. As they settled in the second seats, the Secretary turned to ask how we were.

"Excellent," was Jack's reply.

"Ginny, I'm sorry your visit to St. Petersburg was cut short and all of your Moscow tour erased," the Secretary apologized.

"Your wife and I saw the most important collections. You saved us from seeing three million pieces of art and probably not remembering most of them. What we did see was unforgettable, so thank you for allowing us to have a glimpse of those wonderful treasures at the Hermitage."

"Jack, your wife is turning into a first class diplomat!"

"Thanks to you and Mrs. Stanley," he laughed.

"Be prepared for some choreographed behavior at the funeral. The Brezhnev family will kiss the body as part of the mourning. Then the casket will be moved to Red Square. It will be open for dignitaries to pass by to pay their respects. Members of the public cannot go beyond the roped off area. We will see you back at the limousine," said the Secretary. He and Mrs. Stanley emerged first and were greeted by the Soviets now in power.

Jack and I waited and then stepped out into the brisk air. I put my hat on and pulled the black scarf across half my face. I needed my fur-lined gloves, too. The wind was like a razor. I was glad to have the new hat. We stood behind the American Ambassador and his wife, who stood behind the Vice President, the Secretary, and Mrs. Stanley. We watched the Brezhnev family perform their ritual over the body. Pall bearers carried the casket to the center of Red Square next to Lenin's tomb. One of the bearers dropped a corner of the casket. Everyone gasped. He picked it up again and made it to the spot where they set down the casket and opened it. All of Brezhnev's medals were laid across his feet. A red communist flag was draped at the back of Brezhnev's head.

The press and photographers were located in a tightly roped off area some distance away. They were snapping occasional pictures. The band, in black uniforms, started playing a dirge. Yuri Andropov and his deputy were first to pass and pause at the casket, bowing their heads. The American delegation walked slowly by. I was in front of Jack.

Just as I paused to look at the body, a soldier, carrying a Soviet flag, goose-stepped past me. His right foot kicked in front of my two legs and flipped me in the air, landing me inside the casket. The mob gasped in horror. "Oh no!" they said in Russian and English in unison. I was horrified.

"Oh my God," said Jack under his breath.

The upper half of Brezhnev's body came forward in a slightly upright position and then, his body fell back on the white silk with a thud. At that very moment, the casket door slammed shut over the dead Brezhnev and me. I was wedged inside and too shocked to scream.

Every security officer instantly surrounded the casket, opened it, and yanked me out in a very hostile manner. I didn't understand why because it was their fault, not mine.

Angry and distressed, Jack instructed our Diplomatic Security, "Get her out of here and put her in the Secretary's limousine. Once she's inside, tell her to take off that damn hat. Have her hide on the floor and keep out of sight."

Two of our agents grabbed me and whisked me away to the limo. Photographers were going crazy with their long lenses. "Who is she?" they asked. No one knew, and Jack was hoping they never would, but he knew that was a false hope.

As I crouched on the floor, my teeth began chattering from the incident, from fear, and from the cold. I dreaded the consequences that might result for the Stanleys and Jack.

Once the American delegation finished with the viewing, the Vice President and the Stanleys started to stride to their respective limousines.

Jack caught up with them and said, "Mr. Vice President and Mr. Secretary, under the circumstances, I suggest we go right to the airplanes before the press is unleashed."

"Good suggestion," they said in unison.

Once we boarded the Secretary's plane, and I was safely settled in the private quarters. Mrs. Stanley asked, "What happened?"

Jack replied, "She paused at the casket and bowed her head when a Soviet soldier tripped her and sent her flying into the casket."

"My God," gasped the Secretary.

"And then the casket closed on top of Brezhnev and Ginny."

"How terrifying," said Mrs. Stanley. "Then what?"

"All the guards surrounded the casket, opened it, and pulled her out. Our security moved in front of them and carried her to the limo," Jack said. "No one knows who she is, but we'll be bombarded with questions."

"Ginny, are you all right?" asked the Secretary.

"Yes, but I am mortified. I had no idea this would happen. I am so sorry," I said.

"It was an accident—not your fault," said Stanley.

"But you were so kind to invite me on this trip. I feel truly awful," I said.

"Let's put it behind us," he said graciously.

I was in our private quarters on the plane and hidden from media view while we flew across the Atlantic. It was night time and most everyone was sleeping during the flight. Therefore, Jack was able to avoid the press. I knew Jack probably couldn't sleep because he was figuring out how to handle questions related to my first big, international incident.

Once we landed, Jack made sure the reporters were well out of sight before I was ushered to the car.

However, the next morning, the papers printed distant photos of a woman in black falling into the casket. The headlines: **MYSTERY WOMAN FALLS IN BREZHNEV CASKET; COZY TWOSOME IN BREZHNEV CASKET; WOMAN FALLS IN LOVE WITH DEAD RUSSIAN LEADER; WHO IS SHE?; MOVE OVER BREZH, I'M DYING TO GO WITH YOU! GHOULISH LEAP INTO BREZHNEV CASKET.**

Jack let his deputy take the press briefing the day we returned. The following day, Jack was back at his post and ready to answer the questions about the mystery woman.

"Jack, who was that woman who fell into the casket?" asked a man from Reuters.

"I'll handle this question on background," Jack replied, but the reporters persisted.

"Was she a spy?" asked an American reporter.

"How did it happen?" asked a Pravda newsman.

"Apparently, a goose-stepping Soviet soldier kicked her by mistake, flipping her in the air," said Jack.

"We saw you talking to security," said a television reporter.

"As I said, we'll discuss this on background," Jack repeated. "Next question?"

"Did anything significant come out of your talks with Andropov?" asked a woman from The New York Times.

"It was a 'meet and greet' type of exchange. Nothing else would have been appropriate at a funeral," Jack told him. "Thank you, ladies and gentlemen, it's good to be back. See you tomorrow."

Once the cameras were turned off and notebooks put aside, no reporter left the room. They all crowded around Jack at the lectern for his remarks on background—a sort of semi-off-the-record account of certain sensitive issues. Everyone waited for Jack to speak.

"Ladies and gentlemen, what I am about to say is personally very painful for me, but as spokesman, I owe you an honest explanation of what happened in Moscow, regarding the mystery woman who fell into Leonid Brezhnev's casket. She....is.... my wife."

There was stunned silence. No one knew what to say or what to ask.

"I have no right to ask you to ignore writing about it. I must leave it up to you as to how you will use this information. From your point of view, this is a tantalizing story and I understand that. I have told you the truth. Now, it is in your hands and left up to your consciences. Thank you for your consideration," Jack said as he gathered up his papers and briefing book and left the press room.

Still in shock, the reporters did not move from their circle around the podium. There were no wisecracks or personal exchanges—only silence. They quietly returned to their chairs and picked up their briefcases to depart while pondering how they would write this story.

The next day on the wires, in the papers, and on network news, there were short clips and brief stories about the identity of the mystery woman as being the wife of an American government official, who was accidentally tripped by a Soviet soldier, which caused the woman to fall into the Brezhnev casket.

Fortunately and astonishingly, no names were mentioned. Jack, of course, was as relieved as I was. He had not sacrificed his integrity and had never asked anyone to withhold his name or mine.

A few days later, when all the turmoil over this incident had subsided, there was an invitation from the Soviet Ambassador in D.C. to attend a small reception.

"Do you want to go?" Jack asked.

"You can't be serious," I said.

"I am."

"After what happened in Moscow? That would be stupid," I said.

"Oh, come on, Ginny. You'll be wearing fancy dress clothes, not a Russian hat and scarf."

"Okay, it's your funeral!" I quipped.

"No," Jack said. "It was Brezhnev's funeral." We both started to laugh.

I dolled myself up for the occasion and wore my gold jewelry with a blue Lapis Lazuli stone from Pakistan and Lapis earrings from Afghanistan. The Russians were known for their Lapis, but theirs had more white streaks than flecks of gold.

I picked Jack up and we circled the embassy until we could find a place to park. The Soviets were building a new embassy, set on the highest point in D.C. to intercept all the secret signals roaming around in town and outer space. No one could understand why the Americans permitted this to happen.

Once inside, we joined the receiving line to greet the Ambassador. He was a jolly, but tough looking man—very urbane and witty. Before I could even shake his hand, he grabbed my pendant off my chest and took a close look at it.

"Lapis!" he said. "From our country?"

"From Pakistan," I replied.

"Not as good," he boasted and let go of the pendant, which slapped my chest and quivered for a few moments.

"And her Lapis earrings are from Afghanistan during a trip we made there," said Jack. He intentionally made that remark to highlight the fact that the Soviets were losing in Afghanistan.

"Russian Lapis is the best," he declared again. He shook my hand briefly and gave Jack a hearty handshake. He took him aside, keeping others in the line waiting.

"Mr. Hunter, how was your trip to Moscow?"

"Too brief," Jack answered.

"Did the Secretary have any meaningful talks with Yuri Andropov?"

"There wasn't time. They met face-to-face and that was about all. The purpose was to attend former President Brezhnev's funeral. Did you know, Mr. Ambassador, that President Rowland had written Brezhnev letters for months, asking him to meet with him to talk about disarmament?" said Jack.

"Yes, I was aware," he replied.

"The President never consulted the State Department. He wrote to him as leader to leader."

So I understand," said the Ambassador. "Tell me, Mr. Hunter, about that mystery woman who fell into Brezhnev's casket. Do you know who she is?"

"I think the reporters mentioned it in their stories," said Jack.

The ambassador turned sideways and looked at me. I smiled half-heartedly.

"Such a puzzle," he laughed. "Take your wife to our buffet table for some caviar."

"Thank you."

We ate a couple of crackers spread with caviar and hastened out of there to drive home.

"I think he knows," said Jack when we were in the car.

"Knows what?"

"The identity of the mystery woman."

"Maybe that explains why he looked so strangely at me," I said. I thought to myself that I would never live down that incident. It would go to the grave with me and with Jack, too, even though the press so generously protected him.

CHAPTER NINE

▼

CATERING FOR EMBASSY PARTIES

"Ginnyyyyyy!"

"Nancy Barr, I haven't heard from you in weeks. How's tennis?" I asked. It was good to hear her voice.

"Well, we haven't been able to meet recently. Everyone seems busy," she said. "Also, the three of us are still miffed about the article our fourth partner wrote about you."

"Forget it. I did," I said, though I was relieved to have that news.

"Did Jack get over it?" she asked.

"Eventually. Anything else going on?" I asked.

"I have another favor to ask."

"Uh oh."

"You've been to Pakistan, haven't you?"

"Everywhere. I love the country," I said.

"A friend of mine has a catering business in Georgetown. It's called 'Embassy Parties.' "

"Where do I come in?" I asked.

"She had an unexpected call from the Pakistani Embassy. Their Foreign Minister is coming for dinner tonight and one of their servers is sick. Could you help out?" she asked.

"I probably could."

"Do you have a Pakistani-style outfit?" she asked.

"As a matter of fact, I have two shalwar kamezes."

"I can't believe it. Wonderful. Will you do it?" Nancy asked.

"Yes."

"Thank you. I'll have Angelina Romeo call you. She's the owner."

"Her name doesn't sound Pakistani," I said.

"She's not. She's Italian American, but she can cook for every nationality. Ginny, you're an angel."

After I hung up, I had second thoughts, but knew I couldn't turn her down. It was too late. Jack was away and Max was studying for an exam, so I had no excuse. I thought it would get me out of the house. I went to my closet and looked at the two Pakistani outfits. I decided on the mango colored one with embroidery. Shalwar kamezes were roomy and comfortable. Fortunately, I had a dupatta scarf to match.

When Angelina called, she was gushing in her gratitude. She asked me about Pakistani hors d'oeuvres.

"I thought you knew all about Pakistani food," I said.

"Not everything. Can you help me?"

"Well, there are Samosas."

"Samosas?" she queried.

"Pastries wrapped around ground beef," I said.

"Ah, like ravioli?"

"Somewhat. It's more like pastry than pasta dough."

"What else?" she asked.

"Small kabobs."

"With chicken, onions, and peppers?" Angie asked.

"And pineapple cubes."

"What about a dip?" she wanted to know.

"Yes. Chutney with yogurt, mangoes, and spices."

"Sounds delicious," she said.

"Do you have a main dish?" I asked.

"Chicken Bergani," she said.

"Is that rice with chicken?"

"Yes!"

"And bread?" I asked her.

"Roghani nan—a sort of pita bread that is rich and greasy."

"And curry?" I knew it was a foolish question, but I asked anyway.

"I'm told that curry is the fire of passion. They don't drink, but they set their taste buds on fire. Italians have garlic, Pakistanis have curry. I will tell you that I make a dish called pasta and curry that has a robust taste!" said Angie.

"What about Koftas?" I asked.

"Koftas?"

"Meatballs with curry, along with nine jewels," I said.

"Hail Mary, I can't afford diamonds and rubies!"

"No, no. This is a Mogul dish of nine vegetables—nine jewels," I giggled.

"My dear, Mrs. Hunter, can you come early to help me with all these dishes?" she asked in distress.

"How many are coming to dinner?"

"Twelve."

"What time would you like me to come?" I asked.

"At four, if you could."

"I'll be there," I assured her as she gave me the address.

"Thank you, thank you, thank you! Oh, what about dessert?"

"Let's see—either rice pudding or gujrela," I said.

"Gujrela?"

"It's either a cooked carrot or radish," I stated.

"Oh. Should we do rice pudding?"

"Perfect," I said.

At four o'clock I turned up at "Embassy Parties" in Georgetown, wearing my shalwar kamez. Angelina Romeo opened the door to me and raved about my outfit. She was a large woman and the perspiration was rolling down her cheeks.

"Come in, come in. I need you to help with Koftas and nine jewels."

"I'm ready to do anything," I said.

"Put this Moo Moo over your Pakistani outfit. Curry could ruin it," she said.

We worked side-by-side until everything was ready to be put in insulated boxes. We loaded her van and went together to the Pakistani Embassy and parked around back near the kitchen. She gave me a different scarf because mine was too stiff. It was white and looked fine.

"How shall I introduce you?" she asked.

"Virginia. Just Virginia. No last name, please."

"As you wish," she said.

The ambassador himself came to greet us and to thank us for helping. His cook and assistant cook were both sick as was one server. He commented on the aroma of spices coming from the boxes. That was a good sign.

Once we had the oven working and their warming ovens in operation, we took off our Moo Moos. I put on the scarf Pakistani style, hiding my hair. We were ready to serve hors d'oeuvres at seven o'clock. Soft drinks were offered to the guests because Muslims did not indulge in alcohol. The ambassador gave us the signal to serve the morsels. Everyone marveled at the western way of presenting Pakistani Samosas and Koftas. They looked closely at Angelina and me, knowing we were not Pakistanis. One wife whispered how much she liked my shalwar kamez. I thanked her and said her red and gold was far more beautiful. In a private home, the women were not required to wear their dupattas. Their hair was bedecked with jewels. I was wearing my Pakistani lapis pendant directly from Pakistan. Another wife was very interested and inquired as to its origin. When she knew it was from Pakistan, her pride and pleasure were obvious.

As the guests moved to the dining room and found their place cards, Angelina and I began serving Bergani nan and rice. The ladies couldn't wait to dip their nan in the chutney yogurt we had made. Everyone made pleasing noises. Angelina went back to the kitchen for the nine jewels while I picked up the hot curry with heavy potholders.

The Foreign Minister was the guest of honor, so I approached him first. He was so handsome, I nearly dropped the dish. His eyes were large and a beautiful chocolate brown. His smile was a dazzling white. The fringe end of my scarf fell onto his Nehru-style suit jacket and somehow wrapped itself around the middle button. Once I realized what had happened, I lifted my head, trying to jostle it loose. Instead, it tightened around the button. When I pulled my head upwards again, it snapped the button from his coat and sent it flying through the air like a tiny golf ball and plopped right into the ambassador's water goblet. I put the curry dish down and rushed around the table to retrieve the button from the goblet with a spoon. I snatched the ambassador's napkin from his lap and wiped the button dry, apologizing profusely and offering to sew it back on.

"Please, Madam, the repairs can be done later," said the Foreign Minister.

"Which one is your wife?" She raised her hand shyly and I quickly put the button at her place. She popped it in her evening bag.

I rushed back to the curry dish to serve the Foreign Minister. As I continued to apologize, the curry dish slipped and covered his jacket in a creamy saffron color.

"Oh no!" I cried. I gave the dish to Angelina to take to the kitchen. "Please, everyone hand me your napkins. I began wiping down his jacket and dipping some of them in the water goblets. I did the best I could. He quickly asked that I stop. Then, the ambassador stood and beckoned the Foreign Minister to leave the room with him. When the foreign minister reappeared, he was wearing a beautiful clean jacket, belonging to the ambassador.

At that point, I sincerely apologized. "I've ruined your dinner, your jacket, and your visit. I'll never forgive myself." I felt as though I had let everyone down.

"Madam, please don't be upset," said the Foreign Minister.

"And you probably hate my country because of my horrible mistake," I choked back tears.

"On the contrary, I find you and your country enchanting," he said.

"You do?"

"American/Pakistani relations are very healthy," he said with a disarming smile.

"I'm so glad."

"But, I have a strange feeling that you are not a professional caterer," he said.

"No, this is my first time."

"Dear lady, what do you do?" asked the minister.

"I'm a wife, mother, and a playwright."

"Tonight you are a first-time caterer," he said. "Now, why don't you finish the main course and then, serve our dessert. Afterwards, I want you to join us in the living room for Kawa. You know Kawa?"

"Tea," I said.

"You know Pakistan?"

"Yes, I love it and have visited," I said.

"Then, the evening is not a disaster."

I did join the guests in the living room. They asked me about my plays. I asked them about Pakistan under General Zhia and Ali Bhutto and about his daughter, Benazir Bhutto. They gave me guarded opinions about everything. We had a lovely evening and they all shook my hand with gusto when they left. A couple of the women even gave me kisses on both cheeks.

Then, it was time for me to help Angelina pack up and go back to Georgetown with the empty serving dishes. After we finished unloading at her shop, I intended to go home, but she asked me to stay and listen to her problems, regarding her daughter and a boy friend. How could I refuse? We sat at a table for two in her café as she poured out her heart.

"Virginia, this is a portrait of my late husband, Luigi Romeo. We knew each other since fourteen years of age. There was no one else for me and no one else for him. We had one daughter, Safrina. When he died from a construction accident, my whole world ended. I talk to him all the time in front of the portrait and get angry at him for leaving Safrina and me."

"That is so sad," I said. "Does Safrina help you with the business?" I asked.

"When she can, but she was studying political science and diplomacy at American University and now…"

"And…now?"

"Everything has changed since she met this boy, Amir, in one of her classes. She claims they are in love."

"And you don't approve," I said.

"I don't approve, his father doesn't approve, and my late husband would not approve, would you Luigi?" she declared, looking up at her husband's portrait.

"So, what's happened?"

"She has left home," she said tearfully.

"Oh dear," I said.

"You see, he is a Muslim, and Safrina is a Catholic. It just wouldn't work."

"Both religions spend a lot of time on their knees," I said. "And they each have beads."

"Virginia, this is not helping me," she said.

"Sorry."

"But, his widowed father has visited me several times, trying to solve the situation."

"Did he solve it?" I asked.

"He made it worse."

"Worse?"

"Because he has fallen in love with me!" she said.

"Are you in love with him?"

"No! Yes! I don't know. And one other thing," she said.

"What's that?"

"His country is sending him to London as the ambassador."

"What an honor!" I said.

"But he wants me to go with him."

"Are you going? It would be an honor for you as well."

'Virginia!"

"It sounds like a romantic love story to me," I said.

"You are not helping."

"Where is he now?" I asked.

"In his home country for a briefing, preparing him for his assignment in London. Amir, his son, is with him."

"Where is Safrina?"

"I think she's coming home tomorrow," she said.

"That's wonderful. Does that mean you will let her marry Amir and you will marry his father?"

"I don't know. What do you think?" she asked.

"I think it should be a double wedding…half Catholic and half Muslim."

"Virginia, you're on their side," she said.

"I'm on the side of love," I said.

Angelina left the table to find a Kleenex. On the counter, she sees something and picks it up. It looks like a Western Union telegram. She reads it and bursts into tears. I immediately get up to comfort her.

"Angelina, what is it?"

"It's Moktar," she sobbed.

"Is he Amir's father?"

"Yes."

"What happened?"

"I have to sit down." The tears won't stop. She reads the telegram over and over until her emotions are under control.

"What does it say?"

"He was on his way to the British Embassy when...when a terrorist bomb blew up the car," she sobbed. "He's gone. Moktar's gone—gone to heaven."

"Oh no. That's so tragic," I said. "And Amir, too?"

"He wasn't with him. Why didn't I tell him before he left?" Angelina said.

"Tell him what?"

"Tell him I longed to be in his arms...to become his wife," she said.

"But I thought you didn't know if you loved him."

"I do now—now that it's too late," she sobbed.

"Oh, Angelina, I don't know what to say, except maybe you should let Amir and Safrina marry because their children would be part of their grandfather and so, you would always have him with you," I told her, trying to soothe her emotions.

"Virginia, what a beautiful thought. Perhaps you're right."

"Do you want me to stay the night, so you won't be so lonely?" I asked.

"That is very kind, but you must go home to your family. Besides, you hardly know me. We only met tonight."

"And I apologize for all my terrible mishaps," I said.

"That is nothing compared to this news. My heart is breaking. Thank you for being here. You have helped me decide what to do," she said. I got up, hugged her goodbye, and left with my eyes full of tears.

As I drove home through the deserted streets of Georgetown and across the river to McLean, I thought about the Pakistani people we met tonight. They couldn't have been kinder. That's what I love about Washington—all the different nations and cultures. When Jack returns, I want him to hear this sad story of love gone awry. Maybe I should write a play about two generations held back by prejudice, but united through love. Then again, perhaps I won't mention the social disasters I made at the Pakistani Embassy to Jack or Nancy Barr. If Angelina tells Nancy, then I can explain.

As I pulled in front of our condo, there was no sign of life anywhere. I closed the car door quietly and went inside. Max was asleep, and I soon would be. This would be a night to remember when we were back on Cape Cod, reminiscing.

CHAPTER TEN

▼

MEXICO AND THE SOVIETS

Giles Roberts asked Jack if he would go to Mexico City with him for a UNESCO Conference and help establish press communications between foreign countries and the USA. It would be a long week-end and Giles thought it might be kind of fun for the wives to land in Acapulco, and join their spouses in Mexico City.

"Let me ask the Secretary if he could let me go. I'm sure Ginny would leap at the chance," said Jack.

"I'll count on your coming and have my secretary book two tickets in your name."

"Hold off until I get the green light from Stanley," Jack said.

The Secretary encouraged Jack to go for a change of pace and to take me. He thought Jack could be very helpful with the press. So, the four of us boarded the plane to Mexico. The men left the plane in Mexico City, and we went on to Acapulco on the West coast of Mexico.

"Don't get into trouble down there," Giles whispered to us as he de-planed. I looked at him and laughed. Jack wasn't laughing. He remembered Moscow.

From the air, Mexico City looked enormous—almost like NYC with a cluster of skyscrapers—but bigger. In another hour we were in Acapulco. The water from the air looked like the color of blue and lime, lined with white sandy beaches. We both had our swim suits packed, ready to sunbathe outside our hotel. The warm breezes were a welcome change from a cold January in Washington.

Someone from the consulate was waiting for Janine and me and hurried us to the tourist spot where the La Quebrada cliff divers jump from jagged rocks to the narrow inlet of water below. They looked like human birds, pulled by gravity to splash into the blue-green waters. Fearful that they might slam into ragged spears of rock, we held our breath until they landed safely in the waters between two slices of rocks.

We marveled at their lack of fear and handed them five dollar tips in appreciation. They bowed to us. We found out that there are five divers and five diving performances every day. The most spectacular is at sunset. It is 136 feet to the water below, which is only nine and a half feet deep. I gulped when I heard that from a man next to us. He also said that they have to wait and time the waves coming in to give them more water to plunge into. I realized what a death plunge it was if the rocks were not covered by water. "Furthermore," he said, "over the years, their spinal cords get crushed from the impact of hitting the water." As he explained this, we noticed four men standing together on the deck, commenting on the show and staring at us curiously.

We debated whether to have a late lunch at the famous La Perla restaurant, overlooking the view and the divers, but we decided to go to the hotel instead. The consular car took us there. It sat on the edge of the white sandy, Costera beach. We changed into our swim suits and headed for the beach. It felt good to dig our toes into the sand. We ordered sandwiches from the beach waiter and were provided with towels and chaise lounges. We were drenched in suntan oil and drowsing while baking in the sun.

Soon a shadow fell across our faces. A young waiter asked if we wanted to order a drink. We yawned and asked for iced tea. After we had eaten, we felt refreshed.

"Let's go swimming," I said. "This may be our last chance before going to Mexico City tomorrow."

"Do you feel like it?" asked Janine, who was blonde and beautiful.

"Yes!" We ran to the edge of the surf, letting the foamy sea water rush over our feet. "A little chilly," I winced.

"Run right into it and dive into a wave," advised Janine. "That way, you'll forget about the cold quicker, so you can enjoy it." We ran and dove together. She was right. It was an iceberg at first and then tingly warm afterwards. The color of the water shifted from emerald green to sapphire blue. We swam out quite far until we saw a lifeguard motioning us back.

Obedient, we started to swim towards the shore. I was in front of Janine, but my bathing cap deafened the sounds around me. I stopped for air and turned around, but couldn't see Janine. I shouted for her and saw her head bobbing. I swam back to her.

"Janine, what's wrong?"

"My leg."

"Your leg?" I asked.

"It has a horrible cramp. I can't swim."

I remembered a Red Cross life saving course I had once taken, so I cupped my hand around her chin and began to swim. "Don't worry," I said, treading water. "I've got you. Relax. You're going to be fine." After we reached shore, I gently pulled her to a sitting position and waved the lifeguard to help.

"How's the leg?"

"Still cramped," she said.

The four men we had seen at the cliff divers surrounded us and asked if they could help. I thanked them, but the lifeguard was now taking charge. The foursome bowed and left. I turned to the lifeguard and told him what had happened. "Can you carry her to the hotel and up to our room?"

"Yes, madam. I can carry her as far as the lobby. We do have a wheelchair there and a bell hop can take her to your room," he said.

"Thank you." I walked alongside him as he carried Janine. The front entrance to the hotel was fairly close, so I ran ahead to ask the concierge for the wheelchair. After the lifeguard came inside, he carefully eased her into the chair. We both thanked him, and I wheeled Janine to the elevator that took us to the top floor where our room was.

Our veranda had a magnificent view of the beach and bay. "Look at the sunset, Janine. Its colors are spreading across the whole horizon—like a peacock's feathers. Here, I'll wheel you out," I said. "While you watch the sun sink, I'll draw a hot bath, so you can soak your leg. Any relief yet?" I asked.

"Some," she said.

I was sure it was more painful than she was telling me. After turning on the tub water, I rejoined her to gaze at the sunset.

"Thank you for saving me," she said tearfully. "If you hadn't come back when you did, I could have drowned."

"I had to do it because Giles would never forgive me!" We both laughed as she wiped away her tears.

"Would you rather go downstairs for dinner or order from room service?" I asked.

"If you don't mind, I think eating here would suit me fine."

"Same for me. We won't have to get dressed."

We ordered seafood from the menu. I helped Janine hobble to the tub, and she soaked for a long time before emerging for dinner.

"What do you suppose our boys are doing?" Janine asked.

"Working," I said.

"And unaware of the beauty just a few hours away from them," Janine added.

"I guess we shouldn't rub it in," I smiled.

"No."

A knock at the door signaled our order had arrived. We raved about the sole and salmon, topped with a sweet and sour salsa. Janine and I lingered over our chocolate mousse dessert and coffee as we talked about our kids and life in Washington.

At that point, the telephone rang. It was the consular's office, making arrangements to pick us up in the morning.

"What time will they come for us tomorrow?" Janine asked.

"By 8:00 a.m. Because it takes three and a half hours to drive to Mexico City, they want us to see the countryside. Breakfast is scheduled for 6:30."

We went to bed early and slept soundly. At 5:30 a.m., I awakened Janine and whispered, "How's the leg? Would you like to take a walk on this beautiful beach before we leave it behind?"

"The leg is much better, but I think I'll pack and take things slowly," she answered.

I hit the beach at sunrise. It was deserted, so I ran along the ocean's edge. The smell of salt was strong. A few fishermen were launching their boats and waved to me. I waved to them, walked back to the hotel, dressed, and packed my bag. Breakfast was a buffet, combining American and Mexican selections. There were burritos, scrambled eggs, cheese, salsa, fried tortilla pieces, quesadillas, fruit, and a variety of hot and cold drinks to make a great farewell breakfast. After checking out, we met the consular car at exactly 8:00. Janine tried to stay awake, but snoozed most of the way. Her leg was almost free of the tight, painful cramp.

During the drive, the consular gave us a brief history lesson about Mexico City. "Once, it was the center of the Aztec Empire. Now the city is the largest in Mexico. In fact, many describe it as the 'little Manhattan.' You will notice the old blended with modern buildings. Within and around Mexico City are a dozen or more archaeological sites and of course, many museums. Zocalo is the main square on thirteen acres, which was Montezuma's palace at one time," she said.

"Is there any downside to the City?" I asked.

"Yes. It is a nightmare for driving. Don't ever rent a car and drive yourself. Taxis know the ropes and how to execute maneuvers!" We all laughed. Janine woke up and wanted to know what the joke was. The consular told her.

As we approached Mexico City, it was full of modern skyscrapers--just like our charming guide told us--and throbbing with activity like any city. The shops were colorful and inviting. There were several scary, brake-screeching encounters with other cars and taxis, but the consular had prepared us.

Before noon, we reached the front door of the hotel where the conference was already in progress. We thanked the consular for all her help and for the sightseeing excursion in Acapulco. The driver helped us with our luggage. After our goodbyes, we went inside to the front desk to find out where our rooms were. Janine and I embraced as we were about to part. Fortunately, Janine's leg was as good as new.

Jack was not in the room, but left a note and told me to wait for him and browse through the folder on the bed if I liked.

The contents described UNESCO as the United Nations Educational, Scientific and Cultural Organization. The overview inside began explaining... UNESCO was formed in 1945 and the IPDC (International Program of Development for Communications) was added to the United Nations in 1977 to meet the needs of newspapers. That's why Jack was here—for communications, but I was sure he was helping UNESCO as well. Jack suddenly appeared.

"You're back!" he said as he walked over to give me a big welcome hug.

"Fifteen minutes ago," I said.

"How was it?"

"Spectacular. Janine and I loved every minute. Too bad you and Giles couldn't have been there. Have you had any fun?" I asked.

"Too busy. Let's eat."

"I'm starving, too," I said.

We went downstairs to a small cantina for a sandwich and iced tea. I told Jack about the cliff divers, and he told me about his hectic schedule. There was much maneuvering among the 35 countries represented. Apparently, at 2:00 p.m., Jack and Giles would conduct a press conference. I was curious to attend and Jack said I could.

Since the press room was crowded, I sat at the very back. Giles stood near to Jack as the press pounded him with questions. His answers were diplomatic and skillful. When the queries were specific about UNESCO, Jack deferred to Giles. Across the room, I saw the four men from Acapulco, sitting together. One of them challenged Jack about the effectiveness of a free press as opposed to a nationalized press.

"Of course, a free press creates an environment where it is much more difficult to drive the message as you can see from the questions here, but in the long run, it is the best kind of press. The truth is often uncovered to the benefit of the citizens and helps create a balance of power between the governed and those that govern," Jack replied. "In most cases, but not all, a national press is the extension of the government, which controls the information delivered by its press. One can never be sure about the authenticity of the information and the citizens do not always benefit."

When it was over, Jack was surrounded by American reporters. I stood at the back. As the four men--obviously reporters--passed me, one of them stopped to ask, "Where is your friend?"

"I think she's at another meeting," I replied.

"Are you a reporter?" he asked.

"No," I said.

He nodded and left. His English was impeccable. Jack finished with the reporters and motioned me to join him as he left the chaos.

"Let's go to the room," said Jack.

"Fine. Where's Giles?"

"With Janine. She's not feeling well," he said.

"Oh, no. Her leg was fine when we arrived."

"Leg?" he asked.

"Yes, it was badly cramped yesterday."

"I think it was something she ate and not anything else," he said.

"I hope not."

"The Mexican government is hosting a big bash tonight. Let's rest up beforehand," Jack said.

"Okay with me."

Back in the room, I asked Jack about the four men who were together at the press briefing.

"They're Russians. Two are from <u>TASS</u>, one from <u>Moscow News</u>, and the other from the <u>The Moscow Literary Gazette</u>," he said.

"What are they doing here?"

"They are probably KGB, posing as newspapermen."

"Really? What do you suppose they want here?" I asked.

"Well, behind the scenes, they're probably putting pressure on the East Germans, Yugoslavs, Cubans, Guyanese, Venezuelans, and Nicaraguans to go for a nationally controlled press. You heard their question."

"I did, but who is the US putting pressure on?" I asked.

"Not pressure—encouragement to the West Germans, Dutch, Gabonese, and Nigerians for a free press. We show them how a free press could operate within nationally funded agencies."

"Why not do away with national agencies?" I wanted to know.

"Because they have the money to run everything and to throw away free money in a poor country would not be wise, plus they need to transition slowly. Of course, the United States will assist."

"I get it. Well, I guess I should get ready for the party," I said.

For the occasion, I wore a red and gold dress alongside Jack's dark suit and silver tie. As we entered the ballroom, Mexican girls greeted us and pinned carnation corsages on the women. After socializing during drinks, we found our table. Seated with us were two Chinese men from Peking; a Mexican; a West German; a Canadian; a Norwegian; a Swede; and one other American. The music was very loud, so we had to shout to converse. We just gave up and did a lot of smiling and nodding at each other in between bites of food.

The menu was composed of eclectic spices and exotic dishes. For openers, ceviche was served in a half coconut shell, followed by a lobster bisque soup. The main course was a fish smothered with tomatoes, onions, and rice. Dessert was crème de menthe ice cream.

Following dinner, our hosts had arranged a brilliant fireworks display, which we watched from the veranda. We saw spinning wheels and rockets shooting high above the hotel. The very last firework spelled UNESCO in the sky. We went back to the table for coffee. As we were sipping, someone came and whispered something in Jack's ear.

Jack stood up and whispered to me, "I may be gone for quite a while. Do you want to stay here or go to the room?"

"Stay here," I said. In seconds, he was gone. I watched those on the dance floor. Most people were sedate, but the Russians had invited the German women at a nearby table to dance. The Russian men were wild. If indeed they were KGB, they flung themselves all over the dance floor in crazy abandon. I couldn't help laughing! Of course, it reminded me of the CIA man who spun me around the dance floor during the UN celebrations. Anyway, the poetic-looking man from the Moscow Literary Gazetter was much more reserved.

After the dance was over, all four Russians came over to me. Only the two Chinese and I were left at our table.

"May we join you?" they asked.

"If you like," I said.

They sat down and were slightly uncomfortable. I didn't know what to say.

"Your husband is a journalist?" the one from TASS asked.

"Yes."

"Who does he work for?"

"We own weekly newspapers on Cape Cod," I said.

"Cape Cod?"

"It's a resort area off the coast of Massachusetts."

"Ah. You write, too?"

"I'm a playwright," I said.

"Like Chekhov?"

"I wish." We all laughed. "You are newspapermen?" I asked.

"Yes." They all nodded.

"Not KGB?" They laughed gustily.

"Why do you ask?"

"I thought everyone in the Soviet Union was KGB!" I said. They laughed again.

"Is your husband CIA?" Now it was my turn to laugh.

"No!"

"He's not a spy?"

"Of course not."

"Would you like to dance?" The poetic one asked.

"Not the way you danced to that last song."

"I promise to do the Fox Trot or waltz," he smiled. He took my hand and led me to the dance floor. He was smooth and easy to follow.

"You speak beautiful English. How did you learn?" I asked.

"From language school."

"You speak other languages?"

"Five or six," he volunteered. "And you?" he asked.

"One—sadly. Where have you been posted?"

"London, Paris, D.C."

When the band finished playing, we returned to my table. His three companions applauded. They had ordered Vodka and were feeling no pain.

"Tell us more about your playwriting."

"Well, I was a professional actress before that," I said. They perked up.

"An actress?"

"Yes. I studied the method of your famous Stanislavski," I said to flatter them.

"Konstantin Stanislavski?"

"Yes. American actors worship him," I said.

"Did you know," said the poetic one, "that the finest collection of Stanislavski works is right here in Mexico City?"

"Where?"

"At the Soviet Embassy's library. Would you like to see it?"

"We leave tomorrow," I said.

"What about now!"

"Now?"

"It's not far. We could be there and back in less than an hour."

"Well, I don't know."

"We are gentlemen. You will be very safe with us. Don't worry," he smiled. I was still uncertain, but I decided it was an opportunity of a lifetime.

"All right."

Two of them guided my elbows to the entrance of the hotel and ordered their Russian limo. In Spanish, one of the <u>TASS</u> reporters gave instructions.

They spoke Russian the whole way in between much laughter. Shortly, we were at the Embassy. The door opened when they called up the code, and we entered, taking the elevator to the fourth floor. They opened a special door and there was the most magnificent library in red and gold.

"It matches your dress," one of them said.

"This is beautiful. Oh, and you have a Voltaire Collection. I thought the only one was at the Hermitage," I exclaimed.

"Not as big or as wonderful as the Hermitage," they said all at once.

"Look, here is Stanislavski," said Boris, the poetic one. He took it from the shelf. It was in brown leather with gold lettering. He handed it to me. Of course it was in Russian, but with black and white illustrations. I couldn't have been more thrilled. "We also have it in Spanish and English." My eyes opened wider. The original book by the Russian master of acting was being held in my hands. Gently I gave it back to Boris.

"Over here is a bronze statue of Stanislavski," said the quiet <u>TASS</u> man.

"May I touch it?" I asked.

"He would be honored," said Boris. I stroked the statue with reverence as they all watched in silence.

I circled the room and stood in front of an 18th century table with drawers open. "Oh look at these colorful balloons. Do you have children coming to visit the library?" They looked at each other in horror.

"Yes, yes. They are for children," Boris said nervously.

"Is that sand in them?" I asked.

"Oh yes. Russian children in Atlanta and Chicago and Montreal don't see such beautiful sand as on Mexican beaches," he seemed to stumble over his words.

"That's true. They will be thrilled with those filled with sand. I wonder why some sand is darker than others?" I asked.

"Because the Mexican police do not like us to take their white sand, so we have to go to other beaches where the sand is not so white," said Boris.

Meanwhile, back at the hotel, Jack had come to the ballroom to find me. I was gone. He figured I was back in the room. After unlocking the room, he couldn't find me. He caught the elevator back to the lobby and strode to the table where he left me and asked the two Chinese if they had seen his wife.

"She go with four Russians," they said.

"Russians?"

"Yes."

"Where did they go?" Jack asked.

"I don't know," said one.

"I think they go to Embassy," said the other one.

"Which embassy?"

"Russian Embassy."

"Christ Almighty," exploded Jack. He rushed out of the ballroom and went back to the room to call the American Ambassador.

"Sir, this is Jack Hunter, spokesman for Secretary of State Gavin Stanley. I apologize for calling you at such a late hour, but I have just come out of a UNESCO meeting and found my wife missing.

"Missing?"

"Her companions at the dinner table said that she went with four Russians to their Embassy."

"Good God, I wonder why?"

"I don't know, but would you be kind enough to call the Soviet Ambassador to send someone to the Embassy to rescue her?" Jack said.

"I will indeed."

Boris quietly closed the drawers with the balloons and suggested that we should return to the hotel if I had finished browsing the library. As I was about to reply, the door burst open. Four policemen with rifles pointed at all of us. We instinctively held our hands over our heads. The Soviet Ambassador entered and asked what we were doing there.

"We were showing Madam Hunter our Stanislavski collection of books since she was an actress at one time," said Boris.

"Is this true, Mrs. Hunter?" asked the Ambassador.

"Very true and I'm so sorry to have caused you such concern. These are total gentlemen and I can't thank them enough," I said.

"Your husband called the American Ambassador to contact me."

"Oh dear," I said. "We were just about to leave," I said.

"Our limousine will return you to the hotel," the Ambassador said.

"Thank you." Before I could thank the four journalists, they rushed me out, and I knew the men were going to get a tongue-lashing.

When the limo arrived at the hotel, Jack was pacing up and down at the front entrance, waiting for me.

"Ginny, thank God you're all right."

"I'm fine," I told him.

"Why in hell did you go with complete strangers to the Soviet Embassy?"

"To see the collection of Stanislavski books."

"Who's he?" asked Jack.

"The great master for teaching acting," I said.

"Well, you should have told someone or left a message for me."

"I'm sorry, Jack." Once we were in the room, I wanted to tell him about the balloons. "Jack, I think we should call the American Ambassador to thank him, but also to tell him what I discovered at the Embassy," I said.

"What was that?"

"Drugs."

"Drugs?" he asked.

"Please call him. I don't want to tell the story twice, but this is critical." He dialed.

"Mr. Ambassador, it's Jack Hunter again. My wife is back and we both want to thank you for acting so quickly on her behalf."

"Why did she go with these men to the Embassy at this time of night?" he asked.

"Apparently, these men had promised to show her the Stanislavski collection of books in the Embassy Library, but she discovered something else that I think you should hear directly from her," Jack said.

"Put her on."

"Mr. Ambassador, thank you so much for your assistance," I said.

"How are you, Mrs. Hunter? Were you treated well?"

"I'm fine, though probably I was unwise to go, but to see the Stanislavski collection was too tempting," I said

"You must be a student of the theatre," he replied.

"I am, but I have something important to tell you that I discovered while I was at the Embassy Library. There were tubes of colorful balloons, filled with white sand—that's what they told me, but I knew it wasn't sand. It was heroin—first and second grade. They didn't realize I had a clue. I asked them where they were sending them to Russian children. They said Atlanta, Chicago, and Montreal. I know there are Russian populations in those cities. I also know that the Russian mafia launders money in Mexico, Brazil, and Argentina in collaboration with the Germans. So, I thought you might want to be alerted to these underground activities and alert the FBI and CIA." I said in a matter of fact way.

"Perhaps this little adventure of yours was more valuable to our country than we realize," said the Ambassador. "Thank you."

"You're very welcome. And thank you again for rescuing me!"

As I hung up, Jack's jaw had dropped. "My God, Ginny, I had no idea you knew all this stuff about drugs and heroin."

"Sometimes, I'm not as dumb as I seem!"

Early on Monday morning, we flew back to Virginia. Three months later, Jack read in the newspaper that there was a big drug bust in Mexico City, capturing Soviets and Germans. He couldn't wait to tell me and congratulated me for being such a good informant!

"Perhaps, I should become a CIA agent," I said.

"And perhaps not!" he answered wryly.

CHAPTER ELEVEN

▼

FRENCH EMBASSY AND DINNER AT GEORGE WADE'S

Since that incident in the Chinese Restaurant when I used the Heimlich procedure on the French Ambassador, I had not heard from him and assumed he had forgotten. He had promised to invite us in September, after my arrival, but life is so busy in D.C.

A year and a half later, the French Ambassador sent Jack a printed invitation in gold-lettering to the Embassy for dinner. Nora French was not included. I imagined he had forgotten my association with Jack Hunter and was inviting us because of Jack's appearances on network TV.

Anyway, on a Friday night during a warm and soft rain, Jack and I drove to the French Embassy, set majestically behind gates. It looked like a Gothic, baronial chateau and was most appropriate for a Parisian representative of his country. Most of the guests arrived in their chauffeur-driven cars. Jack dropped me at the front entrance while he found a place to park.

Ordinarily, I would have waited for Jack, but because of the rain, I went inside and made my way to the cloakroom. In the foyer was a large table with names, a guest list, and a guest book to be signed. I looked for our names on the seating plan for five tables. We were not at the same table.

As I waited for Jack, I observed the elegant foyer in the shape of a T. A fireplace was at the center, and the walls were covered with European paintings, except for a modern French painting in needlepoint.

Once Jack joined me, we entered le salon to stand in the receiving line. Suddenly the Ambassador stepped away from his prominent place and rushed over to me.

"At last, my heroine. The lady who saved my life—my Joan of Arc!" He kissed my hand. "I apologize for not inviting you sooner, but I have been traveling. And this is your husband, the handsome spokesman for the State Department?"

"Yes," I replied.

"My dear sir, I shall ever be grateful to your wife."

"I'm sorry, Mr. Ambassador, but I do not know to what you are referring?" Jack said with a blank look upon his face.

"She has not told you?" he asked incredulously.

"Not that I recall."

"Well, Monsieur Hunter, over a year ago, my wife and I and some friends were dining at a Chinese Restaurant when suddenly I was choking. Your wife appeared from another table, demanded I stand up, and proceeded to apply the Heimlich method. The morsel was dislodged and I could breathe again. I shall always be grateful to her. She did not tell you?" he asked again.

"No."

"I imagine she is too modest," smiled the ambassador. "Come meet my wife. Darling, you remember the young lady who helped me in the Chinese Restaurant?"

"Of course. How delightful to see you again," Mrs. Marchant said as she took my hand.

"And her husband, Mr. Hunter, you will recognize from network television for the State Department."

"I thought he looked familiar," she said.

"Madam Hunter, let me escort you to your table. Do you know the number?" he asked.

"Number four," I said. Jack made his way to table one.

The Ambassador took my arm and guided me to my table and found my place card. He pulled out my chair when his valet tapped him on the shoulder.

"Mr. Ambassador, Paris is calling you on the telephone."

Marchant jerked the chair to the right. I went sprawling on the carpet. He dropped the chair and reached for my hand.

"Tell them I will call back later. My dear, Mrs. Hunter, this is terrible. Please take my hand," said the Ambassador.

By this time I was sitting upright. "I was admiring your carpet. The French have impeccable taste in everything, especially your Savonnerie."

"You are too kind, covering my embarrassment. Shall we try again to seat you properly?" The buzz of conversations had come to a halt and everyone was staring at me and trying not to laugh. I caught sight of Jack, turning red and shaking his head. Many of his superiors and colleagues were at the party, and he knew the gossip would circle over the weekend and on Monday morning. Once the Ambassador had safely seated me, he kissed my hand and went back to the receiving line, which also had come to a halt. Mrs. Marchant looked annoyed and concerned. As hostess, she wanted her evening to progress without a hitch, but her husband had created a big hitch!

Nevertheless, she could be proud of everything else. I began noticing the centerpieces on the round tables. They were tall crystal candlesticks with small vases of sweetheart roses and baby's breath set in a circle at the top of the candlestick. At the bottom were four white alabaster cherubs.

Everyone at my table wanted to make sure I was all right.

"It was a great exercise in humility," I laughed as they did, relieving the embarrassment and tension. "Also, I had an opportunity to examine their beautiful carpet." They laughed nervously again.

The first course was a hot lobster mousse, surrounded by endive. The entrée was veal, wrapped around pate. The mashed potatoes were accompanied by very thin string beans and tomatoes. The salad had a touch of red cabbage. For dessert we had a mouth-watering, chocolate torte.

My dinner companions were interesting. To my left was the Ambassador from Switzerland. His wife and children remained in Switzerland (who could blame them!) because his wife was sick of diplomatic life. He collected paintings for a hobby, and he was as enchanted by the paintings in the foyer as I was. To my right was a D.C. lawyer. I couldn't believe how honest he was with me.

"So much public money is wasted here," he said. "Lawyers negotiate for a quick solution and sometimes sacrifice principle to please their clients." He seemed sincerely troubled by this.

A woman on the other side of him had just submitted a thirteen-part series for TV to actor/director, Sandy Meisner. The plot was about five people trying to make it to Broadway. I admitted that I, too, was a playwright and had a comedy musical called <u>Cabbie!</u> about a New York cab driver and all the people who get in and out of his cab, including Elvis Presley and a Broadway producer. The table guests seemed fascinated by the details of the plot.

When everyone finished, Ambassador Marchant made a toast to someone who had a birthday. Everyone sang and applauded. I was completely flabbergasted by his second toast.

"Ladies and gentlemen, I would like to toast a young woman who saved my life over a year ago. My wife and I were eating with friends in a Chinese restaurant here in town, when I suddenly choked on something. Before I knew it, this woman appeared out of nowhere, made me stand up, and applied the Heimlich method. Her husband is at my table and just related another act of courage. A senior government official was in New York for the annual United Nations convention for countries around the globe. Apparently, his wife saved this person from an assassin's bullet."

"Who is she?" shouted someone from table three.

"May I present Mrs. Virginia Hunter. Please stand, Mrs. Hunter," said the Ambassador.

Very reluctantly, I stood up. Everyone clapped. My table gave me a standing ovation.

"Let us adjourn for coffee," announced the Ambassador.

My table companions shook my hand. They seemed to have forgotten about the chair incident.

Jack crossed the room and guided me to the cloakroom. "We should leave right now," he said. "I've told the Ambassador that I have to pack for a trip tomorrow and I delivered our thanks."

"What's the real reason?" I asked.

"Everyone is going to want to speak to you and it will be terribly embarrassing."

"Okay," I said. We found our coats and stepped out into the rain and walked quickly to our car. "Jack, I had no idea he was going to give that toast."

"Nor did I. Why didn't you tell me about the Heimlich encounter?" Jack asked.

"It was over a year ago," I said.

"But you should have told me."

"I think it was when I was down here looking for a house. Back at the Cape, you were leaving for D.C.," I said. "I forgot."

"You should have warned me tonight on the way to the Embassy."

"I told you, I had forgotten about the whole thing," I said.

The next morning, Jack padded down the staircase in his striped pajamas to get the paper. He opened the front door and leaned down to pick up the paper. He let the whole front page drop open and his jaw dropped. Suddenly, the paparazzi, who had been waiting for this moment, flashed their cameras. Jack quickly jumped inside and closed the door.

He stood motionless. A photograph of me, missing the chair and landing on the carpet, went the whole length of the paper. The headline read, **"Spokesman's Spouse Falls For the French!"**

"Oh my God," Jack said under his breath.

The insert at the top of this long photo was of the French Ambassador, giving a toast. The headline read, "**French Toast.**"

Jack grabbed two cups of coffee from the kitchen and came back upstairs to the bedroom. He put the coffee on the bedside table.

"Ginny, wake up!"

"Um?"

"Sit up, NOW!"

I struggled to sit up as Jack held up the front page. I rubbed my eyes to make sure I saw my spill at the French Embassy plastered there for eternity.

"OH NO!"

"OH YES!" Jack said. "Do you have anything to say?" he asked.

"Well…" I started to laugh and couldn't stop.

"Ginny, this isn't funny," Jack said.

"I know." I started to laugh even more.

"This is serious. Don't laugh."

"I can't help it," I said. I was howling uncontrollably by now.

"I hope we aren't the laughing stock of D.C.," said Jack.

"So do I. Sorry, Jack, but the headline is pretty amusing."

When Jack reached the office on Monday morning, he received mixed reviews about events at the French Embassy. Mostly, his colleagues felt pity for him.

Secretary Stanley, aware of Jack's agony, came to greet him, putting his arm around Jack's shoulder and said, "Jack, it wasn't her fault. I read the whole story. Don't forget she saved the French Ambassador from choking, and she saved me from being killed. Didn't she crack a drug ring in Mexico between the Soviets and Germans as well?"

"Yes," replied Jack, still suffering.

"These are worthy achievements," said the Secretary. "This story will fade." Jack gave him a half smile and nursed his humiliation for at least a week.

For a few months, Jack turned down invitations, except for obligatory ones. Work was obsessive. There wasn't much time to socialize.

When the workload eased, Geoff Wade, a conservative columnist, had been trying to schedule a dinner party to honor the Secretary. They finally settled on an evening in April. Wade asked Secretary Stanley if he had any special guests he wanted to invite.

"If it is a stag affair, I'd like my spokesman, Jack Hunter, to come, but if couples are invited, include Jack's wife, Ginny," he said.

"Is she the one who saved your life and fell at the French Embassy?" asked Wade.

"That's the one."

"Then the invitation is extended to her as well," Wade said.

"We look forward to it, Geoff," said the Secretary.

When Jack came home that night and told me about this special dinner party, I was thrilled. It meant I was ready to emerge back into the social scene. Geoff Wade was a well respected columnist and it would be fun to go to his home. I had to find a special dress for this occasion. I found one in a Chinese red. I had a fixation about the color red!

The night of the party in Bethesda, Maryland, we arrived separately from the Stanleys because they lived nearby.

The house was a big, old one that had been remodeled. It had a New England feel to it. Wade's office was in his house. He had two secretaries that came every day to handle his mail and help with the research. There was also a housekeeper to look after his several children.

We waved to the Stanleys and circulated among the guests.

I talked with a former president of Boston University, where I graduated from the theatre division with a Masters. One of his sons had gone there to study acting and was living in NYC, trying to get a break into theatre.

As dinner was announced, the guests looked at the seating diagram on a hall table for the three square tables. There were eight at each table. I was at Geoff Wade's table with Mrs. Stanley sitting to his right and the wife of one of the network news presidents on his left. I sat next to Frank Royal, a doyen of financiers in NYC. Since I could barely balance my checkbook, I knew I would be out of my league in a discussion about economics.

"Do you like Washington?" he asked me.

"It's fascinating. I like the cross-section of cultures and nations. We were at the French Embassy a few months ago and I couldn't get enough of those European paintings in their foyer," I answered.

"As a matter of fact," said Mr. Royal, "I had dinner with Mitterand recently. We are personal friends and had some interesting discussions about the economics governing our two countries."

"Did you agree?" I asked.

"Hardly at all," he said and we both laughed. "But what a charming man."

"Most Frenchmen are charming!" I said. "They are irresistible."

"Tell me about your husband," he asked.

"He's irresistible, too!" I answered humorously.

"Delightful," he said. "I think you know what I meant."

"Of course. Although he is the spokesman for the State Department, he is a lifelong journalist," I told him.

"What's the difference being a journalist and becoming a government servant?" he genuinely wanted to know.

"A journalist only knows one quarter of what goes on in government, but the government servant—especially the spokesman—knows almost 100%. It's frustrating for my husband, because when he learns something no journalist knows, he has to slap his wrist to stop from sharing the tidbit with a fellow journalist. It's complicated," I said.

"I can understand why," said Royal.

At that moment, Geoff Wade told his table how he had considered running for the senate.

"Why didn't you?" asked Royal.

"Because the senators talked me out of it!"

"Why?" asked another guest.

"They said I wouldn't like it."

"Why not?"

"Because you can't get anything done," said Wade.

"That would be frustrating for a columnist," commented Royal.

"If it takes forever to get any legislation passed, I wouldn't have the patience," said Wade. "But let's change the subject. I want to make a toast to Secretary and Mrs. Stanley for their patience in serving our country during difficult times."

"Hear, hear" said everyone as they tapped glasses.

At the conclusion of Geoff Wade's words of praise, Mr. Stanley stood up to make his own toast. "Washington is a town of words—too many words, but I salute our host for his use of words in his insightful columns. Would you agree?"

"Hear, hear," said the guests as they raised their glasses a second time.

"Now, if I may, I'd like to propose a toast to our leader, President Russell Rowland, whose humor and grasp of foreign policy have steered us successfully through dangerous waters."

"Hear, hear," shouted all the guests a third time.

Geoff Wade raised the question of presidential prospects in the next election.

"Who do you think, Geoff?" asked Frank Royal.

"Well, what the American people want in a president is someone who is likable and strong," said Wade.

"So, who falls into that category?" asked another guest.

"I think John Glenn could be a challenge. He's a hero and likable," said Wade.

"It's too early to even think about," said the Secretary.

"You're right. The coffee is on another table. Shall we mingle?" Wade inquired.

As we stood sipping coffee, I was talking to Marge Green, a fabulous columnist for The D.C. Gazette. She had just returned from South Africa and saw Nelson Mandela in prison. Geoff Wade joined us as we discussed South Africa.

"My husband and I lived in South Africa for six years. He was a foreign correspondent for The Boston International," I said.

"When was that?" asked Ms. Green.

"During the bad years of apartheid, our telephone was blatantly tapped. One day I heard my own voice coming back over the phone—obviously a tape recording that backfired," I told her.

"What did you do?" she asked.

"I shouted into the phone, 'If you're going to run a police state, at least run it efficiently.'"

The guests in our group laughed and remarked that I was very courageous.

"Annoyed is the word," I said. They laughed again.

"Any other anecdotes from your time in South Africa?" asked Miss Green.

"As a matter of fact, there was one defiant act that I did deliberately," I confessed.

"How intriguing. Tell us."

"Well, I went into the main post office in Cape Town and sat down in the Non-European section to address an envelope. Apartheid had two sections—one for Europeans and the other for Non-Europeans," I said. "In the American south the separation was known as Whites and Coloreds."

"What happened?"

"An Afrikaans security guard came over. As you know, Afrikaners are a mixture of Dutch and German with a very thick accent. He clicked his heels and clasped his hands behind his back. 'Madam, you are sitting in the Non-European section and that is not allowed. You must move to the European section.'"

"But, I AM Non-European. I'm American," I declared. He huffed and puffed in irritation, spun on his heel, and walked away. "A few Africans witnessed the drama and sniggered behind their hands. They smiled and secretly clapped their hands."

"You were taking a big chance," said Miss Green.

"I know. I could have been deported," I said.

Earl Martin and his wife joined our group. Martin and his wife were both biographers.

"Mr. Martin, who will be the subject of your next biography?" I asked.

"As a matter of fact, I just signed a contract today to do President Rowland's biography," he said jubilantly.

Everyone congratulated him. Signing a contract for an author is the ultimate goal.

"What's your deadline?" I asked.

"It could be ten or fifteen years," he said.

"How do you live and exist for that length of time?" I asked.

"Actually, they give a very handsome advance and my wife has just signed a contract to do one of America's maverick women. So, with two advances, we should be able to eat quite well," he smiled.

"Is it authorized and will you have total access to the President?" I asked.

"Yes and yes," he responded. "Robert Caro took a decade or more on one of his books about Lyndon Johnson. You seem to know a lot about writing, are you a writer?" asked Earl Martin.

"Mostly a playwright, but I've written an unpublished book, tracing five thousand years of theater in China with an emphasis on the revolutionary period," I replied.

"How did you choose that subject?" Martin asked.

"We lived in Hong Kong for six years and I became fascinated by the eight revolutionary operas by Madame Mao Tse Tung," I said.

"How fascinating," he said.

Jack finally joined our group. As I turned to him the long zipper on my red dress separated. I coughed to cover up the noise. Immediately, Jack grabbed the dress at the neck to hold the two pieces together. I had to keep my back to the walls, avoiding anyone from seeing it. Jack helped me maneuver without exposing my back to any of the guests to thank our host and hostess for a wonderful evening.

"We must be going. I have an early morning at the office tomorrow," said Jack. He shifted sides with his left hand holding the dress together, so he could shake hands with his right hand. I backed up to the front door and exited without turning my back. Once outside in the dark, we turned and made a run for it and reached the car before the top half of my dress fell off.

"Thank God you arrived when you did," I said.

"Why did the dress fall apart?"

"I don't know. Maybe I'm getting fat or maybe the dress is cheap."

"Isn't it new?"

"First time I've ever worn it," I said.

"Well, throw it out!"

"I will, but I'll buy two other red dresses that won't disintegrate. Aside from that, it was such an interesting party," I said.

"Those parties all alike," he said.

"I loved every moment,"

"One man said you were the prettiest woman there," Jack said.

"He what?"

"You heard me."

"Imagine that!" I said.

CHAPTER TWELVE

▼

MAX

Max was a typical teenager. His communications to us were usually grunts or one syllable answers to questions. His hair was long and bushy, squashed by a camouflage hat. Why he wore it was a mystery. Fortunately, he had an interesting group of friends, who dropped by the house and enjoyed going downstairs to his private suite. Often I would hear their laughter drift up the stairs and wondered what was so funny.

After the front page photo of me appeared in the paper, he didn't want his friends around for a long time because of his embarrassment, but that soon faded and his friends forgot about it. In fact, they thought the whole thing was kind of wild.

"Mom, how could you miss a chair like that? Were you drinking?" he asked.

"Of course not."

"Well, you made a fool of yourself," he said.

"Did you read the story?" I asked.

"Why should I? The photograph said it all."

"I suggest you read it because you would know it wasn't my fault, it was the French Ambassador's," I told him.

"Well, all my friends were making fun of you," he said.

"I can't help it if they didn't read the story."

I was heartsick that my son was in distress over the Gazette's front page picture, but he was too charming and forgiving to be upset for long.

When his writing class at Langley High School took a field trip to Columbia University for a conference on journalism, Jack and I had no idea how much we would miss him. It was a foretaste of what was to come when he left for college. We had already gone through the empty-nest-syndrome with Wanda.

The class planned to stay at a cheap hotel and go to a Broadway show one night. It was <u>A Chorus Line.</u> What a great show for teenagers to see. Jack and I had seen it opening night and found it thrilling. Max took far too many clothes for this weekend, but who doesn't?

The condo seemed empty without his muffled "hi" after school was over. Even though he said virtually nothing at the dinner table, he was a shambling presence.

After he left, I ventured downstairs to clean up the clutter. Once it was tidy and sterile, it seemed like a death in the family. His scrambled balls of dirty socks and his messy pajamas on the floor meant there was life going on. With everything in place, it was quiet and lonely.

One special summer in McLean, Max decided to become an intern at the White House. Wanda and I reunited on Cape Cod while Jack and Max commuted every day to their respective jobs in government.

Under the distinguished Communications Director, Don George, Max started out clipping articles from the morning newspapers for the president's briefing book before moving onto the wire room of the press office and tearing off stories. They contained the news of the day and were also prepared for the president.

In addition, Max had the privilege of attending one of President Rowland's televised press conference and stood only four feet away as he took questions from the White House press corps. Also, he attended the ceremony for Prime Minister Indira Gandhi of India.

At one point, Max wandered somewhere that he shouldn't have been, and the White House Secret Service pounced on him. He thought he might lose his job and quickly went out to the nearest florist shop to buy flowers for his boss. When he presented them to her, she laughed, hugged him, and forgave him. He was safe!

In fact, a member of Jack's State Department staff had to go over to the White House press office for something and asked what they thought of Max Hunter.

"Max Hunter is a charming and impressive young man. If his father is anything like his son, we are in good hands."

The staffer relayed the information to Jack, who chuckled, but modestly beamed with pride.

Though Max was mature for his age, he was still a teenager. Every once in a while, Max liked to borrow my Ford Bronco. He hadn't had his license too long, but the Bronco was huge and indestructible.

Jack had gone to China with the Secretary while I spent my time at the typewriter, creating and revising my plays at home. One day I was lost in my creative world when the doorbell rang. I didn't hear it at first until whomever it was knocked very hard. I went downstairs and opened the door to find a policeman standing with Max.

"Mrs. Hunter?" asked the policeman.

"Yes? What's wrong, officer?"

"This is your son?" he asked.

"Yes, he is."

"He's been involved in an accident," he said.

My heart sank. "An accident?"

"Yes, with another car."

"Is he alright?" I asked as the shock was slowly sinking in.

"As you can see, he looks fine, except his elbow may be fractured."

"What about the person in the other car?" I asked.

"She's shaken, but seems okay," he said. "The two cars were both totaled."

"Oh, my heavens!" I exclaimed as I was falling apart inside, visualizing Max in this accident.

"You better get his arm looked at."

"I will."

The policeman turned and left as Max came inside.

"Thank God you're all right," I said. "Where did it happen?" Max told me approximately where the cross streets in McLean were. I wasn't quite sure of the exact location. "Let me call the Wests to ask if they could come and take us to the emergency room because your father's car is in the State Department garage." They promised to come in an hour, so I fixed something light for Max and myself beforehand. After we arrived at the Emergency Room, we waited and waited and waited. Finally, they took Max and x-rayed his arm. It was not fractured or broken, but just strained, which was a great relief, and they gave him a sling to wear for a few days. Our friends then drove us home. We were both exhausted and went to bed.

That night I tossed and turned and couldn't stop thinking about Max's accident. I honestly didn't know what to do without Jack's help. I desperately needed him. If only he were here and not in China. I wanted to call him, but what could he do? It wouldn't be fair to upset him. After all, Max appeared to be fine, except for the elbow strain.

Although both of us were still emotional the next day, Max went to school. I finally pulled myself together and decided to call counsel to ask him what to do. I described to him the accident as Max told it to me. He said to sit tight until Jack returned and advised me not to go to trial unless he was back home.

"A trial?" I asked. "Will there be a trial?"

"A formal appearance won't be necessary for a minor, but an informal one will be required," he said.

Even so, the thought of a trial was terrifying. Meanwhile, I had to do something about a car, so I called our insurance company on Cape Cod; they told me to hire a rental car for a week.

Once we had the car, Max showed me exactly where the accident happened. Late the following afternoon, I decided to go to the spot by myself and take photographs at the very time of the accident. Then, I had them all enlarged.

"Ginny, why didn't you tell me while I was in China?" Jack asked when he returned.

"Not to worry you. There was nothing you could do until the trip was over. If Max had really been hurt, I would have contacted you through your assistant," I said.

When the informal trial took place, I was ready. The woman, who was the victim, had the policeman defend her and he testified against Max. I knew the odds were against a teenage driver in a situation like this and probably his license would be suspended.

Once the woman in the other car described the accident, the judge gave me an opportunity to speak.

"Your honor, I went to the very site where this unfortunate incident happened at the exact time of day when the two cars collided," I said.

"What did you find?" His curiosity was aroused.

"I found that the sun hit the STOP sign, so that there was no way he could have seen it. Here's the photograph I took and you will see the time of day stamped on the back."

"May I see it?" the judge asked.

"You certainly may."

The judge looked closely at the photo. "You appear to be right," he said.

"One other thing I'd like to bring to your attention, judge. In Massachusetts, we not only have a stop sign, but also a short white or yellow line that is marked on the street at the very point of the sign to warn the driver twice to stop. Do you see any line in this picture?"

"No, I don't," he said.

"That is why there was an accident. My son could not see the sign and there was no line on the road. It was unintentional. I knew there had to be a reason why this happened because he is a careful driver even at his young age," I said.

"I think this concrete proof calls for a dismissal of this case," said the judge.

Feeling jubilant, we shook hands with the judge, the woman, and the policeman. They were astonished at the outcome. The three Hunters left the courtroom and drove home in Jack's car.

"Ginny, why didn't you tell me what you were doing?" asked Jack.

"I wanted everyone to be surprised, including you and Max."

"Gee, thanks, Mom. You'd make a good lawyer."

Needless to say, as a family, we were relieved, and Jack helped buy me a new Jeep over the weekend.

CHAPTER THIRTEEN

▼

KAREN GRENTHEM'S
FAMOUS PARTIES

To be invited to Karen Grenthem's home in the exclusive area of Georgetown was a coveted invitation in D.C.

Her roots to the publishing world went deep. Her parents had lived in Chicago before moving briefly to NYC where Karen was born. Within a few months, the five children moved with their parents to Washington, D.C. Karen always had considered that she was a native Washingtonian. Of the five siblings, she would be the one who always gravitated back to the hub of American politics.

Much of Karen's addiction to politics came from her father, who was an astute businessman and snatched up The D.C. Gazette newspaper at an auction in 1933. Karen's college education took her to Vassar College and the University of Chicago. Upon graduating, she found a job on a small newspaper to get some experience. She wanted to prove herself.

Somewhere along the way, she met Paul Grenthem, who worked for her father on the business side. He was tall, debonair, wildly intelligent, and articulate. Their romance turned to marriage. She stayed safely in the background while she was raising their four children and was content to let Paul be the shining beacon. He expanded the Gazette holdings to include radio and television and a national news magazine. As Karen and Paul prospered, they bought a farm in Virginia, and a house on Martha's Vineyard to escape the humid summers of D.C. The rich, famous, and powerful would be invited to their home on the Vineyard.

Essentially, Karen was a shy woman and not confident in her own abilities. In their relationship, Paul was the attraction and drew many powerbrokers and visionaries to his ever enlarging circle of friends and contacts. All of this changed in an instant when Paul committed suicide in 1963. No one knew why, except for a possible manic depression problem he had and the pressure from such a giant news organization.

To keep the family bloodlines attached to the powerful Gazette, Karen Grenthem was named as publisher. She tried to cover her terror at the prospect, but decided to learn every aspect of the business. She was coached by administrative assistants and financial wizards of the day. She learned to read Profit and Loss statements and go over the finances with a fine tooth comb. She became knowledgeable about everything concerning the newspaper. As a result, she earned everyone's respect.

She began to move with new confidence in the social and political milieu on her home turf. After all, she had known every president from Henrick Hadley onwards because of her father's and husband's influence. Although difficult in some ways, it was a natural transition. There were decisions thrust upon her that she alone as publisher could make, such as printing the Pentagon Papers and the exposure of the infamous Watergate crime, unraveled by her reporters, causing the eventual resignation of a President. These bold steps made her fame grow even stronger.

When the invitation to a reception at Karen Grenthem's came to the Stanleys and to us, Jack could not hide his excitement. For a newspaperman, The D.C. Gazette was a symbol of excellence. He couldn't wait.

On the night of the reception, we parked our car at the State Department and traveled in the Secretary's limousine because parking was limited at her Georgetown home. We arrived promptly at six to find her Gothic-style home full of guests from the newspaper world as well as cabinet and political dignitaries. Local and diplomatic security agents were trained to make themselves inconspicuous.

As we entered, Mrs. Grenthem greeted the Stanleys warmly, and the Secretary very kindly introduced us. She recognized Jack from network TV and was interested to know of his association with The Boston International. I smiled politely and shook her hand. She looked like a Vassar girl with a pageboy hairdo. I noticed how poised and reserved she appeared. She pointed us toward the back library for drinks, and hors d'oeuvres. The press people from the Gazette and White House Press Corps were in every room. They were probably hoping to gather some tidbits of information.

By seven o'clock, everyone had arrived and Mrs. Grenthem assumed her hostess role by visiting groups in each room. Many journalists, who covered foreign policy, surrounded the Secretary. They asked him a few questions, but nothing too penetrating. Mostly, they talked about sports.

However, one reporter threw out a question, "Mr. Secretary, was there anything of significance that came out of your talks with the King of Norway?"

"Just whaling," he replied.

"Whaling?"

"Yes. We complained to him that harpooning whales was a cruel way to impound their flesh."

"What was his reply?"

"He said that they had considered explosives, but they would completely destroy the flesh. However, he admitted that the Mink Whale was an endangered species and was safe from harpooning and explosives."

"What did you say?"

"Actually, my deputy said, 'Thank God for the Mink Whale!' "

As everyone was laughing heartily, Mrs. Grenthem appeared. "Mr. Secretary, what have you told these reporters to make them so amused?"

He repeated his story about the whales and she joined the laughter. "If only diplomacy had more laughter," she said.

"If only," said the Secretary.

At that moment, I decided to enter the conversation. "Mrs. Grenthem, does your job as publisher bring you any laughter?"

"Rarely. It is serious business. But it does bring me immense joy and sometimes--tears. After all, I am a woman!" she said with a slight twinkle in her eye. They all applauded.

Soon, a waiter came with my ginger ale. I was compelled to ask another question. "Do you ever feel lonely as a woman in this profession?"

"Lonely? Yes. Inadequate? No. At the annual American Society of Newspaper Editors, ASNE, meetings, I have two other female magnates: one from The Boston International, and one from Scripps Howard. We have much in common, not only as women, but as executives. So, I'm not always one of the boys," she said. There was polite laughter.

"I suppose you've seen Presidents come and go," I said.

"I've watched them all since Henrick Hadley from my front row seat. What more could I ask for?"

"Are you going to write an autobiography?" I asked.

"Well, not right now, but I'm thinking about it."

"May I ask you another question?" I asked.

"Anyone object?" They all shook their heads, probably because I was asking questions no one else dared to.

"I've noticed how kind you've been to the First Lady, Mrs. Rowland, since she arrived. The press has criticized her unmercifully for accepting those handsome Swedish goblets."

"Unwarranted criticism," she said forcefully. "The Rowlands have been longtime friends before they ever came to the White House. As you may know, my political leanings are not those of the Rowlands, but I am sensitive to the way people are treated, and she was treated unfairly," said our hostess.

"Have you asked your own paper to stop the criticism?" I wanted to know. You could have heard a pin drop, waiting for her answer.

"Yes. I wrote them a memo saying that this story, above the fold, in the Style section was uncalled for. An American donor paid the Swedish government for each and every goblet and the anonymous donor gave it as a gift to the White House. Is that wrong? I don't think so. With so many critical issues facing this country, that kind of damaging coverage does nothing for solutions. It only furthers gossip."

"Did they do what you asked?" I wondered.

"Yes and no. They kept the stories short and below the fold," she said. All the newsmen laughed.

I finished my drink, felt woozy, and fell to the floor in a dead faint. Jack knelt down immediately. A journalist helped him lift me to a brown, comfortable sofa. The guests in the library focused their concern on me. Mrs. Grenthem was especially attentive.

"Shall I call a doctor?" asked Mrs. Grenthem.

"Wait a few minutes," said Jack. "Can you call the waiter who delivered the drinks?"

"Yes indeed," she said.

Within minutes, the waiter arrived.

"My wife ordered a ginger ale. What was in her drink?" Jack inquired.

"I'm sorry, sir. I think I may have given her champagne and Vodka by mistake and served her soft drink to someone else," he said in apologetic tones.

"Well, she's allergic to alcohol and has passed out," Jack muttered, trying to suppress his annoyance.

"What should we do?" asked Mrs. Grenthem.

"Nothing. Just let her rest and recover on the sofa," he said.

"Do you have any idea what kind of reaction she'll have?" she asked.

"She usually goes into a talkative coma and talks about things she's never told me," said Jack.

"Well, perhaps this should be more interesting than we expected," Mrs. Grenthem surmised.

The reporters pressed closer to me to hear any word I might say. Some leaned closer to the sofa while others stooped down on one knee. They were tempted to bring out their notebooks, but refrained because of the social situation.

I murmured something and Jack leaned over and said in my ear, "What was that, Ginny?" He pulled my hair back and saw my eyes closed. He said, "It's Jack."

"Jack the Ripper?" I asked.

"Jack the Ripper?" Everyone around me looked at each other and tried not to laugh.

"Yes, I know the real story," I said in slurred speech.

"How do you know the real story?" Jack asked.

"Someone close to the Royal Family has read it in the Royal archives. I promised not to tell."

"But it's been a long time—probably in the late 1800s--since that happened. I think you can safely tell the real story," Jack said.

"All right," I said in my semi-conscious state. Everyone was mesmerized. "Jack the Ripper was really the Duke of Clarence, Albert Victor, who is related to Queen Victoria."

"Are you sure?"

"Yes."

"What did Jack the Ripper do?" Jack asked.

"He went to the Whitechapel area in London where the Cockneys lived, and there he kidnapped prostitutes and dismembered their intestines and ovaries. It is even said that in Cockney, the word Ripper is really Raper," I answered. Everyone looked stunned. There were lots of theories, but no one had heard this one.

"What happened to him?" Jack asked me.

"The Royal family didn't know what to do. This would be a terrible stain on the Royals. So they had him institutionalized. The killings stopped and the public assumed the murderer had been caught or died."

"Anything else?"

"Yes," I said.

"What was that?"

"The original London Bridge was sold," I said.

"Sold?"

"Yes."

"To whom?"

"A millionaire from Arizona," I said.

"Where is it now?"

"Arizona," I said.

"Is it still there?"

"I don't know. It could have been sold again," I said. At that instant, I started to moan.

"Ginny? Ginny?"

"What?"

"You can wake up now," said Jack.

I opened my eyes and saw everyone staring at me. I felt disoriented and wasn't sure where we were.

"Is everything all right?" asked Mrs. Grenthem.

"Was I asleep?" I asked her.

"I think you--fainted," she said.

"Oh, that is so rude of me. Please accept my apologies," I said.

"It's not your fault, my dear," she said.

"Would you like to freshen up?" she asked.

"Yes, please," I said.

She showed me to the ladies room. When she came back, she said to Jack and the Secretary, "I'll get one of my investigative reporters to check this fascinating story. Have you ever heard it before, Mr. Hunter?" she asked.

"Never."

"All the more intriguing since it comes from the subconscious," she said.

"I think, Jack, we should be going," said the Secretary.

"I agree. Thank you, Mrs. Grenthem, for this wonderful reception and for answering all my wife's questions. I hope you didn't mind?" said Jack.

"On the contrary, what an interesting wife you have," she said.

"Perhaps you're right," said Jack with a knowing smile.

Feeling refreshed, I joined the Secretary, his wife, and Jack. We made our exit. Everyone seemed very quiet in the car. "I liked Mrs. Grenthem so much. She seems down to earth and easy to talk with," I said. "I don't understand why I fainted."

Don't worry about it, my dear," said the Secretary.

Jack was very quiet driving home.

"Ginny, do you know anything about Jack the Ripper?"

"Nothing. Why do you ask?" I said.

"I don't know. It popped into my mind."

"That's strange," I said.

Stranger than fiction was in Jack's thought. Of course I knew, but I had promised never to tell, and I wasn't going to tell now—even Jack. It was a secret buried in my memory bank.

"Jack, did I really fall asleep?"

"They gave you the wrong drink."

"You mean it wasn't ginger ale?" I asked.

"It was champagne and vodka."

"Oh, no! Did I make a fool of myself?"

"You fell asleep."

"I'm so sorry. I hope the Secretary will forgive me."

"I'm sure he will."

"Oh my God," I said.

"What's the matter?" Jack asked.

"I told the story of Jack the Ripper in my stupor, didn't I?"

"Well…"

"Jack, did I talk about him?"

"Yes," he said.

"Oh dear. This is worse than I thought."

"Forget it," said Jack.

"Will it be in all the papers?"

"I don't know," he said.

"Dear God, I hope not," I said.

"Is the person who told you still alive?"

"No," I said.

"Then, you have nothing to worry about."

"How can you be sure?" I asked.

"Because you said this information is in the Royal Archives."

"What if they've been removed?"

"If you worry, you'll drive yourself crazy."

"Okay," I said. Of course I would worry. This was a shocking story and the conspiracy theories will surface and resurface. I couldn't help that. Maybe I should write a play about it—something different, especially if the masked Jack the Ripper were mentally disturbed. I could consider that possibility. What am I thinking? I could never write a play about this. It would be a betrayal by me, even though my sub-conscious revealed it at Mrs. Grenthem's. My guilt is already overwhelming. Besides, I don't like betraying a confidence given to me, but now that it is out in the open, I'll have to decide how to handle this development. My loyalty is to the person who confided in me. Despite the fact of this person's demise, I want to preserve the trust. If anyone asks me, I will refuse to talk about it or to divulge one word. How I wish the wrong drink hadn't been given to me.

CHAPTER FOURTEEN

▼

THE THORNY MIDDLE EAST

Despite all the different pressures in foreign policy, the Middle East continues to be a thorny situation under any administration. The Rowland presidency was not immune; Secretary Stanley carried the brunt of the burden.

At one staff meeting, Stanley's deputy said, "Did you know, Mr. Secretary, that Yassir Arafat had been offered $100,000 to do a razor commercial?" The Secretary was convulsed in laughter. It broke the tension and he was able to tackle the problems with more objectivity.

In a network televised speech, President Rowland laid out a set of peace proposals for the Palestinians once the PLO left Lebanon. The reaction from both Israelis and Arabs was a storm of anger. They each sent delegations to see Secretary Stanley to state their protests.

Fortunately, Jack was able to sit in on the exchanges from both delegations. Stanley listened intently. After they both had registered their complaints and explained why, the Secretary made them wait for his reply with his eyes cast down and without any facial expression.

"Is there any hope for a solution?" asked the Secretary now looking at them.

"No hope," said the Arabs.

"Absolutely no hope," echoed the Israelis.

The Secretary was silent for a minute or so.

"Then, you give me no choice, but to turn away from the problems of the Mid-East to give my attention to the Soviet Union and other countries," said Stanley poker-faced.

"Perhaps, Mr. Secretary, we overstated our position of 'no hope.' We did not mean the situation was hopeless, but needed deeper thought and consideration on our part and the part of the United States," said the Israelis.

"Indeed, we did not mean to dissuade you from focusing your attention on our area of the world. We may have overstated our views and encourage your continued interest on the complexity of our problems," said the Arabs. "Thank you for your time."

"We hope to meet with you again with less intense emotions," said the Israelis.

Both delegations, surprised by the Secretary's response, stood and excused themselves.

After they left, Jack turned to the Secretary. "Sir, may I applaud your negotiating techniques or psychology. You had them eating out of your hand," laughed Jack.

"Thank you, Mr. Hunter. By the way, did I ever tell you about my unusual call from former President John Carson a few years ago?"

"I don't believe you have," said Jack.

"As you know, the switchboards at the White House and State Department can find anyone in a matter of seconds," Stanley said.

"Yes sir."

"I was working at Beckers when a call came in from John Carson. I picked up the phone and said, 'Hello, Mr. President, how are you?' "

"Just fine, Gavin, just fine," said Carson.

"What can I do for you, Mr. President?"

"Actually, Gavin, I've just realized that I was trying to reach another Stanley. Our operators are so fast."

"Don't give it another thought. As long as you weren't looking for Livingston, we're both in good mental health," said Stanley.

"Clever, Gavin, very clever. Well, I'll let you get on with your day," said Carson.

"Give my best to Mrs. Carson."

"I sure will. And that was the end of the conversation."

"Interesting," said Jack.

"Tell me, Jack, do you think the Jordanians, Saudis, and Egyptians would ever agree to a Palestinian state?"

"Not according to the statement that came out of the FEZ conference in Morocco," Jack replied. "The list of ideas to be discussed weren't realistic. To suggest Jerusalem be capital of a Palestinian state is reaching beyond the moon and the Arab countries know that."

"I agree. And to ask that the Israelis should withdraw from the 1967 War borders is pie in the sky. To ask for the dismantling of Israeli settlements is more realistic, don't you think?" asked the Secretary.

"It's in the realm of possibility as is the request for freedom of religion in the region," said Jack.

"However, to ask for support of Lebanon from all sides is also a shaky request," Stanley stated.

"Again—unrealistic."

"When are you doing the *murder board* to prepare me for the hearings in front of the Senate Foreign Relations Committee?" asked the Secretary.

"Now, if you want to?"

"I'm ready to get it over with," said Stanley.

Jack replied, "I know it is just standard procedure for you and any politician, cabinet member, or even the President who is facing a panel or a press interview, the way you are tomorrow.

Stanley said, "Let's get aides in here to toss out every possible question that might be thrown at me. This way, I won't be surprised or caught off guard by tough questions."

That's what they did for the rest of the afternoon.

When Wanda drove down to D.C. on her way back to college, she and I went together to Stanley's Senate hearings. We had to park miles away from the Dirksen Building. If we went by foot, we would be late. So...I decided the only way was to hitchhike or hail a cab. Wanda was too embarrassed. My hand was half a wave and half a thumb, pointing forward.

A cab with someone in it pulled over. "Where are you going?" asked the man with dark hair and black-rimmed glasses.

"The Dirksen Building," I said.

"Exactly where I'm going," he said.

Wanda and I squeezed into the backseat beside him. "This is very kind of you," I said.

"Ordinarily, two pretty women should not accept a ride from a stranger," he scolded.

"You look too nice to be a horrible creature," I told him.

"Do you know who I am?" he asked.

"I apologize, but I don't think I do, although you do look familiar," I said.

"I'm Senator Justin Hanes,"

"Of course," I said.

""May I have the pleasure of knowing who you and the young lady are?" Hanes asked.

"I'm Mrs. Jack Hunter and this is our daughter, Wanda."

"Ah, your husband is Secretary Stanley's spokesman," he said.

"Yes."

"And you are going to the Senate Hearings?" he asked.

"We are," I said.

"So am I, because I'm on the committee."

"What a wonderful coincidence!" I said.

As we stepped out of the cab, I tried to pay, but he wouldn't let me. He asked if we'd like to see his three offices, assuring us we had time. He introduced us to his secretary. All the walls were filled with awards and photos of the Senator with famous people. There were cartoons, too, making fun of him. He enjoyed those the most. Then, he showed us the conference room.

Instead of standing in the public line, he ushered us into the reserved section—three rows from the front. We whispered our thanks to him while he took his place on the panel to quiz the Secretary. Senator Carlton Pendry was chairman of the committee at that time and made some general opening remarks.

An obscure Massachusetts senator started the questions, coating his words with thick flattery. "After the President's speech about the Middle East, I heard the name 'Stanley, Stanley, Stanley' ripple across the room," he said.

"That's strange," said Stanley, "I heard the name 'Rowland, Rowland, Rowland' bouncing around the nation and world!"

"You are indeed a loyal member of the administration and you have surrounded yourself with a professional team," the senator replied.

There were two tables of reporters while the photographers were on the floor, propped against the wooden modesty-panels. They were focusing their lenses on the Secretary and the senators. Experts from China and Latin America were on each side of the Secretary. Jack sat directly behind him.

Senator Hanes was very soft in his questions and kept looking at Wanda and me, winking every now and then. We smiled politely. The questions seemed to go on for hours. Each senator had his peacock moment in the spotlight.

Finally, the last committee member was ready to conclude with his questions. He said, "I'm told that by the time our esteemed victim reaches the last set of questions, he is invariably too tired to answer them."

"Speak for yourself, senator," said Stanley. A wave of laughter circulated as the senator turned red and was flustered. He finished quickly.

Afterwards, Senator Hanes came over and congratulated the Secretary on his performance. I introduced him to Jack.

"I had the honor of meeting your charming wife and daughter before the hearings," he said.

"I wondered how they were seated in the reserved section," said Jack. "Thank you very much for your thoughtfulness."

"You're doing an outstanding job for the Secretary," said Hanes.

"Thank you, sir."

Only eight days after that hearing, the Middle East exploded. There was a flagrant massacre of women and children in the Palestinian refugee camps in Lebanon, carried out by right wing Lebanese Christians or so the Israelis claimed. The news angered the world.

During this crisis, the State Department and the White House were in constant contact. The days were long and emotions were running high. The massacre happened on the heels of the assassination of the newly elected, 34-year-old President of Lebanon, Christian Bachir Gemayel. The American consensus was that a multi-national force should go into Lebanon to police the violence.

In one of the long sessions, the Secretary turned to Jack and said, "What do you think the press will be doing about this terrible situation?"

Jack offered a possible scenario. "First of all, photographs of the massacre will be picked up and shown on TV and in the press. The President should appear to be waiting on Wednesday. He should be diplomatic on Thursday, angry on Friday, demand a withdrawal of Israeli troops on Saturday. Nothing may happen, but at least he will give the impression of doing something instead of appearing inactive and impotent."

Everyone in the room looked at each other and nodded in agreement. However, the wives of these Foreign Service officers were frustrated by having to wait for their husbands through this lengthy meeting. They were late for diplomatic dinners and preferred not to go alone to them. One high level couple had a rather heated exchange in front of everybody after the meeting adjourned.

The wife stood at the door of her husband's office and said, "I don't want to go to that dinner alone."

"You have to," he said.

"No, I don't."

"It's important--very important."

"It always happens—you're never available. They won't miss me. You're the one they'll miss," she said.

"You have to tell the Italian Ambassador that he is invited to the State Department later tonight for vital discussions and the same with the French Ambassador," he pleaded.

"Can't you make a phone call to them, so I don't have to spend the whole evening there?" she begged him.

"When we're in the middle of a crisis, we need you to pass this information to them. A telephone call won't do it."

"Well, I'll think about it," she said.

"Honey, this is our country—yours and mine. This is an opportunity for you to be patriotic. You can help your country by getting those two ambassadors to our office tonight," he said. "Please."

With that final plea, she left his office. He wasn't sure whether she would go or not. Dejected, he hoped that when she thought about it, she might have a change of heart. He thrust his hands deep in his pockets and went into another meeting.

Of course she did respond to her better instincts and went to the dinner party where, at the appropriate moment, she delivered the messages to the two ambassadors, who excused themselves from the party once dinner was over, and then went to the State Department.

What was on everyone's mind was to consider a multi-national force going into Lebanon to calm the situation.

Meanwhile, I had brought a fried chicken dinner to the office for Jack and me. I assumed he didn't have lunch and was both starved and exhausted. The Secretary spent an unproductive meeting with the French and Italian ambassadors the night before in his office. He needed another session to win them over to America's point of view.

Finally, the President gave a speech late afternoon. It was being changed right up until the time he went on network news. Essentially, he said that the Israelis should be encouraged to remove their troops from Beirut along with other foreign forces. A multi-national force would take their place. Hopefully, it would be composed of our own Marines together with Italian and French forces.

With unflagging support, Jack was beside the Secretary every step of the way in these negotiations. In fact, the Secretary credited Jack with guiding them because of his knowledge of every move the press would make.

"Mr. Secretary, when you have a tough problem to wrestle with, what do you do?" Jack asked.

"When things get really bad, I go to the Lincoln Memorial at night to walk around it and inside it. I read the familiar statements made by Abraham Lincoln and Martin Luther King, Jr., and I feel renewed. Then, I go home," he said.

"You couldn't go to a better place to think," said Jack.

"I don't know how you do those briefings every day."

"It's sort of like making my way through a minefield," laughed Jack.

"Well, I'm glad you can laugh about it," Stanley said. "I'd be terrified to do what you do and face some of those pit bulls."

They both laughed.

When there was a suggestion that Israel should be banned from the United Nations, Secretary Stanley said, "If Israel is banned, the United States will leave the UN and stop paying its bills.

In private, Stanley turned to Jack and said in jest, "If Israel was to be banned, we wouldn't have to go to the UN next year and I could take a vacation instead! Two weeks of golfing would suit me to a tee—no pun intended," said the Secretary humorously.

"Maybe Ginny and I could go to a beach in Hawaii," laughed Jack.

"Of course, I don't really mean any of that, but the two-week trip to the UN is always exhausting."

"True, Mr. Secretary, but necessary and productive," Jack said.

"You're right. I know that. And I keep being criticized for not wearing brighter clothes on television. What do you think, Jack?"

"I think that nothing can compare to your sincerity, and that's what counts," Jack said.

"That's what my wife says."

"If I were you, I'd listen to your wife. She's right," said Jack.

When Yitzhak Shimon, Foreign Minister of Israel, arrived a few days later, Stanley was locked in long meetings with him. Jack was right by his side to witness everything.

At a brief press conference afterwards, Stanley and Shimon put out a joint statement. One of the reporters asked the Secretary a frothy question just before the conference ended.

"Mr. Secretary, we understand that during the repairs to your private dining quarters, some unfortunate discoveries were made."

"Discoveries?" Stanley looked puzzled.

"Mice! Hundreds of mice running all over the carpet. Were they Russian mice or Israeli mice or Arab mice?" The press corps laughed heartily.

With a straight face, Stanley replied, "All three, and they are looking for bugs!"

"Did they find any?"

"Not one," said Stanley, enjoying the banter.

"One more question, sir. Do you think relations between the Soviet Union and the United States might thaw?"

"Well, it takes two to thaw!" said the Secretary with a twinkle. That reply made the headlines next day.

In another meeting with staffers, the Secretary expressed his displeasure over the inertia coming from the Middle East.

"The Arabs are cooperating. Why not the Israelis?" he asked, knowing next week their positions could well be reversed and next month, be changed again.

"We can understand your frustration, but it just takes patience, sir," said his deputy.

"My sources say that the President is equally frustrated by the lack of movement in the Mid-East. The rumors circulating say that the President might fire someone if something doesn't happen soon," Jack said.

"Please God, let it be me," smiled the Secretary and caused a few chuckles around the room.

"By the way, Mr. Secretary, I understand you want to have lunch with the Egyptian ambassador in the same room in which you and Shimon lunched together," the deputy said.

"Yes?"

"Well, the Arabs don't want that room."

"Why not?"

"The carpets are new. They prefer old ones."

"That's what carpets are for—to walk on and spill things on. We'll have it in that room," said the Secretary with a twinkle in his eye. Everyone chuckled. "I don't mean to make light of any situation or problem, but at times we need to relieve the tension. It's so damnable thorny over there with many lives at stake that a few jokes are necessary to keep us sane!"

"Absolutely," agreed Easton.

"All right, I'll tell you a true story, on a different subject, about a question I was asked during a speaking engagement at the World Affairs Council in Dallas. Want to hear it"

"Wouldn't miss it," said Leonard.

"The question was, 'Mr. Secretary, you've been an administrator at a college, an executive of big business, and now head of the State Department in government. What's it like and what's the difference?' "

"This was my answer, 'You have to be very careful because in business if you ask somebody to do something, there's a chance he'll do it and do it quickly. In government, if you ask someone to do anything, you'll be sure it will never get done. And in a college, you have to ask everyone because it's democratic, and no one cares if it gets done or not.' "

As the staffers were chortling over Stanley's clever answer, news came in that a bomb blast in Beirut by Iranian radicals had killed 50 or 60 at the American Embassy, including a CIA expert on the Middle East and the PLO.

"That's it!" said the Secretary. "Let's plan a trip to the Middle East as soon as possible." Once everyone left his office, Stanley turned to Jack. "We'll base ourselves in Jerusalem and shuttle to Lebanon to negotiate the withdrawal of International Military Force, Israeli, Syrian, and PLO troops. Without any fanfare, you and I will bring our wives to see the Biblical sites in Israel while we work and travel in and out. How does that sound?"

"Excellent," replied Jack.

When Jack told me about the trip to Israel, I couldn't have been more excited. He reminded me, though, that he wouldn't be available to do anything, except work. That was fine with me. Mrs. Stanley and I could visit the tourist highlights or I could poke around on my own. I only had two days to do laundry and pack. I had some dressy clothes and some casual ones—nothing conspicuous. Max would be all right and could take care of the dog. Mrs. Stanley and I were taken to Andrews Air Force base much earlier than the press and the government entourage. We boarded, settled down, and assumed a low profile for the rest of the trip.

Once we arrived at the Tel Aviv airport, the press raced off the plane and hired taxis to go to Jerusalem or to hotels in Tel Aviv. After the media went through customs, all the government people were escorted by the American Embassy to the King David Hotel in modern Jerusalem. It was a large, beautiful hotel with an incredible view. Later, in the moonlight, it was an even more spectacular sight.

Throughout the night, rockets were bursting near the hotel. I was afraid to sleep; I kept wondering if one might come crashing through the window of our hotel room. Jack was sound asleep. Just before dawn I drifted off. When I woke up, there was a note on Jack's pillow.

"We are at a private breakfast meeting. Be downstairs to meet Mrs. Stanley at 10:00. An embassy driver will take you to Galilee."

"Galilee?" I said out loud. I quickly showered and dressed in my casual attire, ordered room service, and took the elevator to the lobby. Mrs. Stanley was already waiting.

"Good morning, I hope I'm not late?" I said.

"I'm early. The car is here. Shall we go?"

"I'm ready!" We settled in the back seat of a large, black American car and watched the change in landscape from the dry desert around Jerusalem to the green fertile valley of Lower Galilee, near the rolling foothills of Mount Tabor. We were too overcome to say anything.

Twenty minutes into our journey, the driver pointed to the right. "There's the Sea of Galilee," he said.

"The real Sea of Galilee?" asked Mrs. Stanley.

"It's real," he said.

"It's bigger than I thought," I said.

"Much bigger."

"The emerald color is beautiful," I remarked.

"It looks more like a lake than a sea," Mrs. Stanley said.

"You wouldn't believe how fast a storm can come up and toss the boats to and fro," said the driver.

"Just like in the Bible," Mrs. Stanley said.

"Yes. Would you like to get out?"

"We would," said Mrs. Stanley, expressing my sentiments as well.

We stepped out and felt a soft breeze coming off the water. We walked along the shoreline and stopped to look at the green slopes cascading down to the sea's edge. We both were imagining the slopes filled with people, listening to the preaching of a man whose words were carried up the hillsides by the wind. We savored the moments of a place we had only read about and never expected to see. We looked at each other and smiled.

"Straight across the sea is where the Gadarenes lived. Do you know the story?" asked the driver.

"You mean when Jesus cast out the demons from an insane man and the demons went into the swine, who rushed headlong into the sea?" I asked.

"You're right. The Golan Heights are just above there. Shall we get back in the car and drive around?"

"On the way, could we have a peek of the border between Lebanon and Israel?" I asked.

"Is it safe?" asked Mrs. Stanley.

"We won't get close enough to make it dangerous," said the driver.

The rich greenery in the valley was incredible. Then the car started to climb the hills to the mountainous area. Almost at the top, the driver stopped.

"There's the border," he said.

"It's so close," I observed.

"They look right into each other's eyes," said the driver. As we turned around, there was a loud noise.

"Oh no, we have a flat tire," he said. He stepped out to look and a man in an Arab keffiyeh pointed a gun at him.

"Who you driving?" he asked.

"Two ladies."

"American?" asked the gunman.

The driver nodded.

"Tell them to get out of car," the gunman said in his native language.

"Ladies, would you mind stepping out of the car?"

Mrs. Stanley and I emerged tentatively. He pointed at Mrs. Stanley.

"Me take her," said the gunman.

"No!" I said. You have to take me," I said.

"You? Why?"

"She's not well. Take me," I said.

"Who you?" he asked.

"A reporter," I said. "I can tell your story to the world."

"You come," the gunman said. "You two get in car and not turn around—okay?"

"Okay," said the driver.

The gunman taped my hands behind my back and then put tape over my mouth. He attached a chain from my waist to his. Soon we disappeared behind the tall bushes, growing there. I had no idea what my fate would be. Would he kill me or torture me or rape me or use me as a pawn or a hostage? Would I ever see Jack or my children again? The consequences of what I volunteered to do just hit me and it was scary. The kidnapper yanked me behind him and showed no compassion. His eyes burned like a wild man.

Back in the car, Mrs. Stanley said, "Do something."

"I will. You stay here. Lock the car and here are the keys. I'll change the tire when I get back."

"How do you know where to follow them?" she asked.

"The Mossad."

"What?"

"The Israeli CIA. They've shown me all the trails to the border."

"Then, get going. Don't come back without her!"

The driver ran down the road to the place where he knew there was an opening. He sprinted as fast as he could along the narrow pathway and pulled out his gun. Soon he heard the rustle of bushes and feet ahead of him. He got closer and closer until he saw me stumbling to keep up with my captor. The gunman kept looking back and motioning me to run faster. I shook my head. Then there was an opening. They paused. The driver showed himself and startled the terrorist. He raised his gun and shot him twice before the man could reach for his gun. The driver made sure the gunman was dead. I was thunderstruck. He cut the tape off my hands, pulled it off my mouth, and cut the chain.

Trembling from the thought of what might have happened to me, I gasped for breath and said, "Thank God, you found me!"

"If I didn't, I'd lose my job! Are you okay?"

"I think so," I said, greatly relieved, but scared out of my wits.

"Come on, let's get out of here and back to Mrs. Stanley, before more terrorists come looking for him."

"I guess I missed the scoop of the century," I said in a whisper.

"They would have kept you hostage for years."

We loped back to the car. Mrs. Stanley saw us in the rear view mirror, opened the door, and threw her arms around me. "If anything happened to you, I would never forgive myself." We both started to cry.

"Come on, ladies, we have to get this tire changed quickly before more gunmen arrive. Open the trunk and get out the equipment. I'll get the spare tire," he said.

"No!" said Mrs. Stanley. "Let's leave now. Drive on the rim of the tire until we find a safer place to change it."

The driver jumped back into the car and turned on the ignition. Once the engine roared, we turned around. The metal rim screeched along the highway until he found a safe spot.

As much as I could, I helped with the tire change. Mrs. Stanley watched in every direction for any intruders. When the tire was on, we slid back in our seats. "Do you still want to see the Golan Heights?" he asked.

"No! Back to the hotel!" said Mrs. Stanley.

Once we arrived there, we thanked the driver for his bravery. We offered him a monetary reward, but he refused. We found that the men were not back, so we calmed our nerves by ordering tea and took it to our rooms. Only then did I tell Mrs. Stanley what happened after the man captured me. How he slapped me and jabbed his knee in my stomach. He put his gun barrel against my forehead and then in my ear. She was shocked. I decided not to tell Jack while he was in these sensitive talks, but the next morning the Secretary and delegation had heard every detail. Jack was furious, but relieved we were safe. Although everyone was very solicitous, I didn't want to talk about it and certainly didn't want the press to find out and embarrass Jack.

In a compassionate mood, the Secretary took me aside with his arm around my shoulder and said, "My wife told me you refused to let the gunman take her hostage, but offered yourself instead."

"I couldn't let him do that to you. You need her," I said.

"Well, I just wanted to thank you personally and commend your bravery," he said.

"Besides," I said, "I was hoping to get the scoop of the century!"

"I think there are better things in life," he said.

"You're probably right."

"Why didn't you tell Jack?" he asked.

"I didn't want to add to his worries. All of you have a lot on your minds," I said.

The next day, Mrs. Stanley and I met on the veranda for lunch. When we finished, I suggested we hire a cab to take us to Old Jerusalem to see the sites. She would only go if I felt up to it after yesterday's drama. I assured her that I was fine. The concierge arranged one for us.

"Could you take us to the Mt. of Olives and Gethsemane first and wait for us?" I asked.

"Yes, madam."

We stood on the dry, dusty area of Mt. Olives that looked across to the Old City with its thick walls. Gethsemane was below and was a very small area—much smaller than we thought. An iron gate enclosed it. There were bushes inside. We imagined the description of it in the Bible.

"Let's go inside the walls at one of the gates to see more," I said, my curiosity getting the best of me.

"Fine," said Mrs. Stanley.

"Driver, can you take us to the entrance of Old Jerusalem?"

"Yes, it's not far."

"Where will we find you when we come out?" I asked.

"At the open-air Falafel place across the street," he pointed to it.

"We'll be an hour or so," I said.

"Don't worry," he replied.

Then, we walked through the Moorish arch of one gate, made in thick sandy stone. It was like stepping into another world with its network of tunnels. Small stalls were everywhere; souvenirs, jewelry, and knick knacks were dazzling. Shopkeepers chased after us to bargain. We followed the signs to the Holy Sepulcher and the place of the crucifixion. We found the pool of Bethesda and were amazed how small it was. We overheard a tourist guide say that Jerusalem had been destroyed twenty-one times. We wondered why nothing had changed over the centuries. Finding our way back was like walking through a maze. When we emerged, our driver was sipping tea at the restaurant. He jumped up, paid his bill, and turned his cab around.

"You like?" he asked.

"Very much," replied Mrs. Stanley.

"You want to go to Bethlehem to the Church of the Nativity?"

We looked at our watches and Mrs. Stanley nodded. "If it's not too far."

"Maybe fifteen minutes."

"Yes, we'd like to go," she said, speaking for both of us.

The terrain was very hilly, but we finally reached the church and saw where Jesus was born. We imagined the valley full of shepherds and sheep. The sky would be full of stars at night.

Once we finished sightseeing, it was time to return to the hotel. At the entrance, we paid our taxi bill and went to our rooms. The men were not there. I rested and ordered a light supper from room service. The men returned very late and left very early the following day.

I called Mrs. Stanley in the morning to see if she wanted to do anything. She wasn't feeling well, so I decided to go by myself to Caesarea between Tel Aviv and Haifa. It's a Roman structure, dating back to 22 B.C. and set on the Mediterranean Sea. The ruins of an amphitheatre are still usable for concerts and theatrical productions.

When I boarded the bus, it wasn't full. I sat at the back. There was a young woman with a baby in the middle. An elderly man sat behind her. Two schoolboys were up front near the driver. I was enjoying the view along the Mediterranean and the terraced homes on the opposite side. The bus stopped to pick up a young man. As he stood up, he threw a bomb on the floor of the bus and it rolled right towards me.

"Open the back door!" I screamed at the driver. The bomb exploded between the elderly man and me. "Get out the front," I screamed to everyone, "and run across the street to hide."

I had jumped out and was running to the front of the bus, yelling to everyone through the windows. I saw the terrorist running away and I ran after him as fast as I could. The driver was right behind me. I was so angry that I found speed I never knew existed. I was getting closer. Finally, I made a horizontal leap and tackled him.

"I have another bomb to blow you up!" he said to me.

"So what!" I said.

"You not afraid?"

"No! My children are grown. Why should I care?"

"You stupid," he shouted at me.

The driver arrived next to me. "Take my scarf and wrap it around his neck and choke him to death if you have to," I told him. "Here, put this gun to his neck." It was a metal, cylindrical glasses case that would feel like the barrel of a gun.

"But…" I put my finger to my lips. He understood.

"Put your hands behind your back or we'll shoot you!" He did as I asked. By now, I had taken my shoelaces out of my sneakers and was binding his hands. He tried to wrestle out of the laces and I took his middle finger and pulled it back till he cried with pain and pleaded for me to stop. "Take off your belt," I demanded of the driver. I took the belt and tied it around the terrorist's ankles.

"Turn around and look at me," I yelled. He did. "Look here, whoever you are, I'm not Jewish. I'm an American and I support your cause, but you'll never get anywhere with bombs, bullets, and stones. And that goes for the Israelis as well. Violence won't work. You kill someone and someone will kill you. It will go on and on and never end," I screamed. "Negotiate and work it out. You both are losing families. Get your kids in school. Generations are being wasted by doing what you just did. Start using your brain and smarten up!"

"Then, tell the Israelis to stop building settlements," he screamed.

"I'll tell them this. Every time they build a settlement, they must build one for the Palestinians in Gaza or the West Bank and pay for them. Do you agree?" I asked.

"I agree, but you must tell the Prime Minister," he said.

"I don't know him," I replied.

"Then, write a letter. Do something."

Utterly amazed, the driver was speechless. The sirens started to drone. Ambulances and police cars surrounded the bus and us. The driver explained what happened. Someone was taking photographs. The policeman took off the shoelaces and handcuffed the young man. I started to re-lace my shoes. The driver handed back my scarf and glasses case.

"Don't forget the people from the bus, hiding across the street," I said. A policeman ran across the street to rescue them. The driver asked the policeman if he would take me home.

"What hotel?"

"King David," I said.

"Not the hospital?" he asked.

"Hospital? What for?"

"Your face is all black."

"It doesn't matter. I'd rather go to the hotel," I said.

So, with sirens blaring, he took me to the hotel. I thanked him and ran inside with my scarf over my face. By coincidence, Jack was in the lobby and intercepted me.

"Ginny, what the...?" was all Jack managed to blurt out.

"A bomb was thrown into my bus."

"Oh my God! Let's go to the room," he said.

Once there, he examined my face. He tried a warm wash cloth. Some of the black came off, but most of the skin was burned. He called Stanley's physician and asked him to come to the room. He was there in minutes. After inspecting my face, he assured Jack and me that it wasn't critical and would heal in several weeks. He gave me some cream to put on it.

"Ginny, I'm going to book you on a flight to Washington tomorrow. We'll have Max come meet you. I have to be in a meeting right now, but you can tell me what happened when I come back."

"Okay," I said.

Well, the news story was on Israeli TV that night and in newspapers the next morning. The Secretary and Mrs. Stanley were horrified, and agreed I should go home the next day. Needless to say, my brief time in Israel was an adventure, but perhaps a liability.

Jack told me later that the press corps congratulated him on his wife's courage. They wondered if I might join the NFL because of the way I tackled the terrorist.

The American news networks picked it up, but I refused to talk with anyone since my face was still burned to a crisp and hurt like crazy. I certainly was not at my most attractive.

After a long flight from Tel Aviv, I arrived at Dulles airport, Max was shocked to see my blackened, burnt face, but I think he was secretly proud.

A few days later, the State Department's assistant physician telephoned me to ask how I was. I told him my facial burns were healing. He told me I could come in for treatment because my husband was a government employee and everything was free for him and the family.

"Free?" I asked.

"Yes," he said.

"Well, I couldn't do that. It wouldn't be right."

"Why do you say that?"

"Because all the other people in America have to pay, I should pay, too!" I declared.

"You're an original, Mrs. Hunter, I'll say that about you. Most people would jump at the chance to get something for free," he laughed and hung up, absolutely perplexed.

CHAPTER FIFTEEN

▼

GINGER ROGERS COMES TO D.C.

Because I was a drama critic for our weekly newspapers, I had come to know Ginger Rogers in 1978. She came to the oldest summer theatre in America, the Cape Playhouse on Cape Cod, to perform her one-woman show, <u>An Evening to Remember.</u>

For our papers, I interviewed celebrities; we learned that feature stories about stage, screen, or television stars sold newspapers, so we capitalized on those events. Stars like Henry Fonda, Jean Stapleton, Lana Turner, and Ginger Rogers were the kind of actors drawn to the Cape Playhouse.

Ginger's show was amazing. As a backdrop to the stage, there were video tapes of her dancing and theatrical career. She danced and sang some of the familiar numbers we associate with the team of Rogers and Astaire. She did 73 films in total and yet, only ten with Fred. Just one other person was in her show and that was a male dancing partner of slight build, and perhaps only a little taller than Astaire.

In 1978, she was 69-years-old and still going strong as a dancer and performer. In those days, theatres paid astronomical salaries to the stars for a week long appearance, and they pumped out as much publicity as possible to fill the seats. Of course, for Ginger Rogers, it was no problem. Her name alone had people storming the box office.

After opening night, there was an interview arranged at the bistro diagonally across from the c.1927 theatre. Appetizers and soft drinks were provided for local and Boston TV reporters and journalists.

They were obsessed with her age and kept asking, "Miss Rogers, how old are you?"

"Well, darling," she would say. "I don't like to put a number on myself."

"Why not?"

"It gives me a feeling of limitation, and I don't like to feel limited in what I do," she grinned and batted her eyelashes over those magical blue eyes.

Indeed, she did defy age. Ginger had a dazzling smile and charming personality. She still exuded an allure that captured a man's heart. Without even knowing it, she flirted with men and they fell for her. Katharine Hepburn is attributed with saying about Fred and Ginger, "He made her look classy and she made him look sexy."

"There's a rumor that's been going around about you and Fred not getting along," said one reporter.

"I'm going to have to write a book and put that rumor to rest," she said jokingly.

"So, it's not true?"

"Of course not. Fred and I were perfectionists and we worked long hours to make our routines perfect. Often my feet would be bleeding at the end of the day after rehearsing and rehearsing," she explained.

"Then where did this rumor come from?"

"In the film 'Top Hat,' there was a number called "Cheek to Cheek" by Irving Berlin. I had a satin, ice-blue dress made with Ostrich feathers on the sleeves and tiered down the long skirt. Even though the film was in black and white, I loved to choose colors. However, when Fred began to rehearse with me in that dress, the feathers got in his mouth and he couldn't stand it since it also made him sneeze. The director, Mark Sandrich, was ready to dump it for a dress from "Gay Divorcee.' My mother, Lela, came to the set and there was an almighty fight. We didn't back down. After we watched the rushes, the dress was beautiful. It was Fred who backed down. He sent me a gold charm of a feather with a note that said, 'Dear Feathers, I love ya! Fred.' That is the only possible explanation of this rumor," Ginger replied.

"Do you have children?" inquired another journalist.

"No. I consider the children of the world as mine," she said.

"And a husband?"

"I'm not proud of the fact that I had five husbands. The irony is that I longed for one long-lasting marriage. I loved being married, nesting, and cooking. I had everything else."

"Was there one of the five you hoped would last?"

"Yes, Lew Ayres. He was a wonderful man and a talented actor," she acknowledged. "Can we go to another topic?"

"There's a story about you and Leona Helmsley."

"And her husband Harry, who was a real estate mogul in NYC and owned the fabulous Helmsley Hotel," Ginger volunteered.

"Could you tell us the anecdote?"

"Well, darling, I was in NYC and went to a special dinner party at the home of Mayor Wagner, who was married to my cousin Phyllis at the time. There were about eighteen guests. After dinner, there was a man playing the accordion, and he started playing songs from my Broadway show, <u>Girl Crazy</u>. A tall gentleman asked if I had made many record albums. I told him that albums were very expensive to make. He wondered how much and I told him. I learned this was Harry Helmsley. In a fit of jealousy, his wife Leona insisted they leave immediately. He refused. She stormed out of the house and drove away in their limousine. In another ten minutes, she was back, demanding that Harry come home. This time, he obeyed!"

"Was this the end of the story?" someone asked.

"Oh no. When I was at a Carnegie Hall concert, someone tapped me on the shoulder. It was Leona Helmsley. She showed me the big diamond earrings her husband had bought her to assuage her anger over his talking with me. Jokingly, she asked me to talk with him again, so she could get a pair of ruby earrings!"

"Your mother, Lela Rogers, was a very important part of your life," said a TV reporter.

"She was. She meant everything to me. She made me who I am. I will always be grateful to her. She passed away last year and I still miss her," said Ginger, obviously moved with emotion.

Ginger and her capable, attractive secretary, Roberta Olden, came to our Cape house for lunch and also to our little beach and dock. She was relaxed and charming and was relieved to know my review was positive.

In the 1980s when we were in D.C., our paths crossed again. She called me to see if I could meet her at the airport and take her to the Mayflower Hotel. Of course, I was delighted to do that. The reason for her trip was to donate one of her dresses from "Top Hat" to the Smithsonian. Jack and I were invited to the luncheon, honoring her. It was not the blue feather dress, but the one from the "Piccolino" number. The bodice and most of the long skirt were covered in sparkling sequins that looked like flashing diamonds on the screen. Apparently, the dress is displayed in the museum between Judy Garland's ruby slippers from "Wizard of Oz" and Irving Berlin's piano. Ginger took us to dinner that night. The restaurant was flustered to have her as a guest. They rolled over a bucket with a couple of bottles of champagne, which they presented as a gift.

She graciously thanked them, but said, "I'm so sorry, but I don't drink. Thank you for being so kind." They whisked away the champagne and picked up the dinner check instead.

During her career, Ginger had met seven Presidents at the White House, starting with Forest D. Rosalynne. It was as exciting for them to meet her as it was for her to meet the Presidents. Russell and Clare Rowland invited her to give a short performance at the White House the next night and to dance with some cabinet members afterwards.

In the late afternoon of the following day, we were invited on the Presidential Yacht, a Trumpy, named *Sequoia*. There were hors d'oeuvres and drinks. Ginger stepped down a ladder to the floor below. The Marine in front of her was supposed to help, but he let her foot slip and she sprained it. Of course, she never let on. That night, she went to the White House for dinner and dancing. Although her foot was quite swollen, she didn't want to disappoint anyone.

Jack and I were invited to the dance part of the program. We arrived just as they finished dinner and adjourned to the Cross Hall where the Marine Band was playing.

"And now, ladies and gentlemen, our wonderful guest, Ginger Rogers, has agreed to sing and dance to George Gershwin's "Embraceable You," said President Rowland. Everyone moved as one to form a circle around her off the dance floor as she charmed the whole group with her solo rendition. When it was over, the applause was loud and appreciative. The President invited her for the first dance. Then the Vice-President cut in and twirled her around the floor.

"I have someone who has dreamed of dancing with you for years," he said.

"Who is that?" Ginger asked.

"Our very distinguished Secretary of State," the VP said.

"Gavin Stanley?"

"Yes."

"I never would have guessed," she exclaimed.

"Shall I give him the sign to cut in?"

"Certainly," she said.

Gavin Stanley had been watching her every move. When the VP gave him the nod, he cut in and swept Ginger Rogers around the floor in those minutes of glory. He had flair, and she followed as if they had been partners for years. Photographs were being snapped for posterity.

"Mr. Secretary, your dancing skills are as good as any professional," she said.

"You couldn't have given me a greater compliment," he beamed. There were only a few other men with enough daring to ask her to dance. She sat down frequently to give her swollen ankle a rest.

Before I knew what was happening, Mr. Stanley had taken my hand, led me to the floor, and spun me around in a waltz.

"Were you thrilled to dance with Miss Rogers?" I asked.

"It has made my career!"

"I think she was thrilled, too," I said.

"Ginny, whatever happens during this intricate dance, don't let your head hit the floor."

"Hit the floor?"

"In case you fall, your brain could be damaged forever," he said.

"It is already," I sighed. He laughed at my self-deprecating joke. "I'm ready," I said.

I arched my back and let my head move dramatically from side to side in a stylized waltz I had seen on TV. In a split moment, of course, my heel caught in the hem of my dress. I fell backwards to the floor, making sure my head didn't smack the marble. Not knowing what to do, the Secretary, holding securely to my hands, pushed me between his legs.

Once I was through, he said, "Let go of my hands!" I did and found myself sliding along the dance floor for at least six feet.

Fortunately, the Vice President was there to grab me by both hands, hoist me up, and twirl me around in a fast waltz until my heel again caught in the hem. I fell backwards one more time and slid through his legs. The Vice President almost did a somersault until he released my hands, but Jack was there to pick me up.

"Ginny! What happened?" he asked.

"My heel caught in the hem of my dress. I couldn't help it," I said, laughing.

Frustrated, but knowing I really did pull off a miraculous recovery, I worked my heel free as Jack steered me to the exit. I was too embarrassed to stay another minute as Jack was. We made a hasty exit. I hoped Ginger would understand the reason I didn't say goodbye to her. This dancing fiasco was too humiliating for Jack, the Secretary, Vice-President, and me. Surely Jack would convey my apologies to Secretary Stanley at the office and explain the reason I fell—nothing to do with him.

Despite all the drama, Jack had two copies made of the photo of the Secretary and Ginger dancing together. They both autographed it to the other, and it is a keepsake framed forever.

On this trip to D.C., Ginger had given 60 pages of her autobiography to Jack to read and critique. Unfortunately, he felt it was not publishable for a variety of reasons. When Ginger received his assessment, she was crushed and didn't know if she could pick up her pen to continue. Finally, she did, and it took her eleven years to finish it.

I had no idea that my life in the future would be inexplicably linked to that of Ginger Rogers. But that is another story...to be continued...!

CHAPTER SIXTEEN

SOCIALIZING WITH
THE SECRETARY OF STATE

In Washington, those in high places of government could socialize for lunch and dinner seven days a week, but the days are long and exhausting. That's why the unwritten rule of concluding parties at 9:30 p.m. is a good fallback to those who want to go home and get a good night's sleep. Jack declined 90% of our invitations because of his work schedule. The Secretary had to accept many more. They were obligatory for political and/or international reasons.

The Stanleys enjoyed our company and if we socialized to any degree, it was with them. Often, the Secretary would request that we be included in certain parties. On occasion, Mrs. Stanley would have a ladies coffee, and I would be invited.

One of the reasons we liked them so much was their genuineness. There was no pomposity or desire for self-glorification. They were unpretentious and sincere, and both had a great sense of humor.

For example, they invited us to the theatre on one particular evening while we were in New York. As they stepped out of the limousine and we followed behind them, the name "Stanley" traveled across the crowd.

"Mr. Secretary," I said. "Everyone seems to know your name. It spread through the crowd very quickly."

"Fame is so fleeting," he replied. "I remember after I served in the Norton administration that a colleague and I wrote a book on economics. We thought, because of our notoriety during those years, we would be reviewed by the top newspapers in the country. No one wanted to read it, much less review it."

"That's awful," I said.

"I had the same reaction," said Mrs. Stanley, laughing.

"Don't despair," smiled Stanley. "When I accepted this office, the reviewers rushed to dig it out of the mortuary to read and review it!"

"Were the reviews favorable?" I asked.

"Ginny, perhaps the Secretary would rather not answer that!" said Jack.

"As a matter of fact, it received very good reviews," he said.

After a good laugh, we went inside to find an usher to show us to our seats.

At intermission, we decided to stretch and stand in the lobby. Mr. Stanley recognized a colleague who came over to chat with us. He asked the Secretary if he had heard the latest joke going around about President Rowland.

"No, but I'd like to."

"The right hand doesn't know what the far right hand is doing!" the friend said.

Secretary Stanley laughed so hard, people turned to find out what was so funny. "That's a good one. I'll have to tell the President. He'll enjoy it."

When the final curtain came down, we were invited backstage to greet the actors. They all stood in a line across the stage to shake the Secretary and Mrs. Stanley's hands. Before he started down the line, he spoke a few words to the whole cast.

"You know, I've been playing New York, too, for the past ten or twelve days at the UN," he said. They laughed and applauded. Then, he said something complimentary to each performer.

Once the two weeks in New York were over, the Stanley entourage was happy to return to D.C. and the comforts of their own offices.

One day Victor Walker came to the Secretary's office and appeared very upset. Walker was a military genius and could speak sixteen languages, but in the everyday world, he did not navigate as smoothly.

"What's wrong, Vic?" Stanley asked.

"I've lost my wallet with my money and address book."

"That could be dangerous, Vic, if it got in the wrong hands. All our secrets, and yours too, could be revealed," said the Secretary, who was so amused.

Walker sat down on the sofa and said, "Mr. Secretary, you are very close to the truth."

"Where did you last see it?"

"I don't remember," he said.

"That's not a good sign for a man of your knowledge," spoofed Stanley.

Walker jumped up and said, "Oh my heavens!"

"What's wrong?"

"I think I've found it."

"Where?"

"Here in your sofa." He threw all the cushions on the floor and there, stuffed in a corner, was his wallet. "Thank God."

"Is the money still in it?" asked the Secretary.

"Every dollar and penny," he smiled, looking in various compartments.

"Vic, my office is the safest place to lose anything."

"I believe you," smiled Walker, stuffing his wallet in his back pocket and repairing the sofa.

Not long after this incident, for which Victor endured much teasing, the Secretary took Jack aside and said that he and his wife had been invited to Jean and Tim Barton's for dinner as guests of honor. Secretary Stanley asked Mrs. Barton if we could come as well. "Would you like to go?"

"I'll check with Ginny, but I'm sure we would be delighted to accept," said Jack.

"Mrs. Barton is a very bright woman and enjoys putting the press together with government officials," he said.

"I like her already," said Jack.

Of course we accepted. The day we were to attend, there was a long article in the Gazette about powerful women in D.C. and they referred to Jean Barton as a major hostess who gave smart parties. I told Jack about it, but I wasn't sure if he had time to read it.

On the night of the party, we were the first to arrive just as the security agents finished installing hot line telephones. Tim Barton was slumped in a chair waiting for the other guests to arrive.

"Did you see the article about you in the Gazette?" I asked Mrs. Barton.

"No, what did it say?"

"It was about the most powerful women in Washington, and you are considered a major hostess," I said.

"For someone who has worked most of my life, I resent being referred to as merely a hostess. It is so demeaning," she said.

Soon, the guests were all there. The Stanleys arrived shortly after we did. A famous columnist, who knew the same journalists in South Africa that we did, was among the guests. There was a Union leader with his European wife, a former Secretary of Defense, and a former Secretary of Commerce with other lesser luminaries.

The menu was fairly simple: salmon with capers to start, a Hungarian curry as the main course accompanied by a red cabbage salad, and a hot fruit compote for dessert.

Once we were all seated at the dinner table, Jean Barton tried to start a general conversation directed at the Secretary. He quickly fobbed it off to the Union leader's wife, who was seated next to him.

"As a true European, what do you think about Europe's place in the world today?" asked the Secretary.

"Sadly, Europe has lost its energy and its will, and I don't know why," she said.

Before that conversation could be explored, Tim Barton struggled to his feet to make a toast to the Stanleys. He couldn't remember their names at first. Finally, he did.

"I wonder how good, old, honest Gavin will survive in this town? It reminds me of what Lincoln said, 'I am nothing unless I have something of friendship at the bottom of me.' "

Secretary Stanley stood up immediately to accept Barton's toast.

"Thank you, Tim, for your kind words. For the most part, Abraham Lincoln was rarely wrong. Friendships, in the scheme of things, are very important. Olivia and I cherish the friendships of those at this table."

Jean picked up the conversation and asked the Secretary about his job as head of the State Department and its challenges.

"The hardest thing about being Secretary of State is refraining from giving all my time to the Middle East. I have to fight to make a trip to Canada or to celebrate Costa Rica's democracy. I could send seasoned ambassadors and people with expertise to these countries or I could make good use of the telephone. It is just as good. However, I don't know how long these diplomatic procedures would last!" he responded.

Then, Stanley's good friend, Paul Peters, stood with his wine glass in hand.

"I've known Gavin Stanley for thirty years and played many golf games with him. His character is revealed in the way he plays golf. Gavin drives longer and straighter than anyone else. Well, maybe he goes off to the right sometimes! (Laughter) And Gavin's wife is a diamond—a real gem. My wife and I drove up from New York City just to see them this evening," said Peters.

"Thank you, Paul. It's great to see you both. At this juncture and at the risk of boring our ladies, I'd like to relate a joke that Preston Hazib told me."

"Go right ahead," said Tim Barton. "I love jokes."

"Well, Jesus Christ and Moses were playing golf together. Moses was playing fine, but Jesus Christ couldn't hit the ball straight. Every time he stepped up to drive, the ball went into the woods or in the rough," he said as a few guests chuckled quietly. "Jesus Christ admired Arnold Palmer and wanted to play just like him. When they came up to a water hazard, Moses drove and went over the water near the green. Jesus Christ drove his ball and it went in the water. He walked on the water to go get the ball. Moses walked on the fairway to his ball. Some man in a twosome came up to Moses and saw the other player walking on water. He said to Moses, 'Who does that guy think he is? Jesus Christ?' "

"No," said Moses. "Arnold Palmer."

The men and all the guests laughed. At that point, we each turned to someone on our left or right to engage in conversation.

Bill McNeil, the former Secretary of Defense, and I found common ground about Cape Cod. He had just started to build a house on Martha's Vineyard. Although, Jack and I were on the mainland, McNeil and I were lyrical about the wonders of Cape Cod and its medicinal magic to wash away worries. We agreed how different it was from the pressures of D.C. In further conversation, we touched on the Vietnam War.

"We lived in Hong Kong during the Vietnam years—TET offensive, etc.," I said.

"How did you feel about the War?" he asked.

"At the time, I was hawkish because my husband was, and I thought the domino theory might turn Southeast Asia to communism," I replied.

"Do you feel the same today?" he asked.

"Not really."

"What changed your mind?" he probed.

"Hindsight. Also I felt sorry for General Westmoreland. The White House tied his hands and he couldn't do what a General should do in a war. On the other hand, the terrain in that country was too difficult for big, brawny American soldiers. The Vietcong were small and slight and could move around the dense, hilly jungle without any problems. The purpose for our being there was questioned and protested here in this country. Soldiers felt that the American public was not behind them," I said.

"You really did shift your position," he said.

"If we had remained as advisors instead of participants in the war, maybe things would have been different," I mused. "There is a time for war and a time for peace. The only good thing about any war is that we become familiar with the culture, geography, and ideals of the country we are battling."

"That's an interesting point of view," he said.

"Communism in Asia was never a threat," I said.

At that moment, I felt a woman's hands wrap around my throat. It was the Hungarian wife of the Union leader. She lifted me straight up in the air.

"How dare you! Communism in Europe was brutal and tortuous in the Gulag. My brother spent years in there. It was a dreadful threat. You don't know what you're talking about. Do you understand?"

My eyes were bulging as she held me fast. I nodded as best I could. She started to shake my head. I mouthed "HELP." I was sure I was going to choke to death. All the guests seemed frozen to their chairs. Finally, Bill McNeil stood on my chair and grabbed me under my arms to relieve the pressure of her hands around my neck. As he did so, his jacket ripped right down the middle of his back.

"Oh my God, my suit!" He dropped me and I fell on the floor beside the table. The husband of the woman stood up.

"Katerina, there was no need for that display of emotion. Come back to your seat!" She obeyed him and apologized.

Meanwhile, I had crawled under the table to Jack's knees and pulled myself up onto his lap. The two thumbprints on my neck had turned purple, and I still couldn't speak.

Naturally, the Bartons were embarrassed. Jean tried to get the conversation back on track, and everyone tried to help her in order to distract from the traumatic scene that had just happened. Once I recovered from shock, I slipped off Jack's lap and moved around the table to sit silently in my chair.

As we finished after dinner coffee at the table, everyone started to make an exit with lavish goodbyes. To me, the Jean Barton party didn't disappoint, but my neck was still throbbing. I hadn't meant to offend the European lady, but I must have pushed an emotional button to cause her reaction. Bill McNeil was too distressed over his torn jacket and he was the first one to leave.

Just before the Secretary left, I whispered in a hoarse voice to him, "How was your golf game today. Did you make any birdies?"

His eyes lit up. "On the longest, hardest hole at Burning Tree Country Club, I had a birdie on par 4. My drive was long and my second shot with a 3 wood went up on the green and hit the pin. It bounced six inches from the hole and I sank the putt!"

"Congratulations. That must have been a thrill," I said in a husky voice. "It was."

The Union leader apologized to me for his wife's behavior. So did Jean Barton as we were saying our farewells and thanks for the evening.

$$\ast \quad \ast \quad \ast \quad \ast$$

Our next social meeting with the Stanleys was an unusual one. The Secretary invited his key staff people and their wives to a special viewing of a nuclear war film, called <u>The Day After.</u> It was filmed in Lawrence, Kansas, and showed the after effects of a nuclear attack. We watched the film in Stanley's conference room and then adjourned to a more comfortable area in his office.

As was his custom, the Secretary went around the room and asked everyone's opinion. Without exception, each person, including Jack, praised the film for presenting the reality of such an event in a raw and vivid way. I was seated toward the end of the long line of guests.

"Ginny, do you agree that the film was effective," Stanley asked.

"No, sir," I said.

Everyone sat up in amazement and looked at me with great disdain.

"Why do you say that?" he asked.

"It was badly done and too contrived. Therefore, it was not credible," I replied.

"I think she's wrong," declared one of the wives. "How does she know it was badly done?"

"Ginny, can you defend yourself to this critic?" he said in a humorous mood.

"Well, sir, perhaps my credentials might persuade her to at least consider my point of view," I said facetiously.

"Go ahead and try!"

"Well, I do have a Masters in acting and directing. In my earlier years, I was a professional actress in theatre in New York, East Africa, South Africa, and Hong Kong. For the past six years, I've been a drama critic and written more than 25 plays. More importantly, I've been trained by Elliot Norton, the doyen of drama critics in Boston, how to use a critical eye on films and stage plays. To me, The Day After is overdone and transparent. The scenes and people just aren't believable," I replied. "May I add that if British filmmakers had produced it, I might have an entirely different commentary," I said.

"I still disagree with you," said the woman.

"Do you have anything positive to say about this film, Ginny?" asked Jack's male colleague.

"Yes. Forget the poor quality of acting and directing. The theme of the film makes the United States ever more aware that we have to continue talking disarmament with the Soviet Union to preserve the human family. This is a good thing. Despite our differing viewpoints, we can coexist harmoniously. The film, badly done or not, makes us want world peace more than ever because destruction is an untenable alternative. Therefore, I think the message of the film was more powerful than the visual presentation," I said.

A few people applauded. It was time to leave. Although Jack may not have agreed with me, he knew my professionalism was at least worth considering. I was annoyed at myself for that outburst and didn't mean to extol my own oeuvre, but she got my goat and I just had to respond. She had every right to her opinion as I had to mine.

Soon after the film party, Olivia Stanley gave a coffee in her suburban home in Maryland. It was to welcome two wives of two husbands who had joined Stanley's staff. The Secretary's house was set on a small knoll and was a pretty, white clapboard style with black shutters.

In the hall, one of Mr. Stanley's secretaries was handing out name tags.

"Good morning, Mrs. Hunter. I thought you were very brave to voice your views on that film," she whispered. She handed me my name tag.

"Thank you. I think it was more honest than brave. I just said what I really thought," I said.

"Mr. Stanley seemed to be amused," she said.

"As long as he wasn't upset."

"Oh no. I think he admires your forthrightness," she smiled. "Don't forget to sign the guest book and go right through that archway to the dining room."

"Thank you."

I noticed what a beautiful blue, ultra-suede dress Mrs. Stanley was wearing with a multi-colored gold scarf.

"Mrs. Stanley, you look so pretty in that color. It matches your eyes," I said as I greeted her.

"Thank you, my dear. It's so good to see you. We're serving coffee at this end and tea at the other. On either side are sandwiches, cake, and fruit," she said.

"Looks elegant and delicious," I said.

After my cup was filled and my little plate full of the goodies, I circulated among the guests in the living room. I saw Phil Wolfe's wife, Myra, and gravitated to her.

"Hello, Ginny. You sure were brave to express your views on that film. I also remember that you were the only one to stand up for Martha Covington at the UN dinner in NYC," she said.

"I couldn't sit back and not say what I really believed," I told her. "What are you doing these days?"

"Writing my dissertation," she replied.

"Really? On what?"

"The Javanese language," she said.

"May I join you? I heard you mention Java," said Mrs. Hilder, whose husband had recently been appointed Ambassador to Indonesia.

"The three of us probably share a great love of the country and its people," I said.

"We do indeed," she said. "I'm back on home leave and can't wait to get back. Now what were you saying about the Javanese language?"

"I'm writing my dissertation about it for Johns Hopkins," Myra answered.

"Very ambitious," Mrs. Hilder said.

Then, the Chief of Protocol from the State Department, Laura Remington, joined our group. While Myra and Mrs. Hilder chatted about Indonesia, Laura and I engaged in conversation. She had just come back from Latin America, preparing for the Secretary's trip there. She raved about the orchids that the hotel management had put in her hotel room.

"When you're not in D.C., Ginny, what do you do?" she asked.

"Well, we have several weekly newspapers on Cape Cod that I help run. I write for the papers as a drama critic and also, I write plays."

"How fascinating. Writing plays is something I would really love to do," Laura said. She moved me into a corner for a private conversation. "You know, I've heard that the White House may be looking for someone to handle press matters. It might be perfect for you."

"Really? Can you elaborate?" I asked.

"No. It's a secret and you have to promise me not to tell your husband or anyone."

"Absolutely. No problem," I said. "You know, Laura, I don't think a job like that is for me. I can think of several people who might be perfect, including our friend, Kate Farrell."

"Kate Farrell? My relatives and hers could be related," she said. "Thank you for mentioning her."

The time passed too quickly and it was time to leave. I had a tennis date with Nancy Barr and her group in the afternoon, so I was anxious to get home and change my clothes. I never did tell Jack about the offer. I really didn't think it was serious anyway.

✶   ✶   ✶   ✶

Another special occasion with the Stanleys was down at The Homestead Hotel in Hot Springs, Virginia. The Secretary was speaking to the Business Council. It was a weekend affair, so the Stanleys flew down Friday afternoon.

After lunch on Friday, Jack and I drove through the green hills of Virginia to Hot Springs. Set among the Allegheny Mountains was this enormous old world hotel in red brick and white.

The lobby had ten columns and looked like a British hotel one might find in Singapore or India. We settled in our pristine room and meandered around the grounds. When we came back, there was a note in the box to meet the Stanleys in their suite for drinks at 6:00 p.m.

As we entered their suite that evening, I greeted Mrs. Stanley first and then, the Secretary. "Mr. Stanley, it's good to see you in Virginia."

"Mr., did you say?"

"Yes."

"No, no…it's Gavin," he said.

"But, sir, I've lived among the British too long to change my wicked ways," I said.

He laughed and asked how I'd been. I responded in the positive, but I wondered if he wasn't wooing me to keep Jack from leaving at the end of the year. We felt we had to get back to our newspapers. Money was missing there that couldn't be accounted for, and we had been absentee owners long enough.

The former CEO of Citibank and his wife came for drinks. We had met them before at the memorable UN dinner when I defended Martha Covington. They remembered the incident and me because of it. They were very cordial. That evening, Jack turned down two dinner invitations. Instead, we went to the main dining room to plow through their elaborate menu. After a salad and two appetizers, I skipped the entree because I was getting too full and went directly to the dessert, which was an exotic trifle.

The next morning, we attended the speech shared and given by the Secretary and Peter Vostra. Suddenly, I had a fit of coughing and couldn't stop. I motioned to Jack that I would excuse myself and go out for some water. I returned in time to hear the Secretary's speech.

In the afternoon, Mrs. Stanley invited me to go with her to the famous Warm Springs, five miles away, for a swim in one of the pools heated from the earth beneath. Her security man drove us. The swimsuits appeared to be made of flour sacks—unflattering, but practical. The water temperature was 96 degrees. It was like a sauna and our faces were smothered in steam. Once we were used to it, we floated on our backs, looking at the view through the glass ceiling.

We both almost drifted off to sleep. Even the security agent closed his eyes briefly. Suddenly, I heard some gurgling. I looked for Mrs. Stanley and she had disappeared. I dove under water and found her struggling to come to the surface. Now we both were underwater. I grabbed Mrs. Stanley's chin and pulled her to the surface. She gagged and blew out a mouthful of water. I swam with her over to the edge of the pool for Mr. Security to lift her out. Once she was rested, we went to the locker room and changed into our clothes. On the drive back, Mrs. Stanley kept patting my hand as if to thank me.

Jack and I dined and danced on Saturday night. On Sunday, we had an enormous breakfast, played tennis, packed, and left to drive home before lunch.

It was a change—a dramatic change from the pace of D.C.

★   ★   ★   ★

Because we had been entertained so many times by the Stanleys, I wanted to invite them for dinner at our home. They were the sort of people that wouldn't be offended by a simple, temporary place like this. It was sparsely furnished, but they wouldn't mind. I nagged Jack for two years to invite them, but he refused.

"Ginny, the security people would tear apart our house, installing hotline telephones. It would be a mess. It just isn't worth the trouble. Remember when the President and Mrs. Rowland went to the Stanleys for a home-cooked meal a couple of months ago? Not only did they install the phones, but the police blocked off the street. The place was swarming with security," he said.

"But the Secretary is not the President. It wouldn't be as bad," I pleaded.

"Think of our neighbors and the disruption to them."

"When we were at the Bartons, I don't remember any disruption," I said.

"Because they've been entertaining for years and their house has all the places for wires ready to be reopened. Forget it, Ginny," Jack said.

"Well, I did ask the Secretary once if they would like to come to dinner and he said yes."

"What do you expect him to say? He wouldn't dream of being impolite," Jack said.

"Jack, please ask them for dinner next Friday evening. If they can't come, I promise to drop the idea."

"Alright, alright," he responded.

"And don't pray that they won't be able to come," I said. He laughed in spite of himself.

Every day I nagged Jack about the invitation. I knew he didn't want to ask. One night he came home and said, "They're coming."

I was so excited that I jumped up and down like a child on a Pogo stick.

"You didn't tell me what time they should arrive."

"6:30."

"The State Department Security will come in the afternoon, so do all your shopping in the morning," Jack advised.

"I will. Thank you, Jack. I know you're dreading it."

"You're right."

At dinner, Jack told me about the future trips in the planning stage. They would be going to Mexico, Latin America, Miami, and Augusta.

"Augusta, Georgia?" I asked.

"To play golf with the President."

"That will make both of them happy," I said.

"Yes."

"And Latin America will be a change from the Middle East."

"True," he said. "Ginny, do you need someone to come help prepare the dinner?"

"Of course not," I said. I knew Jack was apprehensive over the whole dinner idea.

The next day, I sat down to plan how I would clean the house—one room at a time, starting with the upstairs. I would save the living room, kitchen, and guest bathroom for last. The dinner menu would be shrimp cocktail to start, steak with string beans, baked potato, and corn, plus some dinner rolls. For dessert, I would make a mango mousse. Oh, and our drink to begin with would be Sparkling Apple Cider. Jack and I didn't drink and didn't have a bar for those who indulged.

On Thursday, I did the final cleaning of the downstairs. It was a major project.

By Friday morning, I did the final food shopping, purchasing Angus beef and the rest of the menu items. After unloading the groceries from the car, I made the mango mousse and put it in the fridge to gel. I set the table for four. I was sorry Max couldn't join us, but he was now in college.

When two security men arrived in the afternoon, we walked all around the complex to determine the best place to drill holes in our condo for the telephone wires.

"If we do it in front, do you think it will be too conspicuous to our neighbors and arouse their curiosity?" I asked.

"Yes. Shall we do it from the back?"

"You can stand on a step-ladder from our deck," I said.

They examined every possibility inside and out. "The back it is," they said. "Would you prefer one big hole or two smaller ones?"

"What do you think?"

"Two smaller ones."

"Fine," I said.

"Where will you be most of the evening?"

"The living room and dining room," I said. "As you can see, they're very close to each other."

"We'll put the telephones in your living room and one of us will stand by them the whole time. One of us will be out front and a third security person out back," one of them said.

"Do you have to do this every day and night?"

"It's a 24-hour-job," he said. "We all have shifts."

"Would you excuse me while I take a shower?" I asked.

"Go ahead. We'll be wandering in and out of the main level," he said.

While the shower was going full tilt, I felt the drilling from outside shake the pipes and could hear a dull buzzing sound. It was unnerving. After washing my hair, I dried it and put curlers in. I slipped into a summery print dress and went down to the kitchen to start cutting the string beans and marinating the steaks to put under the broiler. Everything was on the stove by 6:25. I rushed upstairs to take the curlers out, brush my hair, and put on a dash of lipstick and change my dress.

The doorbell rang on the dot of 6:30. I knew it was the Stanleys and not Jack. Where was he? As I reached the bottom step, smoke filled the dining room and foyer. I dashed to the kitchen and found that the steaks under the broiler had caught fire. I turned it off and opened all the windows. It was too late. The smoke alarm went off. The doorbell rang again. I ran into the living room to ask one of the security agents for help in stopping the alarm.

Out of breath, I opened the front door and the smoke poured out, wrapping me in a cloud of fog as I stepped out of the cloud to greet them.

"Hi, Mr. Secretary and Mrs. Stanley. Do you mind waiting outside while the smoke escapes?" I asked.

"Ginny, is everything all right?" Secretary Stanley asked.

"It will be in a few minutes," I said.

Jack pulled alongside the Secretary's car and jumped out. "What's wrong?"

"A little fire from the broiler," I said.

"Oh my God. The Stanleys can't be subject to that smoke. What are you doing to clear it?" he asked.

"All the windows are open and the security man is stopping the smoke alarm," I said.

"Sir," said the agent. "I think if you drive around and enter from the rear entrance, it might be free of smoke. This will clear shortly," he said.

"Never mind," said the Secretary. "We'll swing around to the back."

"I'm so sorry," I said coughing.

"Everything will be fine," said Mrs. Stanley, who now was feeling quite sorry for me.

Jack and the Stanleys entered through the yard, up on the deck, and through the porch door.

"It seems fine in here," observed Mrs. Stanley.

"Please come in and make yourselves comfortable," I said. "I'll get us something cold to drink."

"Fine," said Mrs. Stanley. The Secretary appeared ill-at-ease.

I dashed to the kitchen and put the steaks in a frying pan to finish cooking. The string beans looked a bit overdone, but the baked potatoes seemed to have survived the fire. I uncorked the cider, poured them in four fluted glasses, and carried the tray to the living room. Jack took the tray and handed them to the Stanleys. I remembered the cocktail napkins, but had forgotten snacks. I did have some mixed nuts in the cabinet and quickly poured them into a dessert bowl that seemed appropriate. I handed these to Jack while I prepared the shrimp cocktails and put them on the table.

I joined our guests and sipped my drink, trying to look calm. Jack and the Secretary were deep in conversation. Mrs. Stanley was looking at me strangely. Jack noticed her staring. Now he was looking at me. He came over to me and leaned down to whisper in my ear.

"What?" I asked.

This time he whispered louder. "You have a curler in your hair!"

"Oh no! Excuse me." I rushed upstairs and saw the mishap. I removed the red curler from the back of my head and brushed it out. That awful feeling in my stomach was growing. Jack was right. We never should have done this.

Sheepishly, I came back to the living room. They had finished their drinks. I picked up mine, but I decided not to apologize. It was too painful.

"The drink was delicious," said Mrs. Stanley. "It's been a long time since we've had Sparkling Cider. I'd forgotten how good it is."

I knew she was trying to save me from utter humiliation. "Shall we go to the dining room for the first course? The smoke has finally disappeared," I said.

There were place cards, so everyone found their seat.

"Shrimp cocktail. My favorite," said the Secretary with an amused look.

"I'm so glad," I said. We all enjoyed the shrimp and talked about the eastern shore of Maryland and the wonderful raw oysters there.

"Excellent, my dear," commented Mrs. Stanley. "May I help you?"

"No, thank you," I said. "I have everything under control, I think." Everyone laughed. Even the security men sniggered.

The steaks looked burnt, so I tried to scrape them with a knife. The string beans were limp, but the corn and baked potatoes were perfect. I fixed each plate and placed them before Mrs. Stanley and the Secretary first. They looked strangely at them.

"You've gone to a lot of trouble with these beautiful Angus steaks," said Mrs. Stanley.

At that very instant, the dog leapt onto the table.

"Ginger! Get down from there!" Jack said. The dog snatched the Secretary's steak, jumped down, and ran to her bed in the living room to chew her way through the whole steak.

Jack ran into the living room. "Ginger, drop that steak." Ginger growled.

"Jack, there's no point in making her drop it. The Secretary can't eat a steak mauled by our dog! I do apologize. She has never jumped on the table before," I said helplessly.

"She's probably never seen or smelled Angus steak before," said the Secretary.

"That's probably true. May I have your plate, sir?" I asked. He handed me his plate and I placed my steak on it.

"I won't hear of it," he said.

"Mr. Secretary, I have lost my appetite," I said.

Mrs. Stanley was now trying to cut her steak. It was so tough that her knife slipped and the meat skidded on the floor. Everyone was speechless.

Suddenly, I found my voice. "Ginger!" I called. She came running and grabbed the steak, taking it to her bed to chew a second slab of wonderful meat. By now, the security men and the Stanleys were laughing uncontrollably. Jack and I were not. I was close to tears and ran to the bathroom to sob and wipe my tears.

Jack knocked on the door. "Ginny, you have to come out and act like a hostess to your guests."

"I will," I said through a film of tears.

"Would you excuse my wife? I think she is pretty upset," said Jack going back to the table.

"Jack, I've never had such a good time. This is better than Irma Bombeck and your dog is the star of the evening!" said Stanley.

When I came out, my eyes were red. The Secretary stood up and put his arm around me. "Don't worry, Ginny, this could happen to anyone. What would you like us to do?"

"Why doesn't Jack go to the Roy Rogers Restaurant down the street for fried chicken, French fries, and coleslaw," I said.

"Perfect solution. Olivia and I like their fried chicken. Let one of the security men pick it up for us," said the Secretary.

"Sir, I insist on paying after this unforgivable disaster," said Jack, pulling out his wallet and giving the agent enough money for our dinner.

"Fine," nodded Stanley.

We adjourned to the living room to wait for the fried chicken. Once it came, we all trooped back to the table. I passed the empty plates and lots of napkins and everyone dug in and seemed to enjoy every bite. After everyone was finished, I served the mango mousse for dessert. The Stanleys loved it and complimented me on such a tasty dessert.

Before we could drink our coffee, the hotline telephone started to ring. Apparently, the President spoke to the Secretary and said there was an international emergency and he needed him to come right away to the Oval Office with Jack. In minutes, the house was empty.

Both Stanleys thanked me and apologized for their early departure.

"My dear Ginny, don't condemn yourself. You have given me something to remember forever. In my daily routine, I seldom have laughter. Your dog has given me such comic pleasure. Now I have to return to the seriousness of global affairs." They both hugged me.

The Diplomatic Security said they would return tomorrow to dismantle the wires.

After I shut the door, the sudden silence in our condo was overwhelming. I died a thousand deaths in recalling every disaster of the evening and suffered a second time. I wished I could start the whole evening over. Even the dog seemed forlorn with her ears down and eyes full of guilt, although she was licking her lips with great pleasure. I was sure the Stanleys were consoling Jack in the limo and assuring him of their great amusement and compassion. The Secretary probably told him of his fondness for the "I Love Lucy" television series and thought he had actually been in an episode tonight.

Did I just go through a nightmare or was this real? Unfortunately, it was all too real. Even painful to write this down in my diary—write here, write now!

▼

CHAPTER SEVENTEEN

GLOBAL MAGAZINE AND THE HOMELESS

During the time we were in Washington, it was full of morning coffees and ladies luncheons at private clubs. I've met some interesting women at most of them. Lucille Post, a military wife on the fringes of society, managed to surround herself with original types. Wearing white gloves and Ferragamo shoes, she could fit into any group as its peer.

One time I was included in her group of fourteen at the City Tavern Club in Georgetown for luncheon. After we all arrived, she went around the table and introduced everyone with a flamboyant, short bio. I was so flustered when she came to me, I don't remember what she said.

Once she finished, someone said for her to give an update on her own activities. With a flourish of modesty, she told of her involvement with the National Society of Arts and Letters and her latest biography on John F. Kennedy for young adults.

Our menu was already selected for us by Mrs. Post.

Deirdre Bradford immediately started the conversation. "My dear Lucille, you forgot to tell your guests that I am a professional woman in the art of marriage."

"My apologies, Deirdre. Would you like to give us a brief synopsis?"

"If your guests will indulge me?" We all nodded. "Well, I met my first husband at a dance. He was a gorgeous 6'4" hunk. All the girls were mad for him. After four dates, he proposed. We married, and he went off to war while I went to university. When he came back, I discovered he was undersexed—once a year to be specific. I knew I'd never get pregnant at that rate, so I divorced him. And by the way, he had four wives after me. Don't ask me if he had children because I don't know, but I suspect not! My number two was a millionaire. I met him in a cab in front of Grand Central Station. I asked him if he would drop me at the Waldorf. He agreed. On the way, he asked me for dinner that evening. He was recently divorced from a cheating wife. When I said I had a date, he told me to break it or he would never see me again. Naturally I broke it. We met in December and married in February. That turned into twenty years of a happy marriage until he died. My third and final husband is a Washington lawyer. And there you have two successful walks down the aisle!"

"Do you recommend three or four marriages to find happiness?" asked Lucille.

"Happiness and wealth. The first husband usually has nothing, but keep trying," she said.

An Alabama debutante, Cassandra B. Portland, was not to be outdone by a Yankee. She leapt into the conversation with a riveting story. "Now, Lucille, if you would forgive me, I'd like to match Deirdre's tale by one of my own."

"The stage is yours, Cassy B.," laughed Lucille.

"I want to tell your lovely guests how and why I managed to be hired by Global Magazine. As you know, I married a lovely, darling man from New Hampshire. I was on my way to an annual reunion with my relatives in Birmingham when I fell in love," she said.

"Cassy B., not you, too. Your husband is every woman's dream," said Lucille.

"I fell in love, honey, but not with a man!"

"A woman?" gasped Lucille.

"A car!"

"A car?" Lucille asked.

"A Studebaker."

"A STUDEBAKER?" we all said at once.

"How could anyone fall in love with that car?" Lucille asked.

"I did."

"What was the catch?" Lucille baited her.

"It cost $80 a month and my husband couldn't swing it," she said.

"What happened?"

"I told my husband of my deep desire and..."

"And?"

"And he wanted to know how I was going to pay for it?"

"What did you say?" I asked.

" 'Sugar, I'll just have to get a job.' Well of course, he didn't believe I could get a job, but I was determined," said Cassy B. "I saw an ad for a filing clerk at <u>Global Magazine</u> and went right over to apply."

"Did you get it?" I asked.

"During the interview, the man said I was overqualified and wondered why in the world I wanted the job. I told him the truth—the car. Maybe he felt sorry for me, but he said they had another job that might be more suitable and they'd been looking for someone for two years. I don't know if he was telling the truth, but I accepted."

"What was the job?" asked Lucille.

"I don't know. I never asked and was afraid to ask. They told me to turn up on Monday in the library," said Cassy B.

"What did you do all day?" I asked.

"Without anyone telling me what to do, I started reading the back issues of the magazine, and I started writing memos to the editor, suggesting story ideas. The first one was to trace Robert Louis Stevenson's steps on the donkey trail. The editor thanked me. Finally, I wrote a memo suggesting we do a series on following the footsteps of Paul in Biblical land. The editor invited me in to the office to say it was about time I started writing for the magazine."

"Did you ever find out what you were supposed to do in the library?" I asked.

"Yes. I was hired as a research assistant for any and all of the writers. They were never told and I was never told, so we just smiled at each other," Cassy B. said. "Thirty years later I did the Stevenson trek and went down the Amazon before becoming editor."

"What about the Studebaker?"

"I bought it and loved it for a couple of decades," she replied.

The conversation came to a standstill as we began eating our meal. Soon people chatted with people on either side of them. I was so impressed with Mrs. Portland that she and I connected on newspapers and on reminiscences of Alabama.

"What do you do at your papers?" she asked me.

"I write feature stories and cover theatre as a drama critic," I said.

"Would you like to freelance for our magazine while you're here?"

"Would I? You bet," I said.

"What's your interest?" she asked.

"The homeless in D.C." I said.

"Send me a memo. I'll get you a photographer and a small tape recorder."

"I'll do that," I said. She gave me her card. I left the luncheon elated and started thinking about the feature story on the homeless. I found the local library in McLean and began researching. I decided not to tell Jack until the story was printed. It was to be a surprise.

In the background search, I learned that Mitch Snyder was the key to learning everything about the homeless in D.C. He was a Madison Avenue advertising executive, who suddenly up and left his wife and two sons and disappeared, stealing a car to get himself across the country. He was caught and landed in prison for a couple of years where the Berrigan brothers were also incarcerated for their protests against the Vietnam War. Once he was out, he returned to his family, but after a year, he went homeless in D.C. There, he took over an empty Federal building and used it to house and feed more than 100 homeless folks. He formed a non-profit company and the Rowland administration leased it to the company for one dollar a year. Mitch became such a celebrity that a movie, starring Martin Sheen, was filmed about him.

I put together a proposal for <u>Global Magazine</u>. Cassy B. called me after she received it and it was a go. She asked me to let her know when I needed a photographer. First, I had to contact Mitch. He seemed pleased to cooperate with the magazine, and we made an appointment at 2:00 p.m. on Tuesday. The photographer met me there and gave me a tape recorder to use if I wanted.

Mitch was charismatic. He greeted us warmly and showed us around the facility. The government hadn't made repairs, so they found volunteers to fix electricity and plumbing. They installed a huge kitchen for feeding large groups every day. The photographer snapped every inch of it.

We went to Mitch's office to talk. He was obsessed with helping the homeless.

"What is the worst thing about being homeless?" I asked.

"Being invisible."

I nodded in agreement.

"Invisible to the public. They treat us as if we don't exist and without respect. Every homeless person will tell you the same thing," Mitch said.

"Are most of the homeless on drugs and alcohol?" I asked.

"Of course not. Some are, but there are those who have mental problems or just don't have any money. Then, too, there are some who are absolute geniuses," he said.

"Geniuses? Why are they on the streets? If they're smart, they must be smart enough to get a job?" I asked.

"The trouble is, geniuses can't fit in. They don't like structure or to be told what to do. They are smart misfits and they can walk rings around us intellectually. Then, there are the wealthy and talented ones like Phil Razen. He had everything—he had a Jaguar and a talent for painting. One day he vanished and was seen homeless on the streets. No one knew why. Maybe he didn't think his art was good enough. You never know."

"What happened to him?" I asked

"He was sleeping under a car and the car ran over him, and he died. There are a million stories like his."

"That's so tragic. Do the non-geniuses accept the structure?" I wanted to know.

"Most of them despise rules. They don't like to come into the building at 5:00 p.m. and out at 5:00 a.m. They feel trapped, but they get food, a shower, and a place to sleep. It's a trade- off for the basics. And they don't trust each other," he said.

"What do you mean?"

"I mean, they are afraid of being robbed of money and possessions by their fellow homeless. So coming in here has its risks for them," he said.

"Do you have any CIA or FBI types that disguise themselves as homeless?"

"Sometimes," he nodded.

"What are they looking for?"

"Drug dealers," he said.

"Anything else?"

"The IRA," he said.

"Why do they mix with the homeless?"

"To sell heroin to drug dealers or individuals," he replied.

"What does the IRA do with the money?"

"Send it to Ireland," he said.

"For what? Weapons?"

"Not so much anymore. It's to buy land and give money to the Catholics," he said.

"Not for the war between the Protestants and Catholics?"

"No. The Protestants in the past have had all the money, power, and land. This is to level the playing field economically, so there is no need for war," he said.

"I've never heard that idea before."

"Most people haven't," he smiled.

"What about Lord Byron?" I asked.

"You know him?"

"Yes."

"He's been a fixture outside the State Department for 15 years or more," he stated.

"How does he eat? I know he sleeps there."

"We feed him once a day and a couple of friends are trustworthy to stay on the grate while he does whatever he has to do," Mitch laughed.

"Well, we want to go over and see him now," I said. "Do you want us to take anything to him?"

"Yes. I'll get his main meal for you to take." We waited and he came back with a Styrofoam box overflowing. We thanked him for his time. He asked me to let him know when the article would appear. I said I would.

We took one car over to Lord Byron's and brought him his dinner.

"Lord Byron, Mitch gave us your main meal," I said. Without even greeting me, he grabbed it and began eating. The photographer took lots of pictures. When he finished, he stretched out on the grate and promptly went to sleep. This was a great shot. I knew I couldn't interview him like this and would have to come back. We left and I drove the photographer to his car. He went to the office and I went home to type up my notes.

As I walked in the door, the phone was ringing. It was Jack. Something terrible happened in Beirut. He would be at the office until late tonight. I offered to bring dinner. He said to arrive about seven. McDonald's, Wendy's, or fried chicken? McDonald's it was. So I changed into something a little dressier. I worked at my typewriter with the notes and decided to do the rest of the interview with Lord Byron after Jack and I finished our fast food. I wired myself with the small tape recorder and tested it to make sure it was working.

At 6:15, I drove to McDonald's and loaded up with hamburgers, fries, and salad before driving into the city. Fortunately, the traffic was coming out of the city and the drive was a breeze. I drove into the State Department garage. They knew me by now and waved me to a place.

"Good evening, Mrs. Hunter. Are you here for a special reason?" Security asked.

"Taking dinner to my hubby," I told them.

"Take the working elevator, Mrs. Hunter," the security guard said.

Jack and I retreated to his office and munched on our dinner. He had missed lunch, so I was glad I had brought three hamburgers for him.

"Wonderful, thanks," he said. "Sorry, I have to get back to work."

"No problem. See you when I see you. Can I ask what happened?" I asked.

"You'll see it on the news," he said. I could see he was distracted.

I waved goodbye to the assistants who were all busy. When the elevator hit the garage, I walked up the ramp and outside. I went around the corner to the grate and saw Lord Byron. He was huddled in a fetal position. I turned on my tape recorder as I knelt down to him.

"Lord Byron," I whispered. No movement. "Lord Byron?"

Suddenly the very still figure sat straight up and flashed a knife at me. "I'm not Lord Byron," he said through gritted teeth.

"Where is he?"

"None of your damn business. Who are you?"

"His friend," I said.

"Well, get out of here!"

"Not till you tell me where he is," I said.

"He's peeing."

"Then, why are you wearing his clothes?" I asked.

"Shut up!" he hissed and pointed the knife at my throat.

"Who are you?" I asked.

"Don't you know when it's time to leave before you get stabbed to death?"

"I want to know who you are!" I said.

"I'm a REVO," he replied, putting his eyes right opposite mine. They were black eyes and wild.

"What's a Revo?"

"You stupid bitch! A Revo is a Revolutionary," he said with utter disdain.

"Are you American?" I asked.

"YES!"

"What is a Revo for or against?" I wondered.

"Against America forcing Democracy on other countries that don't want it," he declared.

"What countries?"

"China, Russia, the Middle East, and Cuba just for a start," he said.

"If you're American, why are you against giving democracy to other countries?"

"Because it should come from within each country. It should be a grass roots revolution—not from the top down—not from missionary Americans," he sputtered. "Our government—our foreign policy doesn't understand this."

"Are you a student?" I asked.

"I go to McGill," he announced proudly.

"Are you Canadian?"

"NO!"

"Where are the Revos based?" I asked.

"Everywhere," he said.

"I mean the headquarters?"

"North Dakota," he said.

"What is your mission?"

"To kill the Secretary of State!" he said.

"You can't do that!"

"I can and I will," he said.

"But he's a reasonable man. He listens to all the countries you mentioned. He doesn't impose democracy arbitrarily on any country," I said.

"Yes, he does."

"Is that why you're here on this grid?" I asked.

"I am going into the State Department through the tunnel under this grid and you're going with me as my hostage," he said, now brandishing a gun. "One wrong move and you'll be my first casualty."

"Tell me one thing," I asked.

"Hurry up!"

"Where is the homeless man who is always here?" I asked.

"Over there in the bushes, tied up with duct tape. He's from the looney bin. Thinks he's some kind of Lord," he said.

It was almost dark. I hoped I had everything on tape. He lifted the grid off.

"You go first. Any false move and I'll fill your brain with bullets. When we reach the garage, open the grid, and get out and hide behind a car. When I get out, I'll take off this masquerade and wear my suit and tie underneath. Do you know where the elevator is?" he asked.

"Yes."

"How come you know?" he asked.

"My husband works here," I said.

"Perfect. If you don't figure a way for us to get up to the Secretary's office, I'll kill you and everyone else who gets in my way until I get to Stanley's office and assassinate him. Do you understand me?" he said.

The thought of the slaughter he planned was too much for me. I had to cooperate with him; there wouldn't be a way to stop him, I was sure. "Yes, I understand."

"Okay, wedge yourself in the tunnel shaft," he motioned with his gun.

I slid down the shaft, aware that the Revo was right above me. When I reached the grid at the bottom, I lifted it slowly out and placed it on the garage floor. I wiggled out and dusted my dress off. The young man came after me. He took off the homeless clothes and folded them right underneath the open grid. He looked quite decent in his dark suit and tie. He smoothed his hair.

"What's your first name?" I asked.

"Richard."

We started walking toward the elevator. My heart was pounding as loud as thunder. The young man had the nozzle of the gun at my back.

"Mrs. Hunter, I thought you had gone home," said the guard.

"No, I wanted my nephew to meet the Secretary for a few minutes. He's from McGill University in Canada. I know they are all busy, dealing with an explosive issue, but we'll only be there a matter of minutes," I lied.

"Fine. I'll call his assistant," said the guard. He went inside his booth and made the call.

"The Secretary would be happy to meet your nephew," he said. "Take the working elevator."

"Thank you," I said. He nodded and smiled.

The elevator seemed to take a century to reach the seventh floor. I was speechless and wondered how this would be resolved. An assistant met us as the doors opened and led us to Stanley's office. The gun was still at my back.

The Secretary came out of his office to the living room area. "Ah, Ginny, I'd be delighted to meet your nephew."

"This is Richard, Mr. Secretary," I said with a shaky voice.

What happened next took place in slow motion. The Secretary put out his hand. The Revo took the gun from my back and raised it toward the Secretary's head. I spun around, grabbed his wrist, and started to struggle. The gun went off and the bullet went right into my shoulder. All hell broke loose. The women screamed and fell to the floor while the men wrestled the man to the ground. Blood from my shoulder was everywhere. Somehow, I didn't feel anything. I was dazed. Alarms began ringing at a high pitch. In minutes the office was swarming with security police, wielding guns. Chaos was breaking all around us.

"My God, Ginny, are you all right?" shouted the Secretary.

I could only nod. My knees were buckling.

"Get Jack up here," he said. "Get some towels to stop the bleeding!"

"Someone get the wheelchair in the closet. Hurry!"

Within minutes, Jack rushed in and was stunned at seeing me in the wheelchair, covered in blood. "What...what happened?"

"She saved my life, that's what happened," said the Secretary. "That lunatic held her hostage and shot her in the shoulder." The Secretary motioned to the subdued man, who was being taken from the room. "The bullet was meant for me, but she took it for me," the Secretary said with emotion.

"Oh my God, Ginny. Are you okay?" Jack asked. For once, he was almost speechless.

I nodded

"Who is he?"

"A Revolutionary."

"You better get her to the hospital, Jack."

"Call an ambulance ," someone said.

"Absolutely not. Jack, you take her," said the Secretary.

"I will, sir!"

I suddenly remembered Lord Byron. "Mr. Secretary, you've got to save the homeless man. He's tied up in the bushes across from the garage," I said, feeling dizzy.

"Don't worry, we'll do it. When you're better, we want to know how this happened," the Secretary said.

"I'll tell Jack," I said. At that point, I fainted.

Jack pushed me into the elevator. When the guard at the exit saw Jack and me, he said, "Mr. Hunter, what happened to Mrs. Hunter?"

"She was shot."

"Shot?" he asked.

"By that young man."

"Her nephew?"

"He wasn't her nephew, he was a Revolutionary."

"Good God, I had no idea!"

"She wants you to rescue the homeless man who is tied up in the bushes across the street."

I tugged on Jack's sleeve to tell him something. He leaned down. I was conscious enough to mumble in Jack's ear where Lord Byron's clothes were.

"His clothes are near the grid in the garage," said Jack.

"I'll do that," said the guard, hoping he wouldn't lose his job.

Jack put me in the back seat of the car and took me to the hospital. The emergency room operated right away and removed the bullet, bandaged the wound, and put my arm in a sling. They removed the wire and tape recorder, giving it to Jack.

"What's this?" Jack asked, mystified.

"I put it on for an interview and was blindsided by that crazy and it's all on tape," I said, still in pain.

"Oh my God."

"Can you take me home, Jack? I don't want to stay here. I'll be all right," I said.

"Are you sure?"

"Yes."

Jack drove me home. On the way, he asked me questions about how this happened. I slowly explained about the homeless story I was writing and how I hoped to tape Lord Byron after I left him earlier. Instead, the Revolutionary was there on the grate, intending to kill the Secretary.

Jack was astonished, and contemplated what might have happened if I or the Secretary or both of us had been killed. It was too awful to think about. Once we were home, he helped me out of the car and walked me slowly up to the bedroom. He gently undressed me and eased me into bed. I wasn't hungry and was soon asleep. Jack sat beside me for quite a time and then headed back to the office, confident that I was well enough to leave and needed uninterrupted sleep. He left me a note and said to call him if I needed anything. I had seen in his eyes that he knew he had almost lost me forever.

Everyone in the Secretary's office was still shaken by the assassination attempt. Jack explained what really happened. They were shocked even more.

"How's Ginny?" they asked. Jack assured them I was going to be all right after the emergency operation and that I had insisted on going home.

"My God, Jack, if Ginny hadn't been here, I'd be a goner!" said the Secretary.

"I don't mean this to be funny, sir, but she would do anything for you and Mrs. Stanley," Jack said.

"Even an assassin's bullet?"

"Apparently so," said Jack.

"I'll never forget this," said Stanley. "Never."

"Sir, this is the tape recorder Ginny was wearing for an interview on the homeless man when the Revo flashed his gun at her and took her hostage. Everything that happened is captured on tape. It should be fascinating."

"My God! That's amazing. I'll get it to security right away."

It took me several weeks to recover. I was glad it was my left shoulder. At least I could use my right hand on the typewriter. I was getting the homeless story ready for Cassy B.

However, the Secretary had Jack ask me not to publish the part about the gunman and my injury. He wanted it kept under wraps in case there might be a copy-cat attempt. I reluctantly agreed, but it was to protect him. I was tempted to tell Cassy B., but I knew it would spread like wildfire.

When the story came out, the photographs were spectacular. The article wasn't too bad either. I dropped a copy off for Mitch Snyder, and he seemed really pleased. Even Jack was impressed.

One afternoon, the Secretary asked me to come to the office for a special occasion to celebrate the homeless feature story. When I arrived, Mrs. Stanley was there, Jack's colleagues, and the Secretary's staff. Someone held up the magazine and they all clapped. I must have turned many shades of red.

Then, the Secretary approached me with a box. He opened it and took out a large medal.

"Ginny, this isn't the Medal of Freedom, but a one-of-a-kind Medal of Bravery, made especially for you. On the back, it says, 'For Virginia Hunter in her heroic display of bravery.' " He placed it around my neck and everyone applauded. Even the security guard from the garage was there. He applauded the hardest.

"I don't know what to say," I said. "Except this is an honor. I'm sure anyone in my position would have done the same thing to protect the Secretary of State."

"Ginny, if you ever considered another profession, I think the CIA would be glad to hire you!" said the Secretary. Everyone laughed and clapped.

CHAPTER EIGHTEEN

▼

TIDBITS AND BEAUTY TIPS

Politics and parties are at the center of Washington life, but not exclusively. The arts play a huge role in filling the niches of the soul. Theatre throbs nightly at the Kennedy Center and a number of other theatres in D.C. Concerts and symphonies satisfy the lovers of music. Dance troupes come and go. Sophisticated lectures abound. There is something for the palette of literary aficionados, too. Art and history exhibitions rotate in and out of the museums. Naturally, there are a whole range of ethnic restaurants to attract any gourmet lovers.

Because of this D.C. variety, I want to record tidbits about some of these from my own personal experiences. They have no particular order, but will help me remember in future years when I thumb through this journal to remind me in a few sentences or paragraphs what I did and what I observed.

✷   ✷   ✷   ✷

Some of our friends from Asia days were posted in or retired to D.C. One such friend, M.V. Trenton, was number three in the political section of the American Embassy in Jakarta, responsible for learning about the women and students in Indonesia; it was an important assignment because the students were part of the uprising against Sukarno and communism during the 1960s.

She invited me to a lecture at the Asia Society by a former ambassador to Indonesia. Jack and I came to know him and rented his house for two months while Jack researched his book on the coup of Sukarno. It was a huge home with eleven servants.

Anyway, the focus of the ambassador's talk was on those four years, resulting in the downfall of Sukarno and the crushing of communism by students and the military. That was familiar territory for Miss Trenton and me. He was very upbeat about the economic recovery of Indonesia after the coup. Inflation was reduced and oil exports were increasing as well as the production of rice. However, he chastised American businessmen for not exercising more patience in working with the Indonesians by opening offices in Jakarta.

At the Kennedy Center, I fed my starved need for theatre by seeing actress Jean Stapleton in The Late Christopher Bean. Although a bit dated and somewhat slow-moving, it was a good vehicle for her talents.

Jean was a personal friend. We visited her theatre in Pennsylvania and met her family. While in D.C., I wrote a comedy for her called, Sin in the Attic. Because she had finished the long TV series All in the Family, she didn't want to do anything that was slightly like Edith Bunker. The character in my play wasn't like Edith at all. Anyway, the play won an award and was produced in Chatham, Massachusetts.

Seeing the plays and celebrities made me long to write reviews again. I missed that.

Another celebrity was Welsh actor, Emlyn Williams, who performed a one-man show of *Charles Dickens* at the Kennedy Center's Terrace Theatre for one week.

At center stage was a table, covered with a rose velvet cloth. On top were a vase of flowers and a glass of water. On the stage floor was a handsome Oriental carpet. Carrying five early editions of Dickens' books, Williams approached the table, wearing a black cut-a-way suit with a waistcoat and white, ruffled shirt underneath. In the buttonhole was a red carnation. To assume the character, he wore a beard and mustache.

In portraying Dickens, he told stories from nine books, accompanied by gestures and special stage lighting. At the conclusion, the audience showed its appreciation by tremendous applause. Emlyn Williams came back on stage to bow to the audience and then to the Dickens' books and quoted from Dickens. What an inspiring evening.

*   *   *   *

The Greek Tragedy, <u>Medea</u>, was performed at Kennedy Center, starring Zoe Caldwell with Judith Anderson as the nurse.

Although Caldwell was graphically dramatic and wailed hauntingly when she killed her children and lost the love of her husband, she sometimes was overdramatic. But Judith Anderson projected the power and majesty in this bit part of the nurse as she did playing the part of Medea for 30 years.

The scenery and lighting were dominant. Medea's house was like a miniature Parthenon, stretching skyward. The lighting was ominous, forecasting the murder of the second wife and of her own two children.

*   *   *   *

<u>West Side Waltz</u> was performed in the Center's Opera House. Katharine Hepburn starred with that unquenchable spirit, which the audience could feel. She defied the tremors of Parkinson's disease and the wobbles in her speaking voice and held back nothing in working with her fellow actors.

There were some structural flaws in the play, but Hepburn's performance of her character, who fights the onset of old age and refuses to give in to arthritis, loss of hearing, and loss of mobility—many of the things Hepburn herself battled against—was superb.

During the whole play, the theatre was very cold. I discovered later in talking with management that Miss Hepburn requested five air-conditioners on stage.

I had asked for an interview with her for our Cape newspapers because I knew her niece. She graciously declined. I also learned from management that she only granted one interview to a woman who was 106 years old and had written a book. Miss Hepburn invited her to lunch.

*   *   *   *

During a spontaneous moment, Lucille Post and I dashed off to a matinee at Kennedy Center to see A. R. Grantley's <u>The Salon Room</u>. Grantley is well-known for pin-pricking the pomposity of WASPs in his plays.

Like its title, the show was set in the salon, exploring the differences between generations. Six people portray 46 characters that are half-defined and situations that are half-suggested. The WASP society is well drawn when a man's family becomes upset over a derogatory remark made at a private club in a sauna.

Unfortunately, the ending was peculiar. The main character stepped out of the play and lectured to the audience. Lucille and I looked at each other in disbelief. I have seen better Grantley plays, most of which I like very much. I have also interviewed him at the Cape Playhouse and I found him a modest, charming man.

Another time, M.V. Trenton invited me to the Baird Auditorium at the Museum of Natural History to see Cambodian dancers. It was magnificent.

Incidentally, this one performance was a year in the making. Refugees had to organize and rehearse. The costumes were rich brocades in gold, green, blue, and occasional velvets. The orchestra was composed of drums, xylophones, recorders, bells, and singers. The dances were long and epic: The Flower Blessing; Fan Dance, and the Demon, abducting the Princess.

Every moment was to be savored.

Once again, M.V. Trenton and I ventured forth to attend the Jefferson Lecture, sponsored annually by the Arts and Humanities. It was in a museum lecture hall with Grecian columns and overstuffed chairs.

Greeks and Barbarians was the subject. A well-qualified archaeologist delivered the lecture to 2,000 people.

A reception was held for the speaker across the street in the Pendulum Rotunda. There were tables full of silver platters, stacked like pyramids with sandwiches, strawberries, and Welsh rarebit. All of this food was set among steam engines, wagons, and other oversized objects.

Afterwards, we mingled among the guests, thanked the speaker, and departed.

During our D.C. days, the bickering and animosity between Republicans and Democrats hardly existed. People put aside politics after five or six o'clock and resumed friendships for dinner.

Jack and I attended a very interesting dinner party, given by one of Senator Kennedy's office assistants. Her husband was a realtor and had shown us some properties. They both were absolutely delightful.

The guests were a young general, a CIA representative, and Director of Voice of America. Our conversation focused on the M-1 tanks, chemical warfare, and the freeze of weapons. Lighter chats centered on theatre, our experiences in Africa, my theatre experiences, and TENNIS!

In the hallway was a gallery of photos with the Kennedys; in the bathroom were framed campaign buttons of Ted and Bobby, much like the Kennedy Compound in Hyannis Port, or so I am told!

Much fun.

On another occasion, we were invited for dinner at the home of a lawyer, who represented all editors in the United States. It was in an exclusive area on Capitol Hill. The homes were very much like those in Boston with three-story brownstones attached to each other. The dining room and kitchen were in the basement, the living room on the main level, and bedrooms on the third story.

As for the guests, they were the V.P. of Doubleday; the head of the National Association of Broadcasters; a Congressman from Oklahoma, and of course, their wives. I was bogged down with a tennis injury and wore one high heel and a slipper. It caused a lot of conversation and amusement.

Other conversations revolved around the defense budget as well as great humor about the President and the Republican far right.

Naturally, the menu was delicious: a chilled Consommé Madrilene; chicken, covered in artichokes and mushrooms; a dessert of lime sherbet, smothered in crème de menthe sauce.

Outside of political circles, we were invited to the birth of a new newspaper, The District Record. The reception was held in the Corcoran Museum. It was mobbed, but picketed outside because the paper was backed by an Asian monk.

In the museum was a full orchestra that lined either side of the marble staircase. Two banners flanked the grand foyer of the museum with a presidential-type seal, bearing the name of the newspaper, and drawings of the Washington Monument and the Capitol building.

On every floor, there were tables of food, laden with hot and cold snacks, crepes, oriental oysters, and lobsters. Drinks and champagne flowed freely. An opera singer bellowed forth, and there were speeches by the new staff, but the noise was so loud, no one could hear them.

Not surprisingly, the Asian monk's temple was the butt of many jokes— all at the expense of this lavish free food! As we left, we were maligned by protesters. Time will tell whether the paper will survive and whether the editorial content will be free from religious control.

The ambassadors of Indonesia, Singapore, and Thailand gave a joint farewell party for the Ambassador of the Philippines, who was leaving D.C., after ten years to become Chairman of Philippine Airlines.

The party was held in the Thai Embassy and we were invited. Since we love all things Asian, we accepted. The Embassy is a beautiful white brick home with a foyer enhanced by an imposing stairway. The rooms are spacious, though sparsely furnished, with carved teak furniture and red upholstery. Large glass cases were ornately carved in gold leaf and housed antique Thai pottery.

The buffet table was full of Far Eastern delicacies: chicken and beef satay, fruits, and cheeses. We spoke to the Ambassador from China, whose interpreter translated for us. He and his wife noticed my white jade buckle and broke into broad smiles when they knew it came from Hong Kong.

* * * *

Traditionally, the State Department and Defense Department have been rivals for decades. They both aspire to gain the ear of the President. Gavin Stanley and Carl Westert had been rivals in business before their government positions pitted them against each other once again. It was fascinating to watch the political dance of these two cabinet members.

In fact, the Daniel Bertram TV show had asked Leonard Easton to appear on their Sunday talk show. When they realized Easton was not a cabinet officer, they apologized and said it would be more appropriate to have both Secretary Stanley and Secretary Westert on the show together. Jack found this to be an unacceptable arrangement.

Knowing the background to the rivalry, Jack had to stall Westert. By coincidence, Westert had called the Pentagon for guidance about going on the TV show. The Pentagon called Jack, who asked them to hold Westert on the line while he contacted the NSC. Jack also tried to reach Stanley. When he did, Stanley agreed that Westert shouldn't go on the show with him. Jack replied to the Pentagon that it might be better if Westert waited until he was back in D.C. to be interviewed. The irony was that the Pentagon wanted to charge the State Department for the nine-dollar- a-minute telephone call for long distance fees.

Not long afterwards, <u>The Nation Talks</u> television show wanted the Secretary to appear. Jack prepared him for the possible questions from four star reporters. It went well.

During a press briefing about the upcoming trip to Canada, a reporter asked Jack where the Secretary would be going in Canada. Jack looked down at his briefing book and said, "Fifty miles north of Montreal, Route 30, Exit 20." All the reporters enjoyed a huge laugh.

On that trip, Stanley told the reporters a joke about things that are free. "On a golf course, if the tees are given away free to the golfers, they can be seen scattered all over the fairways. But if rich people have to pay a quarter for them, you won't see one on the ground!"

Another new newspaper hit the stands in a variety of cities. It's called <u>FAST NEWS NOW</u>, owned by Art Newman of the Gordon Company. Only five weeks old, the Company invited us to a dinner for the American Society of Newspaper Editors at their new building in Roslyn on the 17th floor. It was always fun to circulate with newspapermen.

From their Virginia offices, there was a stunning, panoramic view of D.C. at night. We could see the Washington Monument, flanked by the Lincoln and Jefferson Memorials, the Capitol, and Kennedy Center. Truly spectacular.

At the dinner, there were round black tables with white china. The centerpiece was made of fresh grapes with a spray of small orchids.

After dessert, Mr. Newman spoke about his newspaper baby. He said, "<u>FAST NEWS NOW </u>is for the mobile society—people who have moved around a lot and want their news in small doses." The questions posed to him were tough, hard, cynical, critical, and sarcastic. Although sensitive to the criticism, he retaliated with deliberate, good humor.

As we left, every guest was given a brass paperweight in the shape of the United States. Written on it were <u>FAST NEWS NOW</u> and the individual's name. It was fitted into a small suede bag. It is always on my desk to remind me of that night. I wondered if the publication would last. I hoped it would, even though it seemed very fragile in those early weeks.

Unbeknownst to the Secretary, the State Department reporters had a longstanding bet as to what would make the Secretary lose his composure. He seemed unflappable. They had tripped up his predecessor, whose jaw jutted forward when awkward questions produced answers that would grab headlines. Stanley was too even-tempered for this.

When one of Stanley's secretaries heard about this bet, she volunteered that Mr. and Mrs. Stanley rarely bickered, except over one thing. Mr. Stanley had many personal photos in his office and she wanted some for their home. He won.

In contrast to the press, Secretary Stanley would offer a humorous compliment when one of his colleagues or staff would negotiate very hard on a point of view and succeed. He would say, "You were really good--so good that you tore the sleeves off my vest!"

In a relaxed mood, Stanley recalled a humorous remark someone made at the Office of Management and Budget when he was at the Treasury for President Norton. "Who are the biggest spenders—Republicans or Democrats?" asked Stanley.

The man thought for a moment and replied, "They both are, but Democrats enjoy it!"

$$\ast \qquad \ast \qquad \ast \qquad \ast$$

At a weekly White House meeting, a spirited dialogue erupted about the Catholic Bishops who were coming to D.C. to air their views on an anti-nuclear freeze. Instead of keeping them away from the Secretary or pitting Protestant views against them, Jack suggested that the Bishops should be encouraged to come and that the administration should use the Biblical phrase, "Come let us reason together." Although the idea produced much laughter, they used his suggestion!

$$\ast \qquad \ast \qquad \ast \qquad \ast$$

One of the benefits of Jack working in government was his receiving tickets to attend the Film premiere of <u>Gandhi</u> at the Uptown Theatre in Bethesda, Maryland.

It was a gala affair. Celebrities walked down a red carpet with huge spotlights on them. In the aisle, we saw movie executives and Danny Kaye, Richard Attenborough, Eddie Albert, Martin Sheen, and Ben Kingsley, the star. Ralph Nader, though not connected to the film, was outside.

The film was a stirring epic more than three hours long. During intermission, champagne and cheese balls were offered.

$\ast$ $\ast$ $\ast$ $\ast$

There were a couple of anecdotes during the Secretary's trip to Latin America with the President:

1. After some meetings in Brazil, there was a motorcade to take President Rowland back to the airport. Somehow, inadvertently, the Secretary was left behind. Stanley ran down a pathway to flag down the motorcade, but they were gone in a cloud of dust. Frantic, the Secretary found an old, battered heap of a car with a sleeping driver. He knocked on the window and said, "I, Senor Stanley. Must go with President of America." The driver didn't want to go. Finally, he consented. The car jerked and bumped, but started to chase the President's entourage. Eventually he caught up with them.

2. Within the framework of democracy in Costa Rica, the President gave a speech before their parliament. A Communist stood up and also gave a speech. He was shouted down. "In a Democratic country he could be heard, but I would not be allowed to speak in the Soviet Union," said the President. Everyone got up and cheered.

$\ast$ $\ast$ $\ast$ $\ast$

In a staff meeting, Secretary Stanley asked, "Is there any country in the world we don't have any problems with?" Everyone looked at everyone else perplexed. Before anyone could answer, Stanley answered his own question, "I'd like to go to that country."

Then he turned to Jack and said, "I still marvel at the way you can go before the press every day."

"Ginny won't come to the press briefings."

"Why not?" He asked.

"Because she is afraid she might burst into tears," Jack said. The Secretary laughed.

"I heard what one of the reporters said about you," Stanley said.

"What's that?"

"Hunter always dips his words in Latex before they cross his lips and we always can tell when an innuendo is about to be spoken," repeated Stanley.

"Who said that?" asked Jack.

"You'll never know!"

"I have one for you," said Jack.

"What might that be?"

"When we were coming back from China on the airplane, you were talking at length to the reporters on your favorite subject—economics. You went on and on. Their eyes became glazed. Dinner was about to be served. They didn't know what to do. At last, Mrs. Stanley came up the aisle with a Chinese dragon. She wiggled it at your elbow. You turned and laughed. It broke the tension and everyone could go to their seats and be served dinner," said Jack.

"I knew about that," he mocked.

"How?"

"My wife told me I went on much too long and that reporters aren't interested in economics," the Secretary said.

"I guess your wife is smarter than all of us," Jack said.

On one occasion, we were invited to Chevy Chase to the home of one of the network news correspondents, who was giving a farewell party for friends moving to Vienna, Austria. The brother of this reporter had been in Hong Kong when we were. It was fun to be amongst journalists again who kept their ears open for any kind of tidbit that might drop from Jack's lips.

Columnist Watson Samsir was there. He cornered me in the study area to talk about playwriting. He had never written a play and was interested in the mechanics of it. I kept asking him if he would prefer to join the main group in the living room. He seemed perfectly content to explore this new literary form.

Meanwhile, a few of my plays were winning awards and being produced. Cabbie! is about a New York taxi driver and the people who get in and out of his cab. My comedy won the Maxwell Anderson Playwrights Series Award, in honor of one of our most distinguished American playwrights. I was so overwhelmed to be the first recipient of this award. It was performed in Stamford, Connecticut. Mrs. Maxwell Anderson, Gilda, greeted me warmly and said how much she loved my play; the audience also seemed to enjoy it. One man thought it would make a wonderful musical. So I have it as a play and a musical.

Then, The Tortured Triangle was produced by an off-off Broadway theatre. Many friends came to it. I was rewriting the whole time. The director wanted to take an option on it. When I went from D.C. to NYC for the opening, I left my purse on the plane in Newark. I ran in and out of the planes trying to find it. The stewardess in one asked the flight number. When I told her, she pointed to the plane I had flown on. I ran up the steps and back to my seat and there it was. Too much excitement!

✳   ✳   ✳   ✳

One of my trips down trivia lane was to go to the hair salon in McLean every month or so. It's one of those times when one can read a book and eavesdrop on conversations.

At one of these beauty sessions, two older ladies were having manicures and gossiping. I was half under a dryer about to doze off when my ears picked up on their exchanges.

"Did you hear about that crazy woman over at State?"

"Who's that?"

"Well, she's actually a spouse of someone over there."

"What about her?"

"She is ditsy and gets into more trouble than Lucille Ball."

"What sort of trouble?"

"At the swearing in ceremony of her husband, her shoes became glued to the floor. They had to get two maintenance men to free her."

"Really?"

Now I realized they were talking about me. I pretended to read my book, but couldn't. My heart sank as I listened. It was proof that every misstep I had made reverberated throughout political circles. My biggest concern was the damage it might have caused Jack. Nevertheless, I kept eavesdropping.

"What else has she done?"

"You have to promise not to tell anyone this next one."

"I promise."

"Apparently, she was in Moscow with her husband at Brezhnev's funeral when…"

"When what?"

"She fell into the casket!"

"With Brezhnev?"

"Yes."

"Oh, my God. What did they do?"

"Lifted her out and carried her off to the limousine."

"That's unforgiveable. What did the Secretary say?"

"I understand he would love to get rid of her."

"But, how?"

"That's just it. He needs her husband who is so capable. He's stuck."

"What else?"

"I'm told that when they were in Israel, she was caught in a bomb blast on a bus and ran after the attacker, forcing him to the ground until the police arrived."

"Too bad the bomb didn't take care of her—if you know what I mean."

A tear started to roll down one cheek and then, the other. I couldn't help it. I was totally heartbroken; especially when they hoped the bomb would have killed me. They don't even know me and what really happened in each case. At that very moment, I wanted to die—really die.

"Here's the last incident I'll tell you and this is top secret if you know what I mean."

"Cross my heart and hope to die."

"This is all hush-hush, but there was an assassination attempt on the Secretary in his office and she was involved."

"Involved?"

"I don't know how, but something about her nephew who tried to kill him."

"If you ask me, she should be the one to knock off!"

By now, I was trying to swallow my sobs. I used the towel to wipe my face and eyes. The two ladies went to the counter to pay.

One of them turned to me and said, "That must be an awfully sad book." I nodded and cried some more.

Just before they left, my operator came over to me and said, "Mrs. Hunter, you should be done by now."

The woman who told all the tales about me suddenly stared directly at me. A look of horror crossed her face.

Outside, she whispered to the other woman, "That woman who was crying..."

"What about her?"

"She's the one I was telling you about."

"Good Lord. No wonder she was crying. What are you going to do... apologize?"

"No. It will make it worse. Oh my God, don't tell your husband and I won't tell mine. I feel awful."

"So do I."

On the way home, I could hardly see. My eyes were a watery mess. That night I told Jack. He was more upset than I was and wanted to kill both of them. He suggested getting their names from the operator, but I said to just let it go. It wasn't worth it, since we would be leaving D.C. fairly soon. However, it was painful.

"Jack, does the Secretary really want to get rid of me?" I sobbed.

"Of course not. That must be a rumor the woman heard. Just a rumor, Ginny, don't believe a word. The Secretary and his wife are very fond of you."

I was amazed how angry he was over the women talking about me. Secretly I was pleased at his reaction in wanting to defend me. He couldn't have been more wonderful and sympathetic. When I was at my lowest, he was there for me.

$$* \quad * \quad * \quad *$$

Another time, when I was in the same hair salon, there were two Palestinian ladies having a manicure. I was partly under the dryer and could hear they're halting English.

"Alena, how is your daughter?"

"Working in the West Bank as a teacher."

"Is she happy?"

"Very, but she told me something that makes me frightened for her life?"

"What do you mean?"

"She tells me there is a plot to divert the water into the West Bank."

"I thought the West Bank only had a third of the water and the Israelis have two thirds."

"Everyone knows that."

"So, what is the plot?"

"They plan to dig in the West Bank and find the pipe elbow to divert it."

"How much water will they steal?"

"Half."

"And the rest?"

"They will poison the rest going into Israel."

"Alena, this is dangerous. The Israelis could bomb the whole of the West Bank in retaliation."

"I know."

"How is your daughter involved?"

"Her boy friend is in charge of the whole plan."

"Dear Allah, this is very bad."

"What can I do?"

"Warn her of the consequences."

"She won't listen."

"She must."

"What can I tell her?"

"Tell her to bring her boy friend to the States to study hydrology and find a better way to bring water to the Palestinians."

"I will. You make sense."

They got up to leave. I didn't have time to blow dry my hair. I paid after they did and slid into my car to follow them. They lived in a very nice section of McLean in big houses. I wrote down the addresses of both and drove home to call the man at the CIA that I had danced with at the UN party.

It took a while to get through to him.

"Mr. Ramus, this is Ginny Hunter. Do you remember dancing with me at a UN party a couple of years ago? I lost my shoe on the floor."

"Ah yes, Mrs. Hunter, how could I forget? What can I do for you?" he asked.

"Well, I've just come from the beauty parlor,"

"And you must look beautiful," he said.

"The reason I'm calling is that I overheard a strange conversation between two Palestinian women having manicures," I told him.

"What did they say?"

"The daughter of one lives on the West Bank and is involved with a young man, who is plotting to divert half of the water into the West Bank and poison the water going into Israel," I said.

"I see, and what do you want me to do about it?"

"Give the information to the proper source at the CIA," I said.

"I shall do exactly that, Mrs. Hunter. Thank you for sharing this information."

"Don't you want the address of these two women?" I asked.

"Of course. How negligent of me."

I gave him the addresses. He thanked me and hung up. Six months later I heard on the news that a plot by the Palestinians had been foiled by the Mossad. Although I felt strongly that the Palestinians should have some kind of equal rights, I didn't think this was the right way to achieve them.

My flights of fancy into the CIA world were satisfied! The Hair Salon was my best source of tears and intrigue.

CHAPTER NINETEEN

▼

SAYING FAREWELL

I do hate goodbyes—any goodbye—whether it be to a person, a place, or a country. It seems so final. When my children went to college, my maternal instincts of loss succumbed to heartbreak. They were looking out of the nest as I was looking back into it, missing their presence. When we left Africa, I couldn't bear to leave a continent I had come to love and the friends I would leave behind and perhaps never see again. I was equally emotional when leaving Hong Kong and the enchantment of the Asian culture. Spoiled by cooks and amahs for my children was a selfish sacrifice. But losing friends took its tearful toll.

Now, I had to say another goodbye, this time to Washington—its people and places. Yes, it's a transient political society where nothing ever stays the same, except the buildings and the annual spring buds of pink cherry blossoms. Potomac Fever is very contagious. All I have left is my journal, drawing word pictures of what happened during three and a half years among the high and mighty and the lowly and mighty. It all goes into the memory bank.

In this state of semi-homesickness, I called Nora French one Saturday before we would pack and leave. I was busy all November at rehearsals for my play, White House Secrets.

"Nora, it's Ginny."

"Ginny, I was just thinking about you. I have a horrible feeling you and Jack might be moving back to Cape Cod very soon," she said.

"In about three weeks," I said. "Would you be free to do something with me today since it's Saturday?"

"I am. What would you like to do?" she asked.

"See the sites of D.C., so I won't forget them."

"Sounds perfect. Shall I drive?" Nora asked.

"If you wouldn't mind," I said. "Let's go to lunch where we saved the French Ambassador from choking,"

"Chinese food seems appropriate," she laughed. "What time shall I pick you up?"

"11:30?"

"I'll be there," she said. "By the way, where's Jack?"

"In New York with the Secretary," I said. "Mr. Stanley is giving a speech tonight."

"I'll be over shortly."

"Thanks, Nora," I said. I was beginning to choke up at the thought of leaving her among many others.

When I heard Nora honk outside, I grabbed my purse and off we went to my favorite restaurant.

The owners recognized us from three years ago and made a big fuss. When I told them my husband and I were leaving D.C., they didn't want to hear it. "You must not go. You stay!"

"I wish I could," I said with tears brimming up.

"We give you best table in house!"

"Is the French Ambassador here today?" I asked.

They laughed very much and shook their heads. They insisted on giving us special appetizers for free. We dipped rangoons and spring rolls into spicy sauces. Chicken with cashew nuts and peapods was our main course with stir fry vegetables. Nora and I wielded our chopsticks in an expert manner. She had been to Asia many times for the World Bank and spent Christmas with us once in Hong Kong.

"Ginny, what will you remember most about your time here?" Nora asked.

"Not what you think. Of course, people, places, and events, but I will remember the Golden Moments that no one knows about, except you and me," I said.

"Golden Moments?"

"Yes. They come in the middle of the night when everyone is asleep. It's dark and silent—very silent. But thoughts, not yet verbalized, spin endlessly—thoughts about life, about people, about new plays, and about God and the universe. It's a time to think about the past, the future, and the present. Gratitude for so much becomes volcanic as it gushes upward. One's whole being feels warm and good. The return to sleep is like slipping quietly into an ebb tide."

"That's pretty profound," said Nora.

"There's more," I said.

"More?"

"The other golden moments come at my desk when it is also silent. I'm there alone, except for the hum of the typewriter. Hours feel like minutes when I'm creating. The characters in a new play take shape and move through the plot on each sheet of white paper. The re-typing and re-writing take forever, but the polishing and corrections make up for the tedium," I said.

"When do the ideas come?" she asked.

"Mostly late at night in a dream or very early in the morning. It comes in total form."

"What does that mean?" she asked.

"I see it on stage, in color, with the scenery, and actors in costumes. They move around as if by pre-planned stage directions. They speak already in dialogue. Sometimes the scenes come in snatches. Sometimes the ending comes first and I have to work backwards."

"That's kind of fascinating," she said. "I can't wait to see your play at the Hilltop Theatre. Will you see the opening?"

"I wouldn't miss it. It plays through December, so I'll see the show a few times before we leave."

I paid the bill for us both, except for the appetizers. We hugged and thanked the owners and waiters. They made me promise not to forget them because they would never forget me—us.

Back in Nora's convertible, she said, "Where would you like to go first?"

"The State Department to see my homeless friend," I said.

"That's right. Nancy Barr told me about your first encounter with him."

"I had a few more," I smiled. "Could you pull over to one side and I'll get out and run over to him?" She did. Because it was Saturday, not many cars were around. I pulled the <u>Global Magazine</u> and a fifty dollar bill out of my purse.

"Ginny, that's a lot!"

"A lot to him, but not to us," I said.

Lord Byron was curled up on the grate. I stooped down to look at him. He opened one eye and a smile spread across his face. "My Lady of Mercy! I wasn't sure I would ever see you again," he said.

"Why?"

"I heard the man who tied me, shot you," he said.

"Here I am," I said.

"The security guard said you saved the Secretary of State's life and my life. I might still be rotting in the bushes," he said.

"Oh no, Mitch or someone would have found you!"

"I have a poem I want to recite. Shall I stand on the grate and deliver it?" he asked.

"Be my guest."

Lord Byron gathered himself up and stood with legs spread across the grate. I sat cross-legged at his feet to watch. With his hands on his hips, his Shakespearian voice boomed.

> *"From my grate,*
> *I guard*
> *The Ship of State.*
>
> *Lord Byron*
> *Am I*
> *Under the sun.*
>
> *Though harmless*
> *I be,*
> *I am fearless.*
>
> *Patriot*
> *I am;*
> *Evil I'm not.*
>
> *Give a smile*
> *And I*
> *Will quote a while.*
>
> *As I fight*
> *Demons,*
> *Stalking at night."*

He bowed and I clapped. "Bravo, Lord Byron, bravo. That was magnificent," I said.

"Do you think so, Lady of Mercy?"

"I do," I said.

"Thank you, thank you," he bowed and bowed.

"Lord Byron, I have come to say goodbye," I said.

"Goodbye? No!"

"My husband and I have to go home. We have served our country," I said. I stood up and handed him the fifty dollars.

"No, this is too much, Lady."

"Just think of me with every dollar you spend," I said.

"I will. I will. Will you ever come back?"

"Maybe. Who knows? Oh, I brought the article for you," I showed him the photos of him in the magazine. He was beaming.

"Take the money back. This is a better gift," he said.

"No, you are a star. You deserve both. May we hug goodbye?" I asked.

"We may." His big arms embraced me and the clothes that probably had never been washed smelled earthy. I started to cry and broke loose from his arms and ran back to the car.

"What's wrong?" asked Nora.

"Nothing. I hate saying goodbye."

"Did he take the money?"

"He did. He didn't want to, but he did," I said.

"Now where?" Nora asked.

"I haven't seen the new Vietnam Memorial. Have you?"

"No, but this is the perfect time," she said.

Nora drove to the Lincoln Memorial and parked. I paused to drink in the majesty of that Memorial and what it symbolized for two great men. Not far from it, we walked to the black, shiny granite Vietnam Memorial. It was a simple elegant slab with 58,000 names inscribed for giving their lives to a long war. Single stemmed flowers were scotch-taped to a name. Notes and letters were taped to other names. Small American flags were also hanging from names. Reflections of people could be seen on the wall as they walked slowly past the names. The wind blew leaves hither and yon. They, too, were reflected in the black mirror. They were symbolic of having lost their leaves from nearby trees as the soldiers had lost their lives in a far off land. People spoke in whispers or not at all.

I had strolled halfway and felt frozen and transfixed by the names and reflections. The tears started to fall. From the corner of my eye, I was aware of a man in a wheelchair, speeding down the sidewalk. As he passed me, he grabbed my waist and pulled me onto his lap.

"Ginny!" shouted Nora. "Watch out."

"See, you lost someone, too," he said.

"No, I didn't. I'm crying for all the names," I said.

"It doesn't matter, the war was in vain. They lost their lives in vain!"

"No they didn't. They tried to keep the South Vietnamese free," I said.

"And they didn't!"

"What do you want with me?" I asked.

"You're my shield. I'm going to blow up this whole wall," he said.

"And dishonor all these names?"

"Yes!" he said.

"It's the only place in this country where they get respect—on this wall. Is someone's name here related to you?" I asked.

"My brother, and I don't want to see it here."

"Isn't that rather selfish?" I said.

"Selfish?"

"To blow it up because of one name?" I asked.

"I lost my brother and look at me. I'm half a man without any legs. Who wants a helpless son of a bitch like me?"

"I've known handicapped people worse than you and they make a difference in the world. Why don't you make a difference?" I asked.

"I don't like the way you preach!" he said. "I have two grenades—one to blow up the wall up and the other for you and me."

A crowd had started to back away from the wall and from us. A guard at one end of the wall had a gun pointed at us.

"Drop the grenade," he said.

"No! I'll blow this woman up if you shoot."

"Where's the other grenade?" I asked.

"In my sleeve."

"Are you homeless?" I asked. This was a stab in the dark, but maybe it would work.

"Of course. No one wants me in their home."

"Do you know Mitch Snyder and Lord Byron?" I asked.

"Yeah. Who are you?" he asked.

"Their friend. If you do this, you will disappoint them. They respect you—Mitch gives you free meals. How can you do this to them?" I asked. "You will ruin the name of 'homeless' in this town and ruin the name of 'soldier' in this country. Don't disappoint them. Each name deserves to be written here; especially your brother's. Now, give me the grenades."

He reached in his sleeve for the other grenade and handed them both to me. "Thank you." The guard came forward and pointed his gun at the man in the wheelchair. "Don't shoot him," I said.

"The grenades aren't real," he confessed.

"Not real?" I asked.

"I was hoping the guard would kill me," he said. "What's your name?"

"Lord Byron calls me Lady of Mercy," I said.

"So you're the one who saved him!"

"We all save each other," I said.

"Come on, you, I'm calling the police," said the guard.

"No, don't do that," I said. "Can't you give him the job of cleaning the wall every night and make him feel useful? His brother's name is on this wall."

"Well…"

"He'll do a good job. Won't you?" I asked him.

"I would. I'd like to read all those notes and file them in boxes," he said.

"Please give him a job—even if it's only for a dollar a day," I pleaded.

"Yeah, I could live on that."

"Okay, but no more threats," the guard said.

"I promise," he said.

"Good luck," I said and ran over to Nora. "Let's go."

"My God, Ginny, you almost got killed."

"He was too emotional to kill," I said.

"I don't care. I am stunned by what I just witnessed," Nora said.

"Don't tell anyone," I said. "I mean it."

"Okay, if that's what you want. Where to next?"

"Let's just swing by the Jefferson Memorial, Washington Monument, and Capitol. Oh, and the Kennedy Center. Then, I should be satisfied." As she did what I asked, I threw kisses and waves to each place. Soon, we were back in McLean. I stepped out of the car in front of my condo.

"I'm not going to say goodbye. It's so final. Come to the Cape, Nora, for a visit," I said.

"Now that's an invitation I won't turn down! Anyway, I'll see you at your play." She blew a kiss and drove away. I stood and watched for a long time before going inside to do some gradual packing.

✶   ✶   ✶   ✶

In December, there were a number of farewell office parties for Jack. His secretaries were weeping at the prospect of his leaving. They loved his wit and gentlemanly ways. He was easy to work for. His peers also were sorry to lose a newsman who knew how to handle the media. He understood all too well their motives and manipulations for news when on deadline. He used his skill to deflect their questions when necessary. They respected him because he was a pro. However, to go on as spokesman for another four years wouldn't be possible. It was a burn out job as much as he enjoyed working with the Secretary. Besides we had work to do with our business, after having left it for so long.

The day of the opening of <u>White House Secrets,</u> Mr. and Mrs. Stanley, along with the office staff, held a goodbye and hello luncheon party in the private dining room at State with spouses included. Ben Kline would be taking over as spokesman after Jack leaves. Ben and his wife, Priscilla, would be at the luncheon. We had known them in Hong Kong. Ben had been extremely kind to my mother when she visited us there, so he could do no wrong in my eyes.

Throughout the meal, there were toasts of goodbye to Jack and welcome to Ben. Everyone teased Ben Kline about the job ahead of him.

Just before we left the table, I asked the Secretary, "Mr. Secretary, would you allow me a few moments to give Priscilla a peephole into what her life will be like?"

"I think we would be delighted to allow another point of view, Ginny," he smiled.

I leaned across the table to talk directly to her. Ben was intrigued and wasn't quite sure what to expect. "Well, Priscilla, Ben is just about to go behind the diplomatic curtain, which means he will have a glimpse of life on the other side of the typewriter and the television screen."

"That sounds a bit ominous," laughed Ben who was listening to every word.

"Not really," I said to Priscilla. "Life won't be too different from your life as a foreign correspondent's wife: Ben will be away 50% of the year; there will be many late nights; there will be early mornings, working weekends, and television appearances for the Secretary. Previously, Ben had been with CBS and knew the ropes."

"Sounds exactly like the life I now lead," said Priscilla. "What's the downside?"

"No downside," I said. "The hardest part for Ben will be in knowing the WHOLE story. Instead of scrambling for crumbs of information, Ben will have it all."

"That takes the fun out of it—I like finding the unknown!" said Ben.

"You'll have to slap your wrist and tell yourself, 'If I were a newsman still, what I could do with this juicy tidbit—scoop everybody else!' " I said. Jack and Ben had a secret chuckle over that one.

"And what about the leaks?" asked Ben.

"They'll come from Shallow Throat," quipped Jack and everyone burst out laughing.

"Very clever, Hunter," said Ben.

"What else?" asked Priscilla.

"There will be many receptions, luncheons, and diplomatic dinners. You'll be amazed at how many ways chicken can be fried, tied, baked, broiled, poached and then placed on top of a bed of rice, drenched in creams, wines, and herbs," I said and everyone in the room chuckled and nodded in agreement. Mrs. Stanley thoroughly enjoyed that description.

"What are the benefits?" Priscilla asked.

"The biggest one is the friendships you'll make, starting with two wonderful people—Secretary and Mrs. Stanley. You'll make many others inside and outside of the State Department," I said.

"What's it like working for the government instead of an editor or owner?" she wondered.

"Well, working for the government is an eye opener," I said.

"Eye opener?" asked Ben. "What do you mean?"

"I mean, one discovers that the government is not the 'enemy.' It's made up of people like us who want to do the right thing. And the press is out there to make sure they do the right thing. From secretaries to Foreign Service Officers, they work hard and sacrifice family time and weekends for very little glory," I said.

"Would you say there is any satisfaction to this job?" asked Ben.

"In serving your country and giving back to it in a small way," I finished. "I wish you well in your new career."

"Ginny, what a great piece of PR," said the Secretary. "Let's toast the past and future Spokesmen and their spouses!"

"Hear, hear," said everyone, raising their glasses.

That was my final visit to the State Department.

CHAPTER TWENTY

▼

WHITE HOUSE SECRETS

Before leaving Washington, I became involved with the Hilltop Theatre on Capitol Hill. It was a new theatre in one of the brownstones. The vacant lot across the street made a great parking lot for patrons. Anyway, they wanted to produce my play, <u>White House Secrets,</u> since it has a D.C. setting. Naturally, I was thrilled and was at the theatre every night for four weeks from casting of the play through rehearsals. Jack was away with the Secretary on short trips, so it worked out fine.

The theatre was a sort of an off, off Broadway type with only 200 seats and a smallish, but adequate stage. New works were encouraged from aspiring playwrights. In the basement, all the scenery was made. Dressing rooms were there as well, although the stage wardrobe was on the third floor. There was a small balcony for lighting equipment and sound. There were two special boxes, with seating for four in each, in case celebrities or talent scouts wanted privacy.

Outside the theatre was a marquis. It started advertising <u>White House Secrets</u> two weeks before it opened. The title drew patrons to the outside box office, or reservations were made by telephone. One way to get backstage from the outside was downstairs through a special locked door that opened to a tunnel underground, leading to the stage wings.

On opening night, I was a wreck. Jack's co-workers and the Secretary's staff were coming. Mr. and Mrs. Stanley were our guests and excited to come. The State Department Security insisted on reading the script beforehand. I asked them if they would keep it a surprise for the Stanleys. They agreed.

After reading it, they said the Secretary would have to wait until everyone was seated and then come upstairs unannounced and slip into our special box. Jack agreed to wait in the lobby to meet them and show them to our box. We had to squeeze in an extra chair for the assigned agent.

For the first night, I suggested to all Jack's colleagues and friends that formal attire wasn't necessary in such a small theatre. However, I wore a long skirt and Jack insisted on wearing a tux. The Secretary and Mrs. Stanley also ignored my request for informality. Finally, when the lights faded before the curtain opened, the Stanleys slipped into their seats and whispered greetings. Mr. Stanley was in a tux and Mrs. Stanley in a long emerald green dress.

The director emerged through the center opening of the curtain to make an announcement.

"Good evening, ladies and gentlemen. I am Simon Ford, the artistic director of Hilltop Theatre. We welcome you to the world premiere of a new play. White House Secrets **is by a local playwright, Virginia Hunter of McLean, Virginia, and Cape Cod, Massachusetts. (applause) You will meet her later. The setting is the master bedroom upstairs at the White House. We are delighted to have Simone Paige star in this one-woman show. The time frame is between 1932 to the 1980s. The reason I am speaking before the curtain opens is to warn you that whatever happens, just remember, this is a play—a drama—a suspense drama to entertain you. There may be some surprises at the beginning of the show. Don't be afraid. Don't get up and leave. Just remember, playwright Ginny Hunter has thought up some high-powered drama to startle and delight you. So, sit back and enjoy the one-woman show or... is it?"**

As the lights go down and the curtain opens, the stage is somewhat barren, except for a king- size bed with an exotic, tufted headboard. Enormous pillows are arranged symmetrically against it. They are stamped with the seal of the American President. Simone Paige, an imposing actress, is standing center stage in a long, black, shimmering nightgown with a matching negligee, covered in sequins.

The format below is that of a stage script. Excerpts from the play are in bold print, representing the dialogue or a summary of the play as it progresses. Directions are underneath the speeches in a lighter print. A pinkish spotlight focuses on Miss Paige.

SIMONE
(Center stage, talking to the audience)
Good evening. What a wonderful audience. Tonight, we are going to do some pillow talk. Yes, pillow talk. Isn't that fun? The pillow talk is

going to be with the first ladies of our country from Eleanor Roosevelt
to Clare Rowland. I will play each one of them. Since this is a one-
woman show, you won't hear any of the presidents from Franklin
Delano Roosevelt to Russell Rowland, speaking. BUT, you will hear
the secrets and advice that powerful wives tell their husbands in that
twilight time of night before drifting off to sleep.

(She turns to go to the bed when the lights start to flicker in the theatre.)

SIMONE
(she goes center to talk with the audience)
Whoops. Let's hope there isn't a power failure in this theatre. Ladies and
gentlemen, I assure you, this is not in the script!

(They flicker again, go out, and keep flickering. The audience is probably
tittering and remembering what the director said. They are now onto
something secret.)

Mr. Stage Manager, would you come out here, please.

(By now the lights have gone completely off. The audience sits patiently
in the dark, trying to figure out what is happening. But, they now
understand, this is part of the play.)

Can you bring out some candles or a flashlight?

STAGE MANAGER
(joins her onstage)
Please everyone, stay seated. We hope to get this problem resolved in a
few minutes. We ask you to be patient.

(The audience whispers and laughs in the dark.)

SIMONE
Since pillow talk happens in the dark, let's forget the lights and proceed.
If you don't mind I will plump the pillows and lean against them as dear
Eleanor talks to Franklin. I think you know who I mean. "No, dear
Franklin, you won't be remembered for the Great Depression. No, not
for the War. Not even for Social Security. For what? Your omelets! Yes, for
your famous Sunday night omelets with family and friends. What else?
For Fala, your Scottie dog. He hears every word of history and is your
closest confidante. People can criticize me or the children, but if they
criticize Fala, you are ready to go to war. How could you forget when the
press accused you of leaving Fala in the Aleutian Islands! They said you

spent two million dollars to get him back. I know it was a lie. Sometimes, I wish I were Fala! Thank you, darling. Good night, my dearest one. Remember when we were young and in love? It was the sweetest time. Wasn't it? Franklin? Franklin? Sleep on, my prince, sleep on. I will always love you, and Fala, too!

(Someone approaches Simone in the half-dark and struggles with her.)

Who are you? You're hurting my arm. Stop! I said stop!

(The lights come on again. A Russian soldier is holding a gun to her head.)

SIMONE
Who are you?

(The audience is beginning to understand that this is all part of the play they have come to see and are more comfortable, watching the action unfold.)

PETROV
If you must know, I am Ivan Petrov.

SIMONE
What do you want with me?

PETROV
Not you. I want him and her. (The spotlight goes to the front row. Two actors look very much like the real Secretary and his wife.) **Your Secretary of State, Clark Cabot, and his wife.**

SIMONE
You can't have them.

PETROV
Yes I can and I will. And don't any of you out there try to leave the theatre. My men are guarding every entrance and exit. If you make a move, you will be killed.

(Russian soldiers appear in the wings with rifles. The audience stares at them, realizing they are actors. Now theatre-goers are enjoying the spoof being played on them.)

At this point in the play, I stole a look at Jack. He is mesmerized by the stage action. I notice that the Stanleys are not sitting next to us and the security agent is gone. I poke Jack and point to their empty seats. He brushes my hand aside and shushes me.

PETROV

Bring Mrs. Cabot up here and take her backstage. Don't try to intervene, Secretary Cabot, or we will have to eliminate her.

Obviously, I'm not going to write the whole play in my journal, but I can give a summary of the first act in the text to come.

Through all this dramatic action, Simone Paige continues to do her show, but with Ivan Petrov, who reacts to her dialogue and becomes each one of the presidents by accidental dialogue. For example, she does snatches of pillow talk with Bess and Harry Truman. As Bess, she chastises Harry for getting so mad at the press for attacking their daughter Margaret's singing ability. After her little tirade, she reaches across the bed and pats his hand. Petrov withdraws his hand as Simone pretends he is Harry. "Never mind, Harry, you did what any father would do when his only daughter is criticized. You defended her. By the way, dear, you must do something about your Fedora. It's wearing out, that's why, and looks as if the White House mice have been chewing on it. People do see it--every morning when you take your walk. A President, who was a haberdasher, should have the best. Get a new one. And what's this I hear about showing Ginger Rogers your etchings? A portrait of Dolley Madison? Good heavens, why? Ginger is playing Dolley in a movie? Well, be careful, dear, she's between husbands and likes men with dimples. You're a very attractive man, Harry. Sleep tight, President Valentino!"

Next, Simone and Ivan do some pillow talk as Ike and Mamie Eisenhower. "Why do you care how you're remembered, sweetheart? Well, let me see. As a general? No. For picking up the pieces of war? No. And recharging the economy? No, dear, you will be remembered for golf—the golfing president. That's who you are. I'm serious. Don't you remember when your ball hit the manager's wife in the stomach as she was crossing the fairway in Augusta, Georgia? She said she had been trying to lose weight for years and the President of the United States did it for her. She wasn't mad at all because everyone loves Ike, especially me. Goodnight, darling Ike."

Petrov is fed up with being dragged into these pillow talk scenes and struts away in disgust.

The audience is now very curious to know why Petrov wants to kidnap the Secretary of State, Clark Cabot. "I want an invention from the CIA. It's called CamVac." Now we know his motive. But, no one has ever heard of this invention. CamVac is a laser camera that can bounce off a satellite, take photos, and suck up conversations in the Kremlin or any other major capital in the world. Apparently, the blueprint for the invention is in a safe at the Secretary's home in Chevy Chase.

Petrov learned of the invention and blueprint from the Secretary's personal, most trusted driver. Petrov used KGB tactics to prey upon the driver's weaknesses to extract information. His flaw was a gambling habit that put him deeply in debt. Cleverly, Petrov offers him money to cover his debts and also, he uses a beautiful Russian spy to seduce him. In the end, the money really was the deal breaker that forced him to betray his country and the Secretary of State. The money was too great to resist.

Next, there is a short pillow talk scene between Jackie and Jack Kennedy. It is the summer of 1963. It is a poignant and sweet vignette. He needs her for campaigning, and they feel like sweethearts again. They giggle together over the pony, poking his nose in their pockets for carrots; licking Jack's face and nudging him on the chaise lounge on the patio. They recall how Jack covered his face and curled up in a fetal position, but couldn't stop laughing. They almost acted like a pair of children as they reminisced.

At that crisis point in the play, a young woman stands up in the audience and speaks emotionally. Everyone is startled and strains their necks from the audience. The actors also peer out to see her in the audience. She offers herself to replace the Secretary or his wife as a hostage. She has four children and says her parents can raise them. She lost her husband in the Vietnam War and life for her isn't worth living. Petrov motions her onstage.

For theatrical relief and to keep the audience in suspense, Simone and Petrov reenact a piece of pillow talk between Lady Byrd and Lyndon Johnson. "Honey, sometimes I love these sleepless nights. We never have time to talk until late at night or in the wee hours of the morning. Well, Sugar, I've been meaning to ask you why you invited her into your private bedroom. Who? Why, Karen Grenthem, of course. Did you have to show her your appendix scar? In your pajamas? Completely inappropriate. That isn't the way to gain her sympathy, even if she is publisher of the most powerful paper in D.C. You only won her embarrassment, Lyndon. Your physician and I are the ones allowed in our private, White House bedrooms until we go home to Texas. And then what? To write your memoirs, darling. You have a wonderful story to tell, unless I tell it first! Goodnight, Mr. Longhorn President."

Meanwhile, Simone tries to grab Petrov's gun, but his strength overcomes her. In a fit of frustration, she challenges him to shoot her. Clark Cabot intervenes and offers to call the President to get permission to send someone to get the safe. He makes the call from the stage manager's telephone brought out on stage. Leo Petrov, Ivan's nephew, points his rifle at Cabot.

An almighty verbal fight takes place between Leo and Petrov over the young girl who is now on stage. Leo demands that Petrov give him his independence to live his own life.

For a change of pace and to relax tensions, another pillow talk exchange between Pat and Dick Nixon interrupts the action. "Dick, dear, you won over the press—yes, you did, at least once—when you told college students that you were trying to graduate from college in the fall—from the Electoral College, And the joke about cutting down crime in D.C. by turning on the lights in the White House that Lyndon Johnson had turned off five years ago! Yes, that's your Nixon wit. Watergate? Did you call it a Niagara Falls joke? Not one of your best, dear. Well, no one will ever forget your piano playing. Just play 'Hello Dolly' when things get really bad and all will be well. Goodnight George Gershwin, Irving Berlin, and Jerry Herman!"

Then, the scene switches back to Petrov and Leo who go into the wings to consult on the fate of their hostages. As they exit, two Russian soldiers point their rifles at the hostages onstage. Simone, Clark Cabot, and the young girl do some pillow talking of their own in loud whispers. The girl says she will try to get Leo's rifle away from him by flirting with him.

When the uncle and nephew come back onstage, Simone asks him what is the real reason he's doing this? Petrov finally explains. It is personal. He blames the United States for destroying his nephew's life with drugs. He swears that American women can never be trusted. When Simone asks how much Petrov is being paid, it's only $500 for passing along the CamVac plans to the Soviet Union. The Secretary and Simone Paige are shocked at the small amount for this daring attempt. The young girl shows Leo pictures of her four children to capture his sympathy.

In the middle of this emotional and intense scene, pillow talk between Betty and Gerald Ford sustains the suspense. "Gerry, what was it Emperor Hirohito gave you in Japan? A jeweled sword? Was he suggesting you commit Hara-kiri? Just teasing, honey. And what did you give him? Your WIN button? What did he say? He thanked you and said the Japanese had made them? Gerry, did you just make that up? Well, dear, that's pretty funny. Maybe when you leave office, you can be a stand–up comic. Well, it's better than being a falling-down comic. Chevy Chase wants to do a routine with you? Doing what? Stumbling up and down the Capitol steps? You're not laughing, but I am! Goodnight, Groucho Marx!"

There is a blood-curdling scream backstage. Everyone is stunned into silence. It is Connie Cabot. Everyone realizes Petrov is threatening to do something terrible to Mrs. Cabot. Simone, the Secretary, and young girl cringe in horror. Reluctantly, Simone gives back the rifle.

As she does so, the safe with the CamVac blueprint is rolled onstage from the wings. Cabot warns it will blow up without the code. Connie's fading cries are heard as the curtain comes down on the first act.

The audience is fascinated and talking brightly among themselves. At intermission, Jack goes to the lobby to chat with his colleagues while I dash outside to go underground and backstage. The real State Department Security is outside. They stop me. When I tell them I am the playwright, they let me through.

"Have you seen Secretary and Mrs. Stanley?" I asked them.

"They're inside," they said.

"No, they're not," I said. "They were in our box and then they disappeared."

"We put them in a private box next to yours to make them secure. They're fine. You'll see them after the show."

"Thank goodness," I sighed with relief.

When I arrived backstage, the actors were drinking water and adjusting their costumes.

"Everybody, you were great," I said.

"Do they like it?"

"The buzz is terrific," I said.

"I scooted back through the audience to the lobby and saw Jack holding court with his colleagues.

"Great show, Ginny," said Jack's colleague, the one who thinks I'm the craziest character in the city.

"Thank you."

The lights blinked to announce Act Two. Jack and I waved to his friends and we went upstairs.

"Everyone seems to like it," said Jack.

"Jack, I hear the Stanleys are in the box next to us".

"Didn't I tell you?"

"No."

"It's for safety from any kind of copy-cat crazies who might react to the play," he said.

"But this is fiction—just a play."

"I know."

"The show's about to start," I said.

"I can't wait," said Jack.

Just then, the lights went down to announce the second act. As the curtain pulled back, Mrs. Cabot's stretcher is rolled onstage. She is sedated. Clark Cabot is angry and lets it surface against Petrov.

Before Clark explodes, a pillow talk scene happens between Rosalynn and Jimmy Carter as the spotlight goes to Simone on the presidential bed and Petrov hovers around it. "Jimmy, honey, don't fret over your legacy. Not the hostages, sweetheart—the Camp David Peace Accords. You did it. You brought Sadat and Begin together. History will call you the Peace man. What did you say? The Peanut Man? Darlin' that's not true. It is true, but real funny. What else? Let's see. Ginger Rogers will remember you for showing her your hard hat collection. Now, Jimmy, I didn't call you hardheaded. Anyway, even if you're in love with her, I won't be jealous—I reckon. Goodnight, Mr. Peanut!"

When the scene is over, Mrs. Cabot tries to whisper something to her husband. Clark Cabot puts his ear to her mouth. She tells him not to give in. Therefore, Cabot calls the President again. He promises to send someone with the code. Suddenly, in bursts a bag lady. It is a disguised Simone. She had excused herself earlier to go to the rest room and made a secret telephone call to the local police. She is no longer in her negligee, but wears a red wig, a torn top, and ragged, olive skirt. She uses a Cockney accent, but Petrov recognizes her and roughs her up a bit, shoving her on the bed.

In retaliation, Petrov decides to kill the young girl, who has tried to seduce his nephew with a kiss. As Petrov points his gun at the girl, Leo aims his gun at Petrov. But the driver comes behind Leo with a rifle and makes the nephew drop his gun.

Concerned about the girl, Cabot tries to make a deal with Petrov, saying he would promise a press blackout on this international news story if he lets his wife and the young girl go free. Suddenly, the FBI arrives and captures Petrov, his nephew, and the Russian guards.

When they exit, Clark Cabot walks center stage to apologize to Simone and the audience for ruining the one-woman show. He then comes to the lip of the stage and speaks secretly to the audience. A spotlight is on him.

CABOT

I would like to ask a favor of you. Would you promise not to tell anyone about our White House Secrets that you've witnessed in this theatre tonight; especially about CamVac? The President and I would be very grateful. Thank you and good night."

The curtains close to applause. There is a standing ovation when the curtain opens as the actors take their bows. When the actress who played Mrs. Cabot takes her bow, the audience applauds loudly. She and the actor, who plays her husband, Clark Cabot, embrace.

The director joins the cast.

DIRECTOR

"We would like to introduce you to the playwright of this amazing piece of theatre. Ginny Hunter is up in the balcony. To save her running down to this spot, we have a rope for her to fly to the stage. I understand she had a childhood fantasy, ever since she saw Mary Martin on Broadway as Peter Pan. Ginny, if anybody in the world can do this, you can. The stage manager has tested it, so don't worry. Are you willing to do it?"

"Well, I'll give it a try!" I said. The audience swiveled their heads to watch. This was a dream of a lifetime. I had always wanted to play Peter Pan like Mary Martin, so I grabbed the rope, launched off from the balcony ledge, and soared over the audience to the stage. Everyone cheered and clapped. They rose to their feet and gave me a standing ovation. The director handed me some flowers and I said a few words.

GINNY

I want to thank you, the audience, for coming to support a new piece of work. If your name isn't Neil Simon or William Shakespeare, it's difficult for new playwrights to get their work produced. So, I am grateful to Hilltop Theatre for taking a chance. You can imagine how grateful I am to this amazing cast for putting their heart and soul into this production. Thank you again and if you feel like telling your friends, all of us would appreciate it. Goodnight.

The curtain closed. I again thanked the cast, crew, director, and stage manager for pulling it off without a hitch. They applauded. I left through the center curtain and walked up the aisle. Jack, the Stanleys, and his office colleagues waited to greet me in the lobby, shouting, "Playwright, Playwright, Playwright." The Secretary and Mrs. Stanley hugged me.

"Congratulations, Ginny, you sure wrote a complicated plot. I'm just glad I wasn't kidnapped!" he said. Everyone laughed. "They even had to put my wife and me in a separate box in the balcony in case someone might pick up on that idea."

"Mr. Secretary, are you sure you can trust your driver going home tonight?" asked Leonard Easton. The staff laughed again.

"If I don't turn up in the office, you'll know the answer to that question," Stanley replied. More laughter. "Well, Jack, you certainly have a talented wife."

"Thank you, sir," said Jack, beaming.

After everyone left, Jack and I peeked back at the open stage. It was empty and hushed. The life of two hours was over and yet, something of the truth lingered. The presidential bed was still there, and we surmised that quiet whisperings might be happening after we left. We walked hand-in-hand to our car to drive home.

"Well, Ginny, it looks like you have a hit," said Jack.

"Do you think so?"

"I know so," he smiled, kissed me, and opened the car door for me.

What a night! The best night of my life.

E P I L O G U E

As you know, my discovery of Ginny Hunter's journal, written during her three and a half years in D.C. when she was a political appointee's wife, was an unexpected surprise. It gave me a unique look at our government and how it operates. Using the diary as the framework and foundation for my book, I have taken the liberty to expand and even invent situations, many of which are based on facts before soaring into flights of fiction. I tried to make Ginny Hunter's character as much like a 1980s Lucille Ball as I could to bring a light touch to my novel and to show a woman without pretensions. Washington sometimes infuriates us and at other times, Washington makes us proud, but I felt it was time to pinprick pomposity wherever it exists. Ginny had no idea that she would show us the way and that her experiences would do just that.

Although it often appeared as if Ginny Hunter was a ditsy blonde, who falls and sinks into the most bizarre of situations, D.C. intellectuals, who rolled their eyes at her honesty and accidental scrapes, would come to grudgingly respect what she accomplished.

Her mission to help the homeless has made us stop to think about their plight, for those of us too busy to explore the other side of life. She stops assassination attempts and bomb threats without thinking about herself, and dismisses her bravery as nothing special. She does a lot of dumb things, too, but somehow, they make her more endearing. And yet, we feel for her long-suffering husband, who wavers between embarrassment and pride.

There was a lot I didn't know about Ginny Hunter. It was hard to find out anything. She and Jack divorced a year or so after they came back from D.C.

I never found out why. Apparently, Jack remarried. Ginny never remarried, but she left Cape Cod and lived in Alabama and southern California for a time, but eventually returned to the charms of the Cape. She authored plays, biographies, and a few novels. Because she had two formidable Rhodesian Ridgeback dogs, she bought a small camper and traveled the country with them as her closest companions while doing research for her biographies of heroes for young readers. When her beloved dogs passed away, she moved to Cambridge and wrote in seclusion.

Throughout the post D.C. years, her adventures continued in the same irreverent ways that they had in Washington. I was delighted to learn of the depth of her intellect. She wrote a book on tracing five thousand years of theatre in China with a focus on the revolutionary operas during the Mao Tse Tung years. That was shocking to me after judging her initially in such a different light.

In the sunset of her life, she continued to write plays and musicals—some were produced, some not. Aside from the three plays I had unearthed in the crate, hidden in the storage area of my soon-to-be office in my newly bought Cape Cod house, I uncovered dozens more of her plays with intriguing titles. My eye fell immediately on one that was called The Homeless Exchange, based on a true story in Boston. Another I found fascinating was Tent of Peace, in which she creats an original idea to solve the Middle East problem. Crisis at Cape Cod Inn examines the lives of a young couple, a middle-aged couple, and an elderly couple. I assumed her years of living in Alabama brought forth The Two Mamas about a white mother and a black nanny vying for the love of the white daughter, again based on a true story out of Birmingham, Alabama. And yes, she did write Pasta and Curry as a play and a musical. An Italian American girl falls in love with a Pakistani boy and the parents try to stop the romance, but the widowed parents fall in love, too. The ending is a sad one. On and on, the list goes with fascinating titles.

I found that her association with Ginger Rogers turned into a friendship. The star tracked Ginny down in Alabama, after the Hunters had divorced, and asked her to come edit her autobiography. She did. She lived in the celebrity's house for nearly four months, working every day with Ginger. Six years after she passed, Ginny decided to write a musical about her.

I'm not sure if I ever knew the real Ginny, but what I do know is certainly unforgettable and…..most fun of all for me……only Ginny and I will know which parts of this book are absolute fact, and which are total, complete fiction. See if you can guess which is which! AND best of all, there is so much more that is not in this book………..

Parker Lloyd, Cape Cod, 2028

A CKNOWLEGMENTS

With special thanks to Don Thomas; Carolyn Alexander; Evelyn Reading; and Beverly Gunther.